The Sovereign
of the Seas

STEPHEN SIMPSON

The Sovereign of the Seas
Copyright © 2022 by Stephen Simpson

All rights reserved. No part of this publication may be reproduced,
distributed, or transmitted in any form or by any means, including
photocopying, recording, or other electronic or mechanical
methods, without the prior written permission of the author, except
in the case of brief quotations embodied in critical reviews and
certain other non-commercial uses permitted by copyright law.

ISBN
978-1-959365-10-5 (Paperback)
978-1-959365-11-2 (eBook)
978-1-959365-09-9 (Hardcover)

Acknowledgments

Special thanks to Tammie Currie (Tamantha) for inspiring me to write and to Jane Adams (Lady Jane) and Joe Rickle (Captain Rickle) for their critiques and editing help. Not to forget Kodiak, Klondike, Cheyenne, and Avalanche, my four Alaskan Malamutes.

One

The year is 1824, and my name is Sir Christopher Newly. I am one of the richest men in all England and the Americas, not to mention the rest of the world. I am constantly invited by queens and kings and so-called influential men to come and sit with them to discuss matters of importance and to regale with them my tales of the sea. I never respond to their requests because I do not care for their corruption nor their politics, and I hate their high and mighty attitudes. However, I will sit with the Americans, as I do enjoy their company. They have not had their country or their freedom long enough for the consumption of greed and corruption to set in. I warn my American friends often of the folly.

In my forty-four years, I have made a fortune that would make a king's ransom look like a pittance.

Despite my wealth, and to my fine wife's distaste, I take pleasure in frequenting the taverns down on the docks in Liverpool where I came from. My fortune has not distracted me, as I know if it were not for one man I would not be visiting the docks by choice. I have many friends in the many taverns that do not care about my money, as they are just my mates, and I enjoy their company because it brings me back home to the sea.

Many a night in the taverns I am asked to tell my tales about Captain Pike and of the time I spent at sea with him. Many a night I do, and many a night I do not.

"You have to be worthy of the tale," I'd say, laughingly, sneering at them. "If Captain Pike were here, he'd put a pumpkin ball in your worthless ear. Only the worthy and trusty ones get to hear this tale." When I did decide to tell my tales, a hush would come over the tavern. Even those whom had heard my stories before listened with great attention as if it were their first time hearing them.

I am always asked about the captain, as all knew his name well. People would ask: "What kind of man was Captain Pike?" "Was he a good man, or was he a bad man?" "Was he a hard and cruel man, or was he fair and just in his ways?"

I always answered with a smile and said, "I'll tell you the tales of the time I spent at sea with him, and you can be the judge and jury, mates. "As for me, I like him." When I had everyone's interest and thought them worthy of the tale, I'd put a few logs on the fire, open a bottle of rum, and say, "Listen closely now, mates, I don't want you to miss anything."

It was back in the year 1799 that I had signed onto a merchant ship from England that was headed for the Caribbean with supplies for the king's navy. All I wanted to do was to get away from England to a new life. I did not have any money so I hired on as a deck hand.

The captain of the ship and his crew were the meanest men I had ever came across, They were meaner than my stepfather, the man I was really running from. They would actually whip us, me and the other poor devils on the work detail, if we did not work hard enough or our work was sloppy.

We were no sooner in the Caribbean when we were attacked by pirates. The pirates were the worst-looking lot I had ever seen, and they fought like devils with nothing to lose. Our work detail hid below decks as the fight roared on across the ship, and we were all scared to death. The pirates captured our ship, and all our crew that had not been killed in the fight was assembled on deck. We were found hiding below and drug up before the pirate captain. I was so scared and shaking so badly with the fear I thought my teeth were going to fall out of my head.

The pirate captain walked up and looked us over. He spun me around, looking at the many whip marks on the back of my torn shirt.

The pirate captain then walked over to the British captain, and, getting right in his face, he snarled at him saying "Just what I would expect from you British dogs. Which one of you mates here are in charge of the whip?"

No one said a word.

"Which one of you finely dressed rats here has been beating that boy?"

No one said a word. As quick as you could wink your eye, that pirate captain pulled his pistol and shot the British captain dead on the spot. "Feed the rest to the sharks!" screamed the pirate captain, and the rest of our crew went kicking and screaming over the side except for our work detail.

"Don't worry mates" Help me get this mess cleaned up and get some rum. We will be in Tortola in the morning."

When we arrived the next morning, our new captain gave us each a few coins, smiled, and sent us on our way. I had no way of knowing then that I would meet that captain again.

Tortola was completely lawless except for the law of the sea. It was infested with pirates, thieves, and cutthroats. I spent two weeks there scared out of my mind, not knowing what I was going to do next. *How will I survive here? How will I ever get off this God-forsaken island?* I asked myself over and over again.

One night I came across a great ship down on the docks. It was the blackest night I had ever seen, and I could barely see the ship in the mist. The pay being offered was fair, and the work was going to be hard. I was more than ready to agree to the terms, but the sign-on mate, Mr. Blunk, did not want to hire me because I was too lanky and too young.

"I'm handsome, nineteen, and strong," I argued with him.

"You look to be about a five-foot-eight bean pole with a red, curly top to me, and I don't care how pretty you are. I don't need a dance partner," he argued back. "The sun will burn you to a crisp, and just look at those flea-infested clothes and that hat. Where did you get that hat?" Mr. Blunk said as he continued laughing at me. I picked up a piece of coral and threw it at him.

Still laughing, he said, "Well, now that's different. You didn't say you were a scrapper. Get aboard, Mr. Newly, before you hurt somebody." I was halfway up the gangway with my smile, and Mr. Blunk yelled up to me, "Mr. Newly, if I were you, I'd take a bath and wash them fleas off your carcass. I'd burn them clothes too, before the captain sees you. I saw the captain give a mate like you a bath once. He dragged him behind the ship for ten miles. Poor fellow, the sharks got him."

I was horrified, and Mr. Blunk just looked at me with a big smile as I continued up the gangway. As I boarded the huge ship, I could see it was definitely a ship of war. One of the crew came up to me and looked me over carefully.

"You will do just fine. You will be working for me," he grumbled. "Follow me below and get cleaned up before the captain sees you." Turned out I had just met my first cannon master and did not realize it.

I did clean up, and the next morning the ship got under way. Despite my newfound cleanliness, I was kept below decks under task and training. I did not see the sky again for some time. I was being trained to be a cannon master's mate. Day in and day out all I did was train, train, train. By the time the cannon masters were finished with me, I was exhausted, but I knew everything there was to know about a cannon. I knew everything about how to clean one and how to load one. I knew how to take one apart and put it back together. I knew how to fix one when it was broken. I knew everything about what you could shoot out of one from bits and pieces of metal to mast splitting balls and chain. I especially knew how to shoot one, and I was really good at that.

Two

The first time I saw Captain Ethan Pike I was looking up through a fresh-air opening in the ship. The wind was blowing a warning through the sail rigging, and Captain Pike was peering at an approaching storm. He stood there alone for several minutes chewing on his upper lip, making a nasty sucking sound.

The captain was a tall man at over six foot and appeared a bit thin for his size. Despite his fair skin being sunburned and salt seasoned, he was a handsome man with long blond hair tied back in a tail. Captain Pike sported a nicely trimmed short beard, and the on top of his head he wore a fine Captain's hat with large red and blue parrot feathers mounted to the side. The captain's clothes were covered by a nice sea coat finished off with a fine pair of black boots. He looked exactly what a well-dressed captain should look like. The captain had a disgusted look to his face as he snarled at the storm's scenario unfolding before him. I was sure that he had been in this same scene all too many times in his thirty something years of age, but this particular storm seemed to be in his way.

Captain Pike's hat blew from his head and onto the deck. He snatched it up angrily and began growling orders at the crew. "Stand by to come around hard to port into the storm."

Captain Pike flew up the stairs to the ship's wheel, pushing Jonesy, the wheel man, away and knocking him down. The captain rapidly turned the large ship's wheel himself as fast it would go hard to port. Looking down at Jonesy lying on the deck, the captain screamed at him and said, "I said hard to port!"

Now Jonesy, sometimes not being a very nice fellow himself, jumped to his feet and screamed back at the captain, "You said standby to come around, Captain!"

In a split second, the captain tied off the wheel and grabbed Jonesy up by his shirt. Captain Pike then pulled out one of his pistols from under his coat and stuck it right in one of Jonesy's ears. Jonesy's eyes were as big as two dinner plates. His mouth was wide open, taking in a large gasp of air that he thought would be his last. I, looking through the vent, and the entire crew on deck were frozen in a stare at the scene unfolding before us.

The captain smiled a proud, wicked smile as he whispered into Jonesy's other ear. "Are you questioning me orders in front of the crew there, mate?"

Out of the crow's nest, the lookout screamed, "Land, Captain! I see the island!"

The captain, still holding Jonesy by his shirt, threw him to the wheel and quietly said, "Now steer, Mr. Jonesy, and hold me course into the storm."

Jonesy looked like he had seen the devil himself as Captain Pike turned away and opened his coat, sliding his pistol away and pulling out his seeing glass. The captain began to peer through his glass, looking in the direction the crow's mate was pointing.

As quick as the captain had pulled that pistol, the storm was on us. It was a beauty of a storm too, and we were headed right into her. Thunder, lightning, and hail pounded at the ship as the wind sent huge waves crashing over our bow. The sky had turned greenish in color and looked very strange if not evil. Being new to the ship and the youngest on board, I was terrified, as I did not know if I was more scared of the captain or the storm. In all of my nineteen years, I had not seen the likes of either, and at that moment, I was dead sure that either the sea or the captain would surely be my end.

It was a sight to watch as the crew scrambled in the wind and rain trying to do repairs and attempting to lash things down, all the while trying not to get washed over the side. Then there was Captain Pike who was screaming and cussing orders at the crew.

"Stand by this and stand by that. Secure this and secure that!" he yelled at them. "What's the matter, mates?" the captain yelled. "You scared you might get some of that stench washed off you?"

The entire time Captain Pike was laughing hardily at the entire scene. I could not believe it, but the captain was actually having the time of his life.

To my relief the storm was moving fast and left us as soon as it had come—now all I had to worry about was the captain killing me. As the storm cleared, it left behind a beautiful day and the island the captain was looking for. There on the upper deck, the captain again stood by himself. He stood silent and smiling while wringing his hands in a hungry, greedy way. The gulls seemed to be screaming at him from the distant island like guards sounding an alarm or maybe a warning.

The captain yelled the order, "Drop those anchors, mates!" He began to laugh again as he headed into his cabin.

The crew was nervous because the captain never told them anything. Nary a word as to where we were going, nor a word about what we were looking for. I had heard that you dare not ask either. There was an unspoken tale that the captain had a parchment, a special parchment that was supposedly given to him by some manner of creature for some unknown reason. A parchment that showed all the treasures of the world, and it was supposed to be in his cabin. I did not believe in tall tales, so I dismissed the entire matter.

The captain returned through the cabin door, yelling orders again. "Drop one of the dings over the side and inspect the ship!" he ordered. "And take that new boy that's below with you."

My heart pounded, as I did not know the captain even knew I was aboard. Two mates and I—the O'Hare brothers, Little Tim and his brother Johnny—and a pack of scurvy old fellows from Ireland made our way to the ding. I had never seen the ship from the waterside because I boarded her in the dark and in the mist, and that was pretty much how I was kept—in the dark, training and working for the many days we had been at sea, and I was shocked at what I now saw.

The *Sovereign of the Seas* was a huge ship, a barque class with three of the tallest masts I had ever seen, along with twenty-eight sails. A beauty of a ship she was with magnificent golden carvings and ivory inlays in the wood that covered the entire port and starboard sides, along with the forward and aft. She was herself a treasure afloat.

I asked Little Tim "Is that real gold there?"

"Sure is, mate," he replied.

"Have a look at all that ivory," Johnny added.

"Aye," Tim replied. "And she's got thirty cannon."

Johnny said, "No. She's got sixty!"

They both looked at each other in a disgusted manor, and Little Tim, the smarter of the two, said, "Thirty on the port side, and thirty on the starboard side."

Johnny, with a sour expression, said, "Well, that makes sixty, now don't it? And don't forget the four a stern and the six forward!"

"Where did the captain get her?" I asked as we came around the starboard side.

Both of the O'Hares pointed up at the high mast and started giggling like my little sisters. A flag had been raised and one that seemed too small and much to ragged for this great ship. It was a bit torn and weathered, but a flag that sent shivers up my neck and goose bumps dancing on my arms. The Jolly Roger it was.

My God, I thought to myself, *I have signed onto a pirate ship.*

I must have had the same look on my face as that of Jonesy when the captain had a hold of him at the wheel. The brothers O'Hare were giggling wildly and said, "Captain Pike borrowed her from the British Navy."

My look of worry came quickly back again, if it had ever left, when Johnny said, "Let's get back aboard. The captain wants to see the boy."

As I climbed the rope ladder to board the ship, I thought my heart was going to beat out of my chest. As my head cleared the deck, there the captain stood. "Well, mate, what do you think?" he asked. He had a stern look on his face, his coat opened and his hands resting on his pistols.

Looking at the deck, I mumbled, "About what, sir?"

In the blink of an eye, Captain Pike snatched me up by my shirt and off the deck. My feet were dangling in the air, and terror covered me like a hot, wet blanket. Captain Pike pulled my face right up to his and yelled, "Look at me when I'm talking to you, boy!" His breath was hot and smelled like a dead fish. "What is your name besides boy?" the captain demanded.

I stuttered back, looking him square in the eye, "Christopher, sir. Christopher Newly, sir."

"Well, Christopher, what do you think about the ship?" he questioned.

"It's fine, sir," I replied, scared to death.

"And what do you think of the crew, boy?"

I did not dare look away, but out of the corners of my eyes, I could see the crew gathering around. "I think the crew is fine too, sir."

The captain demanded, "And what do you think of me flag there, Mr. Newly?

"The flag is fine too, sir," I quickly replied.

"Do you know what that flag stands for?" Captain Pike demanded.

"Yes, sir," I said with a stutter."

"Do you still want to be a member of me crew?" questioned the captain.

"Yes, sir," I replied again with a stutter.

Captain Pike slowly lowered my feet back on the deck and exclaimed, "Good, because you don't look much like a swimmer to me!" He started to laugh wildly, and the crew quickly joined in on the joke, laughing with him.

The crew picked me up on their shoulders and started dancing around the deck with me. Just as my fear started to leave me and a smile started to grow on my face, the dancing and laughter stopped cold. The captain's and crew's faces went cold as rock, and my fear came rushing back.

The captain said, "But just in case…" And over the side I went.

The captain and crew all burst into laughter again. "Fish him out." Captain Pike smiled, and the crew hauled me out. "Welcome aboard, mate!" yelled the captain, and all hats were in the air except mine, which had gone over the side with me.

"Don't worry about your hat, mate!" one of the crew yelled out.

"Here it is," said Johnny O'Hare to me as he slammed my missing hat back on my head full of sea water and weeds.

"A pirate is born. Teach him the oath, and give him some rum for the chill," ordered Captain Pike. "We're going to the island in the morning. Be ready," ordered Captain Pike sternly as he turned and walked back into his cabin, slamming the door hard behind him.

Quickly the cabin door reopened, and like the good time had never happened, he screamed the order, "Now get back to work, or I'll have all of you in irons!" He slammed the door shut again, even harder this time, returning to his cabin.

That night we had quite the party. The crew was eating, drinking, singing, and dancing about the ship. Finally we had got a well-deserved break after a long journey at sea. The rum flowed freely as the crew played music on their accordions, bag pipes, and mandolins. I was finally an accepted member of the crew, and this was the first time I had been allowed on deck at night.

The *Sovereign of the Seas* was even more beautiful at night with all her lanterns glowing brightly. The stars, the ocean, the sound of the sea, and, best of all, the hot rum set the pace and the scene of the night. All the crew was there except the captain. I asked about him and was snappily told by the crew, "The captain dines alone."

With a full belly of wild pig washed down with the hot rum, the good time, along with the sounds of the music and singing, were interrupted by my distant thoughts. Thoughts of my home back in England and whom I had left behind ran through my mind.

My father had died from the fever when I was four years old. My mother, three sisters, and I were taken in by a man who owned a large farm. My mother, trying to secure a home for us, married him, and our new troubles began. My stepfather was a tyrant and worked us under the crack of the whip.

I ran away to the ship

yards searching for a better life and planning to someday return to reclaim my family and excuse them from their new master. I also made a solemn promise to return to Katherine. Katherine was a fine, redheaded Irish lass who was forbidden by her family to speak to me because I was English. We had become close friends despite them.

My thoughts from the past and plans for the future were disturbed when I caught the shadow of the captain walking by his cabin window. I was curious to as to what he did in there all by himself, so I crept closer to maybe get a peek. Despite my fear returning, I snuck up and carefully peered into one of his cabin windows. To my surprise, I saw a very handsomely set table with ten inlayed ivory chairs. There were fine china plates with silver forks and knives. Three large golden candleholders with six candles each set the table aglow. A silver platter with an untouched pig on it and several silver bowls full of fruit finished off the scene. The only thing that intruded on this spectacle was an old empty rum bottle lying on its side and a half empty one next to it.

But where is the captain? I wondered to myself.

I knew the captain was inside, so I slid down and around the window and up the other side of it so I could see the interior of the cabin. There was Captain Pike, fiddling around with an old-looking pigeon he kept in a cage. He walked over and sat with his side to me, sitting at an old table and chair, and opened a black iron chest. He pulled out what looked to be a scroll and rolled it open. He began to study it.

I wondered if this could be the parchment I had heard about. Was this the map the crew whispered in secret about?

Three

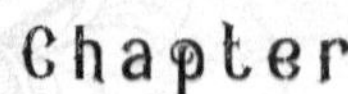

Suddenly, after a brief pounding on the captain's door, a mate burst in. Out of breath and half scared to death, the mate yelled out, "Captain! Captain Pike!"

The captain turned and roared at him, "This better be good, mate."

"The crow's mate reports ship's lights on the horizon off the port bow."

"Very well. Get out."

"But, Captain—"

"I said get out!" and the mate retreated back through the open door, closing it behind him.

Just as slow and smooth as a summer's evening, Captain Pike stood up, rolled up the scroll, placed it carefully back in the chest, locked it, and put it away in a closet. The key went into his coat pocket. He then walked up to the dinner table and snatched out a large chunk of the pig. The captain stuffed the meat into his mouth, almost having to use force to get it all in. A big swallow of rum followed. All of a sudden he seemed to go into a rage. Captain Pike smashed the bottle of rum against the cabin's wall and turned over the table, sending all that was upon it crashing about the room. The captain stalked out the cabin door and headed for the upper deck.

Moments later after peering through the night with his seeing glass, Captain Pike began shouting orders at the crew. "Standby those anchors!" he screamed. "Get them up now, or I'll have your hide on me wall! Get this bucket of barnacles under way! Sound the stations bell, and get those lamps out. If we can see them, they can see us!"

I ran for my station, as did the entire crew. Thank God my station was now with a cannon master on the front of the ship and not down below deck. With all my grueling hours of training complete, I had made the appointment of cannon master's mate. I got to wear a special scarf around my neck to show off my appointment, and I was very proud of that. I did not know why I had to endure such a grueling training, as it appeared I was nothing more than the master's powder-and-ball mate. I just did all the heavy work, and he shot the cannon. The thought had not occurred to me that he might be killed and I would have to take his place.

My cannon master's name was Jeffery Dudly, also an Irish fellow, but he was called Mr. Dudly. Cannon masters didn't live long, I was told.

Just like the captain ordered, we had all scrambled to our stations. The great ship jumped out of the water, and we were hard under way. Dawn was coming as we headed at topsail toward the approaching ship.

The captain stood cold as ice, seemingly not to notice the wind and spray on him. Next to him was Jonesy at the wheel, listening intently for any order the captain might yell out. Captain Pike, looking through his seeing glass, yelled out so all could hear, "It's a British man-of-war, and she's got forty cannon. Twenty on the port and twenty on the starboard."

My heart was pounding as we approached the man-of-war.

"Stand by the forward cannon," the captain commanded.

My cannon master, Mr. Dudly, looked over at me and said with a wink, "That's us, Mr. Newly." I looked over at the other five cannons and crew next to us. It was obvious that I was the only one scared to death, as the rest of the cannon masters and their crew were all smiles.

"Don't worry, Mr. Newly. This will be over as quick as it started. The captain has already won the fight," Mr. Dudly said.

"How?" I questioned.

"Just watch and learn."

Then Captain Pike growled out an order, looking me right in the eye. "If you sink that ship, I'll set you adrift."

"He wants that ship intact!" Mr. Dudley yelled in the wind and the spray.

The wind was picking up, and the sea was building because of it. In rough seas, the front of the ship was the worst place to be. The wind and the spray blinded us all. "Hold your course!" I heard the captain yell at Jonesy from behind me. "Steady on those forward cannon!"

My heart was pounding so hard I thought it was going to explode.

Frantically wiping the sea spray from my eyes, I could see the approaching British man-of-war. They were close enough now that I could see her crew running about her deck preparing for the fight. I could see her captain screaming orders at his crew in his fine red coat. I could see her riflemen, also dressed in their red coats, ready to pepper us. I could see her name—she was the HMS *Ark Royal*.

As the captain knew, the man-of-war had no forward cannon. No front teeth to bite us with, as he put it. They needed to get alongside us to fire their cannon. All they could do until they came alongside was pepper us with rifle fire, which was usually very damaging to the crew I was told.

"Hold steady, mates!" I heard the captain yell. "Easy, easy!"

The *Ark Royal* opened up on us with her rifle fire. There was lead flying everywhere. I saw several of our crew fall dead on the spot. Wood splinters from the *Sovereign* were dancing in the air all over the ship.

"Fire!" screamed the captain, and all forward cannon went off almost at the same time.

The cannon volley we sent over to them almost blew the entire forward section off the *Ark Royal*. The smoke from our cannon blew back in our faces, burning our eyes and leaving a metallic taste in our mouths. The smell of burning gunpowder accompanied by the screams of the dying and the wounded filled the air.

The captain screamed, "Hard to starboard!"

Jonesy, with a quick glance at the captain and remembering his last argument at the helm with him, turned that wheel like there was no tomorrow.

"Aye, hard to starboard, Captain!"

We turned hard at a forty-five angle right at the man-of-war with all our port cannon to bear. We still were not alongside her, so the *Ark Royal* could not fire except for rifle shot, and she was really pouring it on us.

"Fire!" screamed the captain. All thirty port-side cannon went off. The force was so great from all thirty of our cannon going off at one time, the

Sovereign was pushed sideways in the sea. The *Ark Royal* exploded into splinters, and her rifle fire stopped.

We continued our turn to starboard, and we circled around and came up alongside His Majesty's ship with thirty more cannon to bear. The warship was burning badly and was completely destroyed, sinking fast. I'll never forget the sight. Parts of her floated and burned in the water. Many of her wounded and her dead floated in the sea. I watched while what remained of her crew jumped for their lives, leaving the sinking ship. They jumped right into a bloodstained sea where the sharks had already begun to gather. There was a stench about the air, the stench of powder and death.

It was the worst scene I had ever witnessed, and I hoped I would never see anything like it again. I prayed to God and asked his forgiveness, and I prayed for those poor British devils in the sea.

The captain shook his head in disgust.

"Fire," he screamed out, and the warship was gone.

"What about what remains of her crew?" one of our crew asked.

"Give them a Ding" said Captain Pike.

With not agreeing another of our crew, Hank, said, "Why, Captain? Why help them? If it were us in the water, they would all be laughing and betting on the sharks."

"Well, we ain't like them, now are we, Hank? Carry out me orders, or you'll be joining them. As soon as those dings are down, come about and set a course for the island!" He looked directly at me and yelled, "I told you not to sink that ship, Mr. Newly."

I looked at the captain and then looked over at my cannon master, Mr. Dudly, hoping for him to explain. Mr. Dudly was shot dead by rifle fire.

"Too bad," said the captain. "A good hand he was. At least I don't have to shoot him myself for sinking that ship." Captain Pike then paused for a moment and said, "Looks like you're the new cannon master, Mr. Newly. Pick you a mate to assist you. And, Mr. Newly, I expect you for dinner tonight."

The entire topside crew stopped what they were doing and looked at Captain Pike in disbelief, and they began whispering among themselves.

"The captain dines alone," one mate muttered.

"Remember the others!" another mate yelled.

"I claim Mr. Newly's boots," said another.

As usual, together, like they only had one mouth between them, the O'Hare brothers at the same time called out, "I want his tote." They both looked at each other angrily and began to fight like two cats wallowing about on the deck.

"It's better than having him at my window again," growled the captain as he walked away.

I was horrified. The captain knew what I had been up to. For me, the short trip back to the island seemed very long.

I will always remember the horror of my first battle, and I will always remember the HMS *Ark Royal*. She was a magnificent three-tall mast, forty-cannon, nineteen-sail, high-speed ship. The HMS *Ark Royal* was a vicious pirate hunter, and she was gone with most hands lost. Apparently no match for the *Sovereign of the Seas* and her captain.

Chapter

Four

Soon enough, but too soon for me, we were back at the island. We had a busy day making repairs to the ship and preparing the dings with supplies for our excursion to the island the next morning. As the sun began to set, the crew was busy preparing their evening feast and festivities. As their music began to play, dinner was nearly ready to be served at the captain's table, and I was summoned. As I walked past the crew heading for my appointment with the captain, I was really scared. You would think by now the fear of death would elude me but that was not the case.

The crew's music stopped as I reached the top of the stairs in front of Captain Pike's cabin, and I turned back to look at them. The entire crew was grinning ear to ear as one of them signaled the bag pipers to begin to play a funeral song. I was not amused.

I knocked on the cabin door and entered. I began a slow peer around the extra-large cabin, and to my surprise the table was set exactly as I had seen it before. That is, except for the black iron chest in the middle of the table. The captain sat at the head of the table with his boots up on it, chewing on a piece of pig sloppily. Bits of meat were in his beard and on his face as he picked up a bottle of rum and took a big swig. He wiped his coat sleeve across his face and beard, sending the bits of meat flying.

With a mouth half full of rum and pig, he said, "Well, Mr. Newly, are you just going to stand there with that stupid look on your face? Put your carcass in a chair."

It seemed like it took forever for me to walk to the table and sit down. The captain took another big drink of rum that must have been four or five swallows. "Arrrr," he said and tossed the bottle to me. "Drink."

I looked into the old bottle of rum and could see bits of the captain's dinner floating on the top and also bits that had settled to the bottom.

"Drink," he ordered as he leaned forward in his chair staring at me.

I took a big drink of four or five swallows, trying to match the captain. My last swallow did not go down well, and it sprayed out of my mouth all over the table.

The captain burst into laughter, and with a big grin, he said, "Well, Mr. Newly, at least you got salt. I'd rather been keel hauled then to have drank that slop from another man." The captain reached under the table and tossed me a fresh unopened bottle followed closely by a chunk of pig that he flung at me from down the table. "Drink and eat, as I have important matters to discuss with you."

As I ate and drank, I started making light conversation with the captain, and I started to relax a bit. He asked about where I had come from and where I wanted to go. I told the captain of my family back in England and of my Irish lass, Katherine, and how one day I wanted to return to them and set them free. I asked the captain how he had come to this spot in his life, and after a brief minute of chewing, he began his tale of the past.

The captain explained that he was born in England and grew up on the sea. He told me that for a brief time he had retired from the sea and taken a lovely wife that had given him a fine son, but sadly they both had died from the fever. The captain told me that he had returned to the sea as the captain of a merchant ship. He said, "The pirates and the English Navy haunted my life. You had to bribe the pirates not to raid you, and you had to bribe the navy to protect you." The captain explained how one day he had just had enough of it all. He persuaded his crew to follow him as he commandeered his merchant ship and went into business for himself.

"She was a fine ship, Mr. Newly, and when I got done fitting her with hidden cannon and more sail, she was a wolf that looked like a sheep. Those poor devils would come alongside to raid us or to extort us, and we'd give them a broadside. Then we'd steal their ships and leave them for the sharks. After a while, we started openly attacking all of them on sight. It did not take long for the pirates to fear us and the English Navy to hunt us."

All the while when the captain and I were talking I could not help myself and I kept looking at that chest in the middle of the table.

I was careful because I did not want him to see my interest in it, and so far he had not noticed, or at least I did not think he had. One day I would finally learn that the captain did not miss anything.

The black iron chest was nothing fancy and not very big. It certainly did not look like it belonged in the middle of all those fancy table settings.

"I see you have an interest in me chest there, Mr. Newly," the captain observed. I was shocked and almost choked on my mouthful of pig.

"No, sir, Captain," I said. "I hardly had noticed."

He jumped up from his chair, grabbed the chest, and slammed it down in front of me on the table.

"Well, get you a good look." He scowled. "And by the way, Christopher, it's against the law of the sea to lie to your captain." A moment later the captain followed up with, "Unless you got a good reason of course." And he began to chuckle.

The chest was ancient looking but appeared to be in good shape. It was about twice the size of breadbasket, made of a heavy black metal with black metal bands around it. The lock that looked to be made of gold was the only thing on the chest that made it look even remotely valuable. The chest did have some very interesting etchings on it. The etchings showed great scenes, scenes from deep below the sea.

Then out of nowhere, he asked, "Can you read and write, Mr. Newly?"

"Yes, Captain," I replied.

"Good. You're the only man on this ship that can, 'cept me of course. I just ain't real good at it. Are you good at it, Mr. Newly?"

"Yes, Captain. I'm good at it."

"I got something here I want to show you, and if you speak a word of this, I'll cut your throat from ear to ear. Do you understand me?"

"Yes, I understand."

"Yes what?"

"Yes, Captain. Yes, sir, Captain. Of course, Captain, I understand." I guess it was the curiosity that eased my fear because I was no longer scared to death—just half scared to death.

He opened his coat and in a topside pocket pulled out a big black key and tossed it to me. "Open the chest, Mr. Newly," he said with a smile.

"Me, Captain?"

"Of course not, Christopher. I was talking to the other Mr. Newly standing right there behind you!"

My hand was shaking so badly again I had trouble getting the key in the lock. A click and the chest sprung open like it had been waiting forever for someone to unlock it. I jumped back in my chair and almost fell over backward. I stood back up straight, regaining myself, and I began to peer slowly into the chest.

The inside of the chest looked just like outside: cold, black, heavy metal with etchings of undersea scenes. Inside the chest I saw a lone item, the captain's scroll.

"Get the scroll out, Mr. Newly," instructed the captain.

Again my hand was shaking badly as I slowly reached into the chest. I reached in like there was a poison snake inside somewhere unseen and hidden, and I did not want to get bit. With a snatch, I picked up the parchment and pulled it out.

"Well, Mr. Newly!" Captain Pike exclaimed. "You ain't dead!" The captain was looking at me with a surprised and questioning look on his face. "Well, it looks like I chose a proper man finally."

"Dead, Captain?" I asked in a horror.

"Yes! Dead, Mr. Newly," he replied. "The last four dogs that touched that scroll are dead," snarled Captain Pike.

"What did you say, Captain? How did they die, Captain?"

"Well, let's just say it weren't pretty," Captain Pike said with a wince.

I jumped up and threw the parchment upon the table. I slumped back down in my chair and looked at the captain in horror, shaking my head at him, knowing full well that my contempt for him showed plainly on my face.

"This scroll has a curse upon it, and no man can touch it except me," the captain explained. "That is unless I give me permission, and even then the scroll knows the trusty ones." The captain laughed and said, "I guess the other mates were not trusty, and you must be.

"Now that we got that out of the way, pick up the scroll."

"No, Captain. I'm not touching that thing!"

"Come now, Mr. Newly. If that parchment did not want you looking at it, you'd already be dead." I did not move until he screamed, "Pick up that scroll!"

I snatched it up off the table with a quick grab and shut my eyes. When I opened my eyes, Captain Pike laughed. "Now roll it out and put it on the table." My hands were shaking so badly I thought I was going to tear the parchment.

What I saw was truly unearthly. It was a map of some kind that appeared to be made of ancient parchment yellowed with age. The map had its own light to it, like a glow from a thousand candles. It was a flat map of the world with places signed upon it like bright, shining stars. The map had warning pictures of great beasts of the sea that seemed alive.

The map seemed to have a life of its own. The outside edges of it seemed to be trimmed in gold with silver faces of men upon it. The faces of the men also seemed alive and looked to be in great pain. They were squirming about, crying and pleading for their freedom. I could hear them as I listened closely, and I was horrified.

On all four corners of the parchment there was a place for a key to be laid in place like it was some sort of lock. All four keys were missing. My imagination ran wild.

"Those are the un-trusted ones that touched the map," the captain explained

In a second, the captain snatched the parchment off the table, and into the cabin's fireplace it went. The fireplace exploded into a burst and then died back down, and I jumped to my feet as if to rescue the map.

"No need!" snapped the captain as he walked calmly over to the fire and pulled the parchment out with his sword. It was untouched by the flames. "The map of the sea cannot be destroyed by a man," he explained as he knocked the ashes from it back and forth on his leg. Placing the map back on the table, the captain looked at me and whispered, "Open it, Mr. Newly."

Curiosity overcame me again. "Aye, Captain," I answered. I carefully rolled the map back open.

As the captain had explained, the map of the sea was untouched by the flames. The captain leaned over my shoulder and gently blew on the parchment. In a second, right before our eyes, it changed from the world map to an island map with one glowing star jewel.

I again jumped back in surprise, and Captain Pike said, "Relax, Mr. Newly. This is where we be." The map showed an island called Oak Island with three places marked on it. Smuggler's Cove on one side and Smith's Cove on the other. The bright, shining star jewel was marking a spot right in the middle of the island. After a minute of silence and gazing at the map, the captain spoke and said, "That's where the treasure be. We will go for it in the morning."

"Treasure!" I exclaimed.

"The map belongs to the witch of the sea," the captain said in an almost-fearful whisper.

"Witch, Captain? What witch?"

"Those men there," he warned, "the ones whose faces be there on the map, they belong to her now for all time. We will have to deal with her and them later. They are neither dead nor alive."

I jumped up and away from the table and turned to the captain, yelling at him in a horror, "I do not wish to deal with them later or at anytime."

"Too late for that, Mr. Newly," he said, laughing. "The witch is upon you now as she is me! You have touched her map, and she knows who you are." He burst into a fit of laughter and then said, "What hunts me now hunts you, Mr. Newly."

I was not amused as the hot, wet blanket of fear was back upon me.

"She will take any other poor devils in our company too," the captain warned. "But in a special way. She badly wants the ones that have touched her map. She really wants to get her claws on me and now on you, Mr. Newly."

In total disbelief and horror, I yelled, "What is it, Captain? Just what is it that made you bring down this curse on us, your ship, and your crew?"

"Sit down, Mr. Newly," Captain Pike said softly and in a casual manner. "Ask me your questions, and I will tell you your answers. Drink some rum, and put your feet up. You need to relax a bit. You seem to be a bit high strung for your age."

A calm came about the room as we could hear the crew's music and laughter outside in the background. The captain sat sipping his rum, and I guzzled mine in a desperate need. We sat staring at each other in silence, and after a few minutes of thinking, I asked, "Where did you get this fine ship, Captain? Did you fight for it? Did you win it in battle on the seas?"

With a smile, Captain Pike answered, "No, Mr. Newly. I traded for it."

"Traded for it, sir?" I asked in a wonder.

"Yes, Christopher," he said, whining and sneering at my name like he hated it. "Traded for it," he gloated. "I got her without a shot fired. The captain of this fine ship was Admiral George Bennington of His Majesty's Navy, and a fine officer he was 'cept for his corruption and greed. He had heard about me map from someone telling a tall tale somewhere, and he wanted to know more. The good admiral had approached me by messenger and offered in exchange for a share in me map that he would give me this fine ship, so I agreed."

The captain began to laugh and said, "The good admiral wanted to be me partner, you see, and after he sacrificed his crew to the sea and delivered me this ship, I held up me part of the bargain." Getting another big drink of rum, the captain continued, "I showed the admiral the map, just like you, Mr. Newly.

"I gave the good admiral the key, and he opened the chest with a big, greedy smile on his face. As soon as he touched the map, the sea witch was upon him. Admiral Bennington stood back and dropped the map, and he screamed a scream of a thousand screams." Just like that, the captain lost the smile he was wearing and said, "I never heard a man scream like that, Mr. Newly, and I hope I never do again. Bennington was looking at me with horror and contempt as I watched him begin to boil right before me eyes, Mr. Newly."

"Boil, Captain?"

"Yes, boil. Admiral Bennington began to shake widely as what I thought was boiling lava began to run out of his eyes and his ears and his nose. I watched as the man was consumed by the fire, growing smaller and smaller in substance. It was not really a fire, though, Mr. Newly, because it had no heat. All that was left of him was ashes that drifted away in the calm wind, and not even a mark was left on the cabin floor. His head was the last thing to go as he melted away to the witch, Mr. Newly. I could hear her laughing with glee in the back, and the good admiral screamed in his horror to the end.

"Look at the map," the captain ordered.

I looked at the map as fast as my neck would allow me to turn it.

The captain put his finger on one of the silver faces squirming in pain on the map. "There he is, Mr. Newly. There he is, as are the others."

With that, the captain put his finger on each of their poor, cursed faces, and he seemed to dig at them with a nail and with a vengeance scratched at them. "They all have a story, except this one here. I don't know this poor devil, but no matter, in the end they were not trustable, and the sea witch's map knew it. The witch has claimed them for all of time, and not even God can help them now," he whispered as he sat back down in his chair and took five more swallows of the rum. "I'm starting to like you, Mr. Newly. I'm glad your face did not make the map.

I sat in the chair looking at the map with nothing to say. Silently my emotions ran wild with pity for the poor souls on the map and with pity for the admiral's sacrificed crew, not to mention the fact that I was petrified by the witch and her cursed map. I hated the captain for trying me in his court, and my hate and anger for him overcame me. Without speaking a word, I jumped from my chair, drew my sword quickly, and put it to the captain's throat. "I should kill you, Captain Pike!"

"Sit down, Christopher, before you cut yourself," the captain said with a grin. "What is your next question?"

I slowly lowered my sword and placed it back in its sheath and sat back in my chair. The captain was grinning like he knew he could have killed me at any time as he said, "Have another swallow of that rum, Mr. Newly, and relax. What is your next question?"

"What about the four key holes on the map captain?" I asked. "What are they for?"

"It appears to me this map is some sort of lock, and I mean to see what's behind it. That, Mr. Newly, is our mission."

"What about the treasure, Captain?"

"You might as well know this right now. I don't need more treasure. I have more treasure buried in the sand than King George has piled up in the Tower of London. The crew will get their share of the treasure on this island if there is indeed any at all. I'm after these four keys, and it seems to me that if we find the signs on this map we will find the keys."

"Where did you get the map, Captain?" The captain laughed without nerve, but I could tell by the look on his face that he did not like the question.

"I got the map from the Sea Witch, Mr. Newly," he answered.

I again jumped up from my chair and yelled out, "The witch, Captain? You have seen the witch? I thought you found this chest."

"Oh, yes," answered the captain in a strange tone. "I have seen her with me own eyes. "Mr. Newly, do you know of Maidens of the Sea?"

"I have heard stories of them, Captain, but they are fairy tales that don't exist."

"Well, you be wrong, as they do exist. I found one of these maidens a time ago. She was so beautiful it hurt to look at her. She had long, golden hair with smooth, lovely skin. She had deep ocean-blue eyes that could look right through you. She was the finest woman I had ever laid me eyes on. Despite her beauty and her features, she was no woman. She had a big, beautiful tail like a fish, and she carried with her a spell that made all men love her at first sight.

"I found her on the rocks beaten and broken from the waves. We nursed her back, but she could not or would not speak to us except in our minds like a dream. She had a power though, Mr. Newly, and every man on the ship fell under her spell. All of the crew loved her in an unheard of manner, and I, too, began to be consumed and mesmerized by her. I finally caught my sense and ordered the maiden held below in the brig away from the crew.

"We were taking her back to Tortola for more doctoring, and after a day at sea, I went to visit the maiden. Fearing I would be taken again by her thoughts, I came with several mates carrying oil and torches." The captain began to shake with the memory, and he said, "I again felt her overpowering thoughts, and she would not speak. She would not stop her thoughts to control us, Mr. Newly." The captain began to snarl, and a tear ran down his face. "We put the oil and the torches to her. It was the hardest thing I ever had to do, but I had to save me ship and crew. I loved her, Mr. Newly, as did the crew, but we burnt her right then and there. As she screamed from the fire, she finally spoke and said three words. Three words, Mr. Newly, she screamed from the flames, and I'll never forget them.

"'Mother help me!' she cried.

"The sea started to boil, and another great maiden rose up. She also was fine with beauty, except this maiden had nothing to do with the love of men. No word was spoken, but we could feel her anger and hear her demands in our minds. It was the Sea Witch come for her daughter. I ordered the ship hard to port, but it did not move like a great hand from below was upon us. Another demand was made by the witch in our minds, and I could hear her speak to me.

"'Release my daughter, and you shall have all the riches of the sea!' she screamed.

"Then a chest was flung from the sea and upon the deck of this ship as if to pay a ransom we had not asked for. We went below and retrieved the burnt, agonizing creature and tossed her over the side. The sea witch went wild with rage receiving the remains. After her rant, she just disappeared below the waves with what was left of her daughter. She is out there, Mr. Newly, watching us and waiting for her revenge." With a smile and a wink and the tears of the past dried up on his face the captain said, "But we got her map, mate, and that was worth the trouble."

I knew he did not believe that, but I was beginning to learn that that was just how the captain was.

"Let that be a lesson to you, Mr. Newly," the captain said. "I saved that creature from her death on the rocks, and in gratitude it tried to destroy me ship and crew. Now I am cursed for me good deed. Good night, Mr. Newly. That will be all for tonight."

As if to push on my new found luck I asked the Captain, "sir, if I may, ask what's up with that pigeon?"

To my surprise Captain Pike responded saying, "What pigeon?

I looked over and the pigeon was gone.

When I walked out of the captain's cabin and down the stairs, the crew's celebration and music stopped. They looked at me like I was a ghost because nobody that ever had dinner with Captain Pike was seen again.

"Well, we need to take a break here, mates, as I need another bottle of rum and that fire needs a few more logs." Everyone in the tavern was frozen in their tracks listening to my tale.

"Hold on there, Mr. Newly. I'll get you a fresh bottle," said the barkeep.

"I'll get the logs for the fire," said a stranger.

"You just sit there, Mr. Newly, and finish the tale," said a fellow that heard my story at least five times previously. I looked around at all faces in the tavern, and they were all wide eyed and intent. I just smiled and said, "Okay, mates, now listen carefully. I don't want you to miss anything."

Chapter

Five

ell the next morning the captain appeared at dawn from his cabin. He rang the ship's bell three times as a call to all hands to stations. He yelled out with a big grin, "To the island, men! And, Mr. Newly, make sure you are on one of those dings as I may have need of your skills."

A big gulp was all I could produce in reply.

"You men get to the armory and pack yourselves well," the captain said in a most serious tone. "Oh, and give Mr. Newly a pistol or two as we don't want him cutting himself with that sword of his." The crew began to chuckle loudly.

As Captain Pike stepped to board a ding, he looked back and yelled, "Don't forget to feed me pigeon, or I serve all of you up to the sharks when I get back."

It was a strange, almost unreal-looking morning as the sun rose higher and higher in the sky trying to burn off a purple-looking fog and mist that surrounded the island. The high black peaks of the island rose above the fog, and they seemed to be a thousand feet tall. We landed on the shore and stepped into the black sand as the circling gulls above were screaming at us as if we were trespassers and this was their island. One of the gulls made their feelings known well as it relieved itself of its morning fish breakfast all over Mr. Herington's hat. I laughed out loud and got a dirty look from him.

"Do you think that's funny, boy?" Mr. Herington growled as he reached for his knife.

"Now, Mr. Herington," the captain said, "you pull that knife and the crabs will be feastin' on your bones for lunch.

"But, Captain—"

"I don't want to hear it Mr. Herington. This boy, as you call him, has a much larger value to me than you do at this point and since you seem to be so found of him you can look after Mr. Newly on our little visit here."

The captain smiled with an evil look.

"Oh and Mr. Herington, not a bad thing better happen to him either as those crabs look really hungry."

Mr. Herington looked disgusted and replied, "Aye, Captain."

"Oh, and Mr. Herington, one more thing if I may, Mr. Newly's name is not boy. In case you have not noticed, he carries the mark of a cannon master, and you carry that of a cook. His name to you is Mr. Newly from now on."

"Aye, Captain," grumbled Mr. Herington.

Mr. Herington sneered over at me, and I gave him a big, proud smile in return.

I saw no means or way to penetrate the island's wall of black rock without wings. The captain opened his coat and retrieved the sea witch's map. Several of the crewmembers looked away, as it would turn them to stone for a single gaze upon it. The crew had all heard of the map and rumored of it, but none had ever seen it before.

The captain laughed out loud and teased them with the parchment.

"Want to touch it, mates?"

They all jumped back.

"How about you, mate?" Captain Pike teased our master at arms, Mr. Spongy?

He stepped backward in horror. I began to chuckle but was quickly shut up by the captain.

"Watch yourself there, Mr. Newly. Don't push your luck with them crabs neither. I like an even keel, Mr. Newly. I'll not have the crew at you nor you at them. Do you understand me?"

"Yes, sir, Captain. I understand completely," I replied, frowning.

I looked over at Mr. Herington, and in revenge he gave me back my big, proud smile.

"This way mates and be on guard," he said over his shoulder. "Spread out. I could kill all of you at one time with one pumpkin ball from me pistol."

We followed the captain down the beach for about an hour, watching him as he looked at the map and looked about the island. Suddenly Captain Pike stopped dead in his tracks and walked up to the black cliff wall. He pulled at the many vines covering the rock face until he made a clearing. The captain rubbed at the rock as if trying to clean it.

"Here!" he shouted. "Here, Mr. Newly. Get your butt up here!" I ran up and looked at the rock face. "Here be the way in, Mr. Christopher Newly," he said with a big smile.

Sure enough on the rock face was some sort of writing, and on each side of the writing was an odd-looking stone that did not match the rock. They appeared to have been carved in place by someone or something.

"Read to me what it says, Mr. Newly," ordered the captain.

It was then that I finally knew my purpose and my value. The captain could not read a word. Now I had him, and I enjoyed the moment even if it was just for a moment.

"Captain, you can't read that?" I asked aloud so all could hear. The crew looked about at one another as if they were confused.

Captain Pike leaned over my shoulder and whispered in my ear, "Just read what it says, Mr. Newly, and save your comments in front of the crew. The map awaits you."

I decided quickly that it would be in the captain's best interest and my future health's to say aloud, "No wonder you cannot read this, Captain. It is written in French."

-"I like a man that can think on his feet, Mr. Newly. You just made a wise decision."

I cleaned at the rock and looked carefully upon it, and I said to the captain, "It appears to be some sort of rhyme, Captain."

"Rhyme?" asked the captain.

"Yes, sir, a rhyme," I explained.

"Read it," Captain Pike said, and all the crew leaned forward with open ears.

I slowly and carefully spoke the words as my fingers ran them over the rock face. "Those who dare and without a care, turn the stone to the right with all you're might."

The captain and I looked at each other for a second, and I went for the stone. "Hold," the captain blurted out, and I jumped back. "Too easy," he growled as he slowly looked around at the wall and then scratched about the ground. "Stand back, Mr. Newly." He pulled me back and away from the site.

"Mr. Longfellow, get your scurvy carcass over here. It's time you earned your wages."

Mr. Longfellow was one of the most liked men on the ship. He was always polite and apologetic. His name fit him to a tee because he was at least seven feet tall. He was a cannon master on the port side of the ship. I was immediately worried for him. "Aye, Captain. You called," he said.

"Yes," said the captain with a smile of deceit. "See that stone there on the starboard side?" asked the captain.

"Aye," answered Mr. Longfellow.

"Walk up there and turn it hard to the starboard," the captain ordered.

"But, Captain," said Mr. Longfellow, "what if something goes wrong, Captain, and you ain't right?"

"I said turn it." He threw Mr. Longfellow toward the wall.

"Aye, Captain. You know you don't have to get pushy, Captain. I have always followed your orders, Captain," Mr. Longfellow said.

I hated the captain when he acted like that. I was having a lot of trouble figuring him out. One minute I liked and respected the man, and the next I hated him. There was just no way to figure him out. When I think back, I believe that was the way he wanted it.

Turned out those were the last words that Mr. Longfellow would ever speak. He walked up and grabbed that right-side stone, and he turned it with all his might. At first it would not move, but slowly it gave way, and then finally it gave fast. Mr. Longfellow turned and looked at the captain proudly, sporting a big smile. Then he looked at me and then to the crew. With a large noise and in a split second, the ground underneath him fell away to a deep pit, and he was gone. We could hear him screaming as he fell farther and farther down until the screams just faded away.

We all looked around at each other stunned at what had just happened. My heart jumped into my throat, and I could not speak as I fell over backward into the sand. The crew began to run, and the captain's eyes were as big as two dinner plates.

Then we heard a sound coming back up the pit, returning back to the surface from far below and getting louder and louder as it rose. It was the sound of sinister laughing, and it made the hair on the back of my neck stand up. It sounded like an unearthly cackle, a cackle made by some sort of a woman.

Faster and faster it came up and out of the pit. Louder and louder it came. When it cleared the pit and spilled into the air the creature was hard to see plainly because it was moving so fast. In the few seconds I had to look it appeared to have the head of a beautiful woman with long black hair blowing wildly about. The creature's body was not to be seen except for her arms and hands that were a horror. All over them were nasty festering soars. The nails on her fingers were so long they curled around. All I remember about the rest of her was that she wore long red gown that blew about wildly in her wake. It was some sort of banshee, I knew that much. Her laughter was so loud it was deafening. I could feel my eardrums pounding hard, and the pain began to build. All the crew grabbed at their ears trying to stop the sound. Up into the air whatever it was went, and it had a hold of Mr. Longfellow or what used to be him.

Mr. Longfellow's face was a terror, and he looked to be screaming, but he made no sound. Up into the air, the spectacle went dragging Mr. Longfellow along with it by the scruff of his neck. Finally after a minute, it rolled over and down, splashing into the sea and taking its hideous laughter with it. Whatever it was, it and Mr. Longfellow were gone to the sea.

The crew and I were frozen with horror at the scene. The captain seemed untouched and uncaring about the whole event. He walked over to the pit and looked down. Then he glanced over at me and said with a big smile, "Well, Mr. Newly, now you have met her."

"Her, Captain?" I questioned.

"There's your Sea Witch, Mr. Newly. Ain't she a beauty? Still seems a bit upset over her daughter, wouldn't you say?"

I wanted to reply, but no words could leave my lips.

The captain called me over and away from the rest of the crew. He rolled open the map, and to my disbelief, Mr. Longfellow's poor, horrible face began to appear onto the map. He had joined the other poor souls on that curse of a parchment. The captain rolled up the map and put it back in his coat. He was still completely unfettered and said, "Well, I guess that were the wrong stone."

Then the captain began to explain, "I got it figured. The rhyme said turn the stone to the right but did not say turn the stone on the right."

Captain Pike walked over to the wall and eased along a ledge that was still preserved and had not fallen away to the pit. He grabbed the other stone carefully, looking over his shoulder at us, and with a big smile, he turned the stone hard to the right and scurried away quickly. Nothing happened, and we all stood silent staring at the rock face.

"I don't know what else to do here!" yelled the captain. He picked up a large stone and fired it at the rock face, cussing at it.

Turned out the captain had indeed unlocked the way in, but it just needed a little push. When the rock the captain threw hit the rock face, we began to hear a rumble. The ground began to shake wildly, and the rock face began to fall away into the pit. Quick as it started, the shaking stopped, exposing a large opening to a cave.

With a big smile, the captain said, "Fire those torches, mates, and follow me in."

We were all scared to death, except for Captain Pike of course. Maybe it was the greed. Maybe it was the love of adventure that pushed us along. Each of us had to have carried one of these traits in our hearts, or we would have never gone into that cave. The captain, on the other hand, was the only one of us that I was sure had both. Whatever our personal reasons were, we were soon to be regretting our decision to enter that cave. The witch was calling our faces to join her map, and some of us were headed straight into her trap.

The cave was dark, wet, and slimy with roots and such brushing our faces. The entire journey seemed to be downward with lots of bugs and other disgusting things slugging about. The bugs and slugs and leaches would drop on us and crawl on our skin. Some places in the cave were large, and some we had to half bend over to get past. We made our way into the torch-lit darkness, into the unknown. After about an hour, I began to yearn for the light of day, the sight of the blue sky, and the smell of the sea.

We came upon a large arena in the cave with the slimed floor still sloping downward. The smell was practically unbearable. The entire ceiling of the cave was covered with a countless number of bats. The floor of the cave was three hands deep with bugs and roaches that seemed to be one living mass, rolling and tumbling about each other.

The captain turned to me and whispered, "I hate bats, Mr. Newly, especially blood bats."

"Blood bats, Captain?"

"Yes, blood bats, Mr. Newly." He pointed up. "They can suck a man dry in minutes."

"I hate bugs," I said to him back in a whisper.

I could tell by the look on his face that he wanted to laugh one of his hardy laughs, but he held it in. He motioned the crew to come around and join in a group in silence.

As we came together in the torch-lit blackness, I could hear the roaches popping and crunching under our boots. It turned my stomach to hear their sound, but the fear of them crawling up my legs was even more overpowering. We kept burning them off with torches, swatting at them with the flames.

"Easy, mates," the captain said. "We will get through this, but we must be very quiet." Captain Pike turned and started off leading our way again.

"I'd rather be taken by the crabs than eaten alive by bugs," Mr. Livingston whispered. I shivered at the thought.

One of the crew Hutch tripped over something and almost fell into the mix of bugs. Hutch dug about in the bugs with his torch, searching for what had tripped him up. We could hear the bugs popping with the fire and smell them burn. He made a horrifying discovery—it was a man's skeleton cleaned by the bugs.

Hutch let out a scream and took off running. Then poor Hutch tripped again, over a rock this time, and into the bugs he went. He jumped up, thrashing around wildly, screaming, completely covered with bugs. The bugs were crawling in and out of his mouth and ears and his nose. They started to eat him alive from the inside out. The captain pulled out his pistol and shot Hutch dead, and I think a part of me died with him.

Then here came the bats, the blood bats. The entire ceiling of bats descended on us.

The captain screamed, "Run! Run for your lives! Get to the other side!"

All hands took off like the devil himself was after us.

The bats were biting at our heads and at our arms. They were biting at our hands, our faces, and our necks. They had claws that dug into our skin. Their claws held them in place so they could begin their feast. When I would pull at the devil to get it off, it would bite my hands. I did not think I was going to get out alive, but if I did, I knew I was going to be missing some of my fingers and maybe an ear or two.

The cave had plenty of drop-offs, and it was no telling how deep they were. With the bats on him, one of the crew ran right off one of the drops and was gone with what looked a thick cloud of bats following him down.

When he went over, I could hear the Sea Witch laughing and so could Captain Pike. "It's her!" Captain Pike screamed at me.

Another of the crew tripped up and fell into the bugs. The bats were on him in a second and even began eating each other in the frenzy. The poor fellow did not even scream out as I saw his face disappear beneath the surface of bugs and bats like he was sliding under the sea in a peaceful manner.

Then one big blood bat appeared out of the darkness. It seemed fifty times the size of the others, and it had its sights on Captain Pike and me. The bat had great wings upon it, and we could hear them flapping and could feel their air on our faces. Large red eyes lit the bat's face so we could see its great teeth and fangs. It came in fast and swiped at us with its huge claws trying to grab us.

This bat had a large, nasty-looking collar around its neck as if it were owned by someone or something. Its scream was just as bad as the Sea Witch when she had come up and out of the pit. I again could feel my eardrums pounding, and the pain returned. Despite the bat's screams, the captain and I could again hear the laughing of that witch. She was hiding somewhere in the darkness of the cave, waiting for her prizes to be delivered.

The huge bat kept swooping down on me and the captain, badly wanting to carry us away to its master, clutching at us with those huge claws. Several times as it hovered over us, I saw it snap out of the air a smaller bat or two swallowing them down whole.

The witches bat would come out of the cave's darkness and would make a run at us and then disappear back to the darkness. We never knew which way it would come. Captain Pike and I were able to keep it at bay with our swords, but we were losing the battle, and it was only a matter of time.

During one of the bat's runs at us, I pulled out my pistol and shot the red-eyed monster right in the face at pointblank range. The bat, in a rage, just screamed even louder at us and then came back around for another run at us. I yelled to the captain, "We are not going to make it, Captain! We are all dead men!"

"Not so fast, Mr. Newly!" Captain Pike screamed back.

The captain quickly put away his sword and reached into his coat and pulled out the Map of the Sea. He unrolled it with haste and showed it to us.

Instantly the map began to glow the glow of innumerable candles. Not a white color like we had seen before, but a purple-violet color. The map made a sound of ten thousand bees with its hum, and it hurt our eyes to look upon it. The b

Blood Bats began to run away from above us, and the bugs ran from below us. We had a clear floor to walk on except for the slime and the dung. The very large bat was particularly in a rage at the sight of the map but did not approach for another run at us. It just hovered at a distance and screamed at Captain Pike and me.

"The Sea Witch's pet I would guess!" yelled the captain over the bat's rant.

We began to make our way along slowly and approached the other side of the cave and safety was near.

Another one of the mates, Mr. McNairy, fell outside the glow of the map and just like that, the big bat got him. The bat had a hold on the Mr. McNairy's shoulders, and his body dangled from its claws. The look on that poor man's face was one I will never forget. The giant bat took him screaming, off into the darkness. I thought I would never see him again, but as it turned out, I would. Just like the captain had told me when he first showed me the Map of the Sea:

"We will have to deal with them all later, Mr. Newly."

Captain Pike looked over at me and yelled, "Well, Mr. Newly, that winged devil could not have us, so it's settled for him I guess."

What remained of us got to the other side and out of the arena under the protection of the map, which was still glowing. We did not stop running for a good piece, and when we finally did stop to rest, we counted our fingers and ears, all knowing that we had lost four of the crew. What was left of us was covered in blood from being chewed upon by the bats.

I questioned the captain regarding the map's light and how it had saved us from the wrath of the witch and the nasty creatures of the cave. The captain, still out of breath, said to me with a grin, "I told you, Mr. Newly, no man or creature wants to see this map, not to mention maybe being touched by it, 'cept us."

"Did you know the map could do that?" I asked.

"No, Mr. Newly, but I do now." The captain tried to laugh but did not have the breath. "Make camp here," the captain said. He rolled up the map and the light of it faded away into the torch lit darkness of the cave. "Find some fresh water, and get a fire started, as I have had enough of this day. Clean each other up, and when I get back, it better be nice and cozy in here."

Captain Pike began to walk back in the direction of the arena, and Mr. Robinson, the ship's blacksmith, said to me in amazement, "Where in this world is he going?"

I just shook my head and laid back in exhaustion.

The captain reappeared out of the darkness after about a half an hour and he was carrying a half dozen dead bats by their necks. The captain threw them down by the fire and looked around at us with his smile.

"Cook these up and don't forget I like my Blood Bat tender, so you best present them to me that way."

We all looked at the captain as though a fever had come on him.

"Either that or I'll eat one of you."

As it turned out, we discovered the bats did not taste too badly. We sat around the fire with full bellies, picking our teeth with their bones and licking our wounds.

"I'd give me map for a bottle of rum," the captain complained.

The crew started fumbling around in their coats and totes and came up with five bottles or so of the brew. However, not one soul took the captain up on his offer for his map.

"Captain, you can shoot me now, but I'm not going back that way," cried one of the mates.

"That makes two of us," said the captain with a grin.

The captain almost had a look to him like he knew what was around the next turn of half lit darkness. Captain Pike then called me over and showed me the map, and that cursed scroll now showed four more poor retched faces upon it, the faces of the crew lost in the arena.

"One day, Mr. Newly. One day I'll get my chance at that Sea Witch, and I'll have me revenge!"

The next morning, if it was morning, we were awakened by the flicker of the torches. They began to drift a bit back and forth as if there was a breeze. As we all stared in hope at them, the torches blew harder, and the smell of the sea returned to us all. Minutes later after a quick run, we stopped at the great exit of the cave. We had made it through, and all the away crew were smiling and laughing. They lifted each other into the air, turning about in celebration and kissed each other on the foreheads in a glee.

Captain Pike looked over at me and said with a big smile, "Don't even think about it, Mr. Newly, as I don't dance, and if you try to kiss my head, I'll shoot you right on the spot."

Chapter

Six

The view from the cave's exit was as great as I had ever seen. We were not very high up on the side of the mountain, and we were overlooking some sort of inland sea or lake. You could see the other side of the island in the purple mist far away. We had made it to the middle of the island, and again the gulls above seemed to be laughing at us. After the brief period of cheering was over, the captain turned cold in his manner as he retrieved the map from his coat and began to consult it.

After a few minutes, he commanded, "This way, mates. Let's be on our way." As usual, the captain was out in front, but this time he did not get very far in his efforts.

The captain turned the corner of the cave's exit and suddenly stopped. He began to slowly back up. We were all right behind him and as he backed he pushed on us all, causing us to collide against each other until we also began to move backward in motion and confusion. We backed back into the cave in a nervous fashion, one step at a time, slowly.

"What is it, Captain?" I asked.

At that moment, four very large, wolf-like animals came around the corner of the cave and into the entrance to join us. They stood there looking at us as if to size us up. They took two more steps forward, and again they stopped, staring at us with their blue and brown eyes.

Devil eyes, I thought to myself, and I knew the rest of the crew felt the same.

We drew our swords with a combined effort.

"Ice wolves," the captain said in a whisper.

"Ice wolves?" I asked. "There is no ice here, Captain."

"Ice wolves, Mr. Newly," he repeated. "I made a trip far to the north once, up to a place where the world is nothing but ice and snow. I had an encounter or two with a pack of them, just like this lot here. I can tell you they are no friend of man, Mr. Newly. We were lucky to get back to the ship alive. I know an ice wolf when I see one, and there they stand. Never did find the treasure." He scowled.

As the creatures laid their eyes upon us fools standing with our worthless swords drawn, they acted as if we were not worth the effort it would take to tear us to pieces. They turned and walked back to the front of the cave's exit and sat down in a row with their backs toward us, blocking us off.

"I guess we smell too bad to eat," chuckled the captain."

"Must be the bat dung," Mr. Darwin exclaimed.

The Ice Wolves were magnificent creatures full of fur and teeth and eyes like the devil himself. After several minutes, the wolves looked over their backs at us and with a snarl of contempt were gone. They were gone like they had heard or seen something more amusing.

"Do you think someone or something called them, Captain?" I asked.

"I don't, Mr. Newly." Maybe it was the Sea Witch's map they could sense." We were soon to find out.

"Let's go!" the captain shouted. "Follow their tracks down." We all looked at him as if he just ordered us to walk the plank.

"After you, Mr. Newly," he said as he pushed me in the forward position, and down we went, quickly arriving at the bottom in the inland sea's sand.

The wolves were nowhere to be seen, but their tracks went seemingly forever down the beach, in and out of the surf, down the sand and out of sight.

"Well, I guess them devils are gone," said the captain.

With seemingly no danger present, we all looked at the beautiful inland sea that lay there before us.

"I don't know about you, mates, but that sea there is calling me for a bath" said the captain.

The captain laughed hard and loud as he quickly threw off his coat and dropped his two pistols on top of it in the sand. He pulled off his boots and a second later he was in the water, and we were all right behind him.

We were all splashing about each other, playing and laughing like my little sisters, all except for the captain of course. A chance to wash the bat dung off and the stench of that cave would have been worth a bag of silver from each man.

Almost at the same time all of our laughter stopped cold. We all had our backs to the shore enjoying the bath and the view across the sea to the other side of the island. The captain was the farthest out in the water, and we all saw the look on his face when he turned to face us and the shore.

One by one we turned slowly in silence toward the beach, and there she stood with those Ice Wolves. She was a beautiful woman with long red hair, scantily dressed in some sort of animal skin. Even fifty feet away, I could see her beautiful green eyes sparkling in the sun. She was a tall woman with long, beautiful legs that appeared to be tan and smooth like the rest of her fine features. I looked over at the captain, and I thought his eyes were going to pop out of his head at the sight of her.

Two of the giant Ice Wolves stood on her port side and the other two on her starboard. Besides the wolves, it seemed the only weapon she had was a dagger that she wore on her side. The woman's arms were crossed in a confident fashion. She knew that she had the upper hand, as we were unarmed and in the water. She, on the other hand, had two thousand pounds of fur and teeth, along with our swords and pistols, not to forget the map in the captain's coat. All lay before her on the beach and far from our reach.

"Captain, she has the map," I said.

"Shut up, Mr. Newly."

The girl seemed to show a sign of pity toward us with a small smile but still shook her head in disgust. I thought she had taken a liking to the captain's handsome face, and with a big smile, I said, "Captain Pike, I think she likes the look of you, you handsome fellow, you."

Captain Pike returned a sneer to me and said, "Keep it up, Mr. Newly. Just keep it up."

"And just what brings you to trespass on my island?" she demanded.

The wolves started to growl, and we said nothing. That was the first time I had seen the captain without speech. I just knew that this was going to be my last bath in this life. She then put her hands to the wolves, stroking them and whispering to them. They burst into affection for her and danced about her, wagging their great, white, curled-up tails.

"This one is Kodiak," the girl said in a loving way, petting the first wolf.

"This one is Klondike, and this is Avalanche, and this fine beauty here is my princess Cheyenne. She has the mark of time on her forehead."

We all looked at the female wolf's forehead, and sure enough she had an hourglass-looking mark there.

"Watch them," she ordered the wolves, and the four monsters just strolled over a few dozen feet and laid down in the sun looking at us.

Just as I started to relax a bit and began to think I might actually live another day, the loving look on the girl's face turned cold.

"I hate pirates. But those four there really hate pirates. Why are you trespassing on my island?"

"And your name is?" I asked, trying to lighten her mood a bit.

"Tamantha is my name," she aggressively replied.

The captain seemed to like that name because he replied back to her, pouring on his charm, "Tamantha. An unusual but a beautiful name you have there, missy."

"Princess, come!" Tamantha called out loudly, and the big female ice wolf jumped from the sand and was at Tamantha's side in a wink.

Tamantha, stroking the wolf, said, "Princess, if that dog of a man right there calls me missy again, you may eat him."

Both Tamantha and the wolf turned their heads back up toward the captain. Tamantha smiled an evil smile, and the monster female wolf looked at him hungrily. The captain's lips remained closed and silent, and this was now the second time I had ever seen him speechless. All in a matter of ten minutes!

"Come," she said to us. "At least you have had a bath. Get out of the water before something takes a liking to you for breakfast." Then looking right at the captain, she said, "And if I were you, I'd watch your manner, Captain Ethan Pike."

"Captain?" I said. "She knows your name! How does she know your name?"

Judging from the look on the captain's face, I'd say he was shocked too. He did not reply back to her or me. He looked like he wanted to say something, but he did not. Now I was getting worried. This girl seemed to have quickly gotten the upper hand, but I knew that would not last long.

She turned and began to walk away up the beach. Then, she demanded, "I want to see that map the boy was talking about."

If the captain had a pistol with dry powder, he would have shot me dead right there on the spot.

"Now, lass," the captain said as he stumbled out of the water. "Stay calm, as there is no need for harsh behavior. I'll be glad to show you me map. I'll even let you hold it if you want."

"No, Captain," I said, knowing what touching the map would do to her. I did not wish to see her tortured face also captured on that hateful parchment.

"Belay that, Mr. Newly. You already have one hanging coming to you." This time I was the one without speech this time.

I heard later that while all our problems on the island were growing, back at the ship, the *Sovereign of the Seas* and her crew were getting ready to have a big problem of their own, or should I say three big problems.

Mr. Hennery was a fellow that I had never really grown to like. I did not like his manner, nor did I trust him, so I was not surprised when I heard the tale. It was common knowledge that he used to serve in His Majesty's Navy as a lieutenant, but he deserted his post for a chance at getting rich. I guess you could say he was the captain's first mate, but the captain never made it an official appointment. I don't think the captain liked him much either, but he was a very skilled seaman and an asset to the ship. Apparently the captain trusted him because he had left Mr. Hennery as acting captain when we had gone ashore.

As it was told to me later, this is what happened:

The crow's mate yelled down to Mr. Hennery, "I see two ships on the horizon, sir!"

Looking harder through his seeing glass, the crow's mate yelled, "Their headed this way too, sir."

The crow's mate frantically cleaned at the end of his seeing glass and put it back to his eye. Squinting hard, the mate called, "Make that three ships on the horizon, Mr. Hennery. Two in the front, and one farther behind by a mile or so."

All crew stood frozen, dropping what tools they held in their hands to the deck. They all looked up at the crow's mate, hoping he was making a poor joke.

"Hold," the crow's mate said. "Hold, hold!"

"Three British Warships they are, Mr. Hennery.

"Three war ships!" he exclaimed. "All three have the king's flag."

The stations bell began to ring hard.

"Stations!" screamed Mr. Hennery. "Stations!"

He did not even have to give the order to lift the anchors. The twins were already on their way up from the sand below.

"Get them sails down and cinched. Let's get her under way! Helm hard to starboard!"

The great fast ship jumped right up and out of the sea, and she was under way in a hurry.

"Course, Captain?" Jonesy asked Mr. Hennery.

"Steer at two hundred thirty degrees," Mr. Hennery said, looking at the ship's compass.

"Two hundred thirty degrees, Mr. Hennery?"

"Yes, steer two hundred thirty. Are you deaf?"

Mr. O'Kurk had also formally been in the service of His Majesty's Navy as a seaman. He claimed he had deserted because the British treated him like a dog because he was Irish. He was another one I did not like much or trust. He was like a little weasel running about the ship, reporting men when they did something wrong, trying to gain favor with the captain. He was his own self-appointed first mate.

"Belay that order!" shouted Mr. O'Kurk at Jonesy.

"Are you questioning me orders, Mr. O'Kurk?" snarled Mr. Hennery.

"Yes." Both men pulled their pistols at an even draw, but neither fired. They just stood there pointing their shaky-handed pistols at each other as if not knowing what to do next.

"That course will lead us away from the warships and strand Captain Pike on the island!" yelled Mr. O'Kurk.

"Exactly," Mr. Hennery replied with a grin. "And we will live to fight another day."

"Aye, sir. Good plan, Captain," Mr. O'Kurk replied with a wink.

Mr. O'Kurk turned and looked about the ship's crew with an eye for opposition and yelled out, "Proceed with the new captain's orders. Steer two hundred thirty degrees at full. And get them colors up so those redcoats know who we are." The new acting captain, Mr. Hennery, was not amused, but up the mast went the Jolly Roger.

The *Sovereign* was at full speed away from King George's revenge, but not gone for long as it turned out. Through the froth of the sea and the spray and the wind, the crow's mate peered with his glass.

He screamed down to the new captain and said "those two in the front are Interceptor Class. Not sure about the one trailing in the rear, but she is coming up fast to join them."

"Those Interceptors will catch us, "explained Mr. O'Kurk. "Poor on their number of cannon, but they are fast, real fast."

The two front warships were gaining on the *Sovereign of the Seas* quickly, and even quicker the third warship was catching up to her sisters of the king's flag. Then with a surprise, a few miles back, the crew of the *Sovereign* heard cannon fire.

"What the?" questioned Captain Hennery as he spun around looking back. "Crow's mate, what in the blazes is going on back there?" he yelled, scrambling for his seeing glass.

"You won't believe it" yelled down the crow's mate. "That third ship has caught them two British Devils and just blew the back end right off one of them Interceptor's with forward cannon."

"What? What did you say, mate?" Captain Hennery yelled back.

"Aye the back right off her, and she is burning badly! She has lost her steering and she is hard to port in the wind."

Then the crow's mate yelled down, "Captain, that third ship has changed flags and run up the Jolly Roger."

"She's flying the colors?" Captain Hennery asked?

"Hard to port "left" Captain Hennery" screamed out" "And stand by all cannon! Stand by those forward cannon! We will give our brethren a friendly hand and finish both those British devils off."

As the *Sovereign of the Seas* came around, her crew could see the second Interceptor afire and having trouble steering in the sea. She was trying to move off and distance herself.

"The pirate is closing on the other Interceptor," yelled down the crow's mate. "With forward cannon to bare. It looks like he has six cannon forward, sir."

"Six?" Captain Hennery yelled back.

"Aye, sir, six."

"That's not good for us either," Captain Hennery muttered.

"I wonder what clan she is with," said Mr. O'Kurk. "Maybe we should come back around, Captain. Back to continue our run away at the two-hundred-thirty mark. Away from this mess, Captain, and live to fight another day. You know, Captain, just like you said."

Captain Hennery just looked at Mr. O'Kurk and sneered. He did not like being reminded of his earlier cowardly decision to run from the fight.

From above, the crow's mate yelled down with glee, "Captain, it's the *Resolve!*"

"The *Resolve?*" Captain Hennery questioned.

"Yes, Captain. It is the *Resolve!*"

The *Resolve* was Captain Pike's last command before he won the *Sovereign of the Seas*. She used to be the HMS *Resolve*, a fine British Interceptor class ship in His Majesty's Navy. A great pirate hunter she was—that is, until her and her crew met Captain Pike. Now she is the PS *Resolve*, as Captain Pike liked to call her. Now she is one of ours, or should I say, one of his ships. Captain Pike had refitted her with more cannon on the forward and aft along with more sail, and the *Resolve* was now as deadly and quick above water as the sharks were below.

"Hold your course," Captain Hennery told Jonesy.

Now the *Sovereign* was headed toward the fight, and with a smile, Captain Hennery said, "Let's go help out our little sister."

Captain Hennery then looked over at Mr. O'Kurk who had a very worried look about him and said, "What is it, Mr. O'Kurk? It's a fair fight now, two against one. Our two to their one."

Back on the island, we were following our newfound lady friend down the beach. After a few miles of walking at a brisk pace over the sand, weeds, and crabs, the captain asked Tamantha, "Hey, mate, where are we headed?"

"Toward your treasure and to my home. And my name is not mate."

"Another mile and we will arrive," she said. "Can you make it, Ethan, or would you like me to carry you?"

Right then the captain's face started getting red with rage, and he looked like he was going to start a scene. I looked over at him and whispered,

"Captain, have you noticed that we are being followed in the mist, sir?" Reminded of Tamantha's guards, the captain seemed to calm a bit.

"Aye, Mr. Newly, I see them. I hate ice wolves now almost as much as I hate bats."

I looked over at him and said, "I still hate bugs, sir," and we both began to chuckle.

Coming up the beach, we could now see Tamantha's home. It was a large hutch she had hanging on the side of the black mountain. It was half built into the mountain for protection and half over the beach. We followed her up a path that was cut into the side of the mountain and arrived at her home. The entire scene looked very old, many years old in fact, much older than Tamantha.

"Rest," she said. "I'll bring you some food and something to drink."

The four wolves came up and just lay around watching us carefully.

While she was gone, we discussed our present conditions, whereabouts, and questions we had. When she returned, she had a feast of crab, lobsters, and oysters for our lunch. To the captain's special liking, she had several bottles of rum to wash it all down with.

When we had finished our feast, the captain jumped to his feet and said in his most polite tone, "Well, thank you, Tamantha. For the fine meal, of course, and the hospitality, you know. I and me crew best be going now and tend to our business."

It was a nice try by the captain, but we all knew that we weren't going to get out of whatever predicament we were in that easy. Sure enough the trouble began.

"And exactly what is your business here on my island, Captain Pike?" she questioned. Tamantha had a look to her like she already knew his answer. "Let's have a look at that map there in your coat," she said, smiling as she approached the captain with her hand out. All the wolves raised their heads and looked upon us as if to dare us to do a deed that was stupid.

Time was up, and the captain had had enough. He was ready to fight.

"Believe me when I tell you, missy, you don't want anything to do with that map."

"Give me the map, Captain," she said. "And my name is not missy."

"Now, missy, I'm telling you—no, I'm warning you—that you don't want anything to do with that map."

"Kodiak," Tamantha called, and one of the big wolves stood up and growled.

"Fine," said the captain. "But just don't forget, me darling, you be the one that insisted here today."

As he reached into his coat, all the wolves stood up, and I could feel the blood began to pound in my head. I remember thinking to myself, *Well, the jig's up for you, Mr. Christopher Newly.* I just knew that the lunch I had just ate was my last. I wondered how long a man would live while being torn to pieces by four wolves. I looked about the crew, and I could see that they too were deep into their fear.

Out came the Map of the Sea, and the captain started to hand it to her.

"No, Captain!" I yelled. "No, Tamantha, don't touch that thing."

"Belay that, Mr. Newly. If she wants it that badly, she can have it." And with that said, Tamantha took the map from the captain's hand.

The captain stood back because he knew what was to come next. As soon as she touched the map, Tamantha began to tremble and shake, and we all jumped to our feet in alarm. She started to scream and gasped for air. She fell to the ground, rolling around in pain, and I was convinced the witch had her.

Suddenly Tamantha stopped her trembling and shaking. We all just stood there looking down at her in horror. She opened her eyes and looked up at us all and burst into laughter. I was dumbfounded, as was the captain.

"How can this be?" the captain questioned.

Laughing even harder, Tamantha stood up and glared at Captain Pike.

"Where did you get this map?" The wolves began to growl. "Hold," she said to them. "No mortal man can possess this map! It will consume a man and hold him in its curse forever just for touching it." She rolled open the map, and, looking upon it, she exclaimed, "Ah, I see the map has taken several foolish men already!"

She circled the captain, looking him over and asked, "Are you a mortal man, Captain, or some ghost?"

"Aye," answered Captain Pike, "I am a mortal man."

"Then how is it you possess this map?"

"The Sea Witch gave it to me."

"The Sea Witch? Who is this Sea Witch? This parchment belongs to a very powerful sea-maiden, and she is not a witch!"

"Aye," the captain replied, "she is the Witch of the Sea in my eyes."

"And she gave the scroll to you in exchange for what?"

"I had rescued her daughter from the rocks, and I was transporting her," Captain Pike replied in a softer tone, as if the memory of her still haunted him.

"Transporting her to where? You know you were not transporting her anywhere, and you did not rescue her from any rocks. You captured her and were holding her for a ransom, and you know it. You're a pirate, Captain Pike, and that is what pirates do."

Now the captain got mad and snarled back, "I'm done listening to you and your false accusations, as it is very obvious you are not capable of the truth, nor should I expect you to be, missy. But if you were to have the truth, it would be that I was protecting me crew from her wild daughter that showed no gratitude to her saviors except to capture their minds and me ship."

Tamantha stopped her yelling and looked Captain Pike right in the eye. "I'll tell you what pirates don't do. They don't help people or any other manner of creature. They don't try to explain themselves, and they certainly don't proclaim innocence and make excuses for the deeds they have done. I'm starting to think you are not a pirate at all, Captain Pike."

Tamantha had indeed spotted the captain's innocence and said, "I see, so you are the one, the one that burned her daughter?"

Hanging his head with the rest of us, he answered softly, "Yes."

"Well, for your information, Captain Pike, your Sea Witch's name is Miranda," Tamantha explained. "She was one of the most beautiful and wonderful maidens in the sea until she came across you and your lot. Did you just try to use her parchment on me, Captain? Did you just try to murder me and sentence my soul to eternal damnation over a treasure?"

"No, as I recall there, missy, I warned you twice, and then Mr. Newly there warned you a third time. You apparently already knew the Map would not harm you, so you laid this little trap of yours. Why? So you could put on some sort of act?

"You could have skipped over all your theatrics and got right to the talking, but you chose to practice your ranting and raving instead. What is the matter, missy? You don't get much company here, do you? I wonder why."

Tamantha walked up and slapped Captain Pike so hard in the face I thought his teeth were going to fall out of his head.

Tamantha sneered at him and said, "You're a cruel man, Captain Pike, and you shall pay one day, but just not this day. Your s

Sea Witch, as you call her, holds the rights to you."

Then Tamantha looked around at the crew and said, "If I were you gentlemen, I would stay as far away from this man as you can get, or all your faces will be here on this parchment." She shook the map at us all.

Tamantha stormed away, and Captain Pike looked at all of us and said with a smile, "I think she likes me."

Off the island and back at the ship, the *Sovereign* was coming up fast on the battle.

"Stand by the forward cannon!" yelled Captain Hennery. The *Resolve* was coming up fast on the last British Interceptor by the stern, and this was where she did her most damage. She caught a ship and removed their stern and steering with those forward cannon. They didn't have long to admit their defeat and surrender, or to the bottom they all would go.

However, the captain of the second interceptor was no fool and had already seen the *Resolve*'s plan of attack once. He had watched as his sister ship took her measure, and he watched as she limped off badly, trying to steer in the rough sea. These British officers were highly schooled, and Captain Pike said they all just lacked a little mud in their blood as they were just so high and mighty and snippy.

"Half the pirates at sea used to be in His Majesty's Navy Mr. Newly," he had told me.

"That was until they figured out how wealthy they could become as pirates."

The captain of this Interceptor did have an advantage over both our ships, and he knew it. His duty was to destroy us, and ours was to capture him with as little damage as possible so the ship could be commandeered. Captain Hennery, looking through his glass, could see the interceptor's name as the *Sovereign* approached her.

The HMS *Defiant* she was, and the *Sovereign* and the *Resolve* were soon to find out that her name fit her spirit and her captain's. The *Sovereign* came up and was now in range of her with the forward cannon, but Captain Hennery did not want to fire because it would do too much damage to the *Defiant*'s forward section. He wanted to bring this fine prize back to Captain Pike. Captain Hennery knew it was only a matter of time until Captain Pike heard about his cowardly retreat, and he needed a bribe.

Why Captain Hennery ever brought the *Sovereign* in range of that warship's fire and had no plans to deliver any back was beyond all rational thinking. Mr. Hennery must have settled into his final plan too late or changed his mind to late and then panicked.

Just like the other British ships that had been sent to the bottom this devil could not fire at our ship until she got alongside except for rifle fire, at least that's what our crew thought. I was told that when the *Defiant* opened up with her rifle, it was like ten thousand lead hornets were turned loose across the *Sovereign*'s upper deck. I was told several of our crew dropped dead right on the spot, and several more were wounded. I was told a man could not even stick his head up to see what was going on, much less fire back. I would see the damage done to her later, and when I did, I remember wondering how any man survived.

The *Sovereign* could have blown the entire forward section off the *Defiant*, and off to Davey Jones that British dog would have gone. As I just told you, Captain Hennery decided too late and let that Interceptor do her rifle damage.

Now here came the Resolve from the rear and she placed herself up and alongside the Sovereign with an area between the two ships that was about four ships wide.

That Interceptor was really pouring on the speed and headed right for the front of the Sovereign who still did not fire her forward cannon. I was told that you could hear the captain on our other ship, the Resolve, screening and cussing. The crew on both our ships was now screaming, "Fire" but still no cannon fire and here came that Interceptor on what appeared to be his last voyage by choice. He was to ram the Sovereign at full speed head on.

The Resolve could not move quickly enough, nor did it have the room to line up her forward cannon on the Interceptor ship.

Now that Interceptor was coming up really fast and that British captain gambled that in all the confusion not to many of our men would be at their post and that turned out to be a good gamble. Just before he entered the gauntlet fast between our ships he turned her hard to port "left "and went in sideways. This brought one side of her broadside to the Sovereign and one to the *Resolve* and then out the end at full speed. The whole thing was over in a half minute with no damage to the British ship and both ours burning.

It was a brilliant move, and one that took both our ships' captains by surprise. All the crews were watching the scene unfold and not at their stations just like that Interceptor's captain had predicted. You would have thought Captain Pike was at the *Interceptor's helm as smooth as the operation went.*

The crew later told me, "You should have seen it, Mr. Newly"

"That British devil was going to ram us head on at full speed but right at the last second he turned that ship of his and went sideways right between us and the *Resolve*. We were so close to ramming her we could see the color of her captain's eyes. We thought for sure all three of us were going to the bottom, Mr. Newly. That British devil acted like he did not care, like he was ready to go and shake hands with Davey Jones himself or something. He wasn't going to move, Mr. Newly, and we all knew it. If our two ships had not broken off hard when we did, we would not be telling you this tale." "But before our ships could move Mr. Newly that devil gave each of us a broad side as he went by"

As if weren't enough for him that British Captain came back around with its eye on the burning Resolve. As usual that Interceptor came in fast, got along sideways the wounded ship and fired its cannons broadside.

The entire front port "left side forward of the Resolve was now gone. The *Sovereign* also took direct hits on her "right " starboard side and forward section. Half the forward cannon on both ships along with the crews manning them were just gone, along with a big chunk of the ship.

To our dismay that Interceptor came back around again this time staying out of range looking us over. After a minute or two and speeding away, the captain of the HMS *Defiant*, standing on his stern, waved his feathered cap at Captain Pike's two burning ships in a daunting way, motioning the *Sovereign* and the *Resolve* to chase after him and engage him again. We did not, and watched as he set course to his wounded sister ship several miles away on the horizon.

Captain Hennery slammed his hat on the deck and screamed, "That ship there is going to be future trouble, and I could have blown her out of the water! I'll hang for this for sure," he complained. "Just look at this ship, and just look at the smile on that English dog's face!" Then he just stood there with shame and disgust, shaking his head side to side with his hat in his hand.

Back on the island, Tamantha came back in a huff and slapped the map back into the captain's hand. "I'll show you your treasure in the morning," she said. The captain's eyes lit up with greed.

"You know of the treasure, do you?" he calmly asked.

"It's my island, isn't it?"

"Then you must also know of about the key that goes with it."

"Key?" she questioned.

"Well like you said, missy, it's your island. I am here for the map's key, and I'll just bet you know where it is. You can just bet there sweetie that we won't be leaving anytime soon without it."

Then, with surprise, she grabbed the captain by his other hand and squeezed it for a moment. The captain lost his smiley look quickly as Tamantha took a hold on him. She went into some sort of trance for a second or two, and when she opened her eyes, she asked, "Did I just see a good side to you, Captain Pike?"

"I don't have a side. I have no soul. I gave it up years ago when my wife and son died of the fever. You need a soul to have a side, either good or bad. I have no soul."

Now I finally knew what was wrong and right with the captain. The man carried a great burden on his shoulders. One I could not imagine having to carry. I knew his wife and son had died from the fever, but I did not know until now what that loss had done to him. That was why he was always out front of us, leading the way. That was why he fought so fearlessly and did his best to make sure he stayed in harm's way. That was why he laughed at death every step of the way. He wanted to rejoin his family and to do that he would have to die.

"Oh, yes, Captain Pike," Tamantha said, "you have a soul, and I just saw it. You will be glad to know that your so-called sea witch has laid claim to it too. I just saw her mark on it."

"Bunk," the captain said to her.

"You will stay here tonight. They will protect you," Tamantha said, pointing at the wolves.

The captain replied and said, "Protect us! We do not need your wolves' protection."

Tamantha leaned over and got really close to the captain's face, and in a whisper that spooked us all, she said, "Oh, yes, you do, Captain Pike. Yes, you do. Nobody leaves this place in the dark."

"And what do we need protection from?" the captain asked.

"Me," Tamantha again whispered, and then she turned and went inside her cave.

The captain looked around at us and with a grin said, "Well, don't just stand there, mates. Go get something for dinner, as it looks like we are staying the night."

For dinner, the crew fished and crabbed, and we had another feast that night. Tamantha did not join us for dinner despite our calls to her. The four ice wolves just lay in front of the cave's entrance and watched us closely. The sun went down, and the moon came up full.

The inland sea was beautiful and peaceful with its slight slap on the shore over and over by the waves. All of a sudden, about midnight, Tamantha came up and out of her cave. We all thought we were dreaming. To our amazement, the ice wolves stood and snarled at her. They went to

Tamantha and seemed to push at her to get down the path to the beach. She was dressed like a goddess in a long, silk, beautiful gown and her long red hair was flowing in the wind. She seemed to be floating on the mist and appeared to be changing into something as she made her way with the wolves pushing at her as if to hasten her along to the beach.

In the moonlight, I caught a sight of her hand that was hanging by her side. It was like that of a wolf. It looked to be twice its normal size and with long nails. Her other hand, about half into what the other looked like, was clutching her heart. She and the wolves disappeared into the night and the mist.

The captain, seeming a bit nervous, ordered, "Bring up that fire, and post two guards on a two-hour rotation." Then he placed both his pistols on his chest and wallowed his head to its resting place for the night.

I thought to myself, *"How in this world can he sleep after just seeing that?"*

The rest of us followed the example the captain showed. With our pistols at hand and ready, we all laid back. However, it seemed out of us all, only the captain could find his sleep quickly.

Despite the large fire, the Ice Wolves returned to us, and they were very upset and worried. As they walked the fire, they whimpered their feelings of concern. Their thoughts seamed to spill over into mine, and in a strange way, I could almost feel their sadness. Instead of running the beach with their mistress, they were to guard us against her, even to kill her to protect us. They had Tamantha's instructions before the change took her, and they would follow her wishes to the death. That did not sit well with them. After all, who were we compared to their love for her?

I whispered to the captain, "Do you feel the wolves, sir?"

In his usual fashion, he rolled over and said, "I feel their fleas, Mr. Newly. Now get some sleep. The treasure awaits us in the morning."

Chapter

On the other side of the island's mountains, back at sea, the *Sovereign* and the *Resolve* had come to a stop next to each other. The crews began to make repairs and tend to the lost and wounded crew as best they could. Everyone knew that this damage would need to be taken ashore. A ding came alongside the *Sovereign*, and it was carrying the captain of the *Resolve*, which turned out to be Captain Simpson. Captain Simpson was a seasoned and handsome man that had served under Captain Pike for many a year. He was a handpicked by Captain Pike to command the *Resolve*.

It was customary to ask permission to board another man's ship, but this time Captain Simpson chose to forgo the formality. He snarled as he climbed off the rope ladder and his feet hit the deck of the *Sovereign*.

"Where is Captain Pike?" he demanded. "I know he is not aboard this lame of a ship."

Acting Captain Hennery just kind of strolled down the stairs from the helm of the *Sovereign*, and in an unconcerned manner, he said, "Captain Pike is ashore, and I am in charge."

"And you are?"

"I am acting Captain William Hennery."

"Do you know who I am?"

"Of course, Captain Simpson, I know who you are," said Captain Hennery in an increasingly nervous tone.

"When we came upon you, where were you going in such a hurry?" he asked sarcastically. "I guess you were picking up speed in the wind so you could come about to join the fight. I did not think for a moment you were running for your dog of a life. Why did you not fire? Just look at the captain's ships because of you!"

Captain Hennery fired back his answers. "Who did you say you were? You can't be the same Captain Simpson I have heard about. Why did you not fire?" questioned Mr. Hennery.

"Because I think you were in panic and weak at the helm."

Captain Simpson drew his pistol and shot Captain Hennery dead on the spot.

"Any more legal matters need tended to on this ship?" asked Captain Simpson, looking around at the *Sovereign*'s crew. None answered back. "Good. I'm in command.

"Mr. Stevenson!"

"Yes, Captain," Mr. Stevenson called back from the Resolve.

"You have the helm. Set a course for that island and begin repairs."

"Aye, Captain," replied Stevenson, and the *Resolve* began to get under way.

Captain Simpson had the same disposition as did Captain Pike, and all hands knew it by now if they did not before.

"Who is the second in command here?" questioned Captain Simpson.

"I am," Mr. O'Kurk said proudly, wanting to butter up to the new Captain. "I will serve you well."

Captain Simpson pulled his other pistol and shot Mr. O'Kurk dead too and said, "Now that we have the rat problem under task, set a course for the island." All hands ran extra fast to their stations, and they were soon under way.

Back across the island's mountains, the sun was rising on Captain Pike and his away crew. When we awoke, all was well and a beautiful morning was before us. The wolves looked like they had finally settled down and were lying about almost in a peaceful way.

"Mr. McCoy, Mr. Jameson!" the captain called to the last two guards on duty. "Come in!" But they did not come. Again Captain Pike called to them, as did we all, and again they did not come.

"Find them," the captain ordered, and we all set out looking.

"And where in hades is that girl?" the captain questioned. "Find her too."

"Wolves. Find them."

All he got back from the four monsters was a snarl. The wolves made no move to obey the captain's order, and they looked disgusted at the prospect of ever having to.

Mr. McCoy and Mr. Jameson were best friends. They were well liked by the captain and the crew. Both men came from and grew up together in Liverpool. They never did anything without one another, and from what we found, they also went to their maker together.

Turned out Mr. McCoy and Mr. Jameson were just gone, and we never saw them again. We found their tracks in the sand heading down to the inland sea. The tracks stopped about fifty feet from the sea's edge, and from the looks of it, a great commotion had taken place there. The record of it was shown in the sand. The commotion's scar in the sand stopped at the sea. We checked, and their faces were not on the map, so we knew the Sea Witch had not taken them.

Captain Pike scowled. "The fools got eaten by something."

Why the two men had left their posts or where they went, we did not know. They had just disappeared in the night along with the girl.

"Not a bad way to go," the captain said.

"Captain?" I questioned.

"Not the getting eaten part, Mr. Newly. The part about going with your best friend beside you." Then with a disgusted look on his face, he said, "I have had enough of this."

We went back up to Tamantha's hut, and Captain Pike went to go into the cave and the wolves quickly ran to block his path in.

Mr. Langley was a cannon master stationed on the starboard forward section of the ship. He was the funniest man aboard. He always had a joke and a smile for you. He was a bit on the nervous side but a very dependable man.

"Mr. Langley!" the captain called.

"Aye, sir," Mr. Langley replied.

"I want you to take a little walk down that beach," Captain Pike instructed.

"What was that, Captain?" He moved his ear closer and cupped his hand around it as if he thought he had heard the captain wrong.

"You heard me correctly, Mr. Langley," the captain said. Captain Pike looked around a bit and spotted a sash that belonged to Tamantha hanging over a railing. He picked it up, and he tossed it to him. "Yes, Mr. Langley. A little walk."

"To where?" questioned Mr. Langley.

"Just tie the sash around your miserable neck and start walking down that beach before I put a boot on you!" the captain yelled.

"You don't have to be mean like that, Captain. I was just making sure I did right."

"Walk for an hour and return," ordered the captain. Off went Mr. Langley, nervous and looking quite stupid with his new tie.

Just as the captain expected, the four wolves began following Mr. Langley. Looking over his shoulder at the wolves coming after him, Mr. Langley called out in a cry to the captain as if hoping his orders were to change.

"Just walk, Mr. Langley. Just walk," said the captain. "It will be all right."

As the captain turned back at us, he whispered, "Well, maybe it will be all right."

Captain Pike then went up to the entrance of Tamantha's cave home and ordered, "Keep an eye out for the girl, mates."

"Should we post a guard, Captain?" I questioned.

Turning his head back at me from the cave's entrance, the captain replied, "No, Mr. Newly. In case you hadn't noticed, we are running a little low on guards these days. Just stay together, keep an eye out, and try not to get eaten by anything." Then he disappeared into the cave.

What the captain found inside was truly amazing, and I heard all about it. The cave's interior had been transformed into a wonderful treasure-filled sanctuary. The cave was huge inside, as tall as four ships atop each other, including their highest masts, and it was long enough and wide enough to fit ten.

The cave's walls were covered with hundreds of magnificent tapestries inlaid with gold and silver. Ten thousand candles were burning from every nook and cranny in the rock, and each smelled a different scent. Magnificent jewels were in abundance everywhere, just strewn about the caves floor. Great veins of gold and silver ran through the rock face. Countless unmined diamonds, emeralds, and rubies glittered on the stone walls in the great candle light.

Centered right in the middle of the cave was Tamantha's bed. It looked like the bed of a queen. Thousands of candles burned around it in a circle. The bed was made of gold and had long ivory pillars on all four corners that stretched high up into the air. The pillars were all adorned with silver and gold, and atop each a crown of blue diamonds had been laid. A fine lace curtain, made of spun gold, was supported by the pillars and surrounded the bed. The wonderful curtain shimmered in the candlelight as it blew gently back and forth in the sea's breeze. Spun silver made up the curtain's designs that portrayed scenes from the sea. The scenes were like a great play being performed at a wonderful beneath-the-sea theater. The captain was mesmerized at its sight.

Great monsters of the deep were shown and maidens of the sea riding huge undersea dragons. The great Poseidon was also portrayed destroying a ship with his trident. Fabulous treasures from both man and the earth were shown, guarded by indescribable sea beasts, sharks, and giant killer whales.

The great theater showed one scene that was a horror. It looked to be that of a great undersea war between all manners of creatures. Some of the creatures seemed to be attacking ships, and other creatures seemed to be protecting the ships. At the end of the scene, countless were shown dead, strewn across the bottom of sea, and at the end, the oceans were left empty of their existence.

As if the captain was not shocked enough by the spectacular sights and wonders he said he noticed, on the golden lace curtain, a particular scene turned him cold as ice. There was the chest, his chest, the same chest the Sea Witch had thrown upon his ship to pay bounty for her daughter. The chest was shown open, and the map of the sea was lying unrolled for all to see. Many sea-maids were gathered around it, and four giant killer whales were shown to guard it.

The captain told me that what had really spooked him was the next scene he saw as he moved his eyes slowly and nearer to the curtain. The scene showed a great gathering of many maidens and guardians. Neptune stood among them all. Thirty or so giant sea horses as big as a man were pulling a golden sled across the bottom of the sea. Upon the sled was a huge, half-open shell that held of what appeared to be that of a dead sea-maiden with her great tail hang out and over one side of the shell and a dead limp arm hanging out and over the other. Both looked to be burnt.

He said he went into a rage and tried to tear at the golden fabric, but it would not tear. He told that he pulled out his sword and lashed at it, but it would not cut. The captain said he had ran and grabbed up one of the many large candles and tried to burn the curtain, but it would not burn. Continuing his fit, he ran out of the cave into the sun and almost fell down in front of us. We all jumped to our feet,

I yelled, "Captain!" but he did not answer. Again I spoke to him, but he did not answer. The man had a look to his face and his eyes like I had never seen before.

I went over and touched his arm and asked, "Captain? Captain Pike, are you all right, Captain?"

The captain, startled by my touch, jumped and came out of what had a hold of him. He was sweating like he had a fever that had broken.

"Go see for yourselves," he said with a horror.

"I'll stay out here for now. I don't want anyone to touch anything in there, or I'll have your hearts for me breakfast."

Not knowing what to expect and by the condition of the captain, we crept inside the cave slowly. With swords and pistols drawn, we inched in, and I could feel Mr. Wellington's nervous hot breath on the back of my neck. Just as the thought occurred to me as to how and why I was leading the group, the entire wonderful scene unfolded before our eyes. We all just stood there, silent in our thoughts for several minutes, looking and staring at the wonder. One by one we put our drawn arms away and began to spread out and look about in amazement.

Each man's face was aglow in the bright candlelight, and each man's eyes looked in awe. Mr. Wellington reached down to pick up a jewel from the floor, but Captain Pike, who had rejoined us, stepped on his hand.

"I said don't touch anything. Are you deaf, Mr. Wellington?" Captain Pike asked as he pulled out a pistol. "How about I clean out them ears of yours with a pumpkin ball?" He pulled back the pistol's hammer.

Nervously, Mr. Wellington replied and said, "Sorry about that, Captain. I forgot for a minute, but I remember now, sir. I remember plain now that I'm not to touch anything, and I'm sure me ears are fine, sir, and don't need a cleaning."

The captain slowly reset the hammer on the pistol and un-cocked it. Then he turned and looked at me. "Have a gander at this, Mr. Newly." He motioned toward the burial scene on the golden curtain.

I studied at it awhile and then looked up at the captain. "Is that—" I started to ask, but before I could get the whole question out, I was cut off by the captain's answer.

"I guess it is, Mr. Newly," he said, sneering at the scene.

I then asked him in a wonder, "But how, Captain? This thing is old, really old. The sea witch's daughter was just killed a short piece ago, so this cannot be her."

"Can't say, Mr. Newly. I just don't know," he answered. "I do know we ain't touching any of this treasure."

"But, Captain, we came this far," I pleaded as the rest of the crew began to growl.

"I ain't getting blamed for killing that girl Tamantha too. Just who knows who her retched kin might be? I already got a sea witch hunting me, and don't forget: what hunts me hunts us all.

"If that cursed maiden, the daughter of the Sea Witch, had stopped that mind madness on me crew, she would be alive today. It was self-defense. That's what it was. Self-defense. But you can bet if that sea witch ever catches up to me, Mr. Newly, I won't get a fair trial under that ocean."

One of the things I could never figure out about the captain was how he could jump from one mood to another in the snap of a finger. Sometimes I thought there was more than one person living in that body of his. Holding true to form, his mood changed from horror to wit, and he said with a wink and a smile to me,

"Besides, Mr. Newly, I can't hold me breath that long. Let's get back to the ship."

Then pointing to the scene on the curtain where Poseidon was sinking the cursed ship, he said with a laugh, "That is, unless that fellow right there with that big fork has not secured her already." The rest of us did not think it was funny, and I shook my head with a frown.

The crew and I, in a huff about leaving the treasure behind, started to walk toward the exit of Tamantha's cave, muttering to each other. At that same time, Mr. Langley was returning with the wolves in tow, and he entered the cave to meet us head on.

From behind us, the captain asked, "And where do you mates think you are going?" We all turned to see Captain Pike standing there with the map of the sea out. "The treasure and the ship be this way, mates," he said with a smile. He then turned and began walking back and farther into the cave. We all came rushing back to join and follow him with big grins of hope renewed on our faces.

Mr. Langley and the wolves fell a bit behind because he had not seen the wonders and the treasures of Tamantha's home yet. I thought Mr. Langley's head was going to twist off with the looking he was doing. To my surprise, Captain Pike patiently let him have his look around as we waited.

"But ain't this the treasure, Captain?" Mr. Langley asked.

"It's a long story to be told later, Mr. Langley," the captain replied. "Let's go. Fire them torches."

Mr. Langley was last in the line leaving the scene of Tamantha's home. He stopped and looked back at the ice wolves that had stopped following him. They were just sitting there all lined up in a row watching us.

"Captain. Captain Pike," Mr. Langley called out.

"What is it now, Mr. Langley?" asked the captain in an impatient manner.

"What about the wolves, Captain? We just can't leave them here, sir. Tamantha is gone now, and they ain't got nobody now. And besides, Captain, I think they have took a likin' to me."

Captain Pike looked up and over to the wolves and then at Mr. Langley. Shaking his head in disgust, Captain Pike said, "Fine, but you're taking care of those flea-bit monsters."

I thought to myself, *Does Captain Pike have a soft spot in him after all? Maybe Tamantha was right about him.*

Mr. Langley called to the wolves, but they would not come. Back up front, leading the crew farther into the cave, the captain could hear Mr. Langley calling to the wolves to no avail. Captain Pike let out a loud whistle, and the wolves took off running right past Mr. Langley, almost spinning him around as they sped past him. The wolves ran by us all and joined right up with the captain. Captain Pike looked over his shoulder at us all and smiled a sort of childish grin as he continued to walk.

"About time you mangy beasts followed one of me orders." The wolves looked up at him and growled in reply, and to my amazement their tails were wagging.

The journey deeper into the cave was uneventful as if to grant everyone's hopes and wishes. No bats to fly at us and suck our blood or bugs to crawl on us, and, best of all no Sea Witch. The black stone sides of the cave we were following had no marks or writings, and that too was fine with me. We journeyed for about another hour with the captain and his newfound friends, the Ice Wolves. Then to everyone's delight, the torches began to blow, and we all began to feel a cool breeze blow through the cave. The breeze smelled and felt of the sea, and we all knew we were close to the cave's exit overlooking the sea, hopefully our sea.

Sure enough we had come to the end of the cave and found ourselves about a thousand feet up from the shore below. We were overlooking a beautiful day and finally our sea. To make the scene even greater, there sat the *Sovereign of the Seas* and another ship I did not know, at least I did not think so.

"Captain, do you know that ship?" I asked.

"Yes, Mr. Newly. I know her well," said the captain with a huge smile on his face.

"Who is it, Captain?"

"Relax, Mr. Newly. That be the PS *Resolve* and her master, Captain Simpson. She is our sister ship."

What a sight the two ships were to behold. All of us would have been very glad, but we all knew we were missing something. We were missing the treasure promised by the captain and his map, and he was missing his prize key.

Captain Pike was fumbling with the map, looking for his answer. He ordered us to remain, and he walked back inside the cave without a torch.

Into the blackness he went, feeling his way along the black rock sides of the cave.

He did not have to travel far, and he began to see a light ahead. Brighter and brighter the light became as the darkness faded away. The captain came to an area that we had all just walked through minutes before with our torches lit. The natural light of the cave was coming from phosphorous in the rock, and with our torches lit, the phosphorous would not glow. Captain Pike stood there amazed at what he saw.

We had not noticed with our torches lit the size of the chamber we had just passed through. The great cave's hall was ten times the size of Tamantha's cave home and just as tall. There were many pools of the clearest of water that were also lit from their own phosphorous on their sides and seemingly their bottom. Large, magnificent, long-pointed pillars that looked like the tallest of ships' masts were hanging down from the cave's ceiling, dripping water into the pools.

The ice wolves had remained with us outside on our new perch overlooking the sea. All of a sudden, they took off in a flash back into the cave, as they had heard the captain's faint whistle from inside. Catching us by surprise, we jumped from our relaxed manner, and with our torches relit, we followed the wolves back into the cave, and soon enough we came upon Captain Pike.

"Put them torches out," he ordered.

With a questioning look from us all, the crew followed his order, and the torches went out. We all stood about with mouths open, as we too could now see what we could not see before. Even the wolves seemed to be a bit more pleasant at the sight, if that were possible.

As the drops of water from the cave's ceiling landed on the many crystal-blue pools, the pools rippled, sending shimmers of many-colored lights across the entire cave. I was sure that no man had ever seen a sight like this before, as it was like going inside a rainbow.

I asked the captain in a soft tone and wonder, "Captain, is this the treasure?"

"No, Mr. Newly, it's a cave."

I thought to myself and grinned, *Why do you even bother talking to him?*

The captain then turned and looked into one of the clear ponds and pointed. "Here are your treasures, mates!" he exclaimed.

We all gathered around one of the crystal-blue pools and discovered where the colored shimmers were coming from. Huge jewels were everywhere strewn across what seemed to be the pool's shallow bottom. Blue diamonds, yellow diamonds, clear diamonds, rubies, and emeralds were everywhere across the pool's bottom.

"Look at that one there, Captain!" I exclaimed with glee. I had my eye on a large blue diamond that was as big as an apple, and my mind went afire with dreams.

"Get your fill, mates," the captain ordered as he laughed, celebrating his abilities. "Fill those sacks."

Captain Pike started to put his hand into the seemingly very shallow pool, and one of the wolves ran up and knocked the captain down to the cave's floor, away from the pool. It was Kodiak, and he was not letting the captain anywhere near the water.

"Hold!" yelled the captain. "Stay away from the water," he ordered as he picked himself up. Cheyenne and Klondike and Avalanche soon displayed the same manner of behavior. They did not want us anywhere near the wonderful pool of gems.

Captain Pike picked up a rock, and into the pool it went. The stone disappeared from sight. Not just disappeared out of sight because of depth of water, but because the rock just disappeared as it entered the pool.

"Mr. Langley," the captain said, "hand me that rope you have there, and tie a rock on it."

With the rope fixed to the rock, Captain Pike went to the side of the crystal-blue pool, and he began to lower in the rock. As the rock went into the pool's water, it began to disappear right at the surface, seemingly to become a part of the clear blue water. The captain slowly retreated the rock back up, and as he raised the rock ever so slowly, it began to reappear as it came into the air. We all looked at each other in wonder.

"I don't like this," the captain said.

Then he dropped the rock and rope in again. Three fathoms he dropped it, and then ten fathoms it went, and then twenty fathoms, and the rope ran out with the rock still not striking the bottom of the abyss.

"There is no telling how deep this water is," said the captain.

As the rope had gone into the pool, it also was disappearing. When the captain lifted the rope back, it would reappear just like the stone had. The captain was getting frustrated, and it seemed the wolves were getting anxious. Klondike just ran over and jumped into the pool as if to test the water because he knew sooner or later one of us would.

"No!" screamed the captain.

The captain tried to grab Klondike as he went by, but that was a futile attempt. Klondike was gone in an instant, disappearing right before our eyes. We all jumped with alarm and looked hard into the pool, searching for what might have become of Klondike. The other three wolves ran about the bank of the pool, sniffing and whimpering with great concern for their kin.

As the pool cleared and smoothed and became calm again from Klondike's splash in, to our wonder and relief, there we saw him again. Klondike was at the bottom of the pool, or was he at the top of another pool? I was so confused. I shook my head as if to clear it. There Klondike stood on the other side of the pool, seemingly now on his cave's floor looking down and back at us. He paced back and forth, seeming to wait for us to join him. It was like two mirror worlds looking back and forth at each other, and everyone's minds went crazy with thought.

"The treasure's on the other side, mates. Let's get it!" the captain yelled with a cheer, and he jumped right into the pond. Just like Klondike, he had also disappeared beneath the water. Several moments later, after the pool stopped shimmering, we could see clearly again, and there on the other side of the pool stood the captain with Klondike.

"This is crazy," I said to the rest of the crew. "They are standing in another cave looking back at us."

Captain Pike was motioning to us to follow him into the pool. After a quick look about at each other and with a shrug of our shoulders, we all jumped in the pool, including Kodiak, Cheyenne, and Avalanche, as they were more than ready to rejoin their friend Klondike.

In what seemed to be just a moment, despite the depth of the water, we all surfaced on the pool's other surface. Under the pool's water, I realized I did not exist in any physical form. My body was gone, and all that remained were my thoughts. I felt very strange as I swam to the bank of the pool to join the captain and Klondike.

Captain Pike yelled out, "Welcome aboard, Mr. Newly. How did you like that, Mr. Newly?"

I could not speak.

As we all pulled the wolves and ourselves out of the pool to join Captain Pike and Kodiak, our bodies reappeared in full as we left the water. To add additional amazement to the scene, we were not wet from the water but dry to the touch. Again we were all dazzled at the sight of it all. This cave looked exactly like the one we had just left, except for one thing. On this side of the crystal-blue pool was a cave covered with jewels.

I looked over at the captain, and he said, "Figure it out later, Mr. Newly. Get you some treasure. Load all you can into the bags, men."

Then, in a more serious note, Captain Pike said, "Mr. O'Malley, take Mr. Crookshaw back down the cave to where Tamantha's home should be, and report back what you have seen."

"Aye, Captain," Mr. O'Malley said, and off the two went.

Turning his head toward the wolves, the captain said, "Cheyenne, me fine lady. Would you be so kind as to go with them and protect them please?" Cheyenne was gone in a jump after the Misters O'Malley and Crookshaw to help with their trek back to Tamantha's home.

Captain Pike then ordered two more mates and Avalanche to the cave's exit overlooking the sea and our two ships. "Report back what you see," the captain said.

"What do you expect them to find, Captain?" I asked.

"I don't expect them to find anything, Mr. Newly, if my thinking is correct."

"You don't think her home is there, Captain? You don't think the ships will be there, Captain?" I asked.

"I think we are in a different place, Mr. Newly. I think this is a whole new hidden world. This cave might look just like the other, but let's see what happens when we walk away from this mirror made of water," answered the captain with a smile.

I looked at the captain curiously and wondered how he even came up with such a wild idea.

"Oh, Mr. Newly." He smiled. "Let's just hope it's a two-way mirror." I immediately became uncomfortable. The thought had not occurred to me that we had not yet tried to go back into the pool to return to our side where we came from.

We gathered bags and bags of the blue diamonds, white diamonds, and yellow diamonds, along with too many rubies and emeralds to count.

One of the crew yelled out, "Captain Pike, come here! I have found something."

We ran over to see what he had found. What we saw lit the captain's eyes up like two bright stars. There entrenched into the caves stone wall were three keys. Side by side they were set in place. They looked exactly alike and beneath each was a strange writing.

"I'll bet you don't want to pick the wrong key there, Mr. Newly."

I just looked at him.

"Let's have the map of the sea choose."

With that said, out came the map, and as soon as it left the captain's coat, it glowed brightly. There on the wall we saw the last key in the line begin to glow. Brighter and brighter it became until it almost hurt our eyes to look at it. Then, in just a second, it stopped. Captain Pike took out his knife and carefully dug it out of the rock. He held it and examined it carefully. The key looked to be very old. About two inches long and black as coal it was. The head of it was fashioned like the head of a trident and was really very beautiful.

"Well, that was easy enough," I said.

"Really, Mr. Newly," the captain replied. "You might just stumble across this place after ten thousand years of looking and then pick the wrong key. Or you could make it easy on yourself and find a map of the sea, survive touching it, survive that witch, and then find this side of the pool. Nothing to it at all." Then he gave me a big proud smile.

"Are you going to try it out, sir? To see if it fits?

Captain Pike rolled open the map and began to set the key in place. The map of the sea again glowed brightly, and before the captain could finish setting it in place the map just sucked it up, out of hand, and absorbed it. The key was now part of the parchment.

"What now? That's it?" I asked.

"Need three more keys there, Mr. Newly.

Just three more."

We went back and rejoined the crew. Captain Pike reached down and picked up a big blue diamond off the floor of the cave.

"Just one of these stones would make a man very rich, Mr. Newly," said the captain.

"Ten of them would make him a king, and we have thousands of them."

" Mr. MacAfee, come over here."

"Aye, Captain," Mr. MacAfee said as he ran right up.

"I want you to take this rope and jump in that pool again. I want you to return to the other side and get a foothold over there. Prepare a rope line to toss to us as we appear to you. We won't be able to swim with the weight of the jewels, and we will need you to haul us out."

Mr. MacAfee had heard the conversation the captain and I had about the pool maybe being a one-way trip. He hesitated a bit and said,

"But, Captain, what about what you and Mr. Newly were talking about? You know, Captain, about how we might not be able to get back."

"Someone's got to go first, Mr. MacAfee, and today that someone be you," the captain said.

"Aye, sir," he said, and Mr. MacAfee jumped into the pool and was gone.

We all gathered on the side of the pool and glared into it. I didn't know it, but I was holding my breath, and the captain nudged me and said, "Breathe, Mr. Newly".

We waited and waited for the pool's surface to clear from the ripples, and then finally we saw it. On the other side of the pool's surface, there stood Mr. MacAfee. He was standing on the other side with the rope, looking back down at us.

"Kodiak and Klondike, go now. Jump," Captain Pike said to the wolves. The two giants followed his orders and splashed in the pool. Like before, as soon as the pool cleared its ripples, we could see Kodiak and Klondike with Mr. MacAfee standing on the other side of the pool's surface nervously.

"All right, men, after you," the captain ordered. "Into the pool with you, and don't be dropping any of me treasure, or I'll leave you stranded on this island."

One by one, the crew jumped into the blue-crystal pond loaded with the treasure. One by one, the crew and the treasure they were carrying reappeared on the surface on the other side of the pool, and Mr. MacAfee threw them the rope and pulled them ashore.

Besides the scouts, I was the last of the crew to go into the water, and just before I went in, I looked back at the captain and asked, "Aren't you coming, sir?"

"I'll wait till the scout crews come back, Mr. Newly. Wait for us on the other side."

"But, Captain—" I did not get to finish my question because the captain, with a big smile on his face, pushed me into the pool with his boot. I splashed in the pool with a big smile and was gone.

The scouts the captain had sent to the cave's exit reported back that our ships were gone as if they never existed. The scouts he had sent back to Tamantha's home came back and reported it too was gone. The calm beach where Tamantha lived was under a severe storm and wave they reported. There was no beach, and it didn't look there had ever been one.

"Just rocks and waves back there, Captain," they said. "No hutch, no treasure, no sanctuary. Nothing was there, Captain. No trace of anything that would show any of it ever had existed."

"Captain, there is nothing back there but sea grass, ocean foam, sea bugs, and crabs. The place we just left is just not there," reported the scouts.

Captain Pike then realized his theory was correct. On that side of the pool's surface, there existed a very different world and a different time. Captain Pike shook his head back and forth to clear his head from the craziness and ordered the scout crews to fill up their pockets and sacks with gems and jump into the pool.

"They are waiting for you on the other side, mates. Just grab the rope when you come to the surface," he told them. "They will pull you ashore."

Captain Pike, the Princess Cheyenne, and Avalanche were the last left to make the return leap into the pool, to return to our time and to our world.

Together we all now stood back on our side of the pool's surface and back in our own time and our own world where we had started. The captain and the away crew were all very happy as our bags were loaded with the riches of the world and we had the First Key secured.

"Captain, if you don't mind sir, how did you know to pick the right pool? There were hundreds them"

"You ask to many questions Mr. Newly" was all I got back.

"Let's go," the captain said. "Let's get to the end of this cave and to the sea."

As we once again came out of the cave into the sun, the captain seemed to hold his breath as if he were worried the *Sovereign* and the *Resolve* would somehow not be there, but to everyone's relief, there sat our two ships just as we had last seen them. We were all again perched on the side of the mountain far up from the sea, but this time we were loaded with treasure. The captain ordered a signal fire to be built to attract our ship's attention, and *Resolve*'s lookout saw it just minutes after it had be built and lit.

Looking through our glass we could see her crow's mate swinging his arms and pointing in alarm. I saw her captain run out of his cabin, pull out his glass, and look right at us. The smile grew larger and larger on my face. I saw him shouting orders, and I saw the dings hit the water. The *Sovereign* also became a flurry of activity and soon enough they too had dings in the water. Within minutes they were headed for the beach smiling and waving at us.

When the dings hit the beach the men were so excited they tripped and fell about one another in the sand. They all ran up and gathered about a spot below us. I think in their minds they were also asking the same question we had in ours. How were they going to get us down?

There was no way we were going to climb down, as any ropes we had were not long enough and jumping was not even an option. We were so high up we could not even converse with them.

"How are we going to get down there?" I asked the captain.

The captain thought and looked about for a few moments.

"Mr. Newly," the captain said.

"Aye, sir."

"Find yourself a stick."

"A stick, Captain?"

"Yes, Mr. Newly. Get a stick and one of them big green leaves over there."

I fetched the items the captain requested and gave them to him.

"Now give me one of the bigger diamonds, and make it a real beauty," ordered the captain.

In a moment, he had his diamond, and a big, beautiful blue diamond it was. The magnificent stone shone brightly in the sun, and we all grinned wildly at the sight of it. Captain Pike then took the stick and dug it around in the ashes of the signal fire. The captain took the large leaf I had given him and drew a drawing on it. It was a very simple drawing but one that made us all smile as he showed it to us. Captain Pike had drawn a simple harpoon. Then the captain took the diamond and rolled it up inside the big leaf and tied it off with a vine and threw it off the side of the cliff to the men waiting below.

The bundle hit the sand below right in front of Captain Simpson's feet. Captain Simpson leaned over, picked up the package, and unwrapped it. Even way up on our perch, we could hear the crew below all cheer with their glee. The men below were dancing about and laughing and tossing the big blue diamond amongst themselves. The crews on both ships heard the ruckus, and all hands came to the sides to have a gander. Captain Simpson turned to the ships and held the diamond high for all to see. Both ships also exploded with glee and dancing and laughter.

Captain Simpson studied the drawing on the leaf for a second, and then I could see him giving out orders. Seconds later we saw two of his crew scurrying quickly back across the sand for a ding. It took about an hour, but finally we all watched as the harpoon cannon came to the line.

"Watch your scurvy butts, mates, 'cause here she comes," the captain ordered.

With that, we saw the cannon's fire and smoke rise, and a second later we heard the cannon's thunder. A second after that came the harpoon with its line in tow. The harpoon hit the side of the mountain just above us and stuck fast. All of us, the crew on the beach and on the ships, again were dancing with laughter and cheer.

With a little rigging and a lot of sliding down hill, Captain Pike and what was left of his away crew were down on the beach with the others. One by one, as we slid over the edge of the cave, disappearing down the rigging to the beach below, the Ice Wolves were whimpering, as they knew they could not follow us this time. All had the wolves on their minds as we turned to look back at them as we were disappearing away from them.

"How are the wolves going to get down?" I asked the captain as my feet hit the sand.

Captain Pike walked right over to Captain Simpson and grabbed him up in a big hug and a laugh. "Well, if it's not Captain Patrick Simpson of the PS *Resolve*," Captain Pike said. "You're late as usual I see."

Captain Simpson smiled a huge smile and said, "Well, Captain, while you've been sunning yourself on this here beach, I had to keep the British Navy from ruining your holiday. I had to fix your rat problem, and then I had to fix up that old battle wagon you call a ship." Both captains began to laugh hard and loud, as it was very obvious they had a great admiration and affection for one another.

As the treasure packs were loaded onto the dings, both captains talked and laughed. The captains and I were the last to step aboard one of the boats for our quick trip back to the ship.

"Mr. Newly," Captain Pike said sternly, "to answer your question about the wolves. Right this minute I don't care anything about them wolves, but soon enough I better be a petting at them. Build a bridge up there if you have to, but I want them down as soon as possible. We leave the morning after next, and they better be aboard."

Captain Simpson just stood there quiet as I looked at him as if for some relief. We recognized each other, and I was shocked. Captain Simpson was the pirate captain that had attacked my merchant ship and brought me to Tortola.

"Well, you have come a long way in a short time, boy," he said with a grin.

"Captain Simpson, this is Mr. Newly, and do you see that scarf he is wearing, or have your eyes gone bad on you too?" Captain Pike said.

"Well, now, Mr. Newly. My apologies for the boy comment. I see you are a cannon master," Captain Simpson replied. "You *have* come far!"

"I guess so, sir," I replied, smiling.

"Do you two know each other?" asked Captain Pike.

"Acquaintances," answered Captain Simpson.

"Do you understand your orders concerning the wolves, Mr. Newly?" asked the captain, looking at me with a pause.

I looked back at Captain Simpson for support, and he said, "Don't look at me, Mr. Newly, as I'll be the one that has to hang you. I ain't seen these wolves yet, and I don't know their story, but if I were you, Mr. Newly, I'd come up with them."

"By the way, Mr. Newly," Captain Pike said to me as my fate and thoughts were on a hangman's rope.

"In your spare time, I expect my new first mate for dinner tonight with Captain Simpson and myself."

I thought for a moment and asked, "First mate, Captain? Who is the new first mate now? I'll inform him, sir."

Captain Pike looked over at Captain Simpson with a smile and said, "Well, Patrick, you told me you shot the last my last First Mate and his replacement too, so you appoint a new one."

Scratching his beard, Captain Simpson said, "Well, Captain, I just can't think of anyone worthy and trusty enough or stupid enough to take the position. I know! I appoint Mr. Newly as your new First Mate," he exclaimed.

"A fine choice," answered Captain Pike.

"Dinner will be served at eight sharp, Mr. Newly, and try to be on time." Both captains began a hardy laugh together at my expense, and I just sat back in the ding and shook my head side to side.

Then Captain Simpson looked at me and said, "You have come a long way, Mr. Newly, from a whipping boy on a British merchant ship to the First Mate of the *Sovereign of the Seas*."

"I want to hear about you two later," Captain Pike said.

It felt great to back aboard the *Sovereign of the Seas*, and I settled into my new position as first mate smartly. My first order to the crew was grand one.

"Mr. Robinson!" I called out impatiently.

"Aye, Mr. Newly, sir," he said with a snap and a smile.

"Get those wolves down off that mountain."

"But how, sir?"

"Build a bridge up there if you have to, but soon enough I better be petting them. We leave the morning after next, and they better be aboard."

"Aye, Mr. Newly, sir," Mr. Robinson replied. As I walked away, I looked up at the upper deck, and there both the captains stood. They had heard my order to Mr. Robinson, and they were smiling proudly at me. I smiled a big, proud grin back at them, shrugged my shoulders, and continued my duties inspecting the ship.

Chapter

Eight

That night we had the party of parties celebrating Captain Pike's return with the grand treasure. Another beautiful night set the stage for us with its stars and moon and the sea. Both ships looked wonderful in the night with their lanterns aglow, and the sound of the crew's happiness floated on the sea's breeze. As the hot rum began to flow freely, the great celebration began. A fine feast of fresh fish, oysters, crabs, lobsters, and several wild pigs was served. Excitement and anticipation filled the air as the music and dance began. We all knew that it was a truly special night. It was treasure night, and all the crew knew they were about to get their measure. Each man had his own dreams of his future as a rich man. As Captain Pike had explained before, just one of the stones would make a man wealthy beyond his thoughts and ten stones would make him a king.

I had no thoughts of being a king. In my opinion, there were already too many kings and too many queens in this world, and they all seemed to be miserable creatures that were power hungry and cruel. They were persons who were cursed to never be happy, and I wanted no part of their fate. I was going to rescue my mother and sisters from their master and find Katherine. The rest I could figure out from there. But right now I had to get to the captain's table for dinner.

I knocked on the captain's cabin door and entered. A great feast was before me on the grandly set table, and I was hungry. Captains Pike and

76

Simpson were sitting at the table, as was Mr. Stevenson, the first mate of the *Resolve*. They all were sitting quietly, sipping at their hot rum. I quickly lost my smile as I realized the celebration's air was not in this cabin.

"What is wrong?" I asked, sitting down at my place.

The captain opened his coat and pulled out the map and tossed it over to me. "Have a look, Mr. Newly," he said.

I rolled open the map, and there I saw the map's victims all over again. As I had seen before, all the men we had lost on the island, except the two poor devils that got eaten by something, had their poor, retched silver faces upon the map squirming in their agony.

"Look closer, Mr. Newly. There is another now," spoke the captain in a whisper. There in one corner was a great white wolf wrapped in chains and rolling about in its pain.

My eyes filled with tears as I looked up at all in the cabin. "Tamantha." I gasped. "It's Tamantha, isn't it, Captain?"

"Looks to be her, Mr. Newly," replied Captain Pike.

I jumped from the table in anger and threw the map down. "We have to help her, Captain Pike! Captain Simpson, we have to help them," I pleaded. "Give me a ship. I will go to find them myself."

"What about your treasure, Mr. Newly? What about your family, Mr. Newly? And what about your life?" asked Captain Pike. "You will probably lose your life and maybe your soul if you go down this path."

"I yield my treasure and my future to save them!" I cried out.

Captain Pike looked over at Captain Simpson with a smile and said, "Looks like you appointed the right man, Patrick."

Captain Simpson stood and held his glass of rum high and said, "It's settled then. We will go for them."

The rest of us all stood with our rum glasses high in the air. All glasses came together with a loud clank, and all yelled out "Arrr!"

"Don't speak to the crew about this, or we will have a mutiny on our hands, mates," ordered Captain Pike.

"Tell the crew we are going for another treasure."

Then with a big smile, he said, "So, gentlemen, now that we have concluded our business for tonight, let's join the party." He opened the cabin door, and the celebration's sounds and smells poured in carried by the sweet salt air.

We joined the crew in the celebration, and the music and the dancing slowed to a stop as we began to share our stories of our trek on the island. All gathered around as I told of poor Mr. Longfellow and the pit and the witch that got him. The captain told the story of the cave and the bats. All the crew was frozen in time listening, and they laughed with a glee as we told of Tamantha catching us in the waves unarmed. We told of the wolves and of Tamantha's change, and we told of the sanctuary she lived in and the treasures that surrounded it. We told of the pools of light and the treasure we now possessed. We did not say a word about the key. Everyone that knew anything about that key was sworn to the pirate's oath of secrecy and was forbidden to speak of it. When the last breath of the tales ended, you could have heard a pin drop on the deck of both ships.

As if to break the temporary silence from the stories and get back to the celebration, Captain Pike stood and ordered, "Bring the treasure." All hands on both ships burst into a cheer. The stones were poured into a huge chest for all to see, and what a sight it was, a sight that was truly unbelievable.

Captain Pike ordered, "All hands get to a line and receive your measure." After the securing about and after the fighting and a shot in the air from Captain Simpson, we finally had a line of the men.

Just before he began to give out the treasure, the captain gave a little speech and said, "You are all very rich men now. However, a certain responsibility comes with this great wealth. If I have to come for you because of any evil ways you've succumb to or any evil deeds you commit as a result of this great gift it won't be pretty. It won't be pretty at all. There is no where you will able to hide. Do you understand what I'm saying to you mates?

"Arrrrr," yelled the crew.

"Very well then, you have been warned. Let's get to it."

Each crewmember of the *Sovereign of the Seas* and the *Resolve* one by one sat on a barrel before Captain Pike for a talk. He talked to them like they were his mates and like he knew each one well. Captain Pike laughed and talked about their past and about what was next for them in this life.

Captain Pike talked to each crewman about how rich they were and what fine kings they would be. I noticed the captain almost had a tear to him as he sat with each of them, but that could not be. It must have been the rum I was drinking to make me notice such.

Captain Pike gave each man ten stones after he told us he would only give three. The men on the away team got an extra two, and that cannon master that fired that harpoon cannon got an extra two. It took hours, but each man got his talk with Captain Pike. Each crewman seemed to walk away on the mist, floating on their dreams, looking at their treasure. After the last of the crew was presented their prize, the celebration resumed.

The captain walked over to me and said, "I didn't see you in the line, Mr. Newly. Why not?"

"I don't know, Captain. I guess I wanted the crew to get theirs first in case you ran short," I explained.

"Run short, Mr. Newly?" He laughed. "I could have given each man a hundred stones, and we would not have run short. Tell me the real reason for your absence, Mr. Newly."

"I don't know why, Captain. I guess I figured you'd give me something later," I said. "I guess I'm worried more about Tamantha and the others, sir, more than I am about a treasure."

"Come with me, Mr. Newly. I want to show you something."

I followed the captain back to his cabin, and he told me to have a seat. I watched him as he went over and opened up one of the many closets in the cabin. There I saw a large chest. It was just a plain, old wooden chest, but it was very heavy, and the captain struggled with it.

"Mr. Newly, get over here and help me with this thing. Can't you see it's heavy?"

"Aye, Captain. Sorry, Captain," I said as I jumped up and hurried over to help him.

We drug the heavy monster over toward the table, and the captain said, "I made this chest up for myself, but I can always make another. I want you to have it, Mr. Newly. That is, if you live long enough to drag it off the ship."

"What is it, Captain?"

"Open it up, Mr. Newly," he said. "This all belongs to you now."

I opened up the chest, and what I saw made my eyes bug out of my head. There before me lay thousands of gold and silver coins. There were so many gold and silver bars I stopped counting, and then there were hundreds of the jewels we found from the island. I knew where the jewels came from, and I wondered about the gold and silver.

Before I could ask, the captain laughed and said, "Congratulations, Mr. Newly. You are now probably the richest man in the world—besides me, of course, and Captain Simpson."

"No, Captain. I can't take this," I said, trying to gain back my composure.

"Of course you can't take it, Mr. Newly. Not now anyway. You better leave it locked up here for now." The captain laughed. "When the time comes and you leave this ship for your last time, this chest will go with you, Mr. Newly."

"But why, Captain?"

"One day, Mr. Newly, you will know why. For now, let's get back to the celebration."

With the music and laughter in the background, I walked over to the side of the ship facing the island. I thought I could hear Kodiak, Klondike, Cheyenne, and Avalanche talking to the moon. Louder and louder their calls became, and to my great surprise it was because they had been brought aboard the *Sovereign* and were headed up the stairs from the lower deck to greet the captain and me. I was laughing at the sight as I looked over at the captain.

"Well, Mr. Newly, you did it and did it proper," he said with a great smile.

Mr. Robertson ran up to me in a glee and said, "How's that, Mr. Newly? I got your wolves just like you ordered me." I continued to laugh and shook my head.

A second later the entire side of the mountain blew off. The explosion was so powerful it blew our two ships off their anchors. In a second, the captain and I, along with the wolves and Mr. Robertson, found ourselves on the other side of the ship lying on our backs from the blast. Several of the crew were blown over the railing into the sea from the force of the blast. Four huge fireballs flew off the mountain's explosion and went over the ships into the sea. The impact from the fireballs hitting the sea set off a great wave.

The wave was huge and at least thirty feet high, and there was no time to do anything. Not even the captain could get out an order, and with the ships at anchor, this wave was a killer of men and ships. Neither the *Sovereign* nor the *Resolve* would survive its impact. We were busy pulling men out of the water as we watched the wave approach in the moonlit darkness. Just as the wave was upon us, it dropped back into the sea and disappeared below us. Our two ships did not even rock.

With the roar of the wave gone, all was dead calm and silent. The smoke from the explosion still rose from the island in the moonlight. We all stood at a pause wondering what in the world had happened. Captain Pike explained that it must have been the reef that dispatched the wave. Then we heard a large thud on the side of the ship, a dull thud like the ship was banging against a pier piling. Several other thuds were heard and felt on both ships. All hands looked over the side, and there before our eyes were four large whales.

"Those are the biggest killer whales I have ever seen!" exclaimed Captain Pike.

"They usually steer clear of ships too," Captain Simpson said. "Never seen the likes of them in these waters either."

"Not cold enough for them," spoke Captain Pike. The whales scratched at the ships and rolled over on their backs, showing their white bellies to us. They danced about and played in the sea. They placed their heads out of the water and called at us in a laughing tone.

"How do you know they are killer whales, Captain?" I asked, never having seen one before.

"It was that trip north to the land of ice I told you about, Mr. Newly, where I came across the ice wolves for the first time. That cursed land not only had them wolves, but it also had what the natives called killer whales. They would knock the natives out of their dings and eat them, Mr. Newly. Captain Simpson and I saw all of them up close and were lucky to get out alive. Those are killer whales, Mr. Newly! Are all the men out of the water?"

"Do you want me to dispatch them with rifle, Captain?" I asked.

Captain Pike looked them over carefully. "No, Mr. Newly, they seem peaceful enough for now. Post a guard to watch each of them till they move off on their own. If they start any trouble we will deal with them then."

Morning came, and both ships were ready for the sea that waited. I asked Captain Pike as we stood together looking at the island, "Captain, what was that last night?"

"Some sort of volcano, I guess," replied the captain.

The damage to the island's side where the cave's ending used to be was extraordinary. Looking back I think it was to seal it off from mankind

"Maybe we will come back this way someday, Mr. Newly. That is when we run out of treasure."

The captain's thoughts were then distracted by the whales. We walked over and looked over the railing at them.

"Those whales are still here," Captain Pike said.

Captain Simpson saw us looking at them and called over from the *Resolve,*

"Yep, they are still here. Strangest thing I have ever seen, Captain. Those killer whales are no friend of man if you remember, Captain."

"I remember them well, Captain Simpson! But I never remember them to be this large. This batch here has to be three to four times the size of the ones we saw eating those natives."

"I agree, Captain. They are a bit large," said Captain Simpson. "Do you want me to put them to the cannon, Captain?

"Just leave them be, Captain Simpson," ordered the captain. "They aren't bothering anything. Leave them be."

The four huge whales were still in a tickle with their playing about our two ships. Captain Pike studied the killers further and announced,

"Appears to be three large males and an extra-large female."

The wolves seemed particularly interested in them as they ran about the deck sniffing the air, wagging their tails wildly.

The huge female swam up to the ship and raised her head out of the water, looking right at Captain Pike. Its great tail began to thrash about in the water.

I laughed as I said, "Look, Captain, she is wagging her tail at you."

The captain and I caught a sight of something at the same time, and we both stopped dead in our boots and looked at each other. There right on the whale's forehead was the same mark Princess had on hers. The mark of time there was The Hour Glass.

Captain Pike yelled out, "Standby that portside platform!"

"What are you doing, Captain?" I questioned as he walked over to the platform, removing his coat and boots.

"Captain, what are you thinking?" I knew what he was doing and did not want him to do it, as I thought it would be his end.

Captain Simpson, seeing the scene unfolding, yelled over, "Captain Pike, you're not going to do what I think you are going to do, are you?"

With a big laugh, Captain Pike went over the rail and onto the platform.

"Lower me away," he ordered. "Standby to receive me back quickly or what's left of me if need be."

The platform hit the water, and then came the whales.

"I can't watch!" called out Captain Simpson.

All hands in a horror came to the rail to see their crazy captain get eaten. The first of the whales to arrive in a big hurry was the big female. She ran her entire head and neck up onto the platform after the captain. Her huge mouth was open as she slid right up to him. The crews on both ships let out a gasp. To our great surprise, instead of eating the captain in a single gulp, she started to make a whistle noise. Captain Pike reached out and started petting her face. Her tail was thrashing about in that wagging motion again, really stirring up the sea.

Captain Simpson, rubbing his eyes in disbelief, yelled down, "Captain Pike, is that whale glad to see you, or am I as crazy as you?" All the crew through their hats in the air and let out a cheer.

"Look at this mark here on this whale's head, Mr. Newly," Captain Pike said with a glee.

The captain was rubbing an hour-glass-looking marking she had just above her two huge eyes. "Have you ever seen that mark before?" asked the captain, laughing.

I yelled down. "Yes, I have, Captain. Princess has one of those markings and in that same place. That is that mark of time Tamantha talked about."

In a burst of excitement, the big female hurled herself backward off the platform and splashed into the sea. She ran around our ships, jumping out of the water in a dance. The other three whales rushed up to the platform and paid their respects to the captain with their whistles and tails wagging as he was petting at them.

When the captain was finished with his newfound friends, we hauled up the platform. I walked up to the dripping-wet Captain Pike and asked, "Captain, you do not think for a minute that—"

And before I could finish my question, the captain replied, "Of course not, Mr. Newly. Wolves and whales have nothing in common."

Then the captain said with a smile, "But, Mr. Newly, just remember to keep an open mind. We have seen plenty of things that cannot be. Have you heard before of sea witches or giant bats or of maidens of the sea or clear pools of water that take you a different world? I'm sure you have never heard of a woman that will turn into a wolf or of a parchment that will capture you and hold your soul.

"Before this run is over, mate, we are all going to be insane trying figure what is real and what isn't."

Then with a yell, Captain Pike ordered, "Stand by to get under way!"

Nine

Captain Simpson yelled over from the *Resolve*, "What's the heading, Captain Pike?"

Captain Pike was busy studying the map and did not answer for several minutes.

"We're going to need another ship!" yelled back Captain Pike

"And why do we need another ship?" asked Captain Simpson.

Captain Pike still studying the map intently did not answer. We all just stood and waited.

Finally again after several minutes he said, "Where we are going we will need all the fire power we can muster. We're headed over to the Straights and as you know that area is thick with the King's Navy. Those devils run in packs over there too."

Captain Simpson sneered and asked, "The Straights! Why are we going over there?"

"That's where the next sign on the map be. The island is right in the middle of the straights," answered the captain.

"Captain Pike, we have sailed these waters for years, and we both know there is no land in the middle of the straights."

"Me map here says there be an island there so we are going to find it."

"And where do you plan on getting this new ship from if I may ask?"

Captain Pike yelled back with a grin and said, "Oh, I don't know, Mr. Simpson, how about that British interceptor that neatly put you in your place?"

Everyone except Captain Simpson was surprised that Captain Pike would intentionally hunt down a British warship, especially one that had dispatched us so easily on our last encounter with her.

"Let's get to it then," called over Captain Simpson. "Watch yourself with this one, Captain. This British devil is a match for you."

Captain Pike just laughed.

Before long, both our ships were under way. The wolves were trying to get their sea legs, and it was funny to see them stumble about in the sea's motion.

The island was soon just a memory as it disappeared behind us on the horizon.

"Captain," I said.

"I see them, Mr. Newly," he replied, as we watched the four whales swimming right alongside the two ships.

After a few days of searching, we indeed did find that British warship we were looking for. We heard the crow's mate call down and say,

"We got company off the starboard bow, Captain."

Captain Simpson yelled over after consulting his seeing glass, "That's him, Captain! There is your English devil. The HMS *Defiant* she is, Captain, and you had better watch her close. Her master is a tricky one."

With that said, the *Resolve* broke off to the port and put some distance between her and the *Sovereign*. Captain Pike and I stood looking through our seeing glasses at the oncoming warship.

"I'll say one thing for him, Mr. Newly. He's got nerve taking on these two ships to his one," Captain Pike snarled.

"But, Captain," I said, "he has already shamed these two ships before. Why would he be scared of us now?" I got a dirty look from the captain, so I shut my mouth.

"For his sake, let's hope the captain of the *Defiant* has as much greed as he does nerve, or it will be his and that fine ship's end for sure."

"Signal the *Resolve* to move off and standby," Captain Pike ordered.

"Did I hear you right, Captain?" I asked.

"Move, Mr. Newly. If you keep questioning my orders, I'll…Just carry out me orders, Mr. Newly," Captain Pike said calmly.

"Aye, Captain," I replied.

The *Sovereign*'s flagman signaled the *Resolve* to move off, and off she went at full sail.

Captain Pike ordered the *Sovereign of the Seas* to a full stop, and a ding was lowered with a white flag of parlay flying on its small mast. Captain Pike was to be aboard the ding alone except for his smile and a sack full of something he was carrying.

As Captain Pike was going over the side to board the ding, he looked at me and said with a big smile, "Well, Mr. Newly, you don't want my new ship all scratched up do you? And, besides, I have to save this fool's life."

I just shook my head, as I did not have the slightest idea of what all that was supposed to mean.

Captain Pike was careful to stay in front of the *Sovereign* with all those forward cannon to guard him. It was quite a sight as the HMS *Defiant* came up on him to a stop. We were eying them carefully and they us. The captain of the *Defiant* was particularly interested in what our forward cannon were doing.

Then the whales showed up. Those poor British devils did not know what to think or do. There was nothing in their training that covered a crazy man in a rowboat at sea with a white flag of parlay surrounded by huge killer whales, all the while looking down the wrong end of six forward cannon of a pirate ship that had four giant ice wolves snarling at them from its deck. I would have been shocked at the sight if I were the *Defiant*'s captain, but to my dismay, I was getting used to it all and considered it normal.

The Sovereign was sitting two of three hundred feet off the *Defiant*'s stern, so we were close enough to see and hear everything that happened.

"Permission to come aboard, sir," Captain Pike announced to the *Defiant*'s captain.

"Bring him aboard," ordered the *Defiant*'s captain in a typical British, snooty way. All we could see was Captain Pike surround by all those bright red uniforms with rifles and bayonets pointing at him. The captain of the *Defiant* seemed to be disgusted at the sight of Captain Pike, and he seemed to be lecturing him.

All of a sudden it looked like the captain of the *Defiant* had used up his allotted time for chewing on Captain Pike. Captain Pike had finally had enough of the lecture he was receiving and returned one of his own. We saw Captain Pike pointing at our forward cannon and then at the whales and then at the wolves and then at the *Resolve* that was circling at a distance. Captain Pike then opened the sack he was carrying and showed its contents to the *Defiant*'s captain. Big smiles were then exchanged between the two captains, and off they went to the *Defiant*'s captain's quarters.

A few nervous hours passed, and here came Captain Pike and what seemed to be his new best friend, the captain of the *Defiant*. The captain of the *Defiant* called his crew to order, and they seemed to have some sort of vote. It seemed a few of the crew did not like the outcome of the vote because they were set over the side of the *Defiant* in a ding full of supplies. They went cussing and screaming. The two captains shook hands, and with smiles on their faces, Captain Pike boarded the ding for his return. When the captain returned, he was in a jolly mood.

"Well, Mr. Newly, how do you like me new ship?" he asked.

"New ship, Captain?"

"Yes, Mr. Newly. New ship! May I present you all with the PS *Defiant*? I bought her, her captain, and her crew for a sack of gems. I love greed, Mr. Newly! Better than cannon fire any day. She doesn't have a scratch on her and came with a full crew. Signal the *Resolve* to come in.

As the *Resolve* came up, she was nervous and at full quarters. Captain Simpson swung over, and after a brief meeting with Captain Pike, he swung back to the *Resolve*. Captain Simpson then looked to the captain of the *Defiant*, and both men gave a smile and a salute. With the salute being exchanged between these former enemies, all hats on all three ships went into the air with loud cheers.

"Let's get to it, gentlemen!" Captain Pike yelled out.

The captain of the *Defiant*'s name was Captain Joseph Rickle, and a fine, handsome fellow he was. He seemed to be thirty-something years of age, and with his bright red uniform and polished boots and fine-feathered captain's hat, he looked to be every bit of six feet tall. His uniform had medals all over its front, and he wore it well with his slim, trim build. His hair was coal-black and cut short, and he had a clean-shaven face. Captain Pike said Captain Rickle was the snootiest man he had ever met in his life.

All three of the captain's ships got under way at full sail, and what a sight our fleet must have been from a gull's point of view looking down upon us. A British warship and two pirate ships, with four killer whales in tow, not mention the four giant ice wolves running about their decks. The captain had produced the map and was studying it carefully.

"Steer two hundred and sixty degrees," the captain instructed Jonesy.

"Where are we headed, Captain?" I asked, looking over his shoulder at the map.

"Here, Mr. Newly," and he put his finger on a particularly nasty-looking creature that was guarding an island on the map. "We will start looking for them here, Mr. Newly," the captain said with a grin. "At this speed, we will be there in four days."

I looked over at the *Defiant* speeding next to us in the sea and asked the captain, "Sir, why did the captain of that proud ship and his crew sell their loyalty so easily?"

"It was not easy for them, Mr. Newly. It just appeared that way to you. Do not discount them. They have been on their course for years and just needed a reason to turn. They are good and proud men that love their country and their families dearly. The king, however, could give a fat rat's butt about any of them, and they all know it. He treats the officers of his fine navy like trained dogs and their crew like fleas upon their backs. He ridicules some, whips some, hangs some, and disgraces the rest. Captain Simpson told me about your taste of their whip. I'm surprised you would ask. I just gave them all a lifetime of wages one hundred times over and her captain a thousand. I do not have a whip, Mr. Newly. I have only a pistol and an agreement. They all at least know where they stand with me. I will not betray a single one of them, nor will they me."

After one day's sailing, the crow's mate yelled down, "We have company again, Captain!"

Captain Pike, growling as he reached for his seeing glass, said, "It sure is getting crowded out here."

"Three warships!" the crow's mate yelled down. "They are flying a strange flag, Captain. I see a lot of fire power over there, Captain."

After a close inspection of his own, Captain Pike slammed his seeing glass closed and said, "I have seen this flag before, and it is not a good thing for us. Drop those colors quick as you can and run up that French Flag that we have below in the hole.

Our other two ships had already run up their French flags as if they did not have to be told to.

"Signal the *Defiant* to drop that British flag they are so proud of too."

"And tell them to get those redcoats off their deck, or they will go to the bottom for sure.

I heard that Captain Rickle snarled as he read the flagman's signal. He did not like the order at all. He was a fine officer trained to fight at sea and not to hide like a dog, but he complied with Captain Pike's order to him.

"Who are they?" I asked the captain in alarm, looking through my seeing glass.

"Those are pirate hunters of the worst kind, Mr. Newly. The good side to them is that they hate the British Navy even more than I do. They are men that you cannot reason with, Mr. Newly. They can't be bribed or corrupted."

As the warships drew nearer, we took a submissive posture like we were one big happy family at sea except for our hidden teeth. I could now see their flag clearly with its stars and stripes upon it.

"Mr. Newly, I give you the American Navy," said Captain Pike.

The captain almost sounded like he had a certain respect for them.

"Standby all cannon and sail," he ordered. One of the American warships moved off to starboard and one off to port. They begin to circle around and pick up speed, preparing for a run at us. I saw the two ship's names as they turned. The USS *Enterprise* and the USS *Intrepid* they were. The front American warship came on strong, right at us under full sail. She flew by fast, right between the *Resolve* and the *Defiant*, looking us all over quickly.

Captain Pike remarked, "Now ain't she was just dripping with fire power." "Everyone wave to them and smile," Captain Pike ordered. All crew, on all ships, waved and smiled at her under our French flags. As she went by, I saw her name—the USS *Constitution*.

All three warships came around fast to make another run at us. "Hold your fire!" screamed Captain Pike. "They're coming around for another look, and we don't want a fight with these ships—at least not now anyway!"

The warships went by at full speed, looking us over again, and we all waved and smiled. To my relief, they seemed to accept us, and off they went without even slowing down.

"Remember that flag in the future, Mr. Newly, and stay away from it," said Captain Pike.

After the three ships disappeared on the horizon, we resumed our course and speed toward the spot on the map. I continued to be worried about that nasty-looking beast the map showed to be in the area. After another day's sailing, we started to see things in the water. There were odd-looking sea creatures of all sizes and shapes, and they made nice meals for the whales.

In the night sea we began to see what appeared to be shimmering lights. Strange creatures they were, and the spooky part about them is that they seemed to call to us from the depths with whispers we could not understand. It was interesting that the whales had no interest in them at all.

The sea air began to have a stench about it, a rotten stench, and we all wondered what awaited us in the next day and night.

The next morning we found where the stench was coming from. It was a black mass on the surface of the sea that appeared to be quite large, as we could not see across it and find clear water again. The whales did not like it at all and reacted quickly. The *Defiant* would have been the first to cross over into it, but one of the whales came up on the *Defiant*'s port side and hit the ship so hard the ship changed course away from the floating, stinking black mass. The *Defiant*'s wheel was spinning wildly as the helmsman was thrown to the deck. All crew were tossed off their feet as the whale continued to push the *Defiant* away from the floating mass, and Captain Rickle was having a fit. The other three whales stood fast in front of us, blocking our approach to the mass, whistling and making a clicking noise as they warned us off.

Watching the scene, the *Resolve* and the *Sovereign* came about hard to starboard and slowed to a crawl. The whales delivered the *Defiant* nicely alongside us.

"I like your whales!" Captain Rickle called over with his redcoat crew getting to their feet.

"I warned you about them!" Captain Pike yelled back.

"Just imagine if they didn't like you. Stand fast there, I'm coming aboard."

Captain Pike grabbed up a rope and swung over to her. With his feet hitting the deck right in front of Captain Rickle, Captain Pike politely said with a smile, "Let's get a closer look, Captain Rickle."

As the *Defiant* eased up to the mass, we were all staring at the scene intently. Both Captains Pike and Rickle and the crew of the *Defiant* looked like they were all gagging at the smell of the thing. The whales came up whistling and clicking with warning as if to make sure the *Defiant* would not touch it. The nasty black mass not only appeared to be wide, but it also appeared to run deep beneath the surface. In the clear-blue sea, you could see the side of the slick that ran down and out of sight in the water.

"What is this thing?" asked Captain Rickle.

"I don't know, and I don't like it, so let's go around it," replied Captain Pike.

Captain Pike signaled us his intentions, and we all started to move around the slick. We sailed and sailed but could not go around it. Captain Pike snarled out and said, "This thing is moving with us, and if it can move, it must be alive."

Captain Rickle replied, "Well, if it is alive, then it can be killed."

"Full stop," ordered Captain Pike. "Let's see if we can wake this devil up. Load up a ding with powder and lamp oil and set it adrift. Let's see if we can get something to nibble on the bait."

Within minutes, the ding and its load of lamp oil and powder was away and drifting toward the black mass.

As soon as the ding drifted onto the mass, things began to happen. It almost looked like many a man's hands, arms, and heads came up out black mess. The hands, arms, and heads were made of the black goo. You could hear a moaning like sound from them as they rubbed and caressed the ding. The ding began to dissolve and become part of the black devilish puddle of stench. It looked as if the ding was to suffer the same fate that was bestowed on these other poor souls whose ships must have run across it and were caught in the trap.

When the ding was almost completely gone and the barrels of powder and oil began to sizzle in the black mess, the *Defiant* fired at it with three cannon. Immediately the captain got the explosion he wanted, and the burning lamp oil spread out onto the mass. The black mess caught fire and was burning hard and fast.

"Get us out of here, Captain Rickle," Captain Pike ordered.

As the *Defiant* sped away in full retreat, the burning mass began to suck itself back off the surface of the sea. As it did, it began to rise up out of the water higher and higher till what stood before us was just so horrible a man should have never seen it.

It was some sort of creature, and it stood waist deep in the ocean and two hundred feet tall. It was hard to see the creature's features because it was so fluid. You could make out a horrible face that came from men's nightmares. It had large arms with handlike ends or claws or pincers. I could not really tell because the creature kept changing. It appeared to be made up of thousands of men and ship parts and horses and anything else that had been sucked down. All parts of it floated and crawled and squirmed about, in and out, appearing and disappearing, like worms in a ball.

One thing for sure was that this black, slimy devil was on fire and burning badly. It screamed the screams of the thousands of men that made it up as it made its way toward us, dying in the flames. The whales had lined up between the creature and us, and they began to scream back at it. The whales made some sort of sound that came from their heads. I had not heard anything like it before, but I knew it was a sound that could destroy most anything in its path. The sound from the whales slowed the beast's forward advance on us but did not stop it.

"Captain," I yelled, "if that thing gets a hold on us, we are finished!"

"That's what I like about you, Mr. Newly," the captain screamed back. "You're so observant.

"Fire!" screamed the captain.

The *Resolve* and the *Sovereign* opened fire with all forward cannon to bear, and the *Defiant* fired all her portside cannon. The cannon balls just went right through the creature, tearing big chunks of its burning mass away. With one final desperate assault on us, the beast lunged forward and swung at the *Defiant* with a massive, flaming, screaming arm. It was a near miss, and the devil disappeared screaming into the sea.

All ships came together for the night and a rest. As the sun went down, the crew from the *Sovereign* and the *Resolve* mingled together with the crew from the *Defiant*, getting to know their new mates dressed in their bright red coats. The whales seemed calm and content as they scratched at the ships. Hot rum, food, laughter, and music again flowed freely in the night air. The men had a chance to talk about the nightmare they had seen that day and the sweet dreams they each had about their future life as rich men and kings. All captains, first mates, and first officers were invited to dine with Captain Pike in his cabin. After dinner, Captain Pike asked Captain Simpson and me to stay.

"We have map business," he told us.

As the others left, Captain Simpson and I remained at the captain's table. The captain rolled out the map and pointed to the spot where a beast was shown two days ago.

"That beast is gone off the map!" he exclaimed "Gone because we have destroyed it." The captain smiled.

"As you can see, all the other poor souls and Tamantha are still here on the map, squirming in their pain, but that beast we dispatched today is missing. We set that black devil free from its duty, and that means we can set the others free."

"Yes, Captain, that is great news, but you're forgetting one thing here," explained Captain Simpson.

"What would that be?" asked Captain Pike.

"We had to kill it to free it and all its prisoners" said Captain Simpson.

"A mere technicality," replied the captain.

Captain Pike called us to look closer at that cursed map and said, "We are here," pointing with his finger on the map. "This wretch of a rock pile here is where we will be tomorrow and where we will begin to look for our answers."

The captain blew gently on the map, and like before, it shimmered and changed to a local point of view.

"Mr. Newly, what does this say? What is the name of this rock pile?" Captain Pike asked.

"It says Maiden's Island, Captain."

"Arrgh, Maiden's Island," Captain Pike said with a snicker. "Now doesn't that sound like a nice and cozy place?" We all began a big laugh.

"Remember one thing, mates," the captain advised. He looked at us in a strange, serious way like he was worried about what tomorrow would bring. "If you can't outsmart them and you can't outfight them, you have to get nasty mean. Nasty mean like a snake or a rat in a corner. Nasty mean like a rabid dog. It's the only way you will survive. Nasty mean has a strength to its own," Captain Pike explained with a scowl and squinted eyes.

"Dismissed, tend to your duties.

The *Sovereign*, the *Resolve*, and the *Defiant* were drifting quickly in the sea that night. The moonless sky left behind a dark ocean, and the shimmers of light from the depths were back again like ghosts calling at us. It was all very unsettling, and I hung about with the wolves.

"Double the lookouts," I ordered. "I don't want anything crawling over that railing at me."

I could hear all captains laughing as they heard my order, but I just ignored them. I looked over the rail at the whales, and they seemed to be laughing at me also with all their noises that they made. The crew, however, were not amused as they carried out my orders.

One of the crow's mates yelled down and said, "Captain, I have a light off the starboard bow."

"Is it a ship?" questioned the captain.

"In a minute, Captain!" yelled the mate. "I have to get a bearing on it." A minute later, the mate yelled down, "No, sir. Captain, it is a light on land. It does not move, Captain."

"Get a fix on that light. That will be our heading in the morning," ordered the captain. "That is, unless Mr. Newly wants to go tonight." Again I was not amused, but that did not stop the three captains from chuckling.

Ten

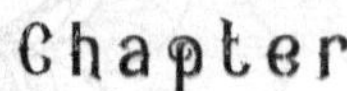

As the sun came up, we got under way and headed in the direction of the light we had seen the night before. We began to see an island on the horizon, and the crow's mate yelled down, "Land off the port bow, Captain!"

When we came up on the island, we all witnessed a great scene. The island was active with so many sights to see it would have been hard for a man to take it all in his lifetime. The island had a strange, many-colored mist surrounding it with great colored waves crashing on to its rocky sides. There was no shore or beach to the island, just rock coming up from the sea. There were hundreds of small volcanic peaks rising up out of the ocean, only ten foot tall or so, spewing their red, hot lava into the crystal-blue water, making the steam.

Lightning was cracking about several seemingly nasty waterspouts that were part of a storm that looked like it had been there for a thousand years. For some reason, it looked to me like a storm that would never end. At the peak of the highest point of the island was the light we had seen from sea. We looked hard but could not make out what was causing the great light that had called to us from so far out to sea. I looked over at Captain Pike and then to the rest of the crew, and they, too, seemed to be as amazed at the sights before us.

"Jonesy, bring us around the island so we can get a look," ordered the captain.

"I know you want to get ashore, Mr. Newly," the captain said in a taunting tone, "But there's no need to get in a hurry."

As we circled the seemingly cursed island, we found no way to approach it with its rocks and waves. When we had almost come completely around the island, to our surprise, there before us was a beautiful calm harbor. As we looked into the harbor, we could see the skeleton of a great ship lying on the island's sand beach.

Captain Pike looked over at me and said with a big smile, "Well, it sure looks to me like someone wore out their welcome here, Mr. Newly."

Just as the captain spoke those words, a great ball of fire came down upon us from high atop the island, right from the direction of the light beacon. We all stood staring as the bright blue fireball came down the side of the mountain and leveled off at the sea. It was headed straight for us. It crossed over all the ship's bows and disappeared on the horizon, seeming to have no limit to its range. It had come in low and fast and just cleared the ships. We could feel the fireball's heat as it went over us, singeing the sails. We got a good look as it went over, and in itself it was a wonder. It was at least thirty feet round, and it crackled and spit with power. Bolts of blue lightning seemed to make up its face, and its insides looked to be made of some sort of molten liquid.

"That, Mr. Newly, was a warning shot! It would seem there is some sort of sentry posted up there!" exclaimed the captain.

"What in Hades was that?" yelled Captain Simpson.

"I don't like this a bit!" yelled Captain Rickle. "No treasure is worth my crew and my ship."

"Maybe or maybe not, Captain Rickle!" the captain yelled back. "Two things I can tell you for sure, mate. We are definitely in range of their cannon, and for sure we are going to find something here, treasure or not."

Captain Rickle just sneered back.

All crew and captains looked up and at the top of this great place from where the fireball had come down. We looked up at the beacon light and squinted hard to make it out in the mist. To the eye, the peak looked like a giant rock candle with some sort of bright light on it. However, looking through our seeing glasses, we could see that on that candle top there sat a great sea-maiden that was like the wick of the candle. A gigantic blue fire burned around her that was so bright it almost outshone the sun, and with that endless storm raging behind her, the whole scene looked like the entrance to hades with her as its sentry.

"What in the world is that, Captain Pike?" Captain Rickle screamed, slamming closed his seeing glass.

"A sea-maiden, Captain Rickle!" yelled Captain Pike. "Ain't she a dandy?" He laughed.

"Sea-maiden?" yelled Captain Rickle. "What is a sea-maiden?"

"Well, there she sits. Ask her!"

Again she looked down at us and flung out another of her fireballs.

"Here comes another one!" screamed Captain Pike.

Down the mountain and across the sea it came fast. We all just stood staring, as there was nothing we could have done to get away. We could feel the heat as the blue flaming ball passed over us again, singeing our sails.

"Another warning shot!" explained the captain.

"How do you know it's a warning shot?" I questioned the captain.

"I think if she had a mind to, we would all be ashes by now, Mr. Newly. We should anchor here," ordered the captain.

"Maybe she will allow us to come ashore if we leave the ships here," Captain Pike said in a nervous tone.

"What in blazes is going on?" Captain Rickle yelled.

"Captain Rickle, if you would you be good enough to please put yourself and six of those fine redcoats of yours in a ding and join my away team, we will see if we can get your questions answered," the captain replied.

Captain Rickle did not like that order, and I could see the surprise on his face. I just chuckled to myself.

"Captain Simpson, drop seven of your mates in a ding to join me also, but I want you to stay here. You are now in command," ordered Captain Pike.

"Mr. Newly, stand by a ding and pick you some mates to go ashore."

We dropped three dings over the side, loaded with the away teams, our supplies, and arms. All the dings joined up together, and off to the shore we went. We were all scared half to death, that is, for Captain Pike as usual. The whales followed us in rubbing and scratching at the dings. Halfway to shore, that sentry atop the mountain let loose with another of her fireballs. Again the great blue fireball came crackling and spitting down the side of the mountain and across the sea, but this one seemed different. It appeared this one was not a warning shot and would not clear us this time. This time the blue devil was headed right at the dings and was meant to take us all. The fireball was almost upon us when the whales, without a care in the world, surfaced and rolled over on their backs with their bright-white bellies showing.

As fast as it had been dispatched, the fireball just evaporated and was gone with only a portion of its heat remaining on our faces. It was as if the maid on top of that mountain had seen the whales and changed her mind about our certain demise.

Only the captain had ever encountered a sea-maiden before, and we were all in for a treat. As with all sea-maids, for some reason, they will not talk to you directly, and this one was no different. Like the captain said before, they go into your mind and speak to you in thoughts. As it turned out, Captain Rickle and the rest of us were not going to enjoy our first thoughtful conversation with a sea-maiden. In our minds, the maiden from atop the mountain angrily began to fire off her demanding questions at us from far away.

"What are you doing trying to approach this island?" she demanded.

"How did you find this place?"

"How did you live past the sea guardian?"

"Are you men or from the sea?"

"Where did you get those whales?"

"Show me your thoughts and answers to my questions," the mighty maiden again demanded in our minds.

We all began to feel a bit dizzy as she searched our minds for her answers. In a second, she stopped her probing and prodding and announced,

"I see you hold the Map of the Sea, Captain Pike, and therefore you and your kind may enter. The answers to your questions are indeed here. Be warned, though, the one you call the Sea Witch may also be here, and she may await you. You are all fools and walking dead men and your ship's bones along with yours will soon be bleaching in the sun on the beach before you."

"I told you this place was going to be nice and cozy, Mr. Newly." The captain laughed.

"Now wasn't she just a dandy? And that was just the housekeeper. Just wait till you meet the mistress of the house."

Captain Pike burst out laughing. The entire away team and I again were not amused, especially Captain Rickle.

"What is this about a map", Captain Pike?

"What about this Sea Witch, Captain?"

"What was that that just took my mind?"

" What in hades is going on here?" Captain Rickle asked.

"Hold your powder there, Mr. Rickle. You'll have your answers soon enough."

As our dings hit the beach, we were all very nervous, except the captain, of course. We loaded our sacks of supplies onto our backs and walked over to examine the skeleton of the once-great ship that lay half buried in the island's sand. The great ship's skeleton looked like it had been placed there as a warning to all trespassers to turn back and leave this place or suffer its fate.

The ship had three large holes on her port side big enough for a man to walk through. Her three masts lay broken in pieces in their rotted rigging. Bits of rotted sail still flapped in the breeze and seemed to sound a warning to all to leave this place. What really spooked us all was the scene we saw on her starboard side. As we came around the ship, we all just stopped in our tracks and stared in silence. There appeared to be giant claw marks running down her entire side. The five large gouge marks went deep into the ship's wood, leaving side planks pulled away and splinted wood everywhere.

"What do you think happened to her?" I asked Captain Pike.

"Maybe that black devil we just burnt dead did not like her taste and spit her up on this beach!" he exclaimed with a grin.

Sometimes I didn't know why I even talked to the captain at all.

As we explored the beach further, we came across a long and wide column of stairs that led up off the sand and up onto the island. It must have been a mile long and rose up many hundreds of feet. It appeared to be made of fine white marble, and its railings were a continuous great marble serpent that ran beginning to end. The many rungs that supported the serpent railing were made of marble carvings of sea creatures. There were landings on the staircase every hundred feet or so. These landings had great scenes from the sea, as we had seen before on Tamantha's bed curtain, etched into the marble at our feet. There were no signs of life anywhere, not even a bird or crab, and that did not sit well with any of us.

Quietly we made our way up the stairs and arrived at the top. To our surprise a small open town greeted us that seemed to be busy with people. The town's buildings were shaped like a horseshoe, with its open end toward the sea and us. They surrounded a large plaza that's roof was the sky, and its floor was made of many-colored stones. The stone's design looked like a great bird's head that had been flattened in a way. Its great eyes and beak welcomed us with a fierce look as we entered the scene. The rest of the stones appeared as the great feathers of the bird covering the floor area of the town's main street arena.

There was a large fountain right in the middle of the plaza that shot water many feet into the air. At the fountain's center was a great, beautiful statue of a sea-maiden.

"Mr. Rickle, there is your sea-maiden." The captain laughed. Captain Rickle and his crew just frowned.

The people of the town seemed to be very friendly and welcomed us, waving their hands and tipping their hats.

"I don't like this a bit," Captain Pike said.

"It's all just too pretty and nice and to easy, keep your guard up."

One very pleasant, but somehow strange, fellow walked up and invited us into his shop for food and drink. He did not talk right. His voice almost sounded like he had a mouthful of water as he spoke to us. Captain Pike looked over at me with a wink like he knew something was up and gracefully accepted the man's invitation with a smile. We all followed behind him to his shop, making pleasant conversation along the way. I could not put my finger on it, but there was definitely something strange about the man, and I could tell the captain felt the same way.

The inside of the man's shop was adorned with beautiful sea sculptures and trinkets from the sea. We sat and had a good meal made up of some sort of bird, and to our delight we washed it all down with a really fine rum-like drink.

Captain Pike looked at us and said with another whisper, "I want you all to listen to and watch this. There is something wrong with this fellow, and I'm going to find out what it is."

With that, Captain Pike went over to the shopkeeper and asked him, "What is your name, sir?"

"Name?" the shopkeeper replied.

"Yes, your name, sir. What is your name?"

The shopkeeper could not answer. He just stood there and looked at the captain with a puzzled look to his face.

"Do you have any fish or oysters or crabs to offer us?"

Again the man just stood silent and looked at the captain.

"What is the name of this town, sir? What is this place, sir? Are these trinkets here for sale, sir?"

Again the shopkeeper just looked at the captain in silence like he didn't understand a word the captain had said. To our surprise, the shopkeeper turned and went out the door in a confused manner and closed it behind him. We all stood and watched him through the window of the shop as he walked away hurriedly.

"Where in this world is he going?" I asked.

"In this world is the right question, Mr. Newly," Captain Pike said as he held up his hand as if to pause my questions.

"Just watch."

The shopkeeper walked over to the large fountain in the middle of the plaza with the statue of the sea-maiden. As the shopkeeper stood in front of the fountain, its waters began to change in color and rose higher into the air. He stood there for several minutes in silence. As the shopkeeper finished whatever it was that he was doing and turned to come back to us, the water in the fountain went back to its clear color and returned to its normal height.

Hurriedly the shopkeeper returned back to us from across the plaza. We all got back to our seats so the man would not see us all staring at him through the window. When the shopkeeper returned, he had a calm manner to him, as he had his answers to the captain's questions.

He walked back through the front door of his shop and said, "Captain Pike, my name is any you wish to call me. This town is named by whatever you wish to name it. This place is where you are standing. This shop does not serve fish and oysters and crabs to eat because that would be disgusting. This shop does not sell anything, but you may take any items you wish to possess."

We all just looked at him in amazement.

I could tell Captain Pike was growing impatient, and that was never a good thing.

"Where did you get your answers from?" asked the captain.

"What were you doing over at that fountain? You weren't by any chance talking to that sea-maiden, were you?"

Again the shopkeeper just stood in silence.

"Well," said the captain, "how about this then, mate? This should be an easy one to answer. Do you know what this is?" He reached into his coat and retrieved the map of the sea. The shopkeeper immediately got a panicked look about him as Captain Pike laid it on the table and rolled it open. The map began to glow another color I had never seen before, and the shopkeeper made a run for the door but did not make it.

The man, or whatever it was, was caught by the map, and he could go no farther toward his escape. Right before our eyes the shopkeeper began to change back to his true form, which turned out to be nothing but seawater. The water kept the man's shape and features as it twirled about in the air. The entire sight was really very beautiful and wonderful, but Captain Pike had not noticed.

"Now," the captain said to the captured creature, "agree to help us, or I'll let me map have you, or maybe I'll just let you splash on the floor in a puddle to dry up to nothing." The creature motioned in agreement, and the captain rolled up the map. Quickly the water became flesh again, and the shopkeeper returned back to us.

Very upset, he said, "Come with me," and he led us outside toward the fountain.

"Captain Rickle." The captain smiled. "In case you were wondering, that was the map you were questioning about."

Again Captain Rickle frowned, and he sneered at the captain. As we followed the shopkeeper, we looked about and saw the entire town had become disserted.

"Where did they all go, Captain?" I asked.

I don't know, Mr. Newly," answered the captain. "But I'll bet that fountain has something to do with it."

At the fountain's edge, the shopkeeper tried to escape us by jumping up and into the fountain's water. Captain Pike grabbed him up by the arm and said, "Not so fast there, mate, as we have a bargain, and you will fulfill your end of it or pay the price."

The shopkeeper turned to the fountain and the statue and began to concentrate on it, not speaking a word. As we saw before, the fountain's water began to change color and spew higher into the air.

As the wind blew the fountains spray over us, the shopkeeper began to disappear into the spray. As he left us, he said with disgust, "What a hideous and vile creature a man is. I have awakened the Oracle of the Sea for you to ask your questions," and he was gone into the fountains mist.

The captain said with a big laugh, "Well, Captain Rickle, it seems everywhere you go you make a new friend." Captain Rickle just shook his head.

We stood in front of the so-called Oracle of the Sea but did not know what we were to do or say. After several minutes of the captain pacing back and forth and cussing about how that water creature had tricked him, something finally began to happen. Into our minds the statue began to probe like the sea-maidens had done in the past. We could feel the Oracle gathering our questions, and then in our minds the Oracle of the Sea began to answer us back.

"This town was created long ago as a gift to mankind so they could come here to visit and to study and to be at peace with the sea," spoke the Oracle. "

"The wonderful water beings you have met here come from the living sea and are called Tresdors. They are also the guardians of this great place and very powerful beings that could easily destroy you, but their compassion prevents them.

"For some unknown reason," the Oracle spoke, "the Tresdors have always had a love of mankind and always believed that somehow man could join with the sea. In their true form, you can only see them as shimmers of light in the night sea. Only here in this place do the Tresdors take mankind's form. They do this in the attempt to make a man's visit here pleasant and act as a mediator between man and the sea. All mankind has been banished from this place now. Banished because of the evil that dwells in their hearts, and I see you are no different by your actions."

Captain Pike, remaining untouched and unmoved by the Oracle's opinion of him, demanded, "Where are the prisoners of this map held? How do I free them?"

"The prisoners of the map are held in the map and in no other place. Only the map's keeper can free them and even then not always," the stone maiden replied.

Captain Pike, in a rage, started yelling at the stone statue and said,

"What kind of double talk was that? You speak in riddles. I am the map's keeper, so what do I have to do to get me mates off this cursed parchment?"

As if trying to aggravate the captain further, the stone maiden replied, "I do not know, as I do not possess the map you do."

He pulled out his pistol and shot the statue at point blank range. The pumpkin ball went right through the statue like it was also made of water with no damage done except to Mr. Smithfield who was standing on the other side. Right through his shoulder the ball went, and he hit the ground with a scream.

Captain Pike snarled and said, "You two men get him back to the ship and get him fixed up."

To surprise us all, the captain began talking to the statue again, only this time he took on a polite tone.

"Sorry about that there, Ms. Oracle."

With his hat off and bowing, he spoke softly.

"Sometimes I lose me temper, and I'm sorry for that."

I was shocked because I never heard the captain apologize for anything.

"I am not an evil man like you say there, missy. I might have the morals of an alley cat, but I have the ethics of a saint. We are all good men on a quest to save our acquaintances from this cursed parchment that I did not want or ask for in the first place."

Well, the captain must have talked for an hour to that stone. Walking around it and pacing before it, telling it his tales about the witch and her daughter and the island and the prisoners of the map. He told the Oracle about how we could have gone home to have become kings, but instead came for our friends, risking our lives. He said he was sorry for the manner in which he treated the shopkeeper but explained how it was necessary. He told that stone everything he could think of to win her over to his side.

After hearing Captain Pike's speech to the Oracle and now knowing all the facts, Captain Rickle and his men looked like they all had just seen a ghost.

Despite the captain's fine performance, the stone maiden stood silent and cold to his pleas. The captain began to pace back and forth and again began to lose his temper.

"You see, Mr. Newly," the captain said with a snarl.

"Let this be a lesson to all men about these fine, so-called respectable creatures of the sea. They are all just so high and mighty with their way, condemning all mankind. But when an honest man does stand before them asking for their help on a truly just and worthy cause, they do not see him because of their prejudices. They are no better than us, Mr. Newly, with their flawed judgment, and they will all report to their maker with the same poor results as that of a man, if not worse."

Well, the captain's speech did not sit well with something, and the ground began to shake violently. The captain shook his fist at the open ocean before him and screamed at it, "Go ahead, you scurvy dogs and kill us! Take our ships and our lives, but we will remain good men, and you will be the killers of the sea. I only ask you spare me whales and me wolves. They are good creatures and don't deserve a death. They are not like that cursed witch that you protect." As soon as he spoke those words, the statue of the sea-maiden fell off its mount and broke into pieces.

We all stood back and watched as the fountain was destroyed by something rising out of the same place where it stood. A molten-fuming mass of earth began to rise up, and as the mass formed up, it began to look like one of the small volcanoes that were all about the island, except this little volcano had a big surprise for us all. When the volcano had finished rising up and the ground had stopped shaking, the scene became dead silent in the smoke and fumes. We all looked at each other and regained our footing. A second later the volcano's top exploded into the air, and it sounded like a hundred cannon firing at once.

The explosion knocked us all to the ground, and out of the mouth of the volcano came a fiery sea-maiden. She was magnificent with beauty as she rose up slowly out of the fire. The maiden appeared to us with the lower half of her body still part of the flames and smoke. Her skin was as white as alabaster, and her beautiful hair seemed to be made up from ringlets of fire that danced in the breeze. She wore a great-jeweled crown on her head and an amulet around her neck that shined so bright we could barely look at it.

Captain Pike seemed to show a great interest in that amulet.

Her arms were above her head seemingly to support a great glowing crystal orb that floated in the air above her.

In our thoughts, the fiery maiden spoke to us and said, "I am the Oracle of the Sea. I can see the future and the past. When I am spoken to, all creatures of the sea can hear the words, and when I speak, I speak for the sea. Captain Pike, we all have heard your excuses and your insults that you have directed toward us so theatrically this day.

"Many of us have taken pity on your case, and many have not," the maiden said, shaking her head.

"A once very beautiful and still very powerful sea-maiden in particular has not been softened by your innocent pleas. Her name is Miranda, and you are the one that destroyed her wonderful daughter. With that horrible act you have also stolen Miranda from the sea," the Oracle said in a sorrowful tone.

"Your deeds have turned Miranda's wonderful and kind heart to cold stone and her beauty to ugliness and her brightness into darkness."

"Don't forget she's really mean too, Mr. Newly," the captain said.

I just looked at him in amazement that he could joke at a time like this.

The Oracle continued, "In Miranda's mind, along with many others that support her cause, she thinks that all men on the sea and all that help them are to be blamed for her daughter's fate and should be destroyed and cursed for all time. Now your words and innocent pleas today have changed the once united sea into two groups. As we speak, a great line is being draw across the sea's floor.

"Despite their pity and compassion for Miranda, on one side of this great scar stands all that oppose Miranda's ugliness and spite. On the other side stand those with revenge and hatred in their hearts. A great undersea war will be the result of all your actions here today. Sisters against sisters and brothers against brothers will come from this. Fathers against sons and mothers against daughters will be the result of your actions,." The Oracle began to cry.

"The sea as I know it will not survive, and in the end, mankind will have this world to themselves. Our race of wonderful and magical undersea beings will only be a wild tale told by your kind in the future."

Captain Pike looked over at me and said, "Now you went and done it, Mr. Newly."

I just looked at him with disgust.

"With all things considered," the maiden said, "I alone make the decision to let you set free from the map of the sea the great white wolf Tamantha."

We all had big smiles, but our smiles faded as we heard the next judgment come forth.

"All others that are imprisoned on the map shall remain imprisoned there for all of eternity," the Oracle commanded.

Captain Pike looked over at me and said, "I wasn't going to let that dog of an admiral off the hook anyway."

"All others in the future that the map takes will also face eternity and you will never free them, unless you or Miranda take their place," the Oracle commanded.

"What about the four keys there, missy? What are the keys for? What happens if all the keys are placed on the map?"

The captain apparently struck a nerve with his question as the Oracle stood silent looking him over.

After a few seconds the Oracle said, "It is highly unlikely that would ever happen, Captain Pike. The Map of the Sea was originally created to imprison a few very evil and powerful sea beings. The keys are gone, scattered to the winds, centuries ago, so these evil creatures that could never again be free. No one knows where the keys are. If someone or something did indeed gain possession of the f

Four Keys of the Sea they would have power over the map and could free all the lost souls held there at will—all except one.

"There is always one that can never be freed because he or she is the Map of the Sea. It does not matter which one it is as long as one remains. The great map needs at least one soul to exist. The more souls the map holds the more powerful it is.

"Miranda in her madness has abused the map as its keeper. She collects souls not caring whether they are good or evil. She collects them to increase the map's power and, therefore, hers. This can no longer be tolerated."

"You have not answered my question there, missy," Captain Pike said.

"What happens if all four keys are laid in place?"

"If all four keys were to be laid in place on the map's face, the lock would be opened, and that last soul could be set free at the keeper's will. That, Captain Pike, would destroy the Map of the Sea.

"For one creature to hold all four keys and the map at one time, in one place, is unthinkable. I cannot tell the outcome if the Map of the Sea was destroyed. It is the greatest treasure of the entire undersea world because it protects us from the evil imprisoned on it. It is also the greatest weapon for those who know how to use it. That is why the keys were scattered and the map locked away. Never before has that lock been removed.

The captain rolled open the map and it began to glow brightly as he said "I do not see any of these so called super devils you are so proud of mate. The ones you and your kind are so scared of or this so called lock."

"Captain Pike, you are to keep the Map of the Sea, and now you are indeed *the keeper of the map* and not just the possessor of it. Miranda no longer has a claim to it."

When the Oracle spoke those words, a crack of lightning went off that almost deafened us all. The wind began to pick up, and the sky began to darken as a severe storm approached. I was sure it was not just a coincidence. With the news of him being named the keeper of the map, a big smile returned to his face that soon faded by the next words to leave the maiden's lips.

"Captain Pike, you will need the map of the sea to protect yourself and your crew and all mankind from the wrath of Miranda and her followers," warned the maiden. "You are now at war with the sea, or at least half of it."

With that said, the lightning began to crack and the thunder sounded like cannon fire. The wind began to build, and the day was turning to night with the approaching storm.

"Captain Pike," commanded the maiden in a loud voice over the storm, "as further punishment toward you, I command that you receive this orb so you can look beneath the sea and watch in horror the great war soon to come. I want you to always see what your actions and words have caused here today. I truly hope that you spend the rest of your life and eternity in misery because of it. Your maker is our maker, and I am sure you will be dealt with harshly in the end."

The rain had come, and it was really coming down. It was blowing wildly in every direction, and the lightning was striking everywhere.

"Captain, we better go!" yelled Captain Rickle.

"I am the Oracle of the Sea!" she screamed above the storm. "I can see the future and the past." With that, the maiden started to turn to stone right before our eyes.

That's when the captain went for it. I had never seen him move that fast. Just before the stone took her, Captain Pike ran up and snatched her amulet right off her neck. She gave the captain a look of horror but it was too late. The captain had it, and she went to stone.

The orb fell from above the maiden's now-stone hands and hit the ground, rolling up to the captain's feet.

Captain Pike kicked the orb to the side with his boot and looked around at all of us in the pouring rain. With a shrug of his shoulders, he yelled above the storm,

"Well, mates, I wonder who will get to us first. The British Navy maybe?" he laughed.

"The French Navy, I highly doubt. "

"The Americans might just do it."

"Maybe even another pirate clan."

That witch has a good chance, but I'll tell you one thing, mates, if we don't get moving, this storm will for sure." And he took off at a run.

"Let's get back to the ships!" he yelled.

"What about the orb, Captain?" I asked.

"Bring it, Mr. Newly, we may have use for that thing."

As we ran along, the captain yelled, laughing at the lightning, "I wonder if there is such a thing as land pirates, Mr. Newly."

"Why, Captain?" I yelled back at a trot.

"I think we better be finding a new high-and-dry profession, Mr. Newly. Our welcome seems to be worn a bit thin at sea." He laughed.

As we reached the bottom of the marble staircase, the storm began to pass as if we had been escorted out of the town by force, and we stopped our run.

"Let's get back to the ships, mates," the captain ordered.

"Can I have a look at that amulet?" I asked.

The captain looked over at me with a huge grin on his face. He reached in his pocket and tossed it over to me. I was amazed at what I saw. There in my hand was a magnificent golden amulet covered with jewels that hung from a broken chain of diamonds.

"Open it up there, Mr. Newly, and have a look."

I cracked the amulet open, and there it was. An old black key resting nicely on a bed of fine pearls. A smile covered my face as I looked closely at the key. The head on it was fashioned to look like a great dragon breathing out a steam of fire. An interesting feature of the dragon was that the fire coming out of its mouth was bright blue. The rest of the key was old and black, but this dragon's fire looked like the key had just been made yesterday. I knew immediately what this key was. I looked up to the captain, and he was all smiles.

"Well now, Mr. Newly, I believe that is key number two, and I believe what you hold in your hand there is worth King George two or three times over, so I'm counting that as the treasure. Can you believe that Oracle would lie to us and tell me us she had no idea where the keys were and all the time be wearing one around her neck? It's getting so you just can't trust anyone," said the Captain.

"What do you all have there? asked Captain Rickle.

I slid the treasure into my pocket and said, "Nothing, sir, nothing at all."

Captain Pike gave me a big grin.

Captain Simpson and all the crews were glad to see us, and they bombarded us with questions about our adventure. Even Captain Rickle's crew, in their fine red uniforms, had taken a liking to us and welcomed us home. The whales were about themselves with happiness when they saw us. Not to mention the wolves. The whales danced on the sea, jumping with joy at our sight, and the wolves knocked us down and licked our faces wildly.

"I like those whales, Mr. Newly," said the captain with a big smile as Princess almost licked his face off.

"Mr. Newly," the captain ordered, "take our new orb and put it in the map's chest, as that should hold it."

"Aye, Captain," I replied, and that was the end of the orb for the time being.

Captain Pike announced a dinner in his cabin for all captains and their first officers. We all now liked to call ourselves first officers since we met His Majesty's Navy. We had grown tall and smart with our new self-imposed proper titles.

"First officer sounds better than first mate," I bragged with a smile.

Captain Pike's dinner was going to be served later than he thought, as our leisure leaving this place was soon to be paid. The sentry on top of the mountain opened fire on us. Three great blue fireballs came down the side of the mountain and across the sea at us, and these were no warning shots. In an instant, off the port side of the ships rose up a powerful maiden that drew up a great wall made of the sea to protect us from the balls of blue fire. As the fireballs hit the wall of water, they exploded and lit the great motionless wave. We all stood watching as the blue lightning danced on the wave, finally to be absorbed by the sea.

But then this maiden that had come to our rescue went a step further that set off the great war beneath the sea. With her hands above her, she drew up the sea and gathered a portion of it into her own great ball of water. She flung it at the top of the mountain and in an instant distinguished the flame that had burned forever and the sentry that had kept it. The mighty sea-maiden looked over at us, and snarling in our minds, she said, "The war has begun with this first blood from my sister drawn. Be gone from this place before I change my mind."

"Dinner can wait," ordered the captain. "Get these ships under way!"

"What course, Captain?" Jonesy asked.

"Away from here as fast as she will sail," replied the captain.

All three ships jumped up and out of the water and were hard under way. As we quickly retreated, we all looked back at the rock island and watched as a great battle began. The sea was shimmering with many colors that seemed to wrestle with each other in the depths.

"Must be those water creatures we saw on the island fighting among themselves!" Captain Rickle yelled out.

We saw great sea beasts come up and out of the sea, fighting with each other. We saw many powerful sea-maidens throw their power at each other, trying to destroy one another. Just like the Oracle of the Sea had said, we all witnessed the sea begin its great war.

Eleven

After several hours sailing as fast we could go, the captain called the ships to a halt. "I think we have come far enough, Mr. Newly. We have business to attend to. Invite Captain Simpson and Captain Rickle over for that dinner we missed back there. Let's see if we can get Tamantha off me map."

He then went up to his cabin, and of course Kodiak, Klondike, Avalanche, and the Princess Cheyenne went with him. As we all assembled in his cabin, it was more than obvious that Captain Rickle was not happy with Captain Pike. Captain Pike opened a bottle of rum and took a big drink. He then tossed the bottle over to Captain Rickle.

"So, Captain Rickle, are you going to pout the entire evening?" asked Captain Pike. I could just tell he was trying to provoke an argument.

Captain Rickle took up the bottle and got a big drink. Then with a snarl he threw the bottle right at Captain Pike's head as hard as he could. Captain Pike ducked, and the bottle broke on the wall behind him, sending rum and glass flying. The wolves growled, and I thought for sure Captain Pike would kill him right on the spot. But as always with Captain Pike, no one could ever predict his next move.

Captain Pike with a grin just looked at Captain Rickle and said, "I see you're a little upset there, mate, but there's no need to waste the rum."

Captain Pike then opened a fresh bottle and set it on the dinner table. He sat back in his chair and put his feet up. "Okay, Captain Rickle, let's hear it."

Captain Rickle yelled, "You lied to me, Captain! You risked my ship and my crew for what? We were supposed to be going after a treasure, and all we got was you with all your devils, sea witches, and cursed maps. You knew there was no treasure and that this all was some sort of rescue mission. I knew you were going to be trouble when you shamed me and my crew by having us hide from the American Navy like scared dogs under a French flag."

Captain Pike replied calmly to the accusations. "First off, Captain Rickle, if you care to remember, that is neither your ship nor your crew. They are mine. Seems to me I hired you and your crew and bought that ship from you for a considerable amount. You work for me, as do they, and I do not expect to have to explain myself to you for anything."

"The way I see it, you have a few choices here as do I. My first choice is that I can kill you where you stand, and no one would care. If I did, I'd get most of the gems back that I gave you, except for giving your crew one each as promised. I'd get to keep your ship, and I'd just be down one captain. My second choice is that I could let you off the hook and out of our bargain completely, which would mean that you give me back that big sack of gems. Of course, you could keep one of the gems for your trouble and leave with your ship and crew."

"Now I know you don't like my first choice, so let's skip to my second. I'm quite sure that your crew would be really unhappy with you getting a gem and them standing with an empty hand. They would either mutiny or, worse, get back to England and tell our little tale, at which time you will be promptly hung for treason. My third choice and yours to pick, Captain Rickle, is that you could just sit down and shut up."

Captain Rickle looked at me and then at Captain Simpson, who shrugged his shoulders at him. Captain Rickle then looked back at Captain Pike and said, "I like the third choice," and he sat down and shut up.

Captain Pike tossed Captain Rickle the rum and with a big smile. "You made the right decision, mate. That's the one I chose too. Drink up. You're a very rich man and no hard feelings. Now that we have that business taken care of, let's try to get the girl off the map."

We all gathered around as Captain Pike unrolled the map that began as usual to glow brightly. Captain Pike did not know what to do next to free Tamantha. There she was on the map, the great wolf wrapped in her chains, squirming in pain. It made me hurt to look at her.

"I don't know what it is I am supposed to do!" exclaimed Captain Pike.

"Are there some sort of words to be spoken? Is there some incantation I have to speak, Mr. Newly?"

I just shook my head with no answer for him.

"Let's have a closer look at the map," said the Captain.

All of us crowed over the parchment except for Captain Rickle. It was plain he wanted nothing to do with entire matter.

We looked and looked, but the answer escaped us.

The map of the sea was hard and confusing thing to look at anyway. Everything depicted on it was fluid and constantly moving in and out twisting and turning about so small details were hard to spot.

The captain reached in his coat and retrieved the second key to the sea and said, "We are wasting our time here, Mr. Newly. There is no clue for us to find. Let's lay this key in place and see what happens.

"No, captain," I said. "Remember the keys must not be laid in place."

"Four keys, Mr. Newly, that's the tale. Never should all four keys be placed on the map. We already have one in place, so what's another matter?"

Captain Pike then took the second key and went to lay it on the map. As we had seen before with the first key as soon as the captain got the second key half laid in place the map sucked it right out of his hand and absorbed it. The map glowed brightly, and the second key to the sea was in place on the map.

Again we all stared intently.

That's when I saw it. Right under the newly placed key there was some sort of writing that had appeared.

"Look here, Captain," I said. "What is this?"

We all stared wide eyed at the writing just under the key.

"Noli Metang El Sea"

Captain Pike frowned and asked, "Now what in the world does that mean?"

Captain Rickle got up from his seat and strolled around the table to look over our shoulders. "That's Latin," he said. It means touch me to her over the sea

Everyone turned and looked at him. He was standing there with a smug look on his face.

"Touch me to her over the sea, that's what that says," Captain Rickle repeated.

Captain Pike sneered as he tried to figure out the new riddle.

"How hard can this be?" said Captain Rickle.

He rudely pushed us aside and went for the map. Captain Pike and I both tried to stop him, but it was too late. He grabbed up the Map of the Sea and went out the cabin's door. Leaning over the side of the ship's rail, over the sea, he impatiently folded the map over.

Sarcastically, like he was talking to a child, he said, "See? Put this here over the sea." And he placed the image of the key onto of the image of Tamantha over the sea.

In an instant the scroll exploded into a great burst of light that blinded us all for second. When the flash was gone there stood Captain Rickle, holding the map of the sea, with a very surprised look on his face. As he held the map open a single drop, of what looked to be blood came out the corner of his eye, dripped on to the map and then into the sea.

A moment later off the port bow the sea began to boil and a light from below the sea came with it. Lightning cracked the area out of a clear dark sky.

"Something coming up captain" I said

"Do you think so Mr. Newly" replied Captain in his sarcastic way.

"I hope it's not that witch" he follow up with.

The whales went crazy and rushed to the area circling where the lighting was continuing to strike the water.

Closer and closer the whales circle closing in on the area while harder and harder the lighting came.

Captain Pike looked over at Captain Rickle, who by how had a horrid look on his face and said, "Now you went and done it, you called up that witch."

As soon as he spoke those words lighting hit ship and the bolt began to crawl all over everything and I mean everything. Bright blue it was and no man or beast was spared. All over us, in and out of our noses, ears, eyes it crawled like it was alive and looking for something. The wolves seem to enjoy it. We could not hear each other screaming over the bolts buzzing sound.

And then, just like that, the Bolt was gone, away from us. It went off our ship and went across the sea over to that area where the commotion was. The area where that witch was rising up out of the sea.

Keep in mind now folks, all this happened in matter of seconds.

Then here she came. Like with a final burst of strength she came up and out of the sea.

It was no Sea Witch though mates. It was Tamantha and she was covered with chains.

Tamantha was gasping for her breath. The chains were trying to hold her back to the sea. Captain Pike went over the side and grabbed her up. Now the chains had them both.

As fast as we could pull the ropes that platform came down to the water. The whales quickly came to help and soon enough we had the two of them onto the deck of the ship.

Kodiak, Klondike, Avalanche, and the Princess ran to Tamantha and were overjoyed at the sight of her. Between the four of them, I thought those wolves were going to lick the skin right off her.

We helped Tamantha up off the deck. She was having a hard time walking, so Captain Pike snatched her up and carried her into his cabin and laid her on his bed. She could barely talk, and she looked horrible. I'd pretty much say she looked like she had just escaped from the devil himself.

Captain Pike and I looked over at Captain Rickle still standing there holding the map.

"He isn't dead, Captain!" I exclaimed. The map did not take him.

"Dead, Mr. Newly?" questioned Captain Rickle.

That's when he realized he had touched the map of the sea. He slowly set the map back on the table and backed away.

Captain pike burst out laughing and then said, "Well, Captain Rickle, I see that map there don't mind you touching it. I wonder why."

Captain Rickle had nothing to say.

"We all thank you much for your help, but I'll tell you this for sure. For your good deed, Captain Rickle, you have just made the witch's list. Now she hunts you too. Welcome to the crew of the damned," said the captain.

Captain Rickle again said nothing. He just sat down in his chair and drank down an entire bottle of rum.

Like I said, Tamantha was really in bad shape. She was going to need a lot of rest. The Captain helped her drink some water and cut up an apple for her to try and eat.

"Thank you all so much," she said.

"I'll join you men in a bit. I'm going see to her for a few hours. I'll join you later," Captain Pike said.

We all walked out of the cabin leaving the wolves and Captain Pike to look after Tamantha.

I asked Captain Rickle with concern, "Captain Rickle, what do you think of Captain Pike?"

Captain Rickle looked over at me with a big smile. He reached over and took my old hat off my head and looked at it. Then he took his fine-feathered captain's hat off and placed it on my head, placing mine on his. Captain Rickle, continuing to smile, said, "A very unusual man, but I like him."

I just smiled back, as did Captain Simpson, because we now knew we had a new loyal captain for sure.

The next morning Tamantha, the wolfs, and the captain emerged from his cabin and walked the deck. We were all so glad to see her already on her feet and feeling better. She still looked really bad, though. The crew was delighted to meet her as they had heard so much about her.

The wolves walked with them with their tails wagging, and then up came the whales. They too were delighted at the sight of her.

"I see the guardians of the map have found you," she said.

Captain Pike was surprised for a moment, but then he remembered back to the scene on the golden curtain around the bed in Tamantha's cave. The scene where the chest lay open, and the map was exposed for all maidens to see—it was guarded by four giant killer whales.

Now the captain finally understood the whales and replied with a smile, "Yes, they found us fine. Signal all ships to get under way, Mr. Newly," ordered the captain.

"Where to, Captain?" I asked.

Wearing one of his big grins, he replied, "We have two more keys to find, Mr. Newly, and the treasure that goes with them. Then in our spare time we're going to have to figure out how to stop this under the sea war you have started."

Captain Simpson yelled over, "I say we get our butts back to Tortola and get some fresh water and supplies!"

Captain Rickle yelled back, "Tortola! I guess I better get to making repairs on the *Defiant* then."

Captain Pike yelled back and asked, "What is wrong with the *Defiant*? Has she been damaged?"

Captain Rickle yelled back, "No, Captain, she is fine! She just looks a little bit like a British warship."

Everyone began to laugh, and I yelled over, "I'd burn those British uniforms too if I were you, Captain Rickle."

"Oh no, Mr. Newly. I'm saving them in case the captain ever decides to get married again."

Well, the laughter really was in the air over that, and when I looked over at Captain Pike and Tamantha with my huge smile, their faces were as red as one of those British uniforms. Captain Pike moved three steps away from her.

"Keep it up, Mr. Newly. The plank awaits you," the captain said. "Set a course for, Tortola," he ordered.

Captain Rickle asked Captain Simpson, his first mate Mr. Stevenson, Captain Pike, Tamantha, and I to have lunch with him in his cabin. Of course, we all accepted and promptly at noon the *Defiant* came up at full sail right between the *Sovereign* and the *Resolve*.

The whales were very happy to be again under way. They jumped and danced in the rough sea, and they acted like they had also been invited to lunch with their thumping on the *Defiant*'s hull. I had never been aboard the *Defiant* or a British warship of any kind, and I was impressed. She was sleek and sweet and to the point of business. She was armed to the teeth, and a killer of ships she was.

The *Defiant*'s crew was at formal attention as we walked by them in the sea spray, and we were escorted to their captain's cabin. Captain Rickle met us at the door and said, "Welcome. Come in, and make yourselves at home."

Captain Rickle had a modest cabin that's décor showed off his past with the king's finest. The cabin displayed all of Captain Rickle's distinguished service ribbons and medals that had been awarded to him by his navy. There was a portrait of King George III above the fireplace. The cabin was at least one-forth the size of the *Sovereign*'s captain's quarters; however, Captain Rickle was quite proud of his home at sea and put on a very nice lunch. Captain Pike looked over at me with a whine as Captain Rickle served tea instead of rum. Tamantha kicked at Captain Pike under the table, and I smiled.

After tea and lunch, to everyone's surprise, Captain Rickle asked, "Tamantha, would you be willing to tell us about your experience while imprisoned on that cursed parchment?"

Tamantha paused for a moment while she looked over at Captain Pike. "I'll tell you the best I can," she said.

Captain Pike jumped up and said, "Hold! Mr. Newly, go and get that cursed orb out of the chest, and let's let everyone listen above and below the sea. This Oracle of the Sea might want me to view the damage I have done for an eternity, so I want her to see hers."

I went up on the *Defiant*'s deck and signaled over to the *Sovereign* to come up so I could return aboard her. Several minutes later the *Sovereign* came up on the *Defiant* close, and over I swung to her. In a short time, I was swinging back aboard the *Defiant* with the chest. We all stared as Captain Pike produced his key and opened the chest, snatching out the brightly glowing orb.

"That orb looks glad to see you Captain," I said with a big grin.

"Keep it up, Mr. Newly. Just keep it up."

The captain set the orb on the table and pronounced to all, "If we have to listen, we have to have a bottle of rum. It's customary, you know, to share a bottle of rum when a tale is told."

Captain Rickle smiled and produced two bottles of the brew with a handful of glasses and said, "We're probably going to need two bottles because I have a feeling this is going to be quite the tale."

Tamantha began her story and said, "As you gentlemen know, I have a slight affliction that affects me when the moon comes up full. I was born with the condition, as were my parents, their parents, their parents, and their parents' parents. The line of our curse goes back to unknown times where our ancestors were also part of the living sea. Somehow at someplace, at sometime, our family was cursed out of the sea to be creatures of the land.

"Apparently a single curse was not enough, so another was added. So our families could never live among men and find happiness, and to insure us being stranded forever on the island, it was deemed that when the moon comes up full, we would be transformed into wolves. We were given a great treasure that as men and women we could never spend. Even crueler, the curse left us with all the memories and knowledge of the sea that lived intact in our minds from generation to generation so we would miss the sea terribly every day of our lives. We have always searched for a cure and the reason for the curse, but it has evaded us to this day.

"We do know that not only did the two curses take us, but it also took all that were close to our family, as if to erase us from the memory of the sea forever like we never existed in this world."

Captain Pike interrupted and said, "Now that's a curse, Mr. Newly, if I ever heard one. How about throwing me that rum."

Everyone in the cabin just shook their heads at him as Tamantha continued. "That night on the island when the change had taken me, Miranda found me alone wandering on the beach. The pack was not with me, so I was easy prey for her. She rose up out of the sea in all her great beauty and began to probe my mind with her thoughts. At first she just thought I was a beautiful white wolf, and she adored me. When she found I was not just a wolf, she probed harder and found my family's history and what she called my contamination by you."

Captain Pike interrupted again and said, "I knew you were going to get blamed for this sooner or later, Mr. Newly. It was only a matter of time." This time I kicked at him from under the table, and Tamantha smiled.

Tamantha continued her tale, giving the captain a look that surely would shut him up. "I then understood why Ethan called her the sea witch. In a rage, her great beauty melted off her like snow melts off a mountain. What was left was a hideous creature screaming like a banshee.

She flew up in the air and grabbed me by the back of the neck, by my fur, and flew me into the sea. All the way down into the depths I went, snapping and biting in vain. I could not get a bite of flesh because there was none there to bite."

Tamantha paused her tale and took a drink of rum. It was the first I had ever seen her drink. Captain Pike sneered and said,

"One day I'll get that witch on me map, and justice will be served." Said Captain Pike

"Captain, we have seen this before. This is what took Mr. Longfellow," I said.

Tamantha continued. "All I remember after that was the darkness and the pain. I felt like I had been immersed in a dark abyss full of hornets stinging at me by the thousands. The hornets' sound was deafening like the banshee's scream, and it never ended. Once in a while, a great light would come, and I think it must have come from you opening the map, Ethan. That drove the witch crazy with rage. In the light, I could see what was left of Miranda stirring about, poking at her prisoners and laughing at their screams. She has gone completely mad in her torture chamber and changed forever from her former beauty. She lives and breathes hatred and is a vial creature that needs to be destroyed. I cannot say how long I was there, but I could hear Miranda's rage as I was excused from her. The next thing I knew I was here."

Silence was about the cabin as we stared at Tamantha in horror at her tale. Captain Pike stood up and walked around the table and kissed Tamantha on her cheek and said, "We have you now, missy, and revenge will be ours. We will run no farther and cower in fear no longer from this Miranda, the Witch of the Sea. I hereby declare war on this Witch of the Sea."

We all stood and raised our cups into the air and yelled, "Arrrr!"

Captain Pike then ran out of the cabin, holding the orb above his head in both hands. He screamed at the sea in the wind and the spray and said, "You have heard the truth here today, you creatures of the sea. You have heard the truth about your cruelty of the past and your cruelty of the present. You are not so far above man as you believed, but in fact you and your kind are far worse than a man. Show me who is there below the waves that will fight against the past corruption and this present-day

Witch of the Sea."

With that said, the orb began to glow like the sun. We all looked in wonder as the entire sea seamed to boil and bubble. Slowly all manner of creatures began to rise to the surface and appear. First, a few came up, and then many more and then thousands and then tens of thousands rose up. As far as a man could see into the horizon, they came. The ships could not sail because of their numbers in our way, and we came to a slow stop. The creatures were not permitted to touch any of the ships because of the whales circling us at a guard. We had all joined Captain Pike and his orb on the deck of the *Defiant*, and we were all speechless at the masses before us. Tens of thousands of them there were, all in a rage and joining our commitment.

Captain Pike quickly climbed the mast up to the crow's nest and held the brightly glowing orb up again and screamed, "I will lead man's assault against the witch, and which of you will lead the sea's?"

Far off in the distance, we could see something coming. Through the masses of sea creatures came a great seaman riding a magnificent giant seahorse, and he looked like a king. I looked at the captain in surprise as the captain looked at me in the same manner.

The seaman looked like the man version of the sea-maiden except much larger. The seaman was dressed in green armor and carried a golden trident. He wielded it in one hand as he held the jewel-encrusted golden reins of the sea horse in the other. The seaman and his horse were magnificently adorned, and all creatures moved to the sides and bowed their heads as he passed by them, approaching the *Sovereign*.

To our surprise he spoke to us not in thought but in speech. He held up his great golden trident and said, "I am Triton, and I have been sent by my father to lead the sea's assault against the sea-maiden known as Miranda."

Captain Pike yelled out as he hurriedly climbed down the mast, "Mr. Newly, get that platform ready to go down. We will all go to him. I'll not have him looking up at us or us down at him."

We all went down on the platform to the sea below. Triton rode up to us and smiled. Instinctively we all removed our hats and bowed.

Captain Pike with his usual gracefulness, that of a mule, said, "Well, mate, it is nice to meet you. Who did you say your father was? What's your plan?"

Triton ignored the captain's questions and said, "Captain Pike, there is nothing to be discussed here about the past concerning your experiences with Miranda. We have all heard your tales through the Oracle of the Sea that set off this great war. Now we have all heard your most recent rant that has escalated matters. Just look at the countless before you that you have summoned to your cause.

"However, there is a matter of the past to be discussed concerning Tamantha," Triton said.

"My father, over many years has had many wives."

Captain Pike interrupted and said, "Who did you say your father was there, mate?"

Triton looked at the captain and completely ignored him again.

"The one of interest to you Tamantha would be Amphitrite, whom upon joining with my father became a sea goddess with all the power that went with the position."

"Your family, Tamantha, was close to my father. They were trusted consorts and advisors."

"Under the influence of your family, and rightly so because of certain evil deeds she was involved with, my father diminished Amphitrite from her prominent position to a mere symbolic representation of the sea. However, she did retain all her powers, as they could not be rescinded."

"As you can imagine, Amphitrite was furious at your family because in her mind they were the ones whom had caused her demise and not her own deeds. Amphitrite cursed your family and their consorts, and that would be the same curse you carry with you today."

Then Triton smiled and said, "As long as Amphitrite was alive, the curse could not be lifted. My father would not sacrifice Amphitrite's life to lift the curse, and all were forbidden to speak of it. However, now with the war upon him because of Miranda's cruelty and the entire sea now knowing the truth of Amphitrite's cruelty, my father has dispatched Amphitrite to the gods for them to deal with.

"My father wishes for your forgiveness, Tamantha, and welcomes you back to the sea. I'm sorry that this comes too late, as you are the last of your family's line. I know you remember well of the day that your last family member was buried in the sea and you stood alone on the island's beach in horror with nothing left but your loneliness. That was also the day that the Four Giant Ice Wolves appeared from nowhere to guard you and love you. My father sent them in his guilt."

With that said, Triton lifted his great trident in the air and spoke in his native tongue. He pointed the trident at Tamantha, and a great burst of light exploded from it, hitting her and knocking her into the sea. We all jumped up in alarm. The trident's light stopped, and what appeared to be a black gum covered the end and hung from it, dangling. Pretty nasty stuff that you just new you did not want anything to do with.

Triton said with a smile, "Here hangs Tamantha's curse." With that, Triton screamed, "I now give it to you, Miranda, as my father wishes!"

Triton went to throw the trident hard at the sea, and Captain Pike jumped and said, "Hold, Triton."

Triton, holding the cursed spear above his head, looked at the captain, puzzled.

Captain Pike asked, "May I have the pleasure of throwing that spear?" Triton smiled as he handed the cursed spear to Captain Pike.

"Here you go, missy!" Captain Pike yelled, and he threw the trident hard at the sea as if he was spearing a huge fish, and it disappeared beneath the waves.

The many sea creatures before us all cheered at the scene, and Triton said, "It's only a matter of time until the trident and the curse it is carrying finds Miranda, as she cannot hide from it. Miranda is too powerful for the curse to keep her out of the sea and on land. However, she will have to go to land at the full moon, and that is when she can be dealt with."

"Captain Pike!" I yelled. "Tamantha has a tail."

Sure enough, there went Tamantha swimming about in the sea with her new, great, beautiful tail. She was laughing and crying with joy, and we all began to laugh and cheer with her.

Captain Pike stopped his laughter as if a thought had occurred to him. "Don't worry, Captain Pike. Your hidden love for her is safe," Triton said. "She can return to the land whenever she seeks to and also to that of a wolf at will. This is a special gift from my father and is a gift that no other possesses except for my father and me."

Captain Pike's face was again red as a British uniform now that his secret was out, and he yelled back, "My love for whom? I have no love in my heart."

Triton ignored the captain again. And we all laughed so hard.

"Am I here, Mr. Newly? Am I here?" the captain questioned. "I must not be here because this man or fish or whatever he is acting like I am not speaking to him."

Triton completely ignored him again.

"My matters are complete here, and I'll see you again in battle, my friends," With that Triton and his great sea horse disappeared beneath the sea, taking his army of sea creatures with him.

"Well now, Mr. Newly, he seems like a nice enough fellow," said the captain. "I'll bet now you are sorry you said all those mean things to Tamantha back on her island. About her being alone and all."

I just gave him a big smile in return.

Tamantha and the whales played for hours as the wolves ran the deck watching them, wagging their great tails and wanting to join the fun. When she finally swam back up to us, she seemed exhausted and became suddenly sad, as she knew her life with us was over. We convinced her to let us help her out of the water with the promise that we had a surprise for her. As her tail disappeared and her legs reappeared under her on the platform, she exploded with laughter and wonder. We set her down, and Captain Pike told her of Triton's gifts of change for her. A smile began to grow across her face as she realized her gifts. Tamantha yelled with delight, and she climbed the rope for the deck as if in too much of a hurry to be hauled up by us mere mortals.

She hit the deck running, and the wolves joined her as she shimmered and changed into a great white wolf again. The five wolves ran and played again for hours. When they had finally exhausted themselves, the great white female wolf walked up to Captain Pike and licked his hand lovingly.

Tamantha reappeared before Captain Pike and said, "I owe this all to you, Ethan. I told you you had a good side."

We all walked away quickly to leave the two to themselves, but Captain Pike was right on our heels.

"Oh no, mates," he said. "I'm coming with you."

We all chuckled and smiled. I looked back at Tamantha, and she was hiding her smile behind her hand.

"I'll tell you what," Captain Rickle said. "This will be the last time I will have you people to lunch." We all began to laugh hard again.

Captain Pike yelled, "Let's get back under way for Tortola. Oh, and, Mr. Newly, I want you to stop talking to strangers at sea, or we will never get there." "And no more fish dinners" he added

Like Triton, I just ignored him.

Twelve

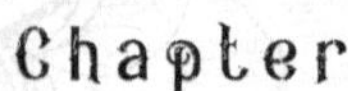

Three days later at noon we arrived back in Tortola. The captain looked over at me and smiled. "Well, Mr. Newly, you have come a long way since your last visit here," he said.

"Aye, Captain," I said. I remembered well my experience after being dropped off by that pirate captain that raided the merchant ship where I was a whipping boy. Who would have ever known that pirate captain had set me down on the road to my future and the adventure of a lifetime? Who would have known that pirate captain would have turned out to be my close, trusted friend Captain Simpson?

As I remembered, the port town of Tortola was a flurry of activity as usual. Many came out to see who we were as the three ships pulled up to dock. A ship arriving in Tortola was good business for the native islanders and their children. There were peddlers everywhere selling their products, along with plenty of cutthroats and thieves. We were of particular interest to the other pirates who were always on the lookout for weak ships and crews. Even as well known as Captain Pike was, there was always a pirate daring enough to challenge him.

To keep those renegades at bay, Captain Pike yelled out one particular order so all could hear on both ships and on shore. "Stand by the portside cannon and triple the guard! We are going ashore."

As the cannons rolled out the sides of the *Defiant*, the *Resolve*, and the *Sovereign*, it was a sight. Between all three ships, we could have completely destroyed a large portion of the town, not to mention a few fools trying to steal a ship. All captains, Tamantha, and I walked down the boarding platforms and went ashore to arrange for supplies.

A particular nasty-looking fellow ran up to Captain Pike and yelled, "Who are you to come here like this?"

Before the captain could speak a word, Captain Simpson hit that fellow so hard in the mouth it knocked the entire front row of rotten teeth out of his mouth. Then Captain Simpson said, "Have some respect, mate, as this here is the tooth fairy come calling, and from the looks of it, it seems like you need a measure coming to you."

The now toothless fellow went into a rage, and Captain Pike called the wolves with a whistle. As the wolves ran down the plank and arrived at the scene, I could see that fellow's attitude change.

"Get your measure from them," Captain Simpson said.

Captain Pike as usual headed right for the nearest tavern. As we walked into the den of iniquity, the laughter, fighting, and drinking came to a silence in an instant. Everyone in the tavern stopped what they were doing and looked at us in silence, and then in another instant the festivities began again.

The tavern keeper ran from behind the bar and promptly stated, "We don't serve dogs here."

Captain Pike pulled his pistol in an instant and placed it under the man's throat with its barrel pointing up. He pushed the tavern keeper's head back with the pistol and asked politely, "Did you just call me a dog?"

Stumbling for words, the tavern keeper said, "Oh, no, Captain. I was referring to your dogs there."

The entire tavern was again in silence as Captain Pike uncocked his pistol and placed it slowly away. "Those aren't dogs. They be Ice Wolves," informed the captain.

"Oh, well then, Captain, that's a completely different matter," the tavern keeper said. "You are all welcome here. I'm particularly fond of ice wolves, Captain." The entire tavern broke into laughter—that is, except for one well-dressed fellow sitting in the corner quietly.

We sat at a table and got a bottle of rum. The captains made arrangements for their ships' supplies as tenders approached them to offer their services. The tavern's music was loud, and the smoke was thick as I watched one scene unfold after the next. That quiet fellow in the corner just kept staring at us, and Captains Rickle and Simpson were getting annoyed.

Tamantha could see the upcoming trouble and thought to diminish it. She stood up and walked over to the fellow in a certain fashion that raised Captain Pike's and all our eyebrows. Before she could say a word to him and as soon as she got close enough to him, that fellow jumped up and spun Tamantha around, putting his knife to her throat.

We all jumped from our seats, pulling out our pistols. The wolves snarled, and the tavern again became silent. The fellow said, "Well, Captain Pike, I see I have something you value here." Tamantha squirmed a bit, and the fellow put the knife harder onto her throat, creating a small trickle of blood to run from it.

"I'll have that scroll you have there in your coat, Captain, or you can speak your last to this fine missy said the fellow."

That's when we recognized him. It was Mr. Longfellow, the crewman that had fallen into the pit on the island.

Out of the tavern's shadows to join Mr. Longfellow came Hutch, the crewman that fell into the bugs and the captain had shot dead. Then came forward Mr. Peterson, the crewman that had run off the cliff in the cave and was eaten by the bats on his way down. Mr. McNally, the crewman that the giant bat had carried off, was the last to appear out of a dark corner. At a closer look, the men looked like they were half dead and half alive. They were snow white and cold looking. They looked horribly sickly with sunken black eyes.

Captain Pike looked over at me and said, "Easy, mate. I told you we would have to deal with them at a later date."

"Miranda wants her map, Captain Pike," Mr. Longfellow said, "and we are here to retrieve it."

Captain Pike replied, "Well then, Mr. Longfellow, did the witch also tell you she was no longer the keeper of the map and that I was? Did she tell you she would grant you your freedom in exchange for the map when in truth she would have to take your place there in order to achieve that agreement? It seems by my count there are four of you and one of her, so three of you would not be excused from your bondage. I'll tell you the truth straight, as you know me well, Mr. Longfellow. If you don't release that girl right now, you will spend eternity in the company of the witch with no hope or future."

With that, Mr. Longfellow released the knife slightly from Tamantha's throat.

"And how do we know you speak the truth here, Captain Pike?" Mr. Peterson asked. Just then, a strange old man came through the door of the tavern, making quite a racket with some sort of incantation he was calling out. As it turned out, he was the native healer on the island and also the local peacemaker. Everyone stopped to look in his direction. He was carrying a small pot of incense in one hand and in the other a small pouch. The incense's smoke smelled like something dead and stunk up the tavern, as if the smell of the place could have gotten any worse.

The old man walked slowly over to our table and opened up his pouch. He reached into it and pulled out a handful of fish bones and tossed them on our table, and they scattered about. We were all frozen, staring as the old man began to laugh and shake.

Then, just like that, he said, "Here comes your witch, mates. We will let her settle your dispute." With that said, the tavern's fireplace exploded, and out of the flames came Miranda in all her glory, and what a sight she was to see. We all jumped back, and the wolves snarled. Our former sickly mates began to laugh an evil laugh as they thought our time was up for sure.

"Last chance, Captain," Mr. Longfellow said.

This was the first time I had seen Miranda in a somewhat human form, and even in the flames she appeared so beautiful. For several seconds, she wallowed in the fire, showing off her beauty, mesmerizing all in a spell. But then she changed from her beauty into a hideous creature with the head of a rabid wolf snarling and snapping at us. She took in a great breath and sucked in the swirling fire that danced about her. Then she spit it into the room, crisping everyone's hair, and let out her usual eardrum-piercing, nail-curling scream.

In our minds, she demandingly said, "Give them the map, Captain Pike, or pay your debt to me now."

I could not believe it, but Captain Pike tried to provoke her by saying, "I see that little curse I sent along to you has found you there, missy. How are those new fleas treating you?"

Captain Simpson looked at me and rolled his eyes and yelled out, "Time to go!"

Well, that seemed to work out for Captain Pike because Miranda went into a rage. As she attempted to come up and out of the fire, snapping and snarling, Captain Pike pulled out the map of the sea and stuck it right in her face. Miranda pulled back, and Captain Pike asked, "Is there some reason you don't want to just take this yourself?"

As the captain pushed at her with the map, she continued to retreat down into the fire, snarling and snapping. Then Captain Pike screamed at her and asked, "Who is the keeper of the map now, witch?"

As quickly as she had come, she was gone, screaming back into the fire. Our former four mates seemed to have disappeared along with her.

Captain Pike looked about the tavern, laughing at the expressions on everyone's faces. He yelled, "How about that, mates? Ain't she a beauty?

All the patrons of the tavern took off running out the door, fighting and pulling each other back so they could be the next through it. The half-scared-to-death tavern keeper was the last to get out, and he yelled back to us, "Help yourself to the rum!"

The only one that had not run, besides all of us, was the old healer with his bag of bones. He just gave us a big, toothless smile and walked slowly out the door with his stinking pot of incense.

Captain Rickle looked over at Captain Simpson and asked, "Do you think I'll ever get used to the sort of life you people lead?"

Captain Pike walked over to Tamantha and examined her throat with his hand. "I would appreciate it if you spared us any further acts like that last one," Captain Pike said.

Tamantha asked, "Why, Ethan, were you worried about me?"

The captain smiled and said, "No, I was worried about Mr. Longfellow."

As we made our way back to the ships, the crowd in the street parted and cleared a path as if we were carrying the fever. Captain Pike looked at me. With a laugh, he said, "Nothing like a little respect, Mr. Newly."

We spent the rest of the day getting our supplies aboard, and the captains let their crews go into town. They rotated the different shore parties on four-hour returns with strict orders to keep their mouths shut about everything.

"Just go and have a good time, and keep your mouths shut, or I'll nail your hide to me wall," Captain Pike told them all.

I objected to the shore excursions, telling all three captains that under the circumstances, there was no way the crew would all keep their mouths shut. I told them, "All we need is one man full of rum trying to impress a lady to run off at the mouth about the treasure, and the entire town will be upon us."

All knew I was right, and Captain Pike replied to me, "We will have to make the best of it, Mr. Newly, because the crew needs to go ashore. Men will be men."

Then Captain Pike ordered to all ships, "Stand by those cannons, and triple the guards. I want one ten-man away team armed and on standby from each ship ready to go ashore. Captain Rickle, have your away team stand below deck with those full-dress British uniforms on with bayonets fixed."

Then Captain Pike walked over to the railing and looked down at the whales. The whales seemed to be having a great time among themselves, clicking and whistling and scratching on the ships. Captain Pike whistled to them, and they all came up to him.

"Watch this side of the ships, mates," he said to them, and the whales took off.

Captain Pike then looked over at me and said, "Is that adequate, Mr. Newly, or do you require more?"

I shook my head in agreement as I checked the powder in my two pistols.

The sun went down, the night came, and so did the trouble. As it turned out, just as I predicted, one of the crew full of rum in one of the many taverns told some hussy how rich he was and disclosed the treasure. The fool had even smuggled one of his gems off the ship and produced it as proof of his claims. The word spread like a wildfire burning the town. Next thing we knew, a huge crowd had gathered on the docks, demanding a share. One fellow ran up with a lit bottleful of lamp oil, and threw it onto the *Resolve*'s deck, and the fire began to quickly spread.

We all jumped from our dinner in Captain Pike's cabin and ran out onto the deck. Captain Pike looked at the crowd and over at the *Resolve*'s deck fire, and he rang the station's bell. "Fire!" he screamed, and all portside cannons on all three ships went off. The captain looked over at me and said with a grin, "I guess I should have said fire on the deck, Mr. Newly, but this will do."

It was a shame to watch what happened in the name of greed. Several hundred were killed in a second, but the hundreds that remained began to storm the ships. It took an eternity of at least two minutes to reload the cannon, and they all fired again, loaded with bits of metal this time. So many more were cut down.

Captain Pike yelled out, "Mr. Rickle, let's see your colors." Captain Rickle yelled at the *Defiant* to raise their flag. With that, the king's flag went up the *Defiant*'s mast and the red coats appeared on the deck and began firing on the riot with their rifles. The crowd went into a panic, screaming about the British Navy being here, and all went into a retreat for what remained of their lives.

Several small crafts had been organized by the rebel to board the starboard side of the ships while we were occupied by the port. That, too, was a shame to watch as the whales destroyed them one by one. The entire scene only lasted ten minutes or so, with most of the town on fire and so many greedy men and women dead. Captain Pike just shook his head in disgust as Tamantha tried to comfort him by taking his hand.

"It's not your fault," she said. "It was their greed that was their demise."

Captain Pike did not like dispatching men to their maker, and we all knew it. But we also knew he would send them in a second if he had to or they deserved the fate.

A shot came from the crowd, and the ball just missed me, exploding the ship's wood next to my head. Captain Pike looked over at me, and when he saw the blood running down my face, I saw his rage begin.

"Fire!" he screamed, and all cannon went off again, resulting in the town's almost complete destruction.

He screamed out the order for the away teams to disperse and retrieve the crew ashore. "Dispatch all that you see, and burn the town. Stand by to get under way as soon as the away teams get back."

I ran up to Captain Pike and said, "No, Captain, there are so many that are innocent. I'm fine, Captain, but you're in a rage."

Tamantha and I looked at him, and his red-faced rage melted into a smile. "Very well, Mr. Newly. As you wish. Belay that order!" the captain screamed, and all the away teams on their way down the gang planks froze in their tracks, looking back at the captain. "Bring back our men, and spare the town. Dispatch only the fools that get in your way." Then he asked, "Is that all right with you, Mr. Newly?"

I just shook my head.

The heavily armed away teams searched the town, and they found our men in several different circumstances. Six had been dispatched to their maker by our cannon, and four others were in a pistol fight, badly outnumbered. That was until Captain Rickle and his redcoats showed up.

Three of our men were found beaten half to death in the corner of a tavern, being held for a ransom that had not yet been demanded. When the *Sovereign*'s away team went through the door of the tavern, the first two in the away team were shot and wounded. The remaining eight on the team laid waste to our crew's captors.

Two more of the crew were found so drunk they did not even know anything was wrong. One was found so scared he had covered himself up with dead men. Captain Simpson's team found another in a tavern with six attentive wenches and a makeshift crown on his drunk head. In his hand was one of his jewels that he had smuggled off the ship. This was the crewman that had started the whole battle and caused the destruction of the town. Captain Simpson was really in a rage, as this man was a member of his crew and a cannon master at that.

The fight in the town was over in about an hour, and the away teams returned, carrying the wounded and the drunk over their shoulders. Captain Simpson's men had the drunk crewman that had caused the entire mess dragging him behind them by a rope, kicking and screaming.

He was brought before Captain Pike, and to my disbelief, he snarled at the captain and said, "Who do you think you are? I am a king, and I could buy and sell you."

Before Captain Pike could even react, Captain Simpson shot the fool dead on the spot. When he hit the deck, his dead hand opened and his precious gem rolled out. Captain Pike reached down and picked up the gem and snarled. Captain Rickle grabbed up the dead man and threw him over the side.

"I take full responsibility, Captain, as that was one of my men," said Captain Simpson.

"No need for that, Captain Simpson. I take full responsibility for this mess. Mr. Newly brought his complaints to all of us, and I dismissed him," said the captain.

"Well, now that we have the rat problem under task, maybe we should set a course," said Captain Simpson.

Captain Pike looked down on what was left of the pier and saw a native woman and her three dirty children. They were crying over a dead native man who was just a peddler trying to make a living when we opened fire he had been caught up in the battle and had been dispatched innocent to his maker.

Captain Pike whistled down at the poor dirty devils, and they looked up at him with their tears and sad faces. "Wrong place, wrong time, and I'm sorry for your loss." The captain then tossed the jewel down to them and said, "Tell no one of your treasure. Live long and well."

It was still dark, but with the tide in our favor, we hurriedly got under way. Within the hour, we were hard under way back at sea. As the sun came up, we could see Tortola burning behind us on the horizon.

"Mr. Newly—" the captain said, but I interrupted him before he could finish.

With a smile I said, "I know, Captain. Wherever I go I make new friends." I looked over at Captain Pike and asked, "Why did you give that treasure to the woman back there, Captain?"

Tamantha turned to hear his answer.

"You have to pay as you go in this world, Mr. Newly. That woman back there had paid enough, and I have not."

Chapter

Thirteen

It was a beautiful morning, and the sea was calm as our three ships made their way across it as free as the wind that pushed us. With the sight of the whales skipping and jumping and the breeze in our faces, I had the feeling that I was lucky to be here at this time, to be part of all about me. I looked around at the mighty ships with their crews smiling and laughing, going about their duties. Tamantha and the captain were smiling and laughing with their conversations and at the ice wolves running about playing on the deck. It was really the first time in my life that I felt like I knew who I was and that I was on the right side of this world's hatred and corruption and its greatness.

The captain retrieved the map from his coat and studied it for a few minutes. He then turned to me with a big grin on his face and said, "Mr. Newly, I think we need a little excitement in our lives and a little more treasure in our pockets before I deliver you back to your family in England. After all," he said, "I wouldn't want you to show up there a pauper."

With that, he walked over to me with the rolled open map and said, "What is the name of this island here, Mr. Newly?"

I looked at the map, and there was an island with a bright, shining point upon it, and I replied, "Well, Captain, that island is called Devil's Den."

Captain Pike replied as usual with his contempt for death and said, "Well, that sounds like a nice, cozy place, Mr. Newly. I don't know about you, but if I was looking for a spot to hide some sort of secret key and a treasure I'd more than likely pick a place with a name like that. Maybe we can do a little witch hunting as we go. Set a course of one hundred and forty degrees, and signal the other ships to follow."

All our ships changed course to one hundred and forty degrees and were headed for our new target, the island called Devil's Den, and we all knew harm's way again awaited us. As if the sea was warning us not to go, a storm started to build in our path. As the lightning and thunder cracked in the distance, the crow's mates on all three ships, almost at the same time, shouted down the sighting of a ship off the port bow.

"Set a course to intercept!" yelled the captain.

We came up on the ship at full sail, and as we went by the sight, what we saw set Captain Pike into a rage. The ship was a whaler under some unknown flag, and they had secured a huge humpback whale with their harpoon gun. She floated in her own blood. The crew of the ship was upon her back, stabbing and cutting at her.

Captain Pike screamed out, "Signal the *Defiant* to come around hard to their port and the *Resolve* to come around hard to their starboard! Jonesy, bring us around one hundred and eighty degrees, bring us up forward of those murdering devils, and come to a stop."

As our ships came up and secured their stations around the whaler, our whales went into a rage as they swam around their wounded kin. The crew of the whaler and its captain screamed at us in their own rage for us to move off. They spoke in a language we could not understand, but it was clear they were set in their ways of killing these creatures. In their rage, they made one big mistake. The fools loaded a harpoon gun and sighted in one of our whales as if to dismiss us.

Captain Pike pulled out his pistol and shot the crewman manning that harpoon gun on the whaler dead on the spot. The whaler's captain went crazy with anger, and Captain Pike yelled, "Roll 'em out, gentleman, and sound the station's bell."

As usual, all our cannon were armed and ready, and as their hatches opened and the big guns rolled out of their holds, the captain and the crew of that whaler knew their time was up.

"Fire!" screamed the captain. The *Defiant* off the whaler's port side gave them a broadside, and the *Resolve* off the starboard offered theirs. The

Sovereign opened up with her forward cannon, and the whaler was gone into splinters. The whaler went down in less than two minutes. We had completely destroyed her. What was left of the whaler's crew was screaming and burnt in the sea, crying to be rescued. Captain Pike looked at them with disgust and said, "This lot here we will leave to the sharks."

We stayed there for many days trying to help that whale. Captain Pike and Tamantha went into the sea every day to rub on her and talk to her. The whale's eyes followed the captain, as he loved on it. Our whales ate every shark that had enough nerve to even approach the scene in the blood slick. On the fifth day, the giant seemed better and responded to the captain's touch, but that evening she went to her maker under Captain Pike's watch.

Tamantha took the captain's hand as he came out of the water. Captain Pike said, "Mr. Newly, it is now the standard operation of these ships to destroy any ship under that flag and any other performing that manner of behavior.

I replied, "Aye, Captain. I will spread the word."

It turned out that there were at least ten ships in the area under that same flag conducting themselves in the same manner of attacking whales. We sent every one of them to the bottom, leaving their heartless crews to the sharks. Captain Pike was obsessed with it, and we continued our patrol for weeks. When the captain was convinced there were no more of the vermin, he ordered that we resume our course. The last thing he said about the matter was for me to make note of the season and the time so we could return and hunt the hunters again.

Finally we were under way again toward the island, Devil's Den. Several days later, our voyage was again interrupted when the crow's mate yelled out the alarm. "Captain, I see four ships on the horizon." Peering closely in his seeing glass, the mate continued, "British warships, Captain, but they are at a stop."

The station's alarm bell rang out, and all our ships went into an attack pattern. Our whales were confused by our sudden increase in speed and direction for a moment, but they quickly caught on to the plan. One of the whales broke off and swam in front of the *Defiant* and one in front of the *Resolve*. The other two moved up and swam in front of the *Sovereign*. It almost seemed like they were joining our attack pattern.

The *Resolve* moved off to the starboard, and the *Defiant* went off to the port. All captains were screaming out orders to stand by their cannons and directions to sail. We came up on the warships fast, and through our seeing glasses, no movement or sign of life was seen on any of them. We went by them at full sail and took a good, close look. The British warships seemed deserted and adrift, but Captain Pike was not to be fooled. This would also be his chance to put Captain Rickle to his ultimate test of loyalty to him and our clan.

"Mr. Newly, signal the *Defiant* to come around and fire on the forward ship," ordered Captain Pike. "If they're up to tricks that will bring them up for air."

Well, Captain Rickle, without a wink, came around and flew by the forward British warship, sending them a broadside as he went by. To everyone's surprise, there was still no sign of life on any of the warships. We all came around and slowed, coming up on them carefully for another close look. We came across a great scene, a scene that sent Captain Rickle and all of us to question our beliefs.

There before us lay four British warships adrift on the sea completely intact except the forward one that Mr. Rickle had just delivered his broadside to. She was burning badly but could be repaired. The warship's crews and captains were missing with no remains of them to be found. No survivors afloat, no bodies in the sea or any proof of a fight. They were just all missing. We boarded the four mighty ships in a search and came up with nothing. It seemed like the British crews had been stolen in their paths with no struggle at all. We were all spooked because we knew well that whatever had stolen the four ship's crews was still out there.

Captain Rickle yelled over, "I knew these ships well, as did I their captains and crew, and they all would have fought to their deaths. What a shame this is."

Captain Pike replied, "Yes, this is a shame, Captain Rickle, but in a way, whatever stole these ships' crews really did us a favor being how they were more than likely hunting us. This could be the work of a friend or the witch."

Then with no remorse and a big smile, Captain Pike said, "Well, I have four new ships, and aren't they dandies."

Captain Rickle turned away in disgust.

"Mr. Newly, fetch that orb out of the chest, and let's see if we can see what has happened here," ordered the captain.

I went to the captain's cabin and opened the chest, producing the orb. The orb began to glow brightly as I retrieved it. With its great light, it almost seemed to be complaining about its imprisonment and celebrating its freedom. I did not like the cursed orb because it seemed to cause trouble every time I had seen it. I covered it in a wrap so I did not have to look at it as I brought it up on deck to Captain Pike.

The captain uncovered the orb from my wrap and said to me, "Do you have a problem with me orb, Mr. Newly?"

"Yes, Captain. I just don't like it," I replied.

We all gathered around the orb to look into it. Since we had never used the orb in this manner, none of us knew what to expect. The orb's glow began to increase until it was almost unbearable to look upon much less trying to see some sort of under-the-sea scene unfolding.

As we were busy squinting at the orb in vain, Captain Simpson yelled over, "Captain Pike, look at the sea!"

To our surprise, we had been looking in the wrong place for our vision. The sea itself- held the key to what we wished to see. The waves had begun to grow smooth, and the sparkles on its surface from the sun disappeared. Right before our eyes the sea began to grow clearer and clearer. The sea, in fact, got so clear it seemed we were looking into air and not water at all. We all were amazed at the sight unfolding before us. All the crew ran to the sides of the ships to get their look on this wondrous scene. Within minutes, we could see what was taking place many fathoms beneath us. It was like we were looking off the top of a mountain into a valley below. What we saw was not good.

There had been a great battle deep beneath us. Thousands of sea creatures lay still on the sea floor as they had all been dispatched to their maker. Along with the dead was strewn a great debris field of undersea chariots and strange weaponry. It was a great massacre of life and a sight I will never forget or ever wish to see again.

"What is this?" I yelled out to the captain.

"It is the war of the sea, Mr. Newly," he sadly replied. "These British warships must have come up on this great battle as it took place, and some manner of creature, maybe even the witch herself, came up and took them."

The whales went down, and we could see them nosing about, nudging and moving some of the dead creatures as if trying to wake them from their sleep. One of the whales grabbed up something and rushed it up to us on the surface. Then another whale found something, as then did the other two. The whales were coming up fast toward us with their cargo.

When the first whale broke the surface, our jaws dropped open at the sight of what it was carrying. It was a badly wounded seaman, and he let out a great moan of pain as he broke the surface. The whale brought him to the ship, and Captain Simpson dove in to retrieve him. Giving the wounded seaman over to Captain Simpson, the whale turned and went back down. The other three whales surfaced, and they, too, were carrying wounded seamen.

The scene went on for hours with the whales carrying up the wounded from below. At first, we hauled them aboard one of Captain Pike's new British warships, but soon it was full. Then we loaded another ship with them and then another. Finally the fourth ship was loaded till it too was filled with the poor devils. Then we started bringing them on board our ships. Finally, we just stopped excepting them from our whales, and the poor devils just drifted back down to the bottom. The whales seemed to know what was happening and stopped their attempts to save any more.

I thought that the slaughter we gave to the renegades back on Tortola was great, but this was just a scene that no man should have to deal with in his lifetime. The seamen had all types of wounds. Many had stab wounds, and many had sword cuts. Many had spears impaling their bodies. Most curious were the burn wounds on many of them.

I asked the captain as we walked about them, "Captain, have you noticed that many of these creatures wear brown armor and some wear green?"

"Aye, Mr. Newly, I have noticed. They must be part of two different armies," he explained.

We also noticed that only the seamen with the brown armor suffered from the burn wounds.

"Did we cause this entire scene, Captain?" I asked him.

"No, Mr. Newly. That witch has caused all you see here. I'm going to get her on me map if it is the last thing I ever do."

We could not give much help to the poor, wounded creatures, as there were just too many lying about bleeding to deal with. The decks ran with their green blood that seeped down through the ship's planks to the lower levels, leaving a great, horrible stain everywhere it touched.

Tamantha seemed to be really affected by her inability to save them. The wolves ran about licking at their faces, seeming to try to comfort them. As the seamen knew their time was near, they would ask to be put back over the side so they could rejoin the sea at their end. In the end, we did not recover one of them. The seamen that were to die we placed over the side, and the ones that were to survive crawled over on their own, thanking us in their own way, as they were to fight another day.

Captain Pike yelled over to Captain Rickle and Captain Simpson, "We need to captain and man these ships. The closest port be Martinique. Get this mess cleaned up, and set sail for Martinique!"

Captain Rickle objected very strongly and yelled back, "Are you crazy, Captain Pike? Those waters are full with the British Navy. If you go to Martinique, you will go on your own. The hangman's noose awaits you all in Martinique."

All the crews on all the ships began to grumble amongst themselves. I thought for sure this was going to be the end of Captain Rickle.

Strangely, Captain Pike sneered over at Captain Rickle and said, "Well now, Captain Rickle, it would appear you be questioning me orders in front of the crew, which is a hanging offense. Do you have a better idea besides setting fire to these fine ships? I'll not have them back in the king's hands."

Captain Rickle yelled back, "Captain Pike, with all due respect, I suggest that we sail the new ships to a remote place and then send for crews and captains for them as we can. Why on earth would we diminish the strength of our ships to man these four more and then sail all with skeleton crews to Martinique, a point where His Majesty's Navy would eat us alive?"

To everyone's surprise, Captain Pike replied, "Agreed.

"Oh, and, Captain Rickle, if you ever question me orders in front of the crew again…" Captain Pike stopped short of finishing what he was going to say. "Let's just say you won't like the outcome if you do."

"Agreed," responded Captain Rickle. "My mistake, Captain," he said.

"Mr. Newly, fetch me pigeon from its cage," ordered the captain.

I gave the captain a strange look, but before I could say anything, he said, "Just fetch the pigeon, Mr. Newly, and let's forego your questions."

I had always noticed the bird in the corner of the cabin, and the captain's attention toward it, but I just thought it was just a strange pet and disregarded it. I reached into the cage, and the bird jumped right on my hand. I brought it over to Captain Pike, and the ragged old pigeon jumped onto the captain's coat, seeming to struggle to get upon his shoulder. All of us watched as Captain Pike removed a very small tote from the pigeon's leg and set it on the table. He then walked over to an old desk, opened a drawer, and retrieved an ink well, feather, and parchment. Tearing off a very small piece of the parchment, the captain set the items down in front of me and said, "Write what I say, Mr. Newly."

"Aye, Captain, I'm ready," I replied.

"Write this, Mr. Newly," the captain ordered. "Captain Adams, bring Captain Bongeorno, Lady Jane, and Joedea, and meet us on the north side of Samana Cay in three days. Bring both ships, and stuff them full of trusty crewmen. Send back your response."

I had a hard time getting all those words on the little piece of parchment, so I had to use both sides of it.

"Here you go, Captain. All finished," I said. He looked it over carefully like he could read what I had written. I looked up at him and said, "Did I spell Captain Bongeorno name properly, Captain?"

We all burst out laughing, except for the captain as he gave us all a sneer. Captain Pike rolled up the small document and put it in the tiny pouch. He tied the message-filled pouch carefully back on the old pigeon's leg and lovingly petted the bird. Then the captain walked over to the cabin's door and opened it to the sea.

"Go!" the captain yelled, and he threw the bird to the wind. Captain Pike with one of his I'm-so-pleased-with-myself smiles said, "Dismissed. Return to your ships, and await me orders."

All of us walked out of the cabin into the sun and into the blue ocean's view, and there was the pigeon disappearing out of sight on its journey somewhere. We all looked at each other.

A few hours later the captain returned out of his cabin and yelled out, "Mr. Newly, have all ships pick a skeleton crew and man those four warships. Have them set a course for Samana Cay and hide on the north side of the island."

Captain Rickle, hearing the orders, looked up, smiling, and saluted Captain Pike with a big grin.

After a few hours, our four new British warships were set off on their course for Samana Cay and as they disappeared on the horizon as Captain Pike ordered, "Continue our course for Devil's Den."

Chapter

Fourteen

It was two days later. The crow's mate yelled down, "Captain, there is land off the starboard side!" We all grabbed at our seeing glasses to get a better look, and there before us was Devil's Den, the island we were looking for.

Captain Pike yelled out, "Set your approach course, Jonesy, and mind the reef!"

About an hour later, on our final approach to the island, the crow's mate yelled down again, "There ain't a reef, Captain, but there be rocks and lots of them!" All captains and crew on all ships were straining to get a better look.

"Captain, the whole area seems to be a bone yard of ships. We better come back around!" yelled the crow's mate. "Something is wrong here, Captain, and I can't make it out."

"Captain?" Jonesy asked.

"Belay that," said the captain. "Continue our course. I ain't about to run from something I ain't even seen yet."

"Aye, Captain," said Jonesy.

As soon as we got close, we could see what the crow's mate was yelling about. The island seemed to be surrounded by a wall of impenetrable rocks that were littered with the bones of hundreds of ships. I wondered to myself why in the world any captain would even approach a place like this. That was until I looked over at Captain Pike smiling at the entire scene.

"Mr. Newly, signal the other ships to remain here," ordered the captain. "Jonesy, bring us around one hundred and eighty degrees. Bring us back out a mile or so and set a course to circle the island."

As the *Sovereign* came around, I looked over at the captain, and he said, "There appears to be plenty of fools and their ships on those rocks there, Mr. Newly. I don't have any plans to join them."

The island was very large, and it took us almost half the day to sail around it. The scene remained the same during the entire trip. Rocks and broken ships with no way in and no way out. We came around the last of the island and came up on our sister ships that were impatiently waiting.

"What did you see, Captain?" yelled over Captain Simpson

"Rocks!" yelled the captain.

"And lots of ship bones," I added.

"Follow us in, gentlemen!" the captain yelled to all ships. "Bring us up closer, Jonesy." When we came up, several hundred yards away from the rocks, the captain ordered all the ships to a halt.

"Drop those anchors, mates," ordered the captain, and all ships came to a standstill. "We will stay the night here and get a hand on this tomorrow at dawn."

"Aye, sir," everyone acknowledged.

The next morning at dawn, we were all ready to greet our new adventure. I don't think anyone got much sleep that night except the ones that had too much rum, the captain being one of them.

"Mr. Newly, I have been thinking," said the captain. "It would appear that many before us have tried unsuccessfully to run this course to the beach, and I wonder why. What did they know? What did they not know? What were they looking for that was so important to them that they would lose their ships and lives over? They could not have known about a treasure nor the map's key. I wonder what became of their crews, as some should have survived."

"Maybe we will find out if we get to the island, Captain," I explained. "Maybe we will find some survivors, Captain."

"I don't think they are here" said the captain. "I don't see any signal fires, and we have been in plain view around this entire island. I just don't think they are here. Set a ding adrift, and let's see what happens to it. Let's see what is really going on here, Mr. Newly."

We set a ding adrift and watched it carefully as it washed in the waves toward the rocks. We all watched amazed as several of the rocks moved toward the ding. "The rocks are moving Captain!" I exclaimed.

Captain Adams yelled over, "Those rocks are definitely under way, Captain Pike."

We all stared intently and watched as the rocks converged ever so slowly on to the ding crushed it in their grasp, sending the ding's splinters shooting into the sea's foam.

"I know one trick those cursed ships did not possess captain," said Tamantha. "One that just might get us ashore."

Captain Pike looked at her and asked, "And what would that be?"

Tamantha walked to the side of the ship and over the side she went with her tail appearing as she hit the sea.

"A tail, Ethan. They had no tail," she yelled up.

The captain yelled, "You get back aboard, missy, or I'll—"

Tamantha interrupted him and yelled back, "Or you will do what, Ethan?" and she was gone toward the rocks.

Captain Pike began to cuss and pace and said, "That woman there will be the death of me."

With a whistle, Captain Pike called the whales. When the giants came up, he said, "Go with her and protect her," and the whales took off after her.

The whales quickly overtook Tamantha and put their giant mouths on her, trying to move her away. They could have just picked her out of the sea and brought her back to the ship, but they did not. Instead, they just warned her over and over again with their nudging and then finally escorted the stubborn maiden into the rocks. To our surprise, the rocks did not move on them and right to the shore they went.

Ashore, Tamantha taunted us and especially Captain Pike. She waved at us, laughing proudly. We could not hear what she was saying, but I was sure it was directed at the captain. The captain just cussed and paced even more.

The whales returned, and Captain Pike finally began to smile with a new idea fresh in his head.

"Tamantha was right about one thing, Mr. Newly," said the captain. "Those wrecked ship's crews did not have tails, but they also did not have something else."

"And what would that be, Captain?" I asked.

"Whales, Mr. Newly. They had no whales." The captain laughed. "Looks like we are going ashore on the backs of whales, mates!" he yelled.

It took at least two or three hours to get all the away teams and our supplies ashore. Three men at a time nervously rode the backs of the whales and were delivered safely to the beach. One of the crew reached over and touched one of the rocks as he went by, and we had to bandage his hand when he got to the beach as it were badly burnt, which sent all our minds wondering again.

Captain Pike and I were among the first to get ashore. Captain Pike in a huff walked up to Tamantha and tried to say something, but he was quickly interrupted by a long kiss from her.

The captain turned and looked at me all red faced and said, "Mr. Newly, I want you to keep this all in mind before I drag your carcass two thousand miles back to England to your Katherine that will surely be your measure of a woman. You're better off at sea, mate."

Tamantha just smiled and kissed him again. I'm pretty sure that's when their romance kicked off.

Then, to our great surprise, here came the wolves. They had jumped the ship and swam all the way to shore, and the rocks for some reason had also left them be. Unlike Tamantha's island or the Oracle of the Sea's, this island had no high mountain tops and looked easy at first sight to walk across.

"Let's get to it, mates," said the captain. As usual, he took off in the lead, looking at the map. We walked down the beach, and soon enough we came upon two giant pillars that marked a path inland. The two pillars each had a statue of a giant man attached to it, giant men that seemed to be guards of some kind.

As we approached the pillars, they gave way, and out came the two giants of men or whatever they were. With a loud commotion, out of the mortar itself they came, like the two statues that had come to life. A great scar showed on the giant pillars where they had been attached. As the mortar dust and bits of broken pillar danced in the air, we just about fell over backward trying to escape the scene.

The two giants seemed to be from a fair-skinned race of beings, but it was hard to tell because they were pretty much covered from head to toe with the mortar dust. The creatures stood at least twelve feet tall and wore the uniforms of warriors. They wore golden armor over their short tunic-like white clothes. They wore a great wide belt that supported a wonderful sword that seemed to be made of some sort of crystal. The creatures also each carried a great golden spear tipped with a long crystal dagger. The giants looked somewhat like men. They were identical twins, and you could not tell one from the other except one wore his sword on his right side and the other on his left. The twins had long white hair that was covered with a warrior's helmet lashed beneath their chins. The twins' extra large, beautiful green eyes shone like jewels in the sun and seemed to look right through us.

"I don't think these fellows here are from this world, Mr. Newly," whispered the captain.

"You don't think, Captain?" I said sarcastically.

One of the giants spoke something to us in a strange language that none of us could understand. Our lack of an answer back to them seemed to aggravate both the creatures, and they snarled at us loudly.

Both the creatures raised their crystal spears to the sky. Just like that, a bolt of lightning came down out of a cloudless clear blue sky. The lightning came down in one large bolt, and with a huge crack it split in two, sending one bolt striking one of the spear's tips and the other bolt striking the other. Each spear's crystal point seemed to gather up the lighting, and it danced about on the tip, popping and snapping. The hair on our heads and arms was standing straight up in the air, and we could feel and hear the power of the lighting in the air. The two giants slowly lowered their lightning-tipped spears and pointed them right at us, and I knew in another second I would meet my maker.

We all jumped back and pulled our pistols; then came Tamantha, pushing through us all with the wolves.

"You fools," she said. "These are the guardians of Lemuria, and you cannot harm them with your mere arms. They are not from this world but from another."

Tamantha looked over at Captain Pike and said, "Ethan, we should not have come here."

To everyone's wonder, Tamantha walked right up to the giants, still pointing their lighting tipped spears at us, and spoke to them. To our amazement she spoke in their tongue. She said something to them and pointed to herself and then pointed to us and then to the wolves.

The spears came up from their pointing at us, and the lighting disappeared, crackling and popping back into the air. One of the giant guards reached down and stroked at Princess. He said something to her in that strange language, and she began to wag her tail wildly. The other wolves ran up and jumped about the two guards as if they were old friends of theirs. The two guards almost seemed like they were not allowed to show an emotion in their duty, but we all saw they had. The two giants quietly backed up to the pillars, back to their previous positions at a guard, and again became part of the giant stone columns. We all just stood there with our mouths open.

"Well, weren't they a charming pair?" said Captain Rickle. "Can't you people go anywhere without something like this happening?"

"What are the guards of Lemuria, Tamantha?" asked Captain Simpson.

"Belay your answer, Tamantha, as I just don't even want to know," said Captain Rickle.

"I have only heard of Lemuria as a child's story," answered Tamantha.

"I did not think Lemuria ever really existed, but I was told many a story about it. These great pillars and their guardians were in those stories, as was the tale of a great rock wall that surrounded the city. I can only guess that we are seeing here is what is left of that great wall after its destruction. The Lemurians were a great and wonderful race of beings that inhabited the land and the sea. I was told they were able to swim the seas and walk the land as I do now. This is definitely Lemuria or a part of it, but how and why it is here is a mystery to me.

"The great city of Lemuria was supposed to have been destroyed many tens of thousands of years ago long along with her great sister cities, Thule, Hyperborea, Mu, and Mar. It was told down through the ages that a great rock from the sky had fallen onto the earth, and all was destroyed. It was taught that the Lemurians watched the night sky and could see the great rock approach slowly for many nights with its giant tail of fire. All that inhabit the sea today come from what was left of the end of all that existed. The language I used to speak to the guardians is called the tongue of the sea."

Captain Pike said, "A tale like that and no rum in my hand. What a shame."

"They are as old as the sea itself, and I am a distant relative of them as I come from the sea. A man would not live a day in this land, and we should return to the ships now," Tamantha demanded.

Captain Pike replied, "I see your point, Tamantha. Let's go."

With relief, we all turned and began to go back in the direction we had come. A minute later we all turned and saw Captain Pike clearing the pillars and heading away from us deeper into the island.

I yelled, "Captain, I thought we were headed back!"

Captain Pike said, "I did not say we were turning back. I just acknowledged that Tamantha had a point. Don't worry, Mr. Newly, as I am quite sure your Katherine will teach you the fine points of getting along with a woman."

Tamantha and I just shook our heads, and we all quick stepped it back and joined up with Captain Pike.

The path before us was more like some sort of great road made of many stones, and it appeared to go on forever. We looked down the road and could see where many other smaller roads joined into it from the sides. As the smaller roads led away, they seemed to go nowhere past a few hundred yards. We could all see in our imaginations how wonderful this place must have been so long ago. All the roads had large toppled-down columns that had once lined their sides. There were many destroyed great stone buildings and statues of strange-looking sea creatures everywhere. We saw many statues that looked just like the guardians we had already met.

"I hope those devils there don't come to life, Mr. Newly." The captain said.

The road seemed to be steadily heading downward, and as we walked it for miles, the land around us rose up like we were walking down into a giant pit. We began to see other roads all around in the distance also heading downward from the island's surface. As we put the miles behind us, the scene of destruction did not change.

"We must be far beneath the sea by now the way this road is heading down," said Captain Rickle. "Is anyone thinking about that but me?"

"Aye, I have been considering just that me self," the captain said.

"I wonder where the sea is and what is keeping it out of this place," said Captain Rickle.

"We better let Tamantha rest. Let's stop here for a bit," the captain said. He was the one that really looked like he needed the rest with his huffing and puffing.

Tamantha just chuckled a bit, and said, "Well, Captain Pike, I just don't know what has come over you, as you are just so considerate lately."

The captain did not acknowledge her sarcasm and lay back in a nice spot he had picked out. I was picking around in the sand when something caught my eye.

"Captain, look at this sand," I said.

"All right, Mr. Newly, I'm looking," the captain replied. "It looks like sand to me."

"No, Captain. It's no longer sand. It has been turned to glass somehow," I explained. Everyone curiously picked up a handful and examined it, and sure enough the sand was now glass.

"Your point, Mr. Newly?"

"You have to have a lot of heat to turn sand into glass, Captain."

"Your point, Mr. Newly?"

"My point is, Captain, that at some time it was really hot here, sir, and I mean really hot."

"Well, it ain't hot now, Mr. Newly," the captain complained. "I guess we better get to it. I can see there will be no rest to be had here."

"Sorry, Captain," I said.

The captain pulled out his seeing glass and looked deep down our path, and a big smile came across his face. "Well I'll be," he said. "Everyone get a look at this sight." We all grabbed up our glasses, and what was in the end of them was really a wonder.

Several miles away a great pyramid lay before us that looked to be made of some sort of crystal. The pyramid was hundreds of feet high and wide. We all stood there quietly, looking through our seeing glasses at the wonder of the scene. The great crystal pyramid was so beautiful glistening in the sunlight I did not want to stop looking at it. The pyramid looked like a giant jewel shining in the sun with all the colors of the rainbow. It appeared that all the roads we had been seeing in the distance led right to it, just like the one we traveled. To make the scene even greater, surrounding the great pyramid were hundreds and hundreds of smaller crystal pyramids equally as beautiful shining in the sun.

As we approached the great crystal pyramid, the wonders we saw began to increase. There were crystal pyramids everywhere in front of us of all sizes shining like the sun. There were some that were almost as large as the great one. There were some that were only half the size of that, big ones, little ones everywhere, even ones small enough to fit in your hand. One of the British crew tried to pick up a really small one that was about the size of an apple. It was so hot he pulled his hand away quickly. He kicked at the small crystal but could not move it because of its great weight. Some pyramids even had other pyramids inside them, and they all glistened like stars. Some had three sides, and some had four. Some had six sides, and some had eight. The entire scene was a wonderful sight.

As the sun shone down upon the great center pyramid, the daylight seemed to be split into the colors of the rainbow. Each of the colored sunbeams split and went off in its own direction and struck other pyramids. Then those pyramids would do the same, sending their color of the collected light off each of their sides to the next pyramids that would do the same, sending their light to the next ones over and over again down the line to finally hit the miniature ones like the British were kicking at. From there, the light shot straight up into the sky, rejoining the other colors and forming a great rainbow that shone a hundred times brighter than any rainbow I had ever seen.

Every time the light beam left one pyramid, it looked to grow in strength and brightness. There were bright, glowing red pyramids and orange ones, yellow ones, and green ones, blue ones, and some that shone the color that the map shone back in the bat cave, a violet color.

Once we had reached the farthest out of the crystals, we were still a mile or so away from the giant center pyramid. As we began to walk into the many-colored beams of light, we were amazed that they went right through our bodies. The colored light would just go in one side and out the other completely undisturbed on its way to the next pyramid. Captain Pike had a beam hit him in the back of his head, and it came right out his eye, and I laughed out loud at his look.

As the light went through me, it was very pleasing. It made me feel warm and good inside, and it offered a peaceful state of mind. I looked over at Captain Rickle, and he had at least a hundred different colors of light passing through every part of his body. I thought he was going to split his face with his smile. Even the wolves seemed pleased at the feeling the light offered as it passed through them. They wagged their great tails as they walked along. Even though the crystal pyramids were much too hot to touch, they offered no heat into the air, or we would have cooked on the spot.

I looked down at my hand as two or three colored beams went through it. I had a fairly large scar on the back of it from an injury I had endured. To my wonder, the scar disappeared right before my eyes. I yelled out and told my tale. Everyone began to examine themselves, and the same was happening to them right down to any gray hair they had, gathering its past color.

One of the British crew exclaimed with great joy, "Captain, I can see out of my bad eye again!"

Another mate yelled out, "My teeth don't hurt me any longer, Captain!"

Another yelled, "My teeth are back!"

Another yelled, "My limp is gone, and me leg don't hurt anymore!"

Even the crewman with the burnt hand was no longer injured. Within minutes, whatever physical afflictions any of us had were gone, and our bodies were completely restored to perfect condition. It was a wonderful, miraculous moment for us all.

"Captain," I asked, "is this the treasure? Is this miracle of life the treasure?"

"Not according to the map, Mr. Newly," replied the captain.

A large storm had begun to cross over the island, and the sun disappeared behind the dark rain clouds. The sunlight no longer reached the giant crystal pyramid, and the scene of light beams just disappeared. As the refreshing rain fell onto our faces, we could hear a loud sizzling and popping noise. The rain was hitting the burning hot crystals and began to cool them. A great steam rose up off the cooling crystals like a thick island mist that we could not see through at all.

I could not believe how quickly the wonderful and beautiful scene had just disappeared, leaving us in a deep, dense fog. We could not see ten feet in front of us, and as the storm's lighting began to crack, I began to get a strange feeling—a gut feeling like something bad was going to happen.

In the mist we began to hear something coming from the direction of the center pyramid. The wolves went crazy with warning and barked and snapped at us to get back.

"We better listen to them, Ethan. This is not good," warned Tamantha.

Louder and louder the racket came, and it started to sound like horses running.

Captain Pike screamed, "Get ready for this!"

All of us put a knee on the ground and pulled our pistols. You could hear the British crew behind us clicking back the hammers on their rifles and cursing. Then out of the steam it came, or should I say they came.

Six horses came through the mist's wall right dead in front of us, followed closely by three golden chariots that each two pulled. The pure black horses were magnificent creatures with great wings; however, the chariots each carried a hideous creature that looked like nothing I had ever seen or even dreamed of.

The creatures looked like they had been dug up out of some sort of undersea graveyard with their goo and seaweed and rot just hanging all about them. They smelled worse than anything I had every smelled before. A horrible stench that made me sick to my stomach, and they ran right over us. The horrible creatures had large, sunken-in, black, glaring eyes that shined in the mist like great black diamonds. They were screaming as they came at us, and their sound was every bit as bad as the sea witch's. It was a scream that pierced our souls and sent fear shouting through our bodies.

Captain Pike grabbed Tamantha and jumped to the side. Captain Rickle jumped and rolled and came up firing. He hit the center rider right in the back of its head as it went by, and off that whole rotten mess came. Captain Simpson shot the rider on the port side in its chest and almost got run down for his trouble, but he jumped clear at the last second. Captain Simpson's shot knocked the ten-foot-tall beast out of its chariot backward, and the wolves were on it in a second tearing it to pieces. Four of the British crew were not so lucky, and as one received one of the large spears the creatures carried right in his chest, the other three fell victim to the horses and the chariots.

As the last beast came around on its turn to make another run at us, Tamantha fired at it and took off what might have been the side of its face, but that did not slow the thing down. We all opened fire on the beast, and it fell apart under the fire, spewing its goo all over us.

Just like that, from behind us, there came three more riders. Just like before, six winged horses and three golden chariots came out of the mist's wall. Again we all jumped away, but now our pistols and rifles were not yet loaded, so this was going to get real close up, and every one of us knew it. As the riders came by, Captain Rickle boarded one of the chariots with his sword drawn. He jumped up in the air and hacked the beast's head right off, and the headless creature's stinking goo again flew all over us.

Princess got another rider as it came by dragging the nasty, oozing mess from its feet and off its chariot. The screaming, ranting creature jumped to its feet and went to take a swipe at Princess with the spear it held. That creature never even got the spear half around when the Klondike was on its back and the rest of the pack joined in quickly. They ripped that creature into ten thousand pieces as if to make an example out of it for daring to strike at Princess.

The third rider came around and began its run back at us, and there stood Captain Pike right in front of its path. Out of his coat came the map of the sea. Unrolling it quickly, the captain showed the map forward of him in the direction of the horses closing on him fast. The map began to glow brightly, and you could see the fear cross over the horses' faces at the sight of it. The charging horses dropped their heads, bent their front legs down, and leaned forward, almost stopping dead in their tracks. They stopped so fast, the chariot and its passenger flew right over their heads, landing on the ground in a wreck in front of them.

The great horses reared into the air, kicking at the sight of the map of the sea. They took off trying to run the other direction, dragging the chariot behind them. I still do not know which killed that creature first. It was either the chariot chewing up the nasty, sticking beast as the wreckage drug him along or those wolves working on it, biting, snapping, and tearing at as it as it was being dragged about. It was not long until that skin bag of nasty rot was gone.

Thank God it was raining so hard because we were all completely covered in the dead creature's goo. There was no way a man could ever carry such a stench for long and not go insane. The captain said that he thought that the stench might have been one of the creature's defenses. Whatever the case, I knew when it got on you, you were desperate to get it off. Even the wolves rolled about trying get clean, and they drank rainwater until I thought they would burst.

"Do you think they worked for the witch Captain?" I asked.

"Can't say, Mr. Newly."

I don't know if it was because of the map being produced or whether there just weren't any more of them, but no more of the creatures came out of the mist. We all looked about at the aftermath of the scene, and there stood the five wrecked chariots with their winged horses standing at a distance in the mist. The other two horses that towed the one wrecked chariot were still attached to it, and they were in a tizzy, as they knew they could not run from any danger we might have in store for them.

Tamantha walked slowly up to the horses and began to talk to them softly. The great steeds were sneezing and pawing at the ground. As she petted and continued talking to them softly, you could tell that the horses had no idea what this new feeling they were experiencing was. As Tamantha ran her hands over their whip scars, she began to cry. You could tell they had never been petted or talked to in a soft tone or treated in a decent manner. Tamantha loved at them and told them none of this was their fault and how sorry she was, and they pushed at her with their heads.

I had never seen the wolves show their tails lowered before. Their great tails were always in a large curl above their backs. Not this time, though. As the wolves came about, they approached the horses slowly, and they seemed to whimper at them, showing their tails down, looking submissive and respectful. It was like they felt sorry for the great steeds' lives of abuse and their requirements to obey their master's wicked orders. At first the horses seemed nervous, but as the wolves came up and licked at their faces, the horses seemed to give into their new, never-before-felt feelings of affection.

We all stood about in the pouring rain as all men and beasts calmed down and came back to their wits.

Captain Pike ordered, "Get that chariot up and rigged back properly."

He walked over to each great horse and petted their faces and talked to them like Tamantha had done. I could not believe it; the horses responded to the captain's touch with pushes of affection and the flapping of their great wings. They all seemed to stand at attention for their new kind master.

"Well, me babies, how about taking us for a little ride?" asked Captain Pike. All the horses flapped their great wings as if they wanted so badly to fly.

"I don't think these horses have ever been allowed to fly," said Tamantha.

"Aye," said the captain. "It looks like they have been tethered their whole lives. What a burden these poor devils have had to endure. Bury the dead, and mark their graves well. As soon as the mist clears, we will go."

About an hour passed, and the storm moved on. As the sun returned, the mist disappeared and, to our great satisfaction, the thousands of colored beams of light returned once again. As the light beams struck the horses, we could see the pleasure on their faces—another emotion we were all sure they had never encountered before. We all watched in amazement as the horses were restored to what their true greatness should have been. We watched as their whip scars disappeared and as the sores in their mouths from the cruelty of the harsh bridles were healed. We watched as the muscles on their backs bulged where their wings were attached. Our new horses were beside themselves with joy.

Captain Pike looked to his map and yelled out, "The treasure, and I'll bet the third key is in that big pyramid there."

Captain Rickle said, "I certainly hope we come across a little quick sand and a couple hundred crocodiles to make this hard.

"Get aboard the chariots, mates, and let's see where home is," ordered the captain. "Mr. Keebler, you stay behind with the wolves and keep an eye out," Captain Pike said to one of the British crew. Needless to say, Mr. Keebler was delighted that he did not have to go with us.

It was a tight squeeze, but all of us managed to get aboard a chariot. Captain Pike grabbed up the reins of his two horses, and with a big smile he looked around at us all and said, "Hold on, mates. This is going to be a ride."

"Captain," I yelled out, "what if the horses take us back to where they came from, and we find that place full of those nasty creatures?"

"I wouldn't worry about that, Mr. Newly. "I don't think these horses are going to go anywhere near a place like that. They have a taste of their freedom and will not soon return to bondage."

"Where exactly are they taking us Pike" asked Captain Simpson

"To the third key and maybe some treasure, I hope, and who knows where that may be." The captain replied.

"That's great just great," said Captain Rickle. "Just the direct answer to the question I was hoping to hear."

Tamantha grabbed Captain Pike around his neck tightly, and Captain Rickle cussed.

"Ya!" Captain Pike yelled, and the horses took off fast. They began to run faster than any horse I had ever seen or ridden, and then even faster they went. As they picked up more and more speed, to our amazement, the horses opened up their great wings, and their hoofs began to leave the ground. Faster and faster we went as if the horses had no limit. We were on the giant center pyramid in a second, and to my horror, the horses did not slow but instead kept building their speed.

We all put our hands out in front of us to brace for the impact into the side of the Pyramid, but we did not crash. We went right through the side of the great crystal, and the horses picked up even more speed, and from that point I still am not sure what happened.

Faster and faster we went, and the world around us went into a blur of lights like some sort of a tunnel. I tried to yell out, but my speech was slow, and it seemed like it took a minute just to say, "Captain Pike." My speech and all my movement went to a very slow motion, and I felt very heavy. Then I heard a loud explosion, and the horses began to slow.

Quickly we came out of that tunnel of lights, and the world began to come back. When I came out of my dizziness, there we all were in the chariots looking at the horses at a standstill in some sort of great crystal hall.

We all stumbled out of the chariots and continued to stumble about the ground.

"I'm not going back that way!" yelled Captain Rickle.

One of the British yelled, "Captain Pike, Mr. Denver has fallen out."

Sure enough, one of the British crewman had fallen out of his chariot and was gone somewhere back in that tunnel of lights. There was no telling where he had wound up or even if he was dead or alive. We all began to look around and realized we were inside the great center pyramid.

"This thing is a lot larger than it looks," said Captain Pike.

"Somehow I don't think we are in that pyramid back on the island. I think we are in another that is far away," said Tamantha.

"I think you are right, Tamantha," said the captain. "Very far away."

As he spoke, the captain was looking up in the air with his mouth open, and we all began to join him in his stare. There floating above us were thousands of crystal pyramids among a huge black night sky full of stars that covered the entire ceiling of this great hall. The crystal pyramids shined like bright beacons, and I remembered the map of the sea.

The captain must have thought the same thing, and we both yelled out together, "It's a map."

"My God," said Tamantha. "It's the map of the Lemuria, or at least that is what it is called back were we came from."

"I need some rum. Who's got the rum?" called out the captain.

"Tamantha, what is this place? What is the map of Lemuria?" I asked.

"I don't want to know. Don't tell us," said Captain Rickle. "Just tell me how to get back to my ship. I have already had enough of this. You can have your key captain and keep any treasure you find for yourselves."

"The map of Lemuria is the map of the cosmos and is fabled to show the thousands and thousands of worlds scattered far across it, including our own world. It is told that everything that exists floats in a vast sea of darkness and that this great ocean is too vast to imagine. The map of Lemuria is fabled to show how to travel to each world," answered Tamantha.

Captain Simpson, pointing up at a still freshly lit trail across the great map's face, spoke up and said, "Here. This is where we must be and here"—he walked a hundred or so paces, pointing—"here is where we just came from."

We all looked and studied and decided he was right. The "here is where we are now" was the part that spooked us all. Where we were, according to the map of Lemuria, was in the center of the cosmos, and all roads from all worlds came to this great center point. Like a wagon wheel with countless spokes. Where we used to be, our world, was clear on the other side of the great black sea.

"This must be how they escaped!" exclaimed Tamantha. "This must be how the Lemurian's escaped their destruction. Just like we saw back on the island with all the crystal pyramids joined by the light, it must be the same everywhere. These pyramids must be in every place that exists and must be connected by the light to each and everyone across the abyss, and you can travel in that light to anywhere you wish to go if you know how. My god, the Lemurian's are alive."

"Well, we better be finding them, as they are probably the only devils that can show us how to get back home," said Captain Rickle.

We all began to walk about studying the great crystal walls of the giant hall. There were thousands of worlds shown with scenes of them etched into the crystal wall of the pyramid. In front of each scene was a large crystal vase filled to the brim with very small crystal pyramids about the size of a marble.

When I touched my hand to one of the etched scenes, it came alive, and I jumped back in surprise. I stared in a wonder at the scene before me. It was almost like I was looking through a porthole to another room, but I was really looking into another world somewhere. I could smell the air from the world and hear its sounds. The view in the porthole would change to different scenes of the world. Some views shown were close up, and some were far away. I yelled to the others to come and see what I had discovered.

There were beautiful worlds and ice worlds. There were hot desert worlds and horrible worlds. There were terrible worlds at war and ones of peace. There were worlds that were at war with other worlds, and the scenes were horrid. Anything you could imagine, there was a world for it.

Captain Simpson called out, "Come here, everyone! Have a gander at this world."

"What do have there, Captain Simpson?" asked the captain.

"I might have just come across the world those stinking creatures came from, Captain," relied Captain Simpson. "Have a look here, Captain, or, better yet, have a smell."

I came running up and asked, "What did you find, Captain?"

"Captain Simpson thinks that this here might be the world those stinking chariot riders came from, Mr. Newly," replied the captain. "They must have wanted to keep us out of this place, so they came for us."

We all looked as Captain Simpson placed his hand back on the crystal etching of the world, and the window opened. Sure enough there they were. It was a horrible place, like a nightmare turned to flesh. We could smell the stench in the air as it leaked out into the great hall. As soon as our horses got a whiff of it, they began to get nervous and jumpy. We could see the nasty, stinking beasts walking about, beating their horses and other poor creatures they held captive. It was a dark, cold world with very little light, and lightning cracked everywhere. It looked to be wet there, and what appeared to be slimy seaweed grew everywhere. In a split second, another scene appeared that showed two of the nasty creatures fighting amongst themselves. All of a sudden, they stopped their fighting and slowly turned to look at us right in the eyes.

"Come get a taste of me map!" the captain screamed at them.

Captain Simpson quickly removed his hand, and the etching closed the scene.

"Have you gone mad, Captain?" questioned Captain Rickle. "Are you trying to provoke them? Did you see the thousands and thousands of them? What will we do if an army of those devils comes out at us?"

Captain Pike replied, "Well, I don't think we will be seeing much of them anymore as they seem to fear me map. Instead of worrying about those dogs, let's see if we can find the third key and figure a way out of here."

"Aye, sir," replied Captain Rickle.

We walked about for what seemed like days looking and looking at all the worlds. It was odd because we did not get hungry or thirsty, nor were we tired. I began to think we were never going to go home.

I started to look carefully at the etching of one of the more pleasant worlds that I had come across, and I put my hand to it to open the porthole. I began to watch the different individual worlds' scenes as one by one they would change to show another. I was fascinated, and then I jumped for joy and yelled out to all to come and see.

"It's our world! It's our world! Come look. It's our world!" I yelled.

Captain Pike and Tamantha were the first to arrive, and sure enough it was our home. There was our great pyramid and the island.

"Aye, Mr. Newly, it appears to be, and now all you need to do is figure how to get back there," said Captain Pike.

As the others came up and gathered around, Tamantha bent down and began to study the etchings on the crystal vase. I knelt down next to her, and I, too, studied hard. There was a particular etching right in the front center of the vase that showed the formation of five of the small pyramids contained in the vase.

Tamantha reached into the vase and picked out five of the crystals and placed four of them in her hand in the exact formation as the etching showed. When she placed the fifth in its place the middle crystal began to gather light and glow brightly, and when it was just so full of light we thought it would explode, it released a beam of light, striking the next crystal to it and from that crystal to the next until all crystals were joined by the beam of light. When the light had made its rounds from crystal to crystal, it returned to the center, and then it shot out and struck just the air twenty feet or so in front of us, seeming to just stop and go no farther.

A great commotion began, right out in front of Tamantha where the light beam stopped. Out of thin air a great blackness began to appear; it was about ten feet across and round. We all jumped back, except Tamantha, who held fast her position and stared into this new devil's face unafraid.

As the blackness formed, it began to pull at the air, and a wind began to build, and the wind appeared to be being sucked into the blackness. Then came the light streaks forming up another tunnel that looked just like the last one that brought us here. Small bolts of what appeared to be lighting flashed and cracked across the face of the tunnel. The tunnel pulled at Tamantha. She closed her hand, and the black tunnel of light streaks vanished in a second, leaving nothing but bits of lightning dancing in the air and disappearing.

Tamantha turned with a huge smile and said, "Here is your treasure, Captain Pike. It is the most powerful thing a man or a woman could ever hope to hold in their hand and the greatest treasure one could ever possess."

"We know the secret, Captain, and now we can control it. Do you know how powerful this is? Do you know what this means? You now have the means go anywhere across the cosmos and return back."

Captain Pike walked up and picked up five of his own crystal pyramids and studied the etching closely. With his always-steady hand, he placed the crystals in their proper position, but as he placed the fifth crystal down, I saw him wince. The light danced in his hand, connecting the pyramids together, and off the light beam went, striking the air in front of him, and the tunnel began to form.

Captain Pike closed his hand and said, "No telling what price a bag of these fine crystals will bring."

We all gave him back a frown. Captain Pike walked many paces back to the center of the great hall. Right there in the exact center of the great crystal hall were placed five larger crystal vases in the shape of the four points of a diamond and one in the middle. Like the other crystal vases in front of all the thousands and thousands of different world scenes these too were full to the brim with small crystal pyramids. Captain Pike paced back and forth, thinking for at least an hour before he finally called us all together.

With the same smile and the same tone, Captain Pike had showed the crew back on treasure night, he said, "We all know by now what we have here. I figure that these crystals here in the center are a way to come back to this place from anywhere in eternity and then to go anywhere you want to go into eternity and then come back again. Tamantha says this is a gift of power and a great treasure with the ability to travel across the cosmos to thousands of worlds with treasures unknown and then return. I agree with her evaluations and believe her theories now be true, but we all need to look a bit deeper into what we have here, into this sea of blackness, and try not to confuse our minds."

The captain paused for a moment, smiled at each of us, and continued. "Look at your bodies, and examine your minds, and question yourselves. Have you ever felt better in your lives? You are all healed from sicknesses and afflictions and scars. Why are you not hungry? Why are you not thirsty? Your broken bones no longer hurt, and you are no longer tired from your travels like you have found the fountain of youth and drank its water. In case no one has noticed, time has no meaning here, and as long as you travel these pyramids and their light, you will never grow old. Ask yourselves who made all of this and what has become of them and how and why we have been given the greatest treasure of all—and that be immortality if you want it."

Again the captain paused. He walked around to all of us, smiling, and put his hand on our shoulders as if he were saying good-bye to each of us.

"As for myself, mates, I wish to get back to the sea and me ship. If I play my cards right, and use these fine new gifts properly, I'll find all the map's keys and free all those poor devils imprisoned on it. I'll also enact my revenge on that witch of the sea and maybe, just maybe, I can save the sea from its great war. I now dismiss any of you that wish to go. As your captain, I no longer have the expectation for you to follow my mere orders in the face of this great gift. I will not and do not expect any of you to disregard your gift of immortality. Those that wish to leave, gather your crystals, and I'm sure our paths will cross again somewhere in some time."

With that said, Captain Pike walked over to the horses and began to pet them.

No man or woman moved, frozen in their thoughts.

Tamantha was the first to say, "I'm with the captain."

Captain Simpson and Captain Rickle, fighting for second place, both yelled out, "Arrrr!"

I was third because they had all beat me to it, and the rest were fourth because we had beat them to it. Not one of us chose the great gift that was offered. Instead, we chose the captain's plan.

The captain turned, smiled, and said, "Just as I expected from this crew. All right then, mates," he said, "this is the plan. You all need to get five stones or more from these center vases so you can always return here some day. Don't forget. You have to remember the pattern, or there is no telling where you will wind up.

"Then in all of this we need to find some sort of water world that be the one the Lemurian's went to and get those five crystals each and remember that pattern."

"Next mates you all need to pick you your own special worlds and get those crystals and remember that pattern."

"One day I'm sure we will all return here for our reward. "For now, spread out and get started finding the Lemurian's," ordered the captain.

"I'll be back I hope," spoke the captain.

When we all turned to look at him, he had the crystals to return there in one hand and the crystals to go to our world in the other.

"Captain, what are you going to do?" I asked.

"Well, Mr. Newly, someone has to go first and see if this all really works, and today is my day. Hopefully I'll be back."

With that, the captain assembled the five crystals in his hand and opened the tunnel back to our world. As before, when the blackness formed up, the lightning danced and cracked across the face of the great tunnel of lights. It pulled at him with its wind and called for him to step in. The captain held his hat in his hand, and he walked into it fearlessly. Just before the tunnel closed, we could see it grab hold of him. It looked like his body was instantly stretched to a thousand feet long, and then he, too, was part of the light. The captain was gone, and the tunnel closed, leaving nothing but bits of lightning floating and disappearing into the air.

A split second later another tunnel opened across the hall, and there came Captain Pike with the four wolves, Mr. Keyblerler, and Mr. Denver, the fellow that fell out of the chariot. The wolves stumbled about, shaking their great heads. Mr. Keyblerler and Mr. Denver both had horrid looks on their faces as they too stumbled about.

"It works!" exclaimed Captain Pike with a big smile.

"But, Captain" I said, "You were only gone for a second, if that.

"Captain, Mr. Newly is right. You were only gone for a split second," said Captain Rickle.

"As I told you before, mind your thoughts trying to figure time, as it will drive you crazy. How many worlds have you searched?" asked the captain.

"None yet, Captain. Like we said, you were only gone for a second not hours," replied Captain Simpson.

"Let's get to it then mates."

Everyone stopped by the center of the hall's crystals and got their share and memorized the proper pattern to open the tunnel back to this great place. Everyone also loaded up with crystals to get back to our world. We all then set off on our search for the new home of the Lemurian's. I walked past Captain Pike and noticed he was looking at a nasty world of fire and smoke, and with a laugh I asked him,

"You going there for your honeymoon, are you, Captain Pike?"

He just laughed and said, "Keep it up, Mr. Newly. Just keep it up."

As I walked away with my smile, I looked back, and to my surprise I saw the captain picking up that world's crystals and studying its pattern.

Then for all I know, in our time it could have been days or weeks later, or even years, or maybe even just a second later that Captain Rickle yelled out from way down the great hall.

"Captain, I think I have something here!"

We all ran down to join him and have a look. He was looking through a porthole he had opened that led to a wonderful world made of sea and land. The smell of the sea came rushing out of the porthole and spilled into the air of the great hall, filling our lungs with joy. The thoughts of being back on our ships filled our heads.

We could see a great, tall people that walked the land, traveling the many roads that joined their great cities together. Not only did the people walk the land, they also swam in the sea with great tails like Tamantha has. We could see all manner of sea creatures like we had been introduced to on our world. We could see great crystal pyramids and the many-colored light beams they produced.

One of light beams came right out of the porthole, and we all jumped back. A brilliant blue beam of light it was, and when it struck the wall of the great hall, the sight was unimaginable. The entire hall lit up with its color sparkling like one hundred blue suns shining on ten thousand seas. The magnificent blue light ran up the sides of the crystal hall and was dispersed all across the map of Lemuria and across the cosmos. All paths to all worlds on the great map above us shined and sparkled, and then the light was gone forever. It was truly a wonderful sight, and everyone's minds ran wild.

"I could go blind right now and would be a happy man after seeing that," said Captain Simpson.

Tamantha was several hundred feet down the hall at a run when the great light came and went. She came running up and exclaimed, "My God! What was that? Did you see that?" She was almost in tears at its sight.

"Have a look here, missy," said the captain.

When she saw the scene in the porthole, a smile covered her entire face as she squealed and jumped with joy.

"Lemuria!" she exclaimed. "It's Lemuria!"

Indeed it was Lemuria, and we all threw our hats in the air and cheered. We all stared and watched as the different scenes changed before us. There were great cities on the land that looked just like the ruins back on our world except these were not in ruin. There were wonderful underwater cities also, deep beneath the sea, which stretched for miles on end. It was a thriving, beautiful, peaceful world, and we all laughed out loud at its sight.

One of the crew reached to get a handful of crystals, and Tamantha pushed his hand away, and she said, "This world is for no man to visit."

The crewman graciously bowed his head and walked away. Tamantha reached down and picked up several of the stones and carefully studied the pattern. Captain Pike watched her with a smile, as he knew of the happiness she carried inside of her. Tamantha then reached down and picked up five more of the crystals. She smiled as she put them into Captain Pike's hand and kissed him on the cheek. She whispered something in his ear that we could not hear, but the captain's face turned bright red.

"Should we go there, Ethan, or leave them untouched and uncorrupted by our world?" Tamantha asked.

"I think it's time we get back to the ships, Captain," said Captain Simpson.

"Aye," replied Captain Pike.

"But first I want to save the horses," said the captain.

"The Map of the Sea is hungry, as I can hear its belly rumble."

We all just watched him and wondered what in the world he was talking about. We followed him back down the great hall until he reached the nightmare world of those stinking devils. He touched the scene and opened it, and the stench was upon us. Captain Pike snarled as he watched those nasty, stinking creatures beat the great winged horses and the other poor creatures they possessed. Our horses again showed their fear as they pawed at the ground, nervously snorting.

Captain Pike reached down and picked up five of the crystals and studied the pattern. I yelled at him and said, "Captain, what are you are going to do? You cannot open a tunnel to that place."

"Belay that, Mr. Newly. Get our horses unbridled off them chariots," the captain ordered.

Then to our horror, Captain Pike assembled the crystals in his hand and open the tunnel to the world. The lightning cracked and danced as the tunnel of lights opened to that horrid world of stench and rot. Captain Pike grabbed the map of the sea from his coat, laughed out loud, and flung the map into the tunnel. Then he cursed at the creatures and closed his hand, collapsing the tunnel.

"Captain, what have you done?" I yelled. "You have given them the map of the sea. Are you crazy?"

Captain snarled back at me and said, "I said belay that, Mr. Newly, or I'll through you in there me self."

He walked over and opened the porthole, and we all strained to get a look. It appeared a great storm had begun to form on the world. A giant storm with a huge whirling wind began to form. It got so large it seemed it could not sustain itself, so it split off into two whirling devils. When they too got so big, then they split to four and then eight and on the process went. The giant storms began to cover the world with their great blackness. Bigger and bigger they became, building and building with power. Then at one time, like the storms had a mind of their own, they began to lay down the curse.

I don't think the captain had any idea of what was about to happen. He had unleashed the entire force of his hatred for this world, and the map of the sea would carry out his wishes. We could see the nasty creatures run for cover, but they could not hide. As the storms crossed over the world, they began sucking up the nasty skin bags of rot. Thousands and thousands of them spun around the outside of the storms, making their way up the sides, screaming and spinning wildly. When they reached the top of the giant cyclones, over into the center they would be sucked, down to their places in to the eternal agony of the Map of the Sea.

We could see all the winged horses and the other creatures with their heads down and their eyes closed, but the storms would not take them. When it was all over no trace of the vile creatures was left, like they never had existed at all. They were gone. The stench was gone, the slime weed was gone, and so was the darkness. A second later a tunnel opened, cracking and popping, and out came the Map of the Sea landing right at the captain's feet.

The captain looked at me with a smile and said, "I wouldn't have really thrown you in there, Mr. Newly."

He walked over and picked up the map and said, "She looks a little scorched from her meal, wouldn't you say, Mr. Newly?"

He rolled open the map, and there appeared a small world sitting in what looked to be a sea of fire. The silver world seemed to spin around slowly as the silver flames licked at it, and we could hear a great faint cry that seemed to come from the many.

"Well, I'm glad me map don't stink," said the captain.

"Tamantha, do you think the Lemurian's will take the horses and treat them well?"

"Of course, Ethan," she answered.

"Open a tunnel to Lemuria then, and then I'll open this one again," said the captain.

Tamantha assembled her crystals and opened the tunnel to Lemuria. Captain Pike walked over to our horses and petted them and talked to them as if they could understand a word he was saying.

"Go and get your mates, me fine babies, as you are free!" yelled the captain, and off the horses flew into the air. They flew about the great hall like it was the first time they had ever been allowed off the ground.

Captain Pike turned and reopened the tunnel to world of rot, and when the lightning cracked, our horses were gone into it. Captain Pike held his tunnel open, as did Tamantha hers. We all watched in a wonder as thousands of horses flew out of the tunnel from their cursed world, circled the great hall, and went right into Tamantha's tunnel to Lemuria.

So many thousands of the different creatures that could not fly scurried out quickly from the nightmare world's tunnel, and off to Lemuria they went.

The last to come out were our twelve horses, and the captain closed the tunnel behind them. The horses all floated to the ground and quickly walked up to Captain Pike and began to play with him. They pushed him about with their faces as they showed their great affection for him.

With a tear running down her face, Tamantha said, "Come on, Ethan. These crystals are starting to get hot."

"Go me, babies, go!" yelled the captain, and the horses jumped into the air and were gone to Lemuria. Tamantha closed her hand, and the tunnel was gone.

"Let's go, mates. Back to the ships. Mr. Newly, open the tunnel for home," ordered Captain Pike.

I assembled the crystals, and as the lightning cracked, we all strolled in to the tunnel back to our world. We returned out of it back on the island where this whole craziness started. As it turned out, we had only been gone for a few minutes. It was a beautiful morning as we made our way back the way we had come. Everyone was quiet and deep in their thoughts trying to make sense of it all. Everyone, that is, except the three captains, who sang pirate songs and laughed and drank on a bottle of rum Captain Simpson had produced that he claimed he was saving for a special occasion.

In between two of the songs, Captain Pike yelled back to us all laughing, and said, "I hope you mates learned them crystal patterns right, or there will be no tellin' where you will wind up."

Soon enough we were back on the ships, courtesy of the whales.

"What about the third key, Captain?" I asked.

"It was there, Mr. Newly. I know it was there. I could feel it in my bones."

I just frowned.

"Don't worry there, Mr. Newly. That key is going to show up as a result of our little visit to this island. I'm very sure of that."

Fifteen

"Heading, Captain?" asked Jonesy.

"Me pigeon has not returned and that can only mean one thing—trouble," replied the captain. "Captain Adams and Bongeorno should have sent me a reply by now about meeting us off Samana Cay to man those four British warships. Set a course for Anegada, we will see what their problem is soon enough," ordered Captain Pike.

"Anegada, Captain?" I questioned.

"You know, Mr. Newly, it's getting to the point where I can't give an order anymore without having to explain myself. Very well then, that's where Captain Adams and Bongeorno are as well as me pigeon. Nothing bad better have happen to me pigeon."

"Set a course for Anegada," I yelled out.

Anegada was a small island just northeast of Tortola and was every bit its twin with the same vagabonds, cutthroats, and thieves making up its lawless population. His Majesty's Navy did patrol the area, but the patrols were few and far between. When they did come into those threatening waters, they came in force with many ships. They would catch and kill as many pirates as they could and reinstall His Majesty's law temporarily back on the island.

Captain Pike was sure that the tale of our encounter on Tortola was well known by the population of Anegada, as well as the king's navy.

"You can bet your last coin that they all have heard the tale of the treasure we're carrying, Mr. Newly," warned the captain.

It was going to take us every bit of the three days to sail off the coast of Anegada. The sea and the wind were beginning to build, which would slow us down even more. After one day's sailing, the sea had changed from being rough to perilous. The wind had picked up to a gale, and the captain looked worried.

Captain Pike looked over at me and screamed through the spray and the wind, "I have seen this type of storm twice before, Mr. Newly, and we always lost men and ships!"

All hands ran about securing things that were breaking lose and flying about the deck.

One of the crew ran up from below decks and screamed, "Captain, one of the portside cannons broke loose from its station and is doing a lot of damage below. We just can't get it secured, Captain. Not in these seas."

The captain looked at me and screamed out with a face full of the sea spray, "Mr. Newly, get below and give me a report!"

I ran down below, following the mate, and what a sight I saw. Sure enough, one of the cannons had broken loose and was flying around the cannon station, damaging other cannons and wounding the crew. It was so rough the men could hardly get their hands on the heavy bronze monster, and when they did, it either flung them off or crushed their bodies, hands, or limbs.

I screamed out, "Get some cargo nets over that beast before it kills someone!"

The crew managed to get the nets over it, and it spun itself into a tangled web and finally came to a rest wedged in the damage it had created.

I made my way as best I could back to the upper deck. The storm had gotten so bad I could barely see with the rain stinging like bees at my eyes and face. I could no longer see the other ships and did not know if they were still even out there. Tamantha had locked herself and the wolves in the captain's cabin. Most of the crew had also lashed themselves to anything that would not blow away. One huge wave came over the front of the ship and washed everything that was not tied down over the side. Men and supplies were gone to the sea, leaving nothing but loose cannon balls rolling about the deck.

I looked up to the wheel, and there stood Captain Pike with his hands grasping it tightly, holding our course into the storm. He had tied Jonesy off and taken the wheel himself, as he knew if the ship got sideways in this storm we would be lost to the sea. It seemed like hours passed, and then just like that, the storm, the sea, and the wind were calming. As we all found our feet, the sky went blue above us, and the sun warmed or cold, wet bodies. It was strange because we could see the storm all round us, but this area was calm. I looked over, and there was the *Resolve* and the *Defiant* looking as ragged as us, but at least they were there.

Captain Pike shouted so we all could hear, "Get repairs under way quickly! We are running out of time." Then he looked at me and said, "Mr. Newly, we are in the eye of a hurricane, and it will come again and even worse this next time."

The whales came up alongside us, and they each were carrying three or four of the washed-over crew hanging about on their backs. As we pulled the men from the whales, the men kissed and petted at them and called them pretty and fancy names.

Sure enough, just as the captain had predicted, the storm began to return. As before, it began to build and build until it was once again a monster hurricane that was hungry for ships. The waves were huge. As they broke over the front of the *Sovereign*, almost half the ship was under the sea. I could not believe the men below were not drowned, but with all hatches closed down tightly, the sea stayed at bay. I did not know how Captain Pike could steer the ship because I could not open my eyes as I thought for sure the rain would surely blind me. Then it happened. One of the cleats broke loose from the ship and hit me right in the head, and that's all I remember except for my dream.

I dreamt I was back on Tamantha's island in that bat cave, and the big blood bat had gotten me. I could see Captain Pike and the crew watching me fly away in its claws. I could hear the laughing of the sea witch and see her ugliness as the bat dropped me before her. She put me to the map, laughing with glee as she poked at me.

When I woke up, I was lying on the deck in a pile of sail with one of the wolves licking my face. Captain Pike and Tamantha were looking down at me smiling. I sat up and looked around, and to my relief there was no sign of the storm.

"How long, Captain…how long have I been gone?" I asked.

"Two days, Mr. Newly, and I'm going to take that time out of your measure," the captain said.

They helped me to my feet, and I looked about the ship that was not in too bad a shape. I looked over, and there sat the *Defiant* and the *Resolve*, still a bit tattered but in fair shape also.

"I see Mr. Newly has had enough beauty sleep!" yelled over Captain Rickle.

"Where are we, Captain?" I asked.

With a smug smart smile he replied, "Off the coast of Anegada! Where else would we be?" That smile was soon gone.

"Two ships off the starboard!" yelled down the crow's mate, "and they be British warships under full sail."

"Sure is getting crowed out here," the captain yelled.

The crow's mates on the *Defiant* and the *Resolve* confirmed the sighting, as they also yelled down to their captains. All captains grabbed at their seeing glasses to view the threat before commanding the station's bell.

"Two more off the port side!" screamed down the crow's mate. Captain Pike turned in an instant and looked through his glass toward port. After exclaiming a few cuss words, he rang the station's bell loudly. The *Defiant* and the *Resolve* went to stations, also ringing their bells loudly.

"Get us under way!" yelled the captain. The sails went down and began to fill with the sea's air.

"Three more British warships forward!" yelled down the crow's mate.

I looked over at Captain Pike and said, "That is seven warships, Captain. What are we going to do?"

Captain Pike just looked over at me, smiling, and said, "Well, Mr. Newly, I don't need any more ships right now, so I guess we don't need to be gentle with this lot."

The *Defiant* was already moving off us to port, the left and the captain ordered,

"Signal her to intercept those redcoat devils to the port side the left."

"Signal the *Resolve* to intercept those devils to starboard, the right."

"Mr. Newly, we will take the three forward. Let's get to it."

"Jonesy!" yelled the captain. "Come over one quarter to starboard, the right and steer twenty-two degrees."

Jonesy and I looked at Captain Pike because we knew that course would take us away from the three British warships.

"Is there a problem with me orders, mates?" asked the captain.

"No, sir, Captain coming up on twenty-two degrees at full sail," Jonesy said. Jonesy gave me a look and shook his head at me in a warning, and I knew to keep my mouth shut.

Just then the crow's mate yelled down in frenzy, "Three more warships on the horizon!" and I thought Captain Pike's head would snap off as quickly as he turned to look up at the crow's mate pointing.

Captain Pike screamed up at him, "What flag are they under?"

"I cannot tell yet, Captain. The distance is too great," replied the crow's mate, and he began to look hard in his seeing glass. The mate called down, "Still can't tell, Captain, but they are not closing and seem to be just having a gander at us all."

Captain Rickle later told me that he had dressed all his men in their fine red coats on deck and had raised His Majesty's flag. As he approached his two targets, the mood was tense, but the crew of the *Defiant* had been ordered to smile and wave and cheer. Captain Rickle said he could see in his glass the captains on the two warships, and their confusion was evident. Captain Rickle knew the thoughts and questions running through their heads: *What is the missing Defiant doing hanging about two pirate ships and especially two that used to belong to His Majesty King George? Maybe the Defiant is having a parlay with the pirates? Where has the Defiant been all this time gone missing, and what on this earth is that whale doing?*

The *Resolve* was well known as a ship captured by pirates, but the *Sovereign* was famous in a class all her own. All knew of the famous ship the *Sovereign of the Seas*. She was once the flagship of the British Navy. She was the king's own lost prized possession, and all knew of the grand price on her head— or should I say on the man who had stolen her.

No one knew what had happened to her or to her crew or to Admiral Bennington that commanded her. That is, except for us, the witch, and the map of the sea. All captains in the British Navy knew that the one of them that secured the *Sovereign of the Seas* back to the king would be famous beyond imagination. They all wanted her badly, and there she was before them.

I always knew that Captain Simpson on the *Resolve* never was one for posturing and planning. He knew he had the forward cannon and how to use them. I had asked Captain Pike once why the British did not have forward cannon, and with a gloat, he said, "That's because every time they saw mine, Mr. Newly, and got the idea, it was the last idea they ever had."

Then with a laugh, he said, "Besides, Mr. Newly, those fine, educated men would probably blow the forward section off their own ship if they had them."

I could see through my glass that Captain Simpson and the *Resolve* were closing fast on his two targets. He told me later that the front interceptor's name was the HMS *Hampton Bay*. She was an interceptor class ship like the *Resolve*, except as usual she had no front teeth to bite with. As in most cases she would have to get alongside the *Resolve* to do any damage except for rifle fire. Captain Simpson told me that as he crossed back and forth across her deck with his glass, he could see all the *Hampton Bay*'s crew at their stations smiling in their confidence and hunger for the *Resolve*'s kill. Captain Simpson could see her captain all dressed up in his fine red coat and his fine captain's hat adorned with feathers blowing in the wind as he shouted orders at his crew.

The *Sovereign of the Seas* was steady at full sail on twenty-two-degree course as the captain had ordered. Just like he knew we had put the three British warships behind us, he looked over at me and Jonesy and said, "They will catch us soon enough. Continue your course. I want them devils to think we are running from them."

Jonesy and I still had nothing to say and watched the scene unfolding and listened for our orders.

"Mr. Newly," the captain said, "while His Majesty's interceptors are still out of range with their seeing glasses, I want you to move two of the top deck cannons to the the back section and cover them. Tell the cannon masters and mates to stay down and out of sight. Then go below and make sure the four aft, rear cannons are stowed back and ready with their sea hatches closed."

"Aye, Captain," I responded. I took off at a run, shouting the captain's orders, and quickly all was ready.

The *Defiant,* as Captain Rickle later told, had now slowed to an approach speed as a submissive gesture. The two British warships were the HMS *Elisabeth* and the HMS *Mary Beth*, both fine and great interceptor-class pirate hunters. Captain Rickle knew their captains well, and he was surprised, knowing them as well as he did, that they had taken his bait so easily. Nevertheless the *Elisabeth* and the *Mary Beth* had also slowed to an approach speed. All crews and captains on the *Mary Beth* and the *Elisabeth* gathered to the side rails of their ships, cheering and waving as the *Defiant* she was coming up to the two of them.

After a few minutes of friendly conversations between the three ships, and when he was sure that the British were at ease, he sprung his trap and announced, "Gentlemen, I have something I want to tell you."

The *Defiant's* crew knew that when Captain Rickle spoke those words they were to pull out every weapon they had to cover the two warships.

"I have always loved this part of Captain Rickle's tale!"

The crew and the captains of the warships just stood with their mouths open. Captain Rickle knew he only had seconds, so he said, "Gentlemen, I have no stomach to fire on my countrymen nor does my crew. I have no fight with you, just your fat king. I know all of you are good men, and I have no desire to turn your wives into widows or your children into orphans. I was sent to destroy you, but like I said, I have no stomach for that.

"I see your cannon masters are on the decks of your ships smiling at me instead of being at their stations. Mine are not!"

With that, all the "left "port and "right"starboard cannon's hatches opened and out rolled the *Defiant's* cannon.

"I want you to surrender your ships and abandon them. Take your dings full of supplies and row away from this place and live to fight another day."

Captain Rickle said that he could already see his countryman's answer to him in their eyes. "At first they froze, but then, like he I expected, they went for their guns."

The *Defiant* opened up on them with both port and starboard cannon. She peppered both the ships with rifle and shotguns keeping them pinned down as she moved away.

"Those poor devils never even had a chance to fire off one cannon, and I did not lose a single man. Not even one wounded," he said.

"We ran off under full sail leaving both warships disabled and burning. And on the back of the ship I waved my hat at them and yelled out to give my regards to the king."

He then set off to help the *Resolve*.

The *Resolve* was now eyeball to eyeball with the HMS *Hampton Bay*, and Captain Simpson said he could see her captain's face clearly.

Captain Simpson later said the man's jaw dropped open when he saw the forward cannons come sliding out of their holds. Captain Simpson was going to use Captain Pike's head-on attack strategy that always worked. Here is the story that was told to me later from Mr. O'Rourke, a cannon master that was on board the *Resolve*:

"The *Hampton Bay* opened up on the *Resolve* with rifle fire and gave us a good peppering, Mr. Newly," said Mr. O'Rourke.

"For me, that was always the worst part of the fight. There was just no place to hide that was safe. I'm glad I was not there.

"Five or six of the *Resolve*'s crew were killed or wounded right on the spot.

"'Fire!' screamed Captain Simpson. All the forward cannons on the *Resolve* went off, and when the smoke cleared, the *Hampton Bay*'s entire front section was almost completely gone. For the moment, the peppering stopped coming from the *Hampton Bay*, and the *Resolve*'s crew jumped up with their rifles and began to do some peppering of their own. Many of the British crew fell dead and wounded.

"Then Captain Simpson went hard to port, the left at forty-five degrees, bringing the *Resolve*'s left side cannon to bare and all the while staying away from the side of the British ship's cannon.

The *Hampton Bay* really started pouring on the rifle fire. They all knew they were now fighting for their lives. Captain Simpson snarled as he watched several more of his crew fall dead in their tracks. Captain Simpson offered the *Resolve*'s broadside at the forty-five-degree mark, and the HMS *Hampton Bay* was gone to splinters.

"Captain Simpson hurriedly looked around at the next interceptor closing on him fast and then toward the *Defiant* far off the back coming toward him at full sail. When he looked back at the baring down British ship, he noticed that this British interceptor was flying a different flag. The flag looked just like the Union Jack, except this one had a black background instead of the usual red.

"Come around one hundred and eighty degrees and head for the *Defiant*, Captain Simpson ordered. The *Resolve* came around wide and picked up speed as she made her turn. The *Resolve* was out of range from the British warship's rifle fire, but His Majesty's ship was not out of range of the *Resolve*'s four hidden back cannons. Captain Simpson fired off these cannon and gave four direct hits on the forward section of the British devil. But on she came from the back end!

"The British interceptor was an equal match for speed, Mr. Newly," said Mr. O'Rourke, "and they followed the *Resolve* closely with no gain. Those two ships could have run around the ocean till the end of days without catching one another. The British interceptor had one big problem though and that problem was the *Defiant* coming up on his forward right side fast.

"Captain Simpson wanted the warship to turn off from behind him so he could come around on her, but that British captain would have none of that. This captain knew his goose was cooked as he had waited too long to break off and maintain a distance between his ship and the *Resolve*. This captain was now committed to the death, and he was going to take as many of us with him as possible.

"That's a dangerous man back there," Captain Simpson yelled to us all"

"Offer him the back cannon again," he ordered.

"Maybe that will turn him."

"As the four rear back cannon rolled back out, the British captain still did not turn. All four aft back cannon went off, scoring direct hits on the warship's forward section, doing a lot of damage. Still the British warship did not turn.

"This man is no captain!' screamed Captain Simpson.

"He is the devil itself"

"Now the *Defiant* was on the scene, to the right side fast, and what a scene it was. But to Captain Rickle's surprise that British Captain was soon to give Captain Rickle a measure of his countryman's wrath.

"You should have seen it," Mr. O'Rourke said.

The *Resolve* opened up on that oncoming British devil again with her back cannon, and for the third time the British interceptor received a crippling blow. This time the British devil caught fire, but still she did not turn.

Here came Captain Rickle fast on the right side and that devil captain turned hard to port and got sideways. The *Defiant* T boned him almost cutting the British ship in half. One half lay burning on that ships forward deck and the other half lay burning on the *Defiant's deck burning. And the fight was on.*

Now it was hand to hand fighting all over the three ships. That British Captain had got his way if you consider three to one good odds with a lost ship and all you're your crew gone. But in the end we won. We never did find that captain.

"We are going to hear about this from Captain Pike" yelled Captain Simpson,

"I would have hated to have been on that British warship that was chasing me," he said.

"They all were watching those cannon balls I was sending to them as they came flying by tearing up everything knowing another one is on the way.

"Captain Pike always said, 'If you have not had a cannon ball almost take your head off, you don't even have an opinion"

"If all British captains were like that one there, I'd retire from this business." said Captain Simpson"

"Mr. Newly that devil Interceptor had a really strange name too, "said Mr. O'Rourke. She was the HMS Never Again. Now why would you give a ship a name like that?

As it turned out, we would see that strange black Union Jack flag again. It was not just this captain or this ship or this crew. King George himself handpicked the men that sailed under this black flag. Some of these men were falsely accused deserters facing the gallows. Some were falsely disgraced captains that had had their lands and fortunes confiscated by the king. Some did not have a friend in the world or a coin in their pockets. Some had fortunes that hung in the balance.

These men were sworn to the death and were to be paid like princes if they succeeded. Their families were held in prison in the case they did not hold up their bargain with the king. In the event of their deaths, their family was supposed to be released and adorned with riches and land.

In the event of their success, the same applied, but since they were ordered to never come back to England without Captain Pike's head, sailing the *Sovereign of the Seas*, the likelihood of their success and their families' well being was limited. If they left the service, their families were put to the axe in the Tower of London. The king had finally had enough of Captain Pike and had unleashed a new private navy to hunt him down. These men really only had one way to go. Death was their only salvation.

Their mission was to hunt Captain Pike down, kill his crew, and bring him and the treasure back to England.

Now to our reaming business. I yelled over to Captain Pike, "Captain, that first British interceptor is getting really close!"

Captain Pike looked over at me and said, "I know, Mr. Newly." Captain Pike reached in his coat and pulled out his seeing glass. He looked back at the warship and mumbled something.

"Captain, did you say something?" I questioned.

"Mr. Newly, I said that her name is the *Sea Maiden*. Are you deaf?"

I snatched at my glass to see.

Sure enough, her name was the HMS *Sea Maiden*, and she was another fine and great ship. I could feel her pride as she sped through the sea winning the race for speed against us. I could almost feel the dreams of her captain and crew capturing back the *Sovereign of the Seas* for their king, and I felt sorry for them as I surely knew that night they would be sleeping forever with the fish.

Soon enough the warship came upon us, and when we began to take her rifle fire, Captain Pike ordered out all aft, back cannons. I can just imagine the look on the HMS *Sea Maiden's* captain's face when we threw off the cover of the two new aft cannons and the other four rolled out below. The *Sea Maiden's* captain was quick at the sight and rolled over hard to port, but she could not get away. She came around and put her back to us.

"Fire!" screamed Captain Pike.

We blistered her starboard, right stern with cannon fire and knocked out her steering. We had no time to come around and finish her off as the other two warships were coming up fast.

The captain yelled out to Jonesy, "Maintain your heading and speed!

"Next "said the captain as he began looking over his shoulder to the next two warships gaining on us.

"If I were them, Mr. Newly, I'd break off the attack and live to fight another day.

Mr. Newly, always remember that you have to have a ship and survive to tell the tale."

Turned out the two warships would not take the captain's advice, at least not yet, as if their captains could have heard it anyway. The British captains had by now come up with a new plan of attack, not wanting to fall prey to the stern back, cannon. The captain looked at Jonesy and ordered him to begin a slight turn to port, left until we had come about one hundred and eighty degrees. The captain had seen the *Defiant* and the *Resolve* on their intercept course for us, and he wanted to join up with them as he had spent all his surprises. Captain Pike had also been watching the three warships hanging on the horizon, watching this entire scene take place.

"Captain!" the crow's mate yelled down. "Those three warships on the horizon have broken their course and are headed for us.

Within a minute or so, the British warships must have seen the same thing because they broke off their pursuit. One went off to starboard, and one to port until they had completed their turns, joined up, and sailed off in the opposite direction of the now-approaching unknown warships. The British ships stopped long enough to pick up any survivors and to get a towline on the HMS *Sea Maiden*. Then they joined up with the *Defiant*'s two new British friends, and off they went, disappearing on the horizon missing three ships.

Sixteen

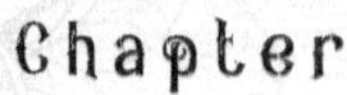

The *Defiant* and the *Resolve* had come up on us, and all ships turned to face the new incoming threat under full sail. The crow's mate screamed down, "Captain, it is those ships we saw earlier under that flag that has the stars with red and white stripes!"

"Ahhh," said Captain Pike, "that's just what we need, the American Navy come to call. Set a course to intercept, as I am done hiding from these ships. If they want a fight, we will offer it today."

All six ships came up on each other under full sail. The Jolly Roger was flying high in the sky on all our three ships, as were the Stars and Stripes on theirs.

"Hold your fire!" screamed the captain. "And signal our other ships to do just that."

There was no way the *Defiant* or the *Resolve* got the signal not to fire in time. Captains Rickle and Simpson with an instinct not to fire just flew by the American ships waving their hats. All ships went between each other head on under full sail, but none offered a fight.

The Americans could read our, "Hold your fire," flag signals between our ships, and one of them came around and reduced to an approach speed. She ran up a white flag of parlay.

Captain Pike ordered, "Mr. Newly, bring us to a stop."

The other two American ships broke off at full sail, one to port, the left and one to starboard, right with the *Resolve* following one and the

Defiant on the other. I looked through my seeing glass at the two American warships as they came around. This was the same three we had met earlier, and they had dismissed us as French merchants. The ship to port coming around was the USS *Enterprise* and the one to starboard was the USS *Intrepid*. It was the USS *Constitution* that was approaching us under the parlay white flag that flew under her Stars and Stripes. They all were just dripping with cannon. The captain told me that he had never seen a ship fly the white flag under their colors before. It was either one or the other.

Captain Rickle later complained that he had to come onto the *Intrepid* while he was still on fire from the fight. "I must have looked like a great threat to them with my tail feathers still burning in the wind, thanks to Captain Simpson. I could almost hear those Americans laughing," he said. Captain Pike and Captain Simpson just burst out laughing.

The American warships out to port, left and right starboard came around on us and also slowed to approach speed. The *Enterprise* came up forward of the *Sovereign* and held steady. The *Intrepid* came up a stern as the *Constitution* came up to rest alongside us. One good, close look at them revealed their teeth, and to everyone's surprise, besides their brisling port and starboard cannon, all the American ships had six forward cannon and four on the back stern. Captain Pike growled at their sight, as he knew he had just been trapped. The American ships could have cared less about the *Resolve* and the *Defiant* circling about, almost as if the Americans knew they had the queen bee and the hive would behave.

A particularly good-looking fellow dressed fine in a bright-blue uniform and a feathered hat walked down off his wheel and leaned over the rail, looking at Captain Pike.

"Captain Pike, I presume," he pronounced.

With a smile he lifted his fine hat off his head with a nod. "I am Captain Chester McCartney, and I am the captain of this ship the USS *Constitution*. We represent the United States of America, and I have someone aboard that wants to meet you. Will you come aboard for dinner?"

Captain Pike looked a bit nervous and uncertain how to answer, so he said nothing in return. He waved his arm in the air above his head and signaled the Defiant and the Resolve to approach. Resolve came to the rear and The Defiant to the front. Both our ships had their forward cannons hatches open and ready.

Captain Pike looked at me and then to Captain McCartney. He gave us both a big smile and said, "Now we have two rats in this trap, and everyone knows that rats in the same trap get along just fine."

The captain of the *Constitution* looked concerned at the sight as Captain Pike said, "I am Captain Pike, and I'd be glad to have your dinner, mate. I'll come aboard in two hours."

I looked over at Captain Pike and asked, "Why two hours, Captain? You could go now."

Captain Pike grabbed up Tamantha's hand and said, "Mr. Newly, everyone knows you have to make an entrance."

Tamantha slapped at his arm, and I kiddingly kicked at him as he turned with a smile, leaving the *Constitution*'s captain holding his hat. I just smiled at Captain McCartney and shook my head.

The two hours went by slowly for everyone except Captain Pike. He acted like he couldn't have cared less about the entire matter. Captain Pike and Tamantha walked out of his cabin, and we were all shocked at what we saw. The captain was dressed in his usual fine captain's apparel, but it looked like he had finally shined up his boots and put new feathers in his hat. It was Tamantha that set everyone back on their heels, and the whistles from our crew began to fly. The captain had produced for her a fine ladies' outfit with all the trimmings, and she was absolutely beautiful.

Captain Pike walked Tamantha up on the wheel deck, and she politely bowed to the *Defiant* and then turned her charm to the *Resolve*. The whistles and cheers were flying from all three of our ships as Captain Pike walked Tamantha down to the awaiting American ding. Her face was as red as the reddest British uniform.

Captain Pike walked by me and said, "Now this is an entrance, Mr. Newly." Tamantha slapped at his arm again, laughing with her red face glowing.

Captain Pike looked at the floating American ding below and looked over at the *Constitution*'s captain and said smugly, "Well, I don't know how your United States does it, but any self-respecting pirate would never make a fine lady crawl down to a ding.

Captain McCartney looked like he had been shot. You could have bought that man for a silver coin. His mouth fell open as he searched for words to reply.

"I'm sorry, Captain Pike. I did not know. How could we have possibly known? How could anyone have known that you would…" He did not get to finish because Captain Pike and Tamantha grabbed up a rope each and swung over to the *Constitution* and landed right in front of her captain.

Captain Pike gave Captain McCartney a big grin and then said, "Permission to come aboard, sir."

Captain McCartney replied with a grin of his own. "Permission granted, and welcome aboard."

Then the captain turned and yelled over at me, "Mr. Newly, are you coming or not?"

I was shocked and so excited. I began to scramble about, not knowing what to do next—comb my hair or brush off my coat or grab a rope and go. I was just a mess of confusion.

"Captain McCartney, I would like to introduce you to this fine lady. Her name is Tamantha."

Captain McCartney took off his fine hat and bowed a great bow. As he stood, he gently took Tamantha's hand and kissed it softly. Then he looked her right in the eye and said, "I have finally sailed the sea long enough to find its true beauty."

I hit the deck of the *Constitution* right next to them all just in time to see the look on Captain Pike's face and the bright-red, all-smiley look on Tamantha's.

Captain McCartney then stepped over to Tamantha's side and gently put his arm in hers, turned, and walked away with her.

Captain McCartney's first officer said, "This way, gentlemen."

"A very good friend of mine is waiting to meet you, Captain Pike," said Captain McCartney. Captain McCartney then looked back at Captain Pike, bringing up the rear, and said, "Captain Pike, this is how a self-respecting American treats a fine lady."

I could see the look on Captain Pike's face, and he was beginning to get mad, so I gave him a nudge with my elbow.

After a minute, and after Captain McCartney had had his fun he turned and said, "Thank you for the honor of letting me hold this beautiful treasure on my arm, Captain Pike, this way please."

Captain Pike and I were looking all about the *Constitution*, and she was a fine, great ship with teeth everywhere. As we made our way up to her Captain's cabin, her crew stood at attention as we passed, and I could see a certain look in their eyes. It was the look of loyalty and pride.

As we approached the cabin's door, it opened smartly. A finely dressed fellow met us and said, "Greetings and welcome. Please do come in. I am James Ripley, and I am the Secretary of the United States Navy, representing the President of the United States of America."

As usual, Captain Pike, with the manners of a shark, shook Mr. Ripley's hand and said, "Nice to meet you, mate. Have you any rum aboard?"

With that said, Captain Pike rushed by him and began looking about the cabin. Mr. Ripley laughed and said, "Why, yes, Captain Pike, I think we can get you some rum."

Tamantha introduced herself, and she received the same bow and kiss on her hand as Captain McCartney had earlier bestowed on her. I introduced myself, and Mr. Ripley shook my hand warmly.

We all stood there in amazement watching Captain Pike walk about the cabin. Captain Pike was completely disinterested in any of us as he looked at everything in that cabin. What was not nailed down, he picked up and studied. Every painting and every award he looked at. Every ribbon and every medal was not safe from his scrutiny. Even Captain McCartney's personal effects were not immune from Captain Pike's study.

Captain Pike turned at looked at us all and said, "You can tell a lot about a captain and his country by his cabin things."

Captain McCartney smiled and told Captain Pike to look around all he wanted and ask any questions he might have.

Mr. Ripley walked up to the captain Pike with a glass in his hand and, offering it to him, said, "Try this, Captain, and let me know how it tastes."

Captain Pike drank the whole thing down and with a big frown said, "My word, Mr. Ripley, I did not think you brought me here to poison me. Me whale's oil would be a better taste than that. Where is the rum, as I got to get that taste out of me mouth?

Everyone just burst out laughing, and then Captain Pike joined in with his.

"You'll have to excuse him, Mr. Ripley. He does not get out much," said Tamantha.

The sun was still high in the sky as our early dinner began to arrive. It was meek offering of dried meats, fresh fish, potatoes, and still no rum. As Captain Pike sat down to the table, he started to get one of his looks, and Tamantha kicked him sternly under the table and gave him a look of her own.

"What a fine table, and thank you for having us," Captain Pike said. With a smile, he grabbed up a piece of the dried meat ignoring the plate in front of him.

"Captain McCartney, would do the honors and say grace?" asked Mr. Ripley. The two men bowed their heads and gave thanks to their maker for their food, and the three of us just froze in our tracks. Captain Pike stopped his sloppy chewing and returned Tamantha's kick under the table back at her, and then she kicked at me. We too bowed our heads until the men had finished their thanks.

Just then, a crewman came through the door with a bottle of rum and handed it to Captain Pike. You just had to figure that if the captain was not going to use his plate, he certainly did not know what a glass was. He opened the bottle and took a big drink, and we all just stared at him in silence. After he got the swallow down, Captain Pike looked at us staring at him, and Tamantha handed him a glass with a sneer.

With a very surprised look, he said, "Oh, sorry about that," as he took the glass and filled it to the brim.

The bottle was almost gone, and the crewman said, "I'm sorry, Captain Pike, but that is all the rum I have for you. I had to get that out of the crew's measure."

Captain Pike placed the full glass of rum on the table and said angrily, "What did you say, mate? Your crew is out of rum, and you give me their last?" He stormed out the cabin door.

Mr. Ripley jumped to his feet, as did Captain McCartney. The crewman was horrified.

We all ran out the door after the captain as he walked over to the side and yelled over to Jonesy and said, "Jonesy, send over fifteen cases of rum to this ship, fifteen to the *Enterprise*, and fifteen to the *Intrepid*. Their crew is out of rum, and they have offered their last to me. No wonder they are so touchy and high strung."

With that, Captain Pike walked back down and back into Captain McCartney's cabin. Jonesy yelled, "Fetch the rum!"

Mr. Ripley walked up to Tamantha and me and said, "That's a very interesting captain you have there. Is he always like this?"

I again just shook my head and said, "Sir, you don't know the half of it."

We all went back down to Captain McCartney's cabin, and there we found Captain Pike with his fine glass of rum, chewing sloppily on a piece of dried meat, looking intently at the paintings on the cabin's walls.

"What is this one?" questioned the captain.

Captain McCartney came over and put his hand on the captain's shoulder and said proudly, "All these paintings in this group are scenes from our revolution against the king."

Captain Pike replied, "It looks like you were getting overrun here," pointing to another painting."

"Yes," replied Captain McCartney. "We lost that battle with many a men dead."

Captain Pike just stared at the paintings, and then he finally asked, "Who is this fellow here?"

Mr. Ripley came up and said, "Oh, you would have liked that fellow, Captain. He was the man that commanded our forces against the British, and he was our first president.

"I hate the King's Navy. I can't imagine his army being any better. They are nothing but finely dressed rats."

The same crewman as before knocked on the cabin door, and as he entered, Captain Pike spotted the two bottles of rum he was carrying. With a big smile, the crewman said, "Here is more rum for you, Captain Pike, courtesy of the *Sovereign of the Seas*."

The captain looked over at me and said, "Mr. Newly, order the crew to stand down and commence with their festivities. By now they need a good time. These fine fellows here are no threat to us. Tell them all to stand down."

With that, Captain McCartney said, "Well, it is against regulations, but I am going to order the same for my ships." Captain McCartney walked out of the cabin and barked his order at his first officer and then returned with a smile. We could hear all the Americans on all three ships cheer as they got the order. It was not long before the music and good time spread from ship to ship as the sun went down.

Captain Pike continued his questions and asked, "What about this painting here? What is this parchment about?"

Captain McCartney replied, "That is the Constitution of the United States and our law that was forged with the blood of our people escaping from the cruelty and tyranny of King George. This ship was named in respect for it."

"What about you, Captain Pike?" Mr. Ripley asked.

"Yes, Captain Pike, what is your story?" asked Captain McCartney.

"You're a pretty famous fellow in our country, as your stories have come ashore," said Mr. Ripley. "You don't seem like the real pirates we hunt, as you do not rob ships or terrorize men. What is it you are doing out here on the sea besides wreaking havoc on the British Navy, which, by the way, our president has no problem with? How did you and your ships learn to fight like you do? We sat off and watched your three ships destroy one half of a British Naval Task Force and send the other half running for their lives. We have heard stories of a great treasure you carry, and we have come to meet you and to hear the story."

Captain Pike had a big grin on his face as he looked the men over carefully. Captain McCartney asked, "What are you looking at, Captain Pike?"

"I was just looking the two of you over to make sure you are worthy of the tale," Captain Pike explained. "Put a log on that fire and hand me the rum, and I'll tell you."

Tamantha and I just rolled our eyes and excused ourselves to return to the *Sovereign,* as we knew this was going to take awhile. I heard the captain say as I walked out the door, "Do you mates believe in maidens of the sea?" and I closed the cabin door smiling.

I awoke the next morning, and Captain Pike was still on board the *Constitution*. I swung over with a sack in my hand, carrying things the captain had told me last night to bring if he was not aboard in the morning. I walked into Captain McCartney's cabin, and I chuckled at the scene before me. Captain Pike was just finishing up the story with the whale killing ships, and he stopped talking with a swig of rum. Captain McCartney and Mr. Ripley were listening carefully. They, too, had begun to drink the captain's rum, and there were several bottles lying about.

"So, Captain Pike," asked Captain McCartney, "do you really expect us to believe in sea witches and maps of the sea and sea-maidens and a treasure that cannot possibly exist? You are a madman, Captain, but I really like you," he said.

I jumped in and said, "Oh, yes, they do exist." I flung the sack on the table. "Show them, Captain, so they may see."

"Calm down, Mr. Newly. Don't get yourself all worked up," said the captain.

"If these fine gentlemen who dismiss me as a loon want to see the proof you have brought over, they will ask."

With that, the captain sat back in his seat with Captain McCartney and Mr. Ripley sitting with their mouths open.

In a second, both men jumped up and said in a choir, "Let's see it."

"Well, I'm glad you asked." Mr. Ripley's and Captain McCartney's eyes were as big as the dinner plates as the captain reached in the sack and produced the brightly glowing orb. "This be the Oracle of Sea's orb, and ain't she a beaut?"

The two men were fascinated at its sight and studied it closely.

Then Captain Pike reached into his coat and pulled out the map of the sea. Flinging the rolled-up parchment onto the table, he said, "This, mates, be the map of the sea," and Mr. Ripley and Captain McCartney jumped back in alarm.

"Easy, mates, just don't touch it, and the witch will leave you be," the captain said. Captain Pike rolled open the map, and I could see the horror on Mr. Ripley and Captain McCartney's faces as Captain Pike showed them the faces upon it squirming about in their pain.

Then Captain Pike called to all to follow him on deck, and he pointed. "Look, mates, there be me whales." And with a whistle, the four giant killer whales came up to the *Constitution*. Captain McCartney and Mr. Ripley could not believe their eyes and neither could the *Constitution*'s crew as the whales showed their affection for Captain Pike.

"Those really are your whales, aren't they, Captain Pike?" Mr. Ripley asked.

"Yep," responded the captain. "It is a good thing your fine crew had not done me any harm because I don't think your ships would have survived me whale's wrath," warned Captain Pike.

Captain Pike again whistled and called the wolves. "There be me wolves too," he said. The four giant ice wolves ran over to the side of the *Sovereign*, and they began to wag their giant white tails at the sight of Captain Pike. Standing on their back legs with their gigantic paws on the railing, those wolves must have stood eight feet tall if it were an inch.

"They would have had you and your crew for lunch if you had harmed me," gloated Captain Pike.

The captain then called for Tamantha, and she came out of his cabin with a big smile. "Tamantha, would you please show these fine gentlemen what a maiden of the sea looks like? They seem to be having their doubts about my tale, so I thought I show them yours," the captain said. With that, Tamantha dove off the side of the *Sovereign* beneath the waves. All ran to the side of the *Constitution* to see, and when she came up, you could have bought the whole ship for a piece of eight.

Captain McCartney, Mr. Ripley, and their crew gasped in wonder as she broke the surface with her fine, beautiful tail. The crew of the *Constitution* and the ones that could see from the *Enterprise* and the *Intrepid* were frozen in their tracks with amazement. None could speak a word.

Mr. Ripley looked over at Captain McCartney and said, "Now, how in this world am I supposed to go back to the president and tell him this? I will lose my appointment, and you will lose your command."

Captain Pike reached again into the sack and picked out a bundle that was all tied up, and he tossed it over to Mr. Ripley and said, "After you tell him the tale, give this to your president and instruct him to buy some rum for his crew with it. Let's go, Mr. Newly." And we swung away.

We hit the deck of the *Sovereign* and looked back upon the Americans with their mouths wide open, holding twenty or so huge gems.

"Get us under way, Mr. Newly," ordered the captain."

As we moved away, Captain McCartney yelled over, "I like your flag! It is better than that French one you were hiding behind at our last encounter!"

Captain Pike responded, "As do I yours, mate. As do I yours. Consider this an accord."

Captain Pike yelled, "Set a course for Anegada, and signal the other ships to follow. We need to find out what has happened to my ships we were to meet and what has happened to me pigeon. If anyone on that cursed island has harmed me pigeon, I'll burn it to the ground."

Chapter

Seventeen

It did not take us long to arrive off the coast of Anegada, another scourge of the Caribbean. Anegada had a large harbor right in the center of it that was famous as a safe haven for ships as the storms raked the Caribbean in the summer. Anegada was also infamous because of its completely lawless population that was far worse than Tortola with pirates, cutthroats, and thieves. The trouble with the harbor of Anegada was that there was only one way in and one way out, and Captain Pike knew it.

There was only a narrow opening maybe two ships wide to come and go. Turns out what we should have done were sail around the island to have a better look, but we did not, and that was a mistake.

"Mr. Newly," ordered the captain, "signal the other ships to come to quarters and follow us around."

The alarm bells rang out on all ships as the *Sovereign* sailed by the entrance to the harbor. The captain, having a better look with his seeing glass, decided there was no threat, and we came around easy to port, left, in a circle, the *Defiant* and the *Resolve* following closely behind. Captain Pike did not see anything that attracted his attention, so we came through the narrow entrance into the harbor's middle section with all cannon to ready,

Captain Pike looked nervously around with his glass and ordered, "Drop those anchors, mates, and prepare to go ashore." As soon as our anchors hit the sand bottom, a signal flare was fired off from ashore, and we all stood with a stare as it went into the sky and made its way slowly back down to the sea.

Captain Pike cussed and screamed out, "This is a trap! Sound the station's bell. Get them anchors up and get us under way!"Just at that moment, four or five British shore cannons were rolled out of their hiding and fired off together a loud warning volley. The cannon balls went over our three ships and splashed into the harbor on our starboard, right side. A British warship came up and blocked the entrance to the harbor, blocking any escape we might have even considered taking. To make things worse, that ship flew that black British Union Jack flag. As we watched, at least thirty or more British shore cannons came out of their hiding, along with at least two hundred redcoats with rifles.

Captain Pike yelled out, "They have us now, mates! Get yourselves mean like I told you before!"

For just a minute, all was silent, and then a real nasty and snooty British officer appeared out of one of the town buildings and began to scream orders at us about surrender and something about us not standing a chance. Captain Pike cursed at him, saying something about his mother, and the British shore batteries opened up on us again.

We were taking their fire and receiving a lot of damage. If their cannons were not bad enough, we could not stick our heads up because of the rifle fire.

Captain Pike screamed out, "Give them a taste of ours!"

We began to return their fire. The ships were lined up in a row, and the town completely surrounded us except for the narrow entrance into the harbor. All of our ships began to lay down nasty broadsides from both their port and starboard cannons. The *Sovereign* was up in front so she could also use her forward cannon. We were really tearing the British up, but there were just too many of them and not enough of us.

We were like fish in a barrel, but just like that, the British stopped firing on us. I looked over my shoulder, and here came Captain Pike holding the orb over his head. Its glow was so bright, the brightest I had ever seen of it yet; it lit the scene like another sun. The British seemed to be stunned at the sight and froze to get a look. Captain Pike whistled to the whales, and he just looked at the British warship blocking our path out. The four giants, seeming to know the captain's thoughts, turned and ran up on the warship as fast as they could swim and hit it a center,amidships. I always knew that the whales were capable of destroying a ship, but as it turned out, I just had no idea. The warship was hit by the whale's entire wrath, sending it many yards sideways before breaking her in half and sending its crew screaming into the sea.

Captain Pike looked to the orb, squinting at its light, and he called out, "Triton, spare me ships so we can fight another day."

The British shore batteries opened up on us again. Just like that, the shore batteries and rifle stopped their assault on us once again, and when we looked upon them, they all seemed to be pointing to the eastern sky. We all looked about and saw something coming up fast and low to the sea.

Whatever it was, it was really large. Tamantha said, "My God, Triton has sent his Dugan."

Captain Pike replied, "What on this earth is a Dugan?"

Tamantha replied, "It is a giant undersea dragon that can swim in the sea or fly in the air, and here it comes. Keep your head down now."

As soon as she got those words out, the monster came by right over us, leaving the sea awash behind it. When it came over us, our ships were blown about like a great storm was upon us. The British went into frenzy, and that snooty officer screamed at them to hold. The Dugan came around and came upon us, flapping its mighty wings above us at a hover. It was so huge it almost blackened the sky above us. It was hard to stand in the wind it produced from the flapping of its great wings.

The Dugan reminded me of the giant bat in the cave, but it was two hundred times larger; however it smelled just as bad if not worse. It looked about at the shoreline as if to set it sights on the British guns. The Dugan snarled and let out a scream that would have sent any man running for his life. A great drool ran from its mouth, and the nasty, sticking mess fell about our ships and crew.

The orb remained glowing brightly on the deck of the *Sovereign*, and she almost looked like she was afire. All four whales jumped out of the sea and sounded their calls. To my surprise, the great dragon returned the whale's calls.

Then that foolish British officer ordered his men to fire on the d Dugan, and that was the last order that fellow's men would ever hear. The Dugan was hit so many times it seemed to twitch and squirm in the air.

The mighty dragon let out a scream that made the sea witch's scream seem small as it took off and began its run.

The Dugan took off from its hover above us and set off across the sea. The British all yelled with joy as if they had run the beast off with their cannons. Their laughter soon could no longer be heard as the Dugan made its turn coming back around fast. We all watched in amazement as it came on shore and the British fools that were upon it.

The dragon spit a great stream of blue fire from its huge mouth. The Dugan's fire looked to be made from the same substance that the blue fireballs the guardian sea-maiden had flung at us. It crackled and spit with its lightning as it shot out of the Dugan's mouth at a great pressure.

It only took a minute for the dragon to circle around the harbor and burn a path of destruction several hundred feet wide, and everything was just gone. The British, the buildings, and every other fool in the path were just gone. The Dugan came back up on us at a hover and let out a scream as it looked us over carefully. It touched its face to the water, and the whales came up and scratched upon it. Then it was gone as quickly as it had come across the sea, disappearing on the horizon.

"Mr. Newly, did you order up a big enough dragon there, did you?" asked the Captain. I could not speak.

For several hours, the captains looked over the damages that had been done to their ships. All crew began the repairs the best they could with what they had to work with. All knew the damage taken was great and would have to be taken ashore to complete the repairs. None of our ships were worthy of what the sea had to offer.

There were no signs of hostile actions on the island, as the redcoats were all but destroyed. We watched as the natives of the island came out slowly and picked around the rubble and the bodies of the British soldiers, claiming anything they could find. Captain Pike laughed and yelled to them, "Get all you can from that devil King George and his mates!"

They cheered and waved in delight.

The captain then yelled over to Captains Simpson and Rickle and asked if they were ready to go ashore. Captain Simpson answered and said, "I'm ready, but my crew needs another hour to get this drool off the deck."

Captain Rickle answered over and said, "Same here, Captain Pike. I'm up to the top of my boots in it, and what about the smell of it?"

"Nice pet you got there"

Captain Pike laughed hard and said back, "Prepare your away crews, and meet me ashore."

Within the hour, all three ships sent off ten-man teams of heavily armed men in dings, and we met on the shore of the island. The captain had left Tamantha and two of the wolves back on the *Sovereign*. Klondike and Kodiak went with us ashore.

In general, the population of the island was glad to see us, the ones that were not were scared to death. All of them had heard the tales about us from Tortola, and now we showed here up sporting a dragon. The British Navy was hated along all the Caribbean islands, as they treated the people like they were an infestation of the land that King George had claimed for himself. Hangings and beating were common and carried out for the smallest of offenses. Captain Pike told me that it was much better to be feared than to be hated.

"Fear, Mr. Newly, will lead to a common respect and a common ground. Hatred will lead to war."

As we began to walk across the vast destruction, the away teams spread out with pistols drawn. Every once in a while we would catch sight of a redcoat, and when they saw us, they would run for their lives. We crossed over the burn and into what was the beginning of what was left of the town. One little, old toothless fellow ran up to Captain Simpson and petted at him and thanked him for saving him from the British devils.

As usual, the first tavern we came to, Captain Pike got a big smile on his face. The tavern's barkeep was even standing outside waving to us and inviting us in.

"Captain Simpson!" yelled over Captain Pike, "take your team to the south, and we will meet up on the other side of the island. Captain Rickle, you do the same to the north, and we will go down the middle."

As soon as the two teams were gone, Captain Pike said, "Well, Mr. Newly, I think we better go in here and see if we can wash the taste of that Dugan out of our mouths. You two men stay here and guard the front, and you two men go around back, and the rest of you come with me," ordered the captain.

There were only a few people in the tavern, and as we walked in, they walked out quickly. The barkeep looked at us and the two giant wolves and said, "Nice pets you have there, mates. Do you think they're big enough?"

We all just stood there looking at him, waiting to see what Captain Pike would offer back.

"I take it they must have been out of the small ones," the keep said.

"You must be the fellows causing all the ruckus around here, but no matter, as I am here to see what you gents are having to drink today."

Captain Pike replied, "Give me men here a drink of rum, and I'll have a bottle. I'll also have some information if you're obliged to give it to me."

"And if I'm not obliged, Captain?"

Captain Pike smiled back as he reached in his pocket and produced a fine gold coin and spun it on the counter.

"I think this should cover the rum, a drink for you, and the information."

"I believe you are right about that, Captain," the keep said, as he turned to get the rum.

"How long has the British Navy been here? How many more are they?" asked Captain Pike.

"The British Navy got here right before the hurricane came through, and I think you might have just about killed them all."

"Where are their ships?"

"There must be a dozen or more of them that are hidden in a cove on the other side of the island."

Captain Pike looked over at me and poured some of his bottle in my glass, and he began to laugh. "Mr. Newly, King George has got to be running a little low on men and ships by now, and I'll bet he wants you really badly. I'll bet His Majesty probably wants you worse than the sea witch does."

"Have you seen some folks by the name of Lady Jane or John Adams around these parts?" asked the captain. "They are a married up couple, and she is a good looker."

"No, can't say I have."

"How about a tall Italian fellow by the name of Thomas Bongeorno? He's about my height with a fine, redheaded lass by the name of Joedea, as they are married up too."

"Nope, Captain. I ain't seen them around here."

Not getting the answers, he wanted I could see the captain's friendly mood was beginning to change for the worse. "You sure about that, Keep? You sure you ain't seen them?"

The keep was really getting nervous and began to fidget around and would no longer look Captain Pike in the eye. The captain knew the barkeep was lying, and he was getting madder by each minute and with each lie. The captain slowly opened his coat and pulled out his pistol and laid it on the counter.

The keep's eyes got big as Captain Pike snarled at him and said, "Well now, mate, I'll bet you have seen me pigeon, now haven't you, as those folks I was just asking about would have been carrying it about in a cage." The wolves looked at the keep and began to growl, and Captain Pike yelled, "Don't worry, mate. I will have shot you dead by the time they get around to eating you. Now, you had better answer me straight. Where are me crew and me ships, and where be me pigeon?"

The barkeep slowly backed away, yelling, "I told you I ain't seen nothing!"

Just as the keep said those words, three doors inside the tavern exploded open, and out poured the British. There must have been twenty-five of them. They had been hidden in the rooms behind the doors, listening and waiting, and they came out quickly with rifle, bayonets, and pistols pointing right at us. We had drawn up all our pistols, and our guards outside came rushing in from the front and back, and there we all stood in a stare down.

Out through one of the doors came a nasty British officer that was full of himself, and he said, "Well, Captain Pike, now what were you saying about my mother?" Right behind him came out our mates, Captain Bongeorno, Joedea, Captain Adams, and Lady Jane with pistols to their heads, and they were not in good shape at all.

They all seemed to have been beaten badly, and Captain Pike snarled and then said, "So it is you? And I see you managed to save your derriere while the rest of your men perished following your poorly contrived orders. Is this not that the way it always is with you fine, better-than-everyone-else people? You would walk, and probably did, across the bodies of your men to save yourself after your fine, educated plans took a turn for the worse."

"This is because you see yourself as one that must survive because you are the smartest of all, even though your plans have killed your crew, and now you blame your failure on good intensions that have gone bad. You are nothing but a finely dressed rat that feeds on the blood of its crew, and you disgust me," said the captain.

The British crew began to look about at each other, as they knew Captain Pike spoke the truth. The British commander went crazy with rage and ordered his men to fire on us and to kill the prisoners, but they did not.

"I said fire!" he screamed, but his men did not. The now well-dressed wild man tried to grab a rifle from one of his men, and the crewman pushed him to the ground. With that, the British crew stood down from their arms and scowled at their soon-to-be former commander scurrying about on the floor to get back to his feet.

He jumped up and ran at Captain Pike, and the captain just moved to the side as he went by grabbing at the air. As he went by, Captain Pike grabbed him by the back of his head of hair and spun him, slamming his face onto the countertop, breaking his nose.

Captain Pike, holding the British rat—I mean British commander's— face down on the counter, spoke quietly to him and said, "Don't worry, mate. I'm not going to kill you. As a matter of fact, I am going to go one better. I'm going to make sure you live forever."

With that, Captain Pike grabbed him up straight and reached in his own coat, pulling out the map of the sea. Captain Pike stuck the map into the British commander's shirt and pushed him away.

"Is that it, pirate? Is that all you have?" scoffed the commander as he pulled the map out of shirt and threw it at Captain Pike.

"I thought you would try to hang me not beat me to death with a soft parchment."

Captain Pike said only two words in reply, "Not quite," and the Witch was upon the British dog.

She came fast, but we could not see her. The sea witch's banshee, deafening scream filled the room, seeming to circle about us, darting in and out in a wind. Just like the captain had told me, the man began to shake wildly and screamed the scream of a thousand screams. He looked about at everyone in a horror as he began to boil from the inside out.

It looked like boiling lava began to run out of his eyes and his ears and his nose. We all watched as the man was consumed by the fire, growing smaller and smaller in substance. His head was the last thing to go as he melted away to the witch screaming in agony. There was no heat from the flames, and in the end, all that was left of him were ashes that drifted away in the breeze. Not even a mark was left on the tavern's floor. The sea witch laughed with her nasty, unearthly cackle as she retreated with her new prize. Captain Pike picked up the map and rolled it open, and there was the commander's face fading onto it, squirming about in his new eternal agony.

Captain Pike looked over at the barkeep slinking in the corner of the tavern and said, "Ain't seen me crew, haven't you?" The captain walked over to the keep and said, "I'll have me coin back, you lying dog, and the rum was on you this time."

The barkeep handed the gold coin back to the captain and said, "They made me do it, Captain. They made me."

One of the British crew said, "We made him do it all right, Captain. We made him do it for a coin."

Captain Pike looked back at the keep and said, "That will be the last lie you tell in this life."

Captain Pike pulled his pistol and shot him dead on the spot.

Captain Pike exclaimed,

"I would give me treasure to put every man to the test of the map, as I know for sure the Sea Witch would be busy enough to leave good men alone! This fine British rat here on me map was claimed justifiably, and there are many more of his breeding. We will all see sooner or later how that has worked out for them! The map of the sea awaits them all!"

To our surprise, one of the British crew came up and said, "Captain Pike, I am Dennis Bride, and I will hold your map as I need to test myself." Captain Pike smiled and handed the map to him. Nothing at all happened to that fellow, which set everyone's minds on fire with thought.

Captain Pike looked at all of us and said, "That is the bravest man I have ever met. Dennis Bride, can you read and write?" asked the captain.

"Aye, sir," answered Dennis Bride.

Then with a big smile, the captain looked at me and said, "Well, there you have it, Mr. Newly. I finally found your replacement." Everyone laughed hard, except me of course.

"All you men here have now been signed on to me crew if you want the position, and a full measure will be applied in your name," said the captain.

The British crew smiled, and they all agreed with hats in the air.

Captain Adams came up and said, "We sure are glad to see you, Captain."

"That makes four of us, Captain," said Captain Bongeorno.

"We all heard the ruckus, and we knew it was you come to call, Captain. I laughed at the British commander and told him he was for sure a dead man."

Captain Pike looked over at Dennis Bride and said, "Mr. Bride, you are the new first officer of whatever ship Captain Adams commands, and I want you to take your redcoats down to the beach and inform your former fellow shipmates guarding their king's warships that they can either join us or meet their maker."

"Aye, Captain," said Mr. Bride, and he and his team left quickly.

"What on this earth did we just see here, Captain Pike?" Lady Jane asked in a horror.

Joedea joined in and said, "Yes, what the world do you have there in your coat, Captain Pike? That man was consumed right before our eyes by something from Hades itself."

The captain just smiled and said, "It is a long story, gals, and you will come to understand it all later."

"Will you also tell us about where you got these fury monsters, Captain?" asked Captain Bongeorno.

The captain, ignoring the questions, ordered, "I want you all to get to your ships and stand by to get under way."

"Captain Pike, you do not know, but all our crew has been hung by that British devil there, and there are only us four," said Captain Adams.

With disregard for the loss of the men, the captain said, "Where is me pigeon?"

"Captain, your precious pigeon is safe on our ship, if someone has not made a meal of it yet. But with its smell, I cannot see that would ever happen," replied Joedea.

Captain Pike put a huge smile on his face and said, "Well, let's get to it, mate. Where is your ship? I want me pigeon back."

"The two ships are this way, Captain, down where your new redcoat friends just went," said Captain Adams.

Captain Pike hesitated for a second and said, "I hope I did not discount a certain possibility, mates. I think we better get a double to our step. If Captain Simpson and Captain Rickle find our redcoats before we get there, no telling how the matter will turn out."

During the trip down to the beach, we were all waiting to hear the sound of rifle fire, but we did not. When we came upon the scene, there was Captain Rickle and Captain Simpson with all the redcoats gathered up in a line with rifles and pistols pointing at them.

"Captain Pike, I would have sent these red coats to their maker but they put up no fight and this one here insisted he and his men were members of your crew, acting upon your orders," said Captain Simpson.

Captain Pike said, "And members of your crew too now Simpson."

Mr. Bride," asked the captain, "I take it that your fellow countrymen here have come to an agreement to join me crew because they ain't dead?"

"Yes, said Captain Pike." "These men here are all sick of the king and his ways."

"Captain Adams, get to your ship, and, Captain Bongeorno, get to yours. These new crew are yours, and you had better make the best of them, or I'll put your women in command."

Joedea and the Lady Jane just laughed and Joedea said, "We will be in command by midnight anyway, Captain."

Captain Pike just laughed and said, "As I suspected, ladies, as I suspected."

"Where is me pigeon?" demanded Captain Pike.

"Take it easy, Captain. I'll bring the retch," answered Joedea. She took off in a trot and boarded one of the ships. Within minutes, she returned with the cage and its feathered inhabitant. Captain Pike was delighted at the sight. We were all amazed as the captain talked and petted at the scraggly old pigeon, and no one dared to say a word.

"Captain Adams, Captain Bongeorno, we are going back to our ships and sail them around here for repairs. I want you and your new crew to strip everything you can off those British warships, and burn what's left. We will be here for two days, and I want all the ships completely repaired and seaworthy. I have had enough of this place, and we still have another two keys along with some treasure to find," ordered the captain.

"Aye, Captain," they replied.

"And might we be asking about these keys and treasure you're talking about there, Captain," asked Captain Adams.

Captain Pike just ignored him and walked away.

"Well then," said Captain Adams. "I'll take that as a no then."

Captain Rickle burst out laughing.

On our way back to our ships, Captain Rickle said, "Captain Pike, if you keep going this course, you are going to have your own British Navy, and King George will be raiding you." We all laughed hard.

Reaching the dings still floating in the harbor, our ships were a good sight to us all. The whales also were a welcome sight. They seemed to have been waiting for us and also were very glad to see us. Boarding our ships, we were all in a particularly fine mood and Captain Pike said, "Well, mates, I guess we have cheated death again. Let's get under way before it catches us."

As we sailed back through the harbor's narrow entrance, the natives of the island waved good-bye to us with big smiles.

"Don't let it go to your head, Mr. Newly, as they are probably just glad to see us gone," said the captain.

"I don't know, Captain. As you know, I make friends wherever I go," I replied.

"You certainly do, Mr. Newly, you certainly do."

The *Sovereign*, the *Defiant*, and the *Resolve* were completely repaired in three days—a day longer than the captain wanted to stay, and we all heard about that. Two ships Captain Bongeorno and Adams still remained for minor repairs. Finally our three ships sailed out past the reef to keep an eye out waiting for Captain Bongeorno and Captain Adams to join us. We could see the smoke rising from King George's burning fleet

"A shame, Mr. Newly," said the captain. "I know the Americans could have put those ships to good use."

Two days later and to the captains aggravation from around the reef here came what looked like two brand new Interceptors flying the Jolly Roger high on their masts. As the Interceptors came up on us, we could see Joedea and Captain Bongeorno at the helm of one and Lady Jane and Captain Adams at the helm of the other. Captain Adam's fine new Interceptor's name was the HMS *Dreadnought* and Captain Bongeorno was the HMS *Valiant.*

As Captain Adams came alongside us, he yelled over and said, "Sorry it took so long. These new Red Coats are having a problem listening to plain English and following orders except for one. He says he is my first mate. Imagine that?

Captain Pike smiled and yelled back, "I'm taking the cost of the time out of your measure. Get some cannons forward and back on those dog ships you are rowing."

"Aye, Captain. They are already there." He yelled back.

"Your naps are getting too long, Captain Pike" said Captain Adams as he broke off into the lead with his big smile on his face.

Captain Bongeorno was right on his heels.

"Come around to three hundred and twenty degrees, Jonesy," Captain Pike ordered. "Let's see if the children will follow us sailing their new toys."

I was shocked, but I actually saw Jonesy smile as he said, "Aye, Captain. Three hundred and twenty." And all five ships were gone from Anegada hard under way.

"It's two days back to Samana Cay, Mr. Newly," said the captain. "We will meet up with our skeleton crews and man those four British warships. Then we're going for the next key. What does it say here, Mr. Newly? What is the name of this island?"

I looked the bright shining point on the map and said, "Thirteen Skulls, Captain, it says the Island of Thirteen Skulls."

The captain did not say a word.

Chapter

Eighteen

Just like the Captain said, two days later we arrived off Samana Cay. It turned out that our four British interceptors hiding off Samana Cay and waiting for crews to man them had indeed been discovered. The American Navy had come across them on their patrol and, thinking they were pirates, had come up to secure them. Once the Americans realized the ships belonged to Captain Pike, they attempted to move off, but it was too late for them all. The British Navy had showed up in force looking for their lost ships.

The Americans had won their freedom and independence from the king, but the tensions between them were still high.

The way I heard it was that the British Navy had showed up and accused the Americans of conspiring with pirates to steal their ships. I heard that the negotiations quickly went downhill from there.

When we arrived on the scene, the Americans were badly outnumbered and under heavy fire by the British Navy. Our hidden interceptors, still undercrewed, were still at an anchor off the reef and were not under way. There were fifteen British warships attacking the Americans, who were long sworn enemies of each other. All the British Navy needed was an excuse to attack them, and they had that excuse. The Americans were completely on the defensive and could not bring a fight. They were running for their lives.

Captain Pike yelled, "Mr. Newly, have the flagman signal all ships to get their colors up and engage those well-dressed rats of the sea."

This is a great part of the tale, mates, so listen closely.

I watched the entire scene through my glass.

Captain Simpson and Captain Adams broke off and picked out the five British devils running down the USS *Enterprise*. Captain Rickle and Captain Bongeorno picked out the five chasing the USS *Intrepid*. Captain Pike had his eye on the rest that were chasing after the USS *Constitution*. The whales were having no trouble at all keeping up with us as we picked up our speed. They seemed to know exactly what was happening as the station's bells rang loud, and they also broke off their formation. One of them went off with the *Defiant* and Captain Bongeorno ship and one of them with the *Resolve* and Captain Adam's ship. The other two whales stayed with us,. All the whales took off, leaving all our ships completely behind, and began attacking the British warships.

Captains Simpson and Adams came up and passed the last of the five British warships that were chasing the *Intrepid*. Their whale escort had already overtaken; it and she was broken in half and sinking. Captain Simpson came up on the fourth British warship in the line, and with his forward cannon, he blew the stern of it, sending His Majesty's ship off without steering and burning badly. Captain Adams came up on the third and did the same.

The British Navy, in this wolf pack, was completely unnerved by the whole situation. They had one ship sunk; two disabled, burning badly; and now the odds were different. They had two interceptors left out of five with a giant killer whale bearing down on them along with two pirate ships with all forward cannon to bear. Then they had to worry about the USS *Intrepid* coming around, and the way she was turning, anyone could tell she was tired of running. She was coming to the fight. The two remaining British warships came around hard to starboard and were gone for the horizon.

It was pretty much the same case for Captains Rickle and Bongeorno as their whale got one of the interceptors, and they each got another with their forward cannon, sending the other two fine representatives of King George's navy sailing for their lives for the horizon.

Our two whales each got one of His Majesty's finest, and we got one. The USS *Constitution* had come around fast and hungry and got another of the interceptors for herself, leaving the last running for her crew's life. Out of fifteen British warships, only a third got away clean, and that was only because we showed no interest to pursue them, and they all knew it.

The remaining wounded British warships floundered in the sea as we each approached them for the kill.

Captain Pike screamed out, "Signal all ships to secure their cannon, and leave them be! I want them all back in King George's court telling this tale."

All ships broke off their attacks and just flew by the British devils, leaving them all with a pause as to why their lives had been spared.

Just off shore from Samana Cay, all our ships and the Americans came up slowly on each other, and the USS *Constitution* again came alongside the *Sovereign of the Seas.* With a huge smile on his face, Captain McCartney yelled over, "Well, Captain Pike, it is good to see you again. I am certainly glad I was able to pull your tail feathers out of the fire this day."

Then he yelled over, "You are a very strange man, Captain Pike. What in heaven has created a man like you and your mission in this life? You are a killer of men but only the ones that deserve their fate. We all just saw you spare the disabled British warships, and I wonder why. You call yourself a pirate, but you really are not one at all. You sail these seas with some sort of rule that escapes us all. You sail under a flag that dismisses your beliefs and your behavior, and a pirate you truly are not. Who are you really, Captain Pike?"

Captain Pike answered with a smile, "I am the same man as you, Captain McCartney. Despite who you think you are, you are not. You think yourself to be a fine officer of the American Navy, but in fact you are just a pirate with ethics as am I. You serve a clan under a fine flag that is moral and just in a great sea of corruption. The difference between us, Captain McCartney, is that you have a great land to return to, and I, on the other hand, do not. Me and my fine crew have only the sea."

Captain McCartney yelled back, "Captain Pike, I would like to offer you and your fine crew a country that you can belong to. I have an invitation from the president of our United States to join us and become part of our new country. I was sent back here by the president to find you and invite you to a grand parlay to discuss just that. Unfortunately for King George, his ships came upon us and accused us of aiding his enemies."

"Well, I don't know about all of that, Captain McCartney, but I hope you will take these fine British interceptors and give them to your president so I don't have to burn them, as I really do not have enough crew to man them properly."

"Come on, Captain. At least hear what the man has to say."

"Bring him to me on the sea." Tell your president I have something I wish to show him. How long will it take for you to return?"

"Seven days if the weather holds and we have a good wind! However, I cannot tell you the president will come."

"Very well, Captain McCartney. We will sit here for seven days and await your return. On the eighth morning, we will be gone, and after that, you, my friend, will be on your own."

"Unless my tail feathers get in the fire again" smiled back the captain.

"As you wish, Captain. I will return in seven days with or without the president." With that, the Americans gleefully took Captain Pike's gift of the four British interceptors and headed home.

As we watched the Americans sail away, Captain Simpson said, "I don't know, Captain. Seven days is a long time to sit here like ducks waiting for the hunters to come."

"Captain Adams and Captain Bongeorno, take your ships out to the horizon and commence a patrol of the area," ordered Captain Pike. "Stay together, and at the first sign of trouble, get back here with a warning."

"Aye, sir," said the two captains, and shortly thereafter both ships were under way.

"We have seven days to kill, so we might just make the best of it. Get to fixing and cleaning, as we may have a president coming to call," ordered Captain Pike. "Mr. Newly, send four dings ashore and see what the natives have to trade."

Samana Cay was a small island that was surrounded by a reef. The native population was a few hundred, and all seemed friendly enough and appeared to welcome our away team with their smiles, speaking the King's English. The dings returned in a few hours and were loaded up with barrels of fresh water, fresh meat, and fruit. One of the away crew had heard of

Captain Pike's liking for eggs and bacon, and his ding carried six cages with two chickens each, and they were already laying eggs. Captain Pike smiled big at the sight, and then the mate, with a big smile of his own, showed off fifty or so pounds of fresh salt-cured bacon.

Like one ding was trying to outdo the other, a mate yelled up to Captain Pike and said, "Look here, Captain!" With his big smile, the mate threw off the large tarp he had hiding his cargo and showed off that his ding was completely full with bottles and barrels of fine island rum. Captain Pike looked at me and let out a big laugh.

The first day went by quickly with all the work that was badly needed. The crow's mates kept their eyes on the horizon, but the only ships to be seen were Captain Bongeorno and Captain Adams's. We all had noticed a lot of activity in the sea with the huge fish population. The natives were all busy harvesting the catch, and they smiled and waved as they went back and forth in their small boats loaded with fish.

On the third day as our hard work continued, the sea was even busier with life. Thousands and thousands of fish schooled everywhere, and I pointed out several dozen really large sharks in the area.

One of the crew looked at me and said, "I hate sharks, Mr. Newly, especially big ones like that. They could eat you in one bite, Mr. Newly, with them big, black eyes rolled back in their heads."

Our whales knew the sharks were there but seemed disinterested in them. The natives knew the sharks were there too, and seemed to be a bit nervous.

On the morning of the seventh day when the Americans were due back, the sea was thick with life. Captain Rickle yelled over and asked, "Captain Pike, what do you make of the sea?"

Captain Simpson yelled out, "I've never seen so much sea life in one place."

Captain Pike, looking over the side, said, "It is a bit thick, ain't it?"

"Have a look at them sharks, would you?" yelled one of the mates. Sure enough, the shark population had gone from dozens to hundreds, and they were big, really big.

Captain Pike sneered and said, "They ain't just your run-of-the-mill reef sharks either, Mr. Newly. Those big fellows there be tiger sharks. The worst and meanest of the lot, and I make them all to be at least sixteen footers."

Even the native fishermen were not going to sea this day because of the sharks. I looked over toward the island and did notice three islanders' boats leaving the shore and seemed to be headed for us.

"Looks like we are going to have company," I said to the captain.

The crow's mate yelled out, "Captain Bongeorno and Captain Adams are headed this way in a big hurry, Captain! It looks like they are trying to outrun a fog bank that has come up on them."

"Fog?" questioned the captain. "There ain't any fog out here today," he said.

We all grabbed up our seeing glasses, and sure enough here they came, and just like the crow's mate had called down, they were in a big hurry. There was not one sail on either of those two ships that was not full of wind, and they appeared to be trying to stay clear of the fog bank that was quickly overtaking them.

Captain Pike snarled and said, "Fog don't move like that. This be the deed of that sea witch, and she is after me ships and crew.

Our attention was distracted for a minute as the three island boats arrived, and these fellows were not in a pleasant mood at all. They were all dressed up in some sort of colored silk body wrap and all sported a big fancy headdress of brightly colored bird's feathers.

When they came up alongside us, one fellow started shouting at us and demanded that we leave. "Look at the sea!" he yelled. "You have brought up the sea's curse to us, and you must leave before it is upon us all." Another fellow was chanting an incantation of some sort, and to our surprise, he began to throw what appeared to be blood on the side of the ship.

Captain Pike snarled at them and said, "Belay that, mates, or those sharks there will be feasting on you for their dinner."

The crow's mate yelled down and said, "Captain, we have six ships— no, make that seven—off the "right"starboard." Squinting in his glass, the crow's mate yelled down again, "It's the Americans, Captain!"

We all looked with our glasses in the direction the crow's mate was pointing, and indeed it was the American Navy.

"I can no longer see Captain Bongeorno or Captain Adams, as they have gone into the fog, Captain!" the crow's mate yelled, and Captain Pike began to curse.

Those island fellows off the port "left" distracted the captain again with their shouting, and Captain Pike snarled at them again and said, "I told you to belay that mumbo jumbo." Then the captain looked right at that fellow throwing the blood on the side of our ship and said, "One more drop, mate! You throw one more drop of that blood on me ship, and I'm going to cover that little ding you got there in yours."

The crow's mate yelled down, "Captain, Captain Bongeorno and Captain Adams just cleared the fog!"

Captain Pike smiled and shook his head in relief. As it turned out, his relief was short lived.

The crow's mate screamed down, "Captain Bongeorno and Captain Adams have changed course and came around to intercept the Americans!"

"What did you say?" screamed the captain.

"Aye, Captain, just as I said. They are moving to intercept the Americans and have formed up in their attack pattern."

"Get these ships under way, and I mean now, or I'll have all your hides on me wall!" screamed Captain Pike.

That one native fellow was still throwing the blood on our ship, and Captain Pike took a grenade and lit it. He tossed it into their boat and yelled, "I have had enough of you." "Throw some blood on that, mates!"

The finely dressed natives dove in the sea for their lives. Their boat exploded and was gone to splinters, and they thrashed and screamed for their lives in the water.

"Captain Pike, our ships are going to attack the Americans?" I asked in horror.

"The Americans will not know till it is too late for them. My God, what if their president is aboard one of those ships?" I asked.

"The Sea Witch has Captain Bongeorno and Captain Adams along with their crew, Mr. Newly," yelled Captain Pike.

"I'll bet you that this cursed fog is what took the crews of those four British warships we gave the Americans.

We were all shocked when we heard the cannon fire in the distance as our two ships attacked our American friends, and Captain Pike went into a fit.

The sharks began to approach the native fellows in the water, and they were screaming pitifully. As their fellow islanders pulled them in to their other two remaining boats, the sharks were closing on them fast. Those natives paddled for shore like there was no tomorrow.

"I see you made some new friends again, Mr. Newly," said the captain.

"Captain one of them Interceptors we gave the Americans just went to the bottom courtesy of Captain Adams, and Captain Bongeorno is just about to get another!" the crow's mate yelled down.

Captain Pike began to cuss hard and screamed, "Get us under way now!" Finally all three ships were hard under way toward the battle.

"Captain Pike," the crow's mate yelled down, "there went another American Interceptor, courtesy of Captain Bongeorno!" Captain Pike went wild with rage.

We were all peering and squinting in our glasses, and to our dismay, we watched as the USS *Intrepid* came around and blew the port "left" side off the *Valiant*. Captain Bongeorno brief reign of terror under the Sea Witch's flag was over as quickly as it began. The *Valiant* sank into the sea, taking him and Joedea and his poor crew with it.

The captain again went wild with rage and said, "Mr. Newly, signal the *Defiant* and the *Resolve* to attack the *Dreadnought*. Send Captain Adams and his crew to the bottom."

"But, Captain," I complained, "maybe we can save them."

"Just do it, Mr. Newly!" he screamed.

Tamantha touched my hand and said, "Carry out his orders, Christopher, they are already gone."

As we approached the battle, we could see that Captain Adams's luck had run out as the *Constitution*, the *Enterprise*, and the *Intrepid* closed on him.

"Signal the Americans, Mr. Newly. Send them my apologies," he said.

"Tell them that we will take care of our own. Tell them if they fire on Captain Adams I will engage them," ordered Captain Pike.

"But, Captain—" I replied.

Tamantha again touched my hand and said, "Just do it, Mr. Newly."

For some reason, the Americans took Captain Pike at his word and broke off their attack. With tears in our eyes, we came up on Captain Adams. The first run we took at him Captain Pike just wanted to have a good look at what had happened to his ship and close friends. As the *Sovereign* flew by them, Captain Adams opened fire on us with cannon and rifle. We could see Captain Adams as he stood at the wheel with Lady Jane next to him, cold as ice.

They were gone to the witch, as was their crew. Their eyes were cold, black, and sunken back in their heads, and their skin was white as a ghost. They stood stiff and cold in the wind with their hair blowing, and they snarled at us with contempt as we went by them under their fire.

"Bring us around on them, Jonesy," said Captain Pike.

"Aye, Captain," said Jonesy, and the wheel came around.

The *Defiant*, the *Resolve*, and the *Sovereign* came around with our colors high on the mast.

"Fire!" screamed out Captain Pike, and all our forward cannon sent their death wish over to Captain Adams and the *Dreadnought*. When we came back around, there was not much left of the *Dreadnought*, as she was burning badly and sinking into the sea.

What was left of the crew was just a terrible sight. They looked as if their souls had been stolen and now were just a shell of their former selves. Most of them floated in the sea and did not try to swim as if they longed for their death to finally come and free them from the witch. That is, if they were still able or permitted to die.

Many a shark had already shown up on the bloodstained sea. The sharks would approach the men in the sea and then turned hard as if they were too rotten to eat.

Only the aft "back"portion of the ship was still above the waves, and I looked in horror and screamed, "Captain Pike, there they are!"

Captain Pike turned and caught the same sight. There stood Captain Adams holding Lady Jane in his arms with a great horrid look on his face. He had Lady Jane wrapped up in the Jolly Roger and her arm hung out limp and cold. Their scene blew in the wind and the spray and the fire and the smoke. We all watched in a horror as the *Dreadnought* slipped beneath the waves. Captain Adams and Lady Jane were the last of the ship to go down, and as his head disappeared beneath the sea, Captain Adams let out a great mournful cry and was gone.

We could hear the Sea Witch laughing, and Captain Pike yelled out to her, "I am glad I killed your retched daughter, and I would do it again! I wish you had another so I could burn her too and feed her well-done carcass to the sharks!"

In a split second, the laughing stopped, and right in front of the ship rose up the Witch of the Sea, Miranda. She looked so small and lonely in that huge ocean as she swam about in all her beauty. She circled our ship, and in our minds we could hear her sing a song.

"That is the song of the dead," said Tamantha.

Captain Pike screamed down at Miranda and said, "Release me crew, witch, or that fine song of the dead you are singing will be for yourself."

The sea witch just smiled and sank beneath the sea.

"She really is crazy mad, Ethan, and you should not taunt her," advised Tamantha.

"I'm going to get that witch, and I am going to send her to a very special place. She will be singing a different tune there," snarled Captain Pike. Tamantha held the captain's hand tightly and kissed him on his cheek.

"Get us under way, Mr. Newly, and set a course over to the Americans or what is left of them. Signal the *Defiant* and the *Resolve* to help the Americans fish their survivors out and help them with their wounded," ordered the captain.

Nineteen

We came up on the Americans, and to my wonder, instead of the Americans being at full arms against us, they had retired their anger and awaited our arrival. We came up on the *Constitution*, and Captain McCartney stood with a finely dressed man at his side.

"Captain Pike, I am Jonathon Adams, and I am sorry we have had to meet like this. We all saw your poor ship's crew as they went by us Captain Pike. What in this world happened to them?" asked the president.

"It be that Sea Witch," Captain Pike answered.

President Adams looked over at Captain McCartney, and Captain McCartney, looking back at him, said, "I told you, sir."

"Please come aboard," asked President Adams. "I'd offer you lunch, but I feel none of us have the stomach for it."

Captain Pike looked at Tamantha and I and said, "Let's go, mates," and we all swung over.

Captain Pike in his usual manner went to walk right up to the president, and the *Constitution*'s marines were on him. Captain Pike pulled out one of his pistols and stuck it right in the face of one of the marines. Captain Pike backed him away hard, with the barrel of the pistol pushing into the skin on the man's face. Everyone froze.

"Easy there, mate," said the captain. "If you ever touch me again, I'll feed you to me whales—or worse, I'll give you to the witch."

The president walked up quickly and slid in between Captain Pike and his guard, easily pushing Captain Pike's hand and pistol down. President Adams ordered, "Stand down, marines." He quickly grabbed Captain Pike by his arm and spun him around and said, "Please walk with me. I want to know everything."

As they walked away down the ship, the president looked over his shoulder back at Captain McCartney with a look of disbelief at what had just happened, and Captain McCartney, with a smile, said, "I told you."

Captain McCartney then looked over at the marines and said, "I think in the future we should just leave Captain Pike be. What do you men think?"

They all smiled back and said, "Aye, sir."

After a brief talk with the president, Captain Pike stopped and put his hands on the *Constitution*'s railing and stared at the horizon.

"What is it, Captain?" asked President Adams.

Captain Pike turned and looked up to the crow's mate on the *Sovereign* and yelled, "Are you keeping your eye on that fog bank, mate?"

"Aye, Captain, I am. It is just setting off to the right "starboard" on the horizon with no movement!" yelled down the mate.

"What is that fog?" asked the president.

"No doubt you have heard the tale of the Sea Witch and her map, have you not?" questioned the captain.

"Yes, I have, Captain Pike, but I am having a small problem believing in a tale that tall. I am sure you can understand that." Said the president. Captain McCartney told me he has seen that map, but a Sea Witch is another matter to consider," President Adams explained.

"That fog there is one of the Sea Witch's tools," Captain Pike explained.

"Did you get a good look at my lost crew when they came up on you to attack?" Those fine men and women were all friends of mine. "

"Did you see them, Mr. President?"

"Did they look like they belonged to this world?"

"Did they look to you like they were following any man's orders?"

"They were running from that fog last I saw of them. When that fog finally caught them, they went into it as men and came out the other side as mindless, half-dead and half-alive slaves to the witch.

"Now that you have seen her work, what do you think?" asked Captain Pike.

"Why do you think that fog is not moving on us now, Captain?" asked the president.

"Because the sea witch fears the map, as she no longer is its keeper," answered Captain Pike.

Then the captain reached in his coat, and out came the Map of the Sea. The President's eyes went huge at its sight as it began to glow.

Seeing the map had been produced, we all thought it might be best if we strolled down to join Captain Pike and the president.

"You see here, Mr. President," said Captain Pike, pointing at the map. "Those men that I just lost to the witch, they did not make it onto the map here like these other poor devils. They are not here because the witch no longer controls the map. As keeper of this map, I alone now decide who makes the map and who doesn't. To me, this means she has them imprisoned somewhere else and I might just be able to get them back."

The President had the same reaction as everyone did at their first sight of the map. Complete wonder at its existence and complete horror at the poor devils imprisoned in it.

"Don't worry about them, Mr. President," said the captain. "The good men held on this map are soon to be released. That is our mission. As for the bad ones on the map, well, they're on their own, mate, and will get no mercy from me."

"How are you going to get them out of the map, Captain?"

"A mere technicality is all that stands in me way there, Mr. President."

"Technicality, Captain Pike?"

"Yes, a small bump in the road, Mr. President. I just have to find two more keys."

"Keys asked the Present?"

Captain Pike did not respond.

The President looked over at Captain McCartney and said, "I'm sorry I ever doubted you."

"Captain Pike, what is it you wanted to show me? I came here despite the warnings of many. I came here to meet the man that has bestowed on my country a great treasure of jewels that will indeed secure our future on this earth."

"I hope you bought your crew some rum."

"Yes, Captain, I did and so much more. It is time for you to show me why you have summoned me, Captain Pike."

"Are you sure you and your fine crew can handle the truth, mate?"

"Yes, Captain, we can handle the truth, and I wish you would call me Jonathon."

"Very well, Jonathon. Do you recall the tale that Captain McCartney must have told you of the great war beneath the sea?

"Yes, I do know the tale, Captain Pike, but to be honest, I had a bit of a problem believing ittoo. However, it would seem that I also doubted the tale about your map and that sea witch, and you can see how that worked out for me."

"Mr. Newly, bring me the orb."

I returned with the orb, and as Captain Pike retrieved it out of the chest, President Adams gasped at its wonder.

"Jonathon, please secure these fine marines of yours, and tell them whatever happens not to show any hostilities, or it will surely be their demise and probably yours," said Captain Pike.

President Adams, looking over at Captain McCartney and then at the marines, said, "Stand down," and they all nodded their heads in agreement.

The captain held the orb above his head and yelled, "Get ready for this, mates!" The orb glowed like the sun as Captain Pike said, "Triton, I call you for an audience."

A minute went by and nothing happened, and President Adams waited patiently. Another minute passed, and the sea remained calm with no sign of Captain Pike's request being answered. The marines began to chuckle, and they all turned to walk away, dismissing Captain Pike as a crazy man on the sea.

Captain Pike, looking unconcerned, in a sarcastic way said, "Well, I am just so sorry, mates, as it might take him a few minutes to get here. What do you think, this is some sort of fairy tale?"

Captain McCartney said, "If I were you, men, I would not be so fast to discount this man." President Adams agreed.

Just as he spoke those words, the sea exploded right next to our ships, and out came that Dugan with Triton riding on its back.

Our ships were covered in the wash like a great wave had come over us all. As we all so vividly remembered, the great dragon was so big it almost blackened the sky above us. As Captain McCartney, President Adams, and their marines tried to stand in the wake of the Dugan's flapping of its wings, Captain Pike yelled over to the president with a huge smile and said, "I hope you don't mind, John, but they were all out of the big dragons."

The president looked horrified, and his marines grabbed at their rifle. Captain Pike screamed, "Stand down, you fools, or this will be your last day for sure!"

The Dugan took his great neck and head down on the marines and drooled all over them, licking its chops like it had not eaten well in a week.

Captain Pike laughed at them and said, "My favorite part is the smell, mates. Don't you just love the smell of that thing?"

Triton just looked down on us all and smiled, and he kicked at the great dragon to behave itself.

"What can I do for you this day, my friend?" yelled Triton.

"First off, I would like you to meet the American Navy and their fine president. Then I have a great gift for you that is beyond your wildest hopes and dreams," said Captain Pike.

Triton looked down from the Dugan at President Adams and held up his great golden trident and said, "I am Triton, sent by my father to be the commander of all the sea that stands against the sea-maiden, Miranda."

Captain Pike looked over at the president and Captain McCartney and said, "Miranda be the sea witch."

The captain then whispered to me and asked, "Who did he say his father was again there, Mr. Newly?"

President Adams stepped forward and could barely speak as he was completely over taken with wonder and amazement at the sights before him. Standing boot high in drool, he said, "I am the president of the United States, and I am very glad to meet you, Triton."

"Jonathon, see if you can get him to tell you who his father is." whispered the captain.

"Triton, if I may be so bold, who did you say your father was?" asked the president.

Triton completely ignored the question.

"Triton, do you know of a place called Lemuria?" Captain Pike asked. Triton looked at the captain and squinted in question.

"I do indeed, Captain. The real question here is how do you know of it?"

"Seen it I have and could have put me feet on its shore if I had a mind to," Captain Pike said.

Triton leaned down off the Dugan and said, "Captain Pike, as you know, I have many duties to attend to, and I really do not have the time for your tales."

With that, Triton kicked at the Dugan, and it began to move away.

"I'll bet you think Lemuria was destroyed, don't you, Triton?" yelled out the captain.

With that, Triton turned back, and again the great dragon hovered over us.

"I'll bet you think Lemuria does not exist, don't you, my friend?" asked Captain Pike.

"I know it does not exist because I know it was destroyed countless years ago replied Triton"

"Is that so, mate?" Captain Pike replied.

"And if it did exist, you would more than likely want to go there, would you not?

"If it was not destroyed and you and all your kind could rejoin the world you descended from, you would more than likely jump at the chance, would you not? I'll even bet such a treasure would stop the great war of the sea and reunite them again, wouldn't you say, mate?"

President Adams looked around at everyone and said, "What in this world are you people talking about?"

Captain McCartney said, "I told you not to discount this man."

Tamantha walked up, and Triton stared at her for answers. She nodded her head to confirm where Captain Pike was headed with his questions.

Triton began to smile and said, "Captain Pike, I do think the answers to all your questions is yes. Yes, I would want to go there, and yes, all the sea would gladly do anything to rejoin with Lemuria, and yes, that would reunite the sea and stop the great war."

"Well then, mate, do you have room on that dragon for a few more to ride?" asked Captain Pike.

Triton kicked at the Dugan, and it lowered its great neck and head to the deck of the *Constitution*. Everyone just stood about looking stupid and hoping that the Dragon's invitation to come aboard was not for them.

"Tamantha," said Captain Pike as he held his arm and hand toward the awaiting monster. Tamantha just jumped right on the Dugan's head, and up its neck she went, arriving at her new seat behind Triton.

I knew it was coming, and sure enough I heard the captain say, "Mr. Newly, get aboard."

Then Captain Pike looked over at President Adams, and the president said, "Oh no, Captain Pike, I am not going anywhere on that monster."

"Come now, Mr. President, you will enjoy the ride," the captain said.

"I'm sure Captain McCartney will make sure nothing happens to you."

Captain Pike laughed as he looked over to Captain McCartney to get aboard the Dugan.

Captain McCartney just shook his head, and up the Dugan he climbed, followed by the president. We all must have been quite the sight sitting on the back of that huge dragon. The American warships' crews were just having a fit at the sight of their president on the back of that great dragon. They all knew if anything happened to him they would never be able to explain the circumstances to any rational man.

"Aren't you coming, Captain?" Triton asked.

Captain Pike said, "Not this time, my friend. I do not care for dragons." Triton laughed as the Dugan spun around and began to move off. The rest of us were pitching a fit that Captain Pike would do this to us and then not come himself.

Triton thought a little show would be appropriate for his new guests. Triton yelled, and off the Dugan went fast. We were all screaming and cussing as we crossed over the sea as fast as lightning, making quick turns and circles. At one time, the Dugan looked around at us all and snarled almost to laugh at our screaming. Triton was laughing so hard I thought he would fall off, and if he had, Tamantha would have surely gone with him as hard as she had a hold on him. After an eternity of ten minutes or so, we came back around and approached the *Constitution*. President Adams yelled out, "I hope that was the worst of it."

Captain Pike yelled back, laughing hard, and said, "You ain't seen anything yet."

"All right, Captain Pike. What now?" asked Triton.

"Tamantha, are you sure you have the crystals to get back here?" asked Captain Pike.

She just smiled, opening her hand and assembling her crystals. I could see the amazed look on everyone's faces as the light joined up the five crystals and shot out in front of the Dugan. All were astonished as the tunnel for Lemuria began to open right before their eyes.

As before, the blackness formed up and the lightning danced and cracked across the face of the great tunnel of lights. The great tunnel pulled at the Dugan in the wind. This tunnel was huge in its size as if to be able to swallow a mouthful like a king-size dragon. The Dugan looked as if it did not want to go in as did Triton, the president, and Captain McCartney.

"Let's get to it, Triton. These crystals are starting to get hot!" yelled Tamantha. With that said, Triton kicked his flying monster, and in we all went.

Everyone on all the ships could see us instantly get stretched to a thousand feet long and become part of the light. They watched as the tunnel closed, leaving nothing but bits of lightning floating and disappearing into the air.

I heard that Captain Pike laughed hard and threw his hat in the air. All the crew on all the ships stood with their mouths open.

"In complete horror and astonishment one of the marines asked him, "Where did they go, Captain Pike?"

Captain Pike knew what was coming next and said, "You are all going to really like this next part." Just as he spoke those words, the lightning began to crack and dance in the air, and with a bang, the tunnel reopened and out came the Dugan and its passengers.

"You're a little late, Tamantha, I was getting worried!" yelled Captain Pike. "I counted five seconds. What kept you?" he asked.

"Oh, Ethan, I could not pull them away. We must have been there for a week," Tamantha answered.

Captain Pike looked about the ships and their crew, and he laughed so hard at the looks on their faces he almost fell into one of the holds.

We all unloaded off the Dugan that itself still looked a bit stunned by its trip through time. As each one of us hit the deck of the *Constitution*, Captain Pike looked into our eyes as if he could see the wonder.

"How did you like that, Jonathon?" asked the captain.

"How about you, Captain McCartney?"How about that?"

The two men and Triton were stunned to know they had only been gone five seconds or so but spent a week in Lemuria.

"I just don't know what to say, Captain Pike," said President Adams.

"Don't worry, mate. It will come to you, as it is a bit much to think about all at one time," explained Captain Pike.

Captain Pike then looked up to Triton, who looked like he could cry from happiness. When he looked down at the captain, he could barely speak. After a moment and a few hard swallows, Triton asked, "Captain Pike, do you know what you have done here today?"

The captain smiled and asked, "Do you have your crystals, mate?"

Triton opened his hand and showed his two sets of the fine crystals: one set for Lemuria and one set for this world.

"Don't get them mixed up, or there will be no tellin' where you will wind up," said Captain Pike.

Triton turned away on the Dugan. Just before the great dragon left the scene, it looked back at Captain Pike and gave him a big snarl and then was gone fast across the sea.

"I think the Dugan likes you, Captain Pike," I said to him.

"Jonathon, we will be leaving this place in a few hours. Would you care to do a little key hunting with us? A great adventure waits on you and maybe a portion of a great treasure for your country. What do you say?"

Captain McCartney shook his head no, and President Adams said, "Well, we better go with you to keep you out of trouble, Captain Pike."

Captain Pike rolled out the map and brought it over to President Adams and said, "Jonathon, this is where we are headed. The Island of Thirteen Skulls."

Captain Pike laughed at the look on the president's and Captain McCartney's faces and said, "Well now, mates, doesn't that just sound like a nice, cozy place, and just look at the size of that jewel on the map." Captain Pike turned and headed off for the *Sovereign*, and we all just stood looking at each other.

Within a few hours, Captain Pike yelled over to the *Constitution* and asked, "Are you ready, Captain McCartney?"

"Aye, Captain Pike, we are indeed." President Adams walked up and had a big grin of excitement on his face.

"Mr. Newly, get us under way," Captain Pike ordered.

"What course, Captain Pike?" yelled over Captain McCartney.

"Steer eighty-five degrees and try to keep up," Captain Pike said. With that, Captain Pike looked over at the *Defiant* and the *Resolve* and yelled out, "Let's get to it, mates," and off we sailed.

"Two days, Mr. Newly. Two days and we will be there. The Island of Thirteen Skulls awaits you. Begin your preparations," ordered Captain Pike. "Dinner is at eight sharp. Come join us, Mr. Newly. I want to hear the tale of Lemuria. Also, signal Captains Rickle and Simpson to join us as I am sure they want to also hear this fine tale too."

"Aye, Captain," I replied.

I looked back on the sea, and it was quite the sight. Right behind us was the *Defiant* and then the *Resolve* and then the five American warships with all our whales running in and out of all.

That evening sharply at eight, we all gathered in the captain's cabin. We had a fine feast of fresh meat and fish and washed it all down with some hot rum.

"Okay, Mr. Newly and Tamantha, it's time we heard the tale of Lemuria," said Captain Pike.

Tamantha began and told everyone what a great, wonderful world Lemuria was. She said that it was a beautiful water world with areas of land just like our world.

I jumped in and said, "Captain, you should have seen the look on the Lemurian's faces when that tunnel opened up and out came that Dugan with all of us aboard. We came out right over one of their big pyramids right in the middle of a great city."

Tamantha smiled and said, "Yes, Mr. Newly is right. They did give us a look, but it was a not pleasant one."

I jumped back in and said, "Yeah, Captain, when they first saw us, several of those big fellows grabbed up their spears and started gathering that lightning tip on their ends like those big stone pillar guards did back on the island. Titan landed the Dugan in a great blue pool, and him and Tamantha dove in, swimming to shore. As soon as the Lemurian's saw

Titan's and Tamantha's tails, those spears came right down, leaving the lightning dancing in the air."

"Hold on right there," said Captain Pike. "I have to get me another bottle of rum."

"The Lemurian's are a great civilization of creatures that swim the seas and can also walk the land," Tamantha said. "They possess the same gift as I do: being able to change my tail for legs at will. They were shocked when Titan and I walked out of the great pool and began to speak to them in the tongue of the sea. Then they knew who we were."

Tamantha continued, "As you know, we had to have been there for a week, and all we did was ask questions, as did the Lemurian's. The President and Mr. Newly had a fine time but had a little trouble discussing matters."

Everyone at the table began to laugh when I jumped in and said, "A little trouble speaking to them, Tamantha? It was downright impossible. Tamantha and Triton were our interpreters though, so me and the president had a grand time.

"Captain, we sat at fine feasts and festivities the Lemurian's held in our honor. They put on great plays for us in huge theaters, Captain. The whole place was in celebration of the two worlds uniting back together. I told of you, Captain Pike, and of our adventures. The Lemurian's were fascinated by every word."

"They were also sad to hear of the great war of the sea and of Miranda," said Tamantha.

I jumped back in and said, "Tamantha changed into a wolf for them, and that really set them back in their seats."

Captain Rickle asked, "Did you see the captain's horses?"

Captain Pike's eyes looked big as he sat up in his chair and awaited an answer.

Tamantha smiled as she looked over at Captain Pike and said, "Oh, yes, Ethan, we saw your babies. They were everywhere flying about and being pampered by the Lemurian's, as were all the other creatures you set free."

I said, "Captain, the Lemurian's could not figure out where they had all come from until I told your tale about us finding and figuring out the crystals and how you saved the horses and the others from that cursed world."

"The Lemurian's are really looking forward to meeting you, Ethan. All know or soon will know the name of the man that has made possible the reuniting of these two civilizations once again," said Tamantha.

Captain Pike asked, "How come the Lemurian's never came back here and reclaimed their lost brethren?

"The Lemurian's thought this world had been completely destroyed and no longer existed," Tamantha explained. "They thought if they opened the tunnel back here, whoever traveled in it would walk into nothingness and never return."

"Now that the Lemurian's know this world was not destroyed, are they going to travel here?" asked the captain.

"A little bit at first, but it was agreed that Triton should bring his kind there, as this world now belongs to mankind," she replied.

"That's a shame because I think they are all a fine lot, except for that witch and a few of them monsters," said Captain Pike.

"When is Triton going to begin this great migration to Lemuria?" asked Captain Simpson.

"As we speak, they are traveling in the tunnels," Tamantha replied.

"Are they are going to take that sea witch with them?" asked Captain Pike.

"No, Ethan, the Lemurian's made it very clear that she will not be welcome, so that means Miranda will have a new curse. If you do not get her, she will spend a long time swimming alone in the sea."

Captain Pike laughed and said, "Well, she deserves her fate. Speaking of fate, I guess there goes my apology from the Oracle of the Sea." Then with a grin and trying to mock the Oracle, the captain said with a whine to his voice, "I am the Oracle of the Sea. I can see the future and the past. Bunk."

"That was quite the tale, and I enjoyed it. Let's get some rest for tomorrow awaits us," said the captain.

"There is one more thing, Ethan," said Tamantha. "The Lemurian's gave me this to give to you. They said you would know what to do with it."

I looked hard because I never saw the Lemurian's give Tamantha anything to present to the captain.

Tamantha reached over and picked up the captain's hand, and we all strained to get a look. She handed him the smallest chest I had ever seen. Captain Pike was delighte and he tried to open it. "It's locked," said the captain.

"Any chance the Lemurian's gave you the key to this chest?"

"No, Ethan, they did not," replied Tamantha.

"They told me that only you would know the secret that will open this chest."

It was almost like the captain knew what was in the chest and what he had to do to open it. He gave Tamantha a big smile and then he reached in his coat and pulled out the Map of the Sea. He laid the Map down on the table and placed the little chest right over one of the empty key holes on the parchment. The map began to glow brightly. Its light grew and grew and grew, brighter and brighter, and then, as quick as it had started, the map's light diminished and was gone.

The little chest sprung open like it had been waiting ten thousand years for someone to finally open it. We all strained to get a look inside and there it lay. The third key of the sea!

"Well there it is, Mr. Newly," said the Captain. "There is the third key."

He picked the key out of the chest and held it up so we could get a good look. It was an old, plain black key with a head that was fashioned after some sort of squid with great big red eyes. The squid's tentacles seemed to wrap down and all around the key's shaft. It was really very beautiful.

"I told you this key would show up as a result of our little visit back there on Devil's Den now didn't I, Mr. Newly?" said the captain. Without any emotion at all, the captain took the key and put it in his coat pocket.

I thought the captain would be happy that now he possessed three of the four keys to the sea, but he was not. Sometimes the captain was really hard to figure out. You would think he would be jumping with joy. But he was not.

Chapter

Twenty

The next morning the crow's mate yelled down, "Captain, we have land off to the "right "starboard!"

We all ran to the side of the ship to have a look, and there it was, the Island of Thirteen Skulls. Captain Pike seemed to be puzzled that we had arrived a day early, but we really had not. What we were seeing was a large volcanic peak a day's sail away. The rest of the day as we sailed toward the peak, all our minds wondered as to what we might find in this place. After all, we were still a day away and could already see the island's maker that stretched so high into the sky its top was covered with snow and ice, which was unheard of in the Caribbean.

The next day as we came up on the island, we all searched it with our seeing glasses for any sign of life. Along with the many gulls that were always about screaming and yelling their warnings, the island was covered with life. Birds, parrots, and monkeys were everywhere. There were large iguanas scurrying across the white sand beach, and to our dismay there was a large selection of salt-water crocs sunning themselves, awaiting their next meal to appear.

The island looked to be fairly large and was covered with a great forest. Many waterfalls spilled down the side of the overgrown volcanic peak and fell into the sea.

Captain Pike said, "This is a good thing, Mr. Newly, as we always need fresh water, and that timber will come in handy for repairing the ships."

Another strange feature of the island was that it had no reef, so we were able to almost sail right up to its beach. Captain Pike said that the reason for the lack of reef was that the island was young in its years.

"Captain, this island is not young," I complained. "Just look at that peak, and look at that forest," I said.

Sarcastically the captain complained back to me and said, "Well, all right then, Mr. Newly. I guess this island has just been hiding here for thousands of years and no one has just ever bothered to see it. Or else maybe it just appeared for us out of thin air."

Then Captain Pike seemed to pause for a moment as he searched his mind remembering everything else that was impossible in our lives, and he said, "Very well, Mr. Newly, you may indeed be right."

We dropped our anchors almost right on the beach, sending the crocs running into the sea as the Americans came up to join us.

"What do you think, Captain Pike?" yelled over Captain McCartney.

Captain Pike turned and said, "This should be a good adventure as we already seem to have a tale, and we have not put a boot on the sand."

Captain Rickle yelled over and disgustedly said, "It just figures if we had to have crocodiles we would get stuck with this lot. I hope you all know those are salt-water crocs, and they don't come any meaner or grow any larger than them."

Everyone looked at the huge devils as they swam around the ships just waiting for one of us to dare step a foot into the water or onto the island. All crews on all ships retrieved a pistol or a rifle, and we all opened fire on the big crocs, laying waste to most, and what remained swam off quickly.

"Set a camp on the beach!" yelled out Captain Pike. That order was not hard to follow, as all we had to do was get off the ships and wade ashore. "Gather up them dead crocks. Captain Simpson knows what to do with them."

Captain Simpson smiled and said, "I love crocodile stew."

Within a few hours, we had a large camp set up and teams of men began to break off and begin exploring the island. Captain Rickle was still unnerved by the salt-water crocs, and as he watched their many tails go into several big cooking pots for dinner, he sneered and said, "This is all fine and dandy, but just wait till they come back tonight." You know at night all you can see of those devils are their brightly glowing eyes in the dark, and that's when they will take you."

We all just laughed at him and assured him the whales and the wolves would keep us safe.

President Adams was particularly happy and enjoying his new adventure. I told Captain Pike that I did not think the poor man got out much anymore, as he seemed to have traded for his love of life and its adventures for his love for his country and his duty.

Captain Pike nodded his head in agreement and said, "Well, Mr. Newly, that is not entirely a bad thing as long as the price of his sacrifice is not squandered by his future generations.

"I do not place my faith in the future of mankind as he does, Mr. Newly, as they will more than likely build the foundations of their homes on his bones and the many like him. They will not see the blood and the lives sacrificed. They will slip into complacency wrapped up in their comfort and disregard the sacrifice as if it had never happened at all, which will be their undoing. Most men sit comfortably in their warm houses never to have had a cannon ball fly by their head, but they will claim the lead. I say they have no opinion and should all be dismissed as the finely dressed rats that they are, running about the picked-over bones of the past, learning nothing at all," said the captain.

As the cooking pots boiled with the fresh croc meat, a group of marines that were off exploring came running back fast and reported that they had found something. All the captains, the president, Tamantha, and I ran back with them to have a look at the find. What the marines found appeared to be the skeleton of some sort of creature that had not been dead long, as it still had bits of flesh on it that the birds and the crabs had not got to yet. The creature appeared to be standing upright on its back legs wedged in between two large rocks.

The creature looked to be about the size of a man and appeared that it walked about upright on those back legs. Its feet were large, and each had eight of what appeared to be toes with a huge claw attached on the end of each. It had two long arms with what appeared to be large hands, and these hands each had three fingers also sporting large claws. Its large head was like that of some sort of reptile, and it was packed full of long, sharp teeth. Hanging from its body, it had a tail that did not quite touch the ground, and from the top of its head to the tip of its tail and all along its back ran a line of spikes. The spikes the creature wore on its head and down its neck were at least two feet long, and as they approached the tip of the tail, they had tapered off to five or six inches.

"This ain't good," Captain Rickle said, frowning.

Captain Pike laughed out loud and asked, "How would you mates like to come across one of these fine fellows that ain't dead?"

President Adams walked up to the skeleton and examined it closely, fascinated by it.

"I just hope this thing was full grown and not some sort of baby something," Captain McCartney said.

"It looks like it was trying to go between these rocks and got stuck," explained the captain. Captain Pike reached over and grabbed a hold of the nasty skeleton and pulled at it. One of the marines joined in and grabbed a hold to help, and they both pulled hard. When the skeleton broke free, one of the spikes on the creature's back cut the marine's arm.

Instantly the marine started screaming in pain. He fell to the ground and began rolling about wildly. We all tried to secure the marine and hold him down, but he grew stronger and stronger. He threw us all off him like we were rag dolls along for the ride. The wolves were snarling and snapping at him. We all stood there and watched as he screamed, and as he screamed he began to change. His entire body started to stretch, and the man's skin just started to tear off his body as some scales began to take his skin's place. Two of the man's fingers fell to the sand, and the remaining three began to grow a skin web between them and grow claws. When the first of the spikes began to grow out of his back, we all knew what he was changing into.

Captain Pike pulled out his pistol and went to shoot the now half man and half creature, and Captain McCartney slapped the pistol down and yelled out, "Like you, Captain Pike, I will take care of my own." He pulled out his pistol and shot his former marine dead on the spot.

Captain McCartney looked calmly over at the president, who was completely horrified, and said, "I told you we should not have come here."

President Adams just shook his head and said, "How am I going to explain this to his family back home?"

"Tell them he died bravely in battle. What else do you think you can say?" asked Captain Pike. "That you had to shoot him because he was taken by some sort of devil?"

"You want me to lie, Captain Pike?" asked the president.

"Yes, I do, Jonathan. When the truth will do no one any good but a lie will, then that is when a lie will do," said Captain Pike.

Captain McCartney looked at the other marines and said, "Bury him deep, and mark his grave well."

Captain Pike began to examine the area between the rocks the creature had been stuck in, and sure enough there was a gap in the rock leading into the mountain. Cold air was coming out of the gap in the rock, and we all looked at each other in question.

I said, "Oh no, Captain, don't tell me it is a cave."

Captain Pike smiled and pulled out the map. As usual, most gasped at its sight as Captain Pike rolled it open and began to study it.

He looked up at me and said, "All right, Mr. Newly. It is not a cave, but whatever it is, the treasure is in that general direction, and this is the way in."

Our wolves seemed excited, and they all took off into the opening in the rock face. Tamantha kept calling them back, and finally after a few minutes, they returned setting all our minds wondering. As they came back out, each of them shook off and threw a sort of white powder off their bodies. Captain Pike walked over to them and touched his hand to Kodiak's back and picked up some of the powder.

"It is snow," said Captain Pike.

"Snow?" questioned President Adams. He too then retrieved some of the white powder off Avalanche. "We are in the middle of the Caribbean Sea. There is no snow here," said the president.

Captain Pike laughed and said, "I believe as we speak you are petting an ice wolf, and there ain't any of them around these parts either. For that matter, Mr. President, when was the last time you ever saw a killer whale in the warm sea? But we have four of them too, don't we? We will go through in the morning. Let's get back to camp."

When we arrived back at the camp, the sun was getting low in the sky, and Captain Rickle ordered the entire beach to be lined with torches, as he had no intention of getting eaten by a croc in the middle of the night. As the sun went down and torches covered the beach with their light, we all enjoyed a big feast of croc tail and potatoes, and it was delicious. Captain Simpson laughed at Captain Rickle, as he would have none of it. Captain Rickle would not even eat a potato that had been boiled in the same water as the croc.

"They don't eat me, and I won't eat them," said Captain Rickle.

Just to be mean and encourage worry, Captain Pike yelled out, "I don't know about you, mates, but I think you are all looking in the wrong direction! I'd rather get taken by a croc than by one of them other spiny devils that live on that mountain behind you."

That seemed to work because all the crews that night slept in pairs back to back, leaning on each other with their port to the sea and their starboard toward the mountain with pistols and rifle ready.

I really don't think anyone got much sleep. Just when we would dose off, something would happen. Several times in the night the wolves chased off something that was attempting to come down the beach to us. Several more times the water just off shore would explode into a great frenzy, and we could see crocs being run off by our whales. Several other times we heard a great fighting and screaming between some sorts of creatures high up on the mountain. The one scene that really spooked all of us was when there was a great commotion just behind us up the mountain, and at least two hundred monkeys jumped for their lives on to the sand and ran right through our camp screaming wildly. Whatever it was, it did not come any closer because of the wolves were really putting on a show of force.

The next morning we all were really glad to see the sun come up. Everyone had been scared half to death all night long. Even the crew left behind on the ships was spooked and awoke at their cannon stations. I laughed at the sight of Captain Rickle, as he was really mad.

"I don't need this, Captain Pike! I really do not need this at all!" yelled Captain Rickle.

We all laughed hard when Captain Pike replied and said, "Come now, Captain Rickle. Don't get yourself all worked up this early into the trip. We both know matters are only going to get worse from here."

Captain Simpson had sent out some scouts to the north, and they came back and reported that just down the beach past the point where the wolf's tracks stopped; there were definitely large animal tracks and lots of them. Something was out there, but we did not have a clue as to what it was.

Captain Pike yelled out, "Listen up, mates, as I have pondered our situation well, and here is my decision! If we stay on this beach for long, it is only a matter of time until something bad happens. This is a very dangerous place, and I'll give you all a slim chance of surviving it. I want all ships to move offshore of this retched place where the crews will be safe. I will not order any man to go with me in my search; however, when I return with any treasure I might have found along the way, I will gladly share it with all of you. If any man wants to volunteer to go with me, I will gladly accept their company, and those that do not, I only ask you take care of your ships and mine until I get back. Oh, and me pigeon of course. Make sure nothing happens to my pigeon, or I'll feed you to the crocs."

The crew followed Captain Pike's orders and broke camp, and they all lined up on the shore, but none would leave to board the ships. Captain Pike yelled at them all to get aboard their ships, but none would move from their stance.

"Get aboard, mates, as you will surely die in this place!" Captain Pike screamed. No one moved.

One of the marines stepped up and said, "Forgive me, Captain, but I believe you have the loyalty part all showed up, so you might as well get started on the matter of the getting under way on the quest."

Captain Pike just burst out laughing and said proudly, "That is exactly the response I expected from this crew."

President Adams walked up and stood next to Captain Pike and said, "I am going."

We all picked up our bags stuffed with supplies and formed a line behind President Adams, ready to go. Captain Pike asked, "Captain Rickle, will you stay behind and command the ships?"

Captain Rickle said, "No way, Captain. I'm going with you. Bring up one of them crocs, and I'll give him a big kiss before we go."

Captain Simpson, producing a handful of crystals, said, "Well, if it comes down to it, I'm going to open up a tunnel, and we all will be gone into it.

"Great plan." Captain Pike laughed. "Unless what if whatever you are running from follows you in."

Captain Simpson was silent.

Time was up, and we all stood in front of the large crack in the side of the mountain. There were at least thirty-five of us waiting to go in. All the ships had moved offshore away from the island's dangers with all the first mates in charge, Jonesy in my place aboard the *Sovereign*.

"Let's go, babies," Captain Pike said to the ice wolves, and they led us into the cave.

As we all went in, I thought back to Tamantha's island and to my now-natural fear of caves. As it turned out, this cave was nothing like that bug-infested, bat-filled, slimy place that I remembered so well. We could all feel the cold on our faces, but we had no idea what was awaiting us.

Within just a few minutes or so, we came out into a great frozen world of ice and snow. It was a spectacular wondrous place that went on forever. I told the captain that I would bet that all of London itself would fit easily into this place. We did not need our torches because sunlight came through many other cracks in the rock face, not to mention the top of the cone of the volcano. We could all look up and see the blue sky way up the volcano's shaft; it was like we were looking through a seeing glass at the sky.

This huge volcano was completely hollow on the inside. Its ice-covered rock face and all across where we stood was covered with thousands of magnificent natural ice sculptures. As the sunlight snuck in through the many cracks and struck the ice, the entire place shimmered and looked like a great ice palace. The ice palace was quiet, and all we could hear was the sound of our boots crushing the snow beneath our feet and the cold wind. The laughing sound the wind made almost seemed real as it danced around our faces, biting our noses and ears.

A little bit further in and off in the distance we began to hear the sound of water running. Then it began to run harder and then harder, then it begin to rush like the gates of a lock had just been opened.

Captain Pike told everyone to spread out and keep their eyes open as he consulted the map of the sea. We began to walk toward what appeared to be the center of this ice mansion. We were all nervous as we walked in between the huge ice sculptures disappearing and reappearing in and out of each other's sight like we were walking through a forest of giant trees. All the while the sound of that water rushing kept getting louder and louder. As it turned out, this great ice volcano was just the top hat of what was below our feet.

As we came up on the middle, the water's rushing sound had now become a great roar. We could barely yell and hear each other above its sound. We came across what appeared to be the continuation of the volcano's shaft downward into the earth. Looking down into the great hole, we could see the other side of it. We could see the ice floor we were standing on was four or five hundred feet thick before the rock began. We could also see that somehow, all of a sudden, this ice floor under our feet had all began to melt and would soon be gone.

We looked down into the huge shaft to where the ice floor met the rock. There was a great waterfall that circled it and looked like it fell into the forever down the shaft.

Captain Pike yelled to me and said, "Now you went and done it, Mr. Newly."

"Did what, Captain?" I yelled back.

"You triggered some sort of trap and set the ice to melting," yelled the captain.

"We don't want to be here long, or we will be washed over those falls. When this ice floor is gone, we better be too."

We also noticed that about a hundred feet down from where we were and several hundred feet above the steadily building waterfall was a large cave and several smaller ones. It appeared that someone or something had carved these caves into the side of the ice shaft.

"What does the map show, Captain? Which way?" asked the president. Captain Pike just smiled and pointed down into the shaft to the ice cave.

"Let's get to it, mates, as we are running out of time!" he yelled.

Captain Simpson, screaming over the sound of the water yelled out, "Which cave?"

"We will only get one shot at this. I'm guessing the big one!" yelled Captain Pike.

We threw several ropes down the side of the ice shaft, and Captain Pike was headed for the rope. Mr. Drummer from Captain Simpson's crew ran up and grabbed the rope from Captain Pike's hand and said, "I'll go first, Captain, as we should send down a scout before the captain of a ship."

Captain Pike looked Mr. Drummer in the eye and gave him a grin and handed him the rope. Poor Mr. Drummer did not even get halfway down before trouble began. Here came those spiny devils out of the other smaller caves, and they came by the hundreds. The creatures ran up the side of the ice like they were running on flat land, using their claws to dig the ice. They were like a spiders scurrying from a nest that had been kicked, and when they were almost on Mr. Drummer, he looked up at us and smiled. He smiled but he had a look to him like he knew his days were over.

Mr. Drummer pushed himself off the wall of the shaft out past the creatures' reach and let go of the rope. As he let go, he pulled his pistol and shot one of the beasts right in the face, and down they both went into the falls below. All of the creatures stopped dead in their tracks and watched as their fellow devil disappeared from sight. Then they all turned their heads slowly back up at us and snarled and screamed as they began their run on us again.

We opened up on them with our pistols and our rifles and sent at least a hundred of them to the falls below, but we could not load our guns fast enough, and we all knew this was to be our end.

As the creatures came up and over the edge of the shaft, they all slowed and walked around us until they finally had us all backed into each other in a circle. As we got a good look at these beasts, we could see their obvious similarity to that skeleton we had found earlier. The wolves ran the circle between the creatures and us, snapping and snarling at them. These spiny monsters did not want anything to do with those ice wolves and would come no closer. The creatures wanted us badly, but they would not get near those wolves.

This all was buying us time, and as each man got his rifle or pistol reloaded, he would fire it off and bring down another of the beasts. Klondike ran up and managed to get one of the spiny devils by its foot and dragged it back toward us. To our surprise, the creature seemed to be scared to death and came along screaming and almost crying in its horror. Klondike tore the retch into pieces in a minute and went for another.

The other wolves began to do the same, and we also continued to fire on them as we loaded. The creatures finally had enough and ran for their lives. They did not run back down the shaft but ran up any ice they could find, disappearing with their screams into the tangles of the ice sculptures above us.

We all just looked around at each other as if we could not believe we were still alive. Captain Rickle looked over at President Adams and said, "This is always the way it is when you are in the company of this man."

"I believe that" replied the President.

Captain Pike yelled, "Let's get to it."

"Tie them wolves off and swing them down," ordered the captain. "I ain't going in there without them." That was easier said than done, but soon enough they were down the shaft. We left a dozen men to stand guard, and down over the side of the shaft the rest of us all went on the ropes, reassembling in the mouth of the large cave below. We all looked at the ice melting below us, and it appeared we had used up about a quarter of our time.

Captain McCartney said, "We better get a move on because that ice fuse we lit is burning quickly."

We fired up our torches and in we went. The first thing we noticed was the sides of the cave were made of clear ice, and you could see into it; what we saw was not good. Side by side frozen in the ice were the ones that the witch had been gathering. There stood all the poor, half-dead-half-alive men and sea creatures with their black, sunken eyes like some sort of frozen army. The poor devils seemed to watch us as we walked past them in the torch light. We were in such a hurry we did not have time to be scared, but as it turned out, we were just a little too much in a hurry. We came up on a large chasm in the floor of the ice, and right over the edge went the first three men in the lead. The forth would have gone over, but President Adams grabbed him by his pack and pulled him back.

We looked down into the great crack and could see the ice water rushing along toward the waterfall and the shaft behind us.

President Adams said, "That fuse is burning quickly, gentlemen."

We could all now see the ice beneath us had used up about a third of our time.

Captain Pike sneered as we all looked around in the torchlight. The walk around the chasm was easy enough, but we still had to look at the so many frozen prisoners the witch had taken.

"Captain, your witch has been quite busy," said Captain Simpson. Captain Pike just shook his head and sneered again, and off we went.

We came into a huge chamber and stopped so fast we all ran up on each other in a pile. We slowly moved forward and spread out, pulling out our pistols and raising our rifles as we all stared at the scene that lay before us. There were twenty or thirty of the sea witch's slaves, but these particular ones were not frozen. They completely ignored us at least for the time being, as they were busy tending to a great treasure. All about the chamber were many lamps burning oil, and their black smoke filled the air that burnt at our eyes.

We quietly walked farther into the chamber and gazed around in wonder. The first thing that caught my eye was the magnificent, golden, jewel-encrusted skulls that were arranged around the chamber in the ice face. I quickly glanced at each one and counted them, and sure enough there were thirteen of them that surrounded us from their icy perches. The golden skulls seemed to be fashioned after that of men but were much larger than a man's head. The skulls had huge red rubies that were their eyes, and they seemed to glow in the torchlight staring back at us. All about the chamber were piles and piles of jewels and gold and silver.

We walked in a bit further, and all the slaves stopped their duties and turned to look at us.

I just knew that was it. We had just walked our last step forward in this place.

The slaves all threw off their hoods and pulled the swords they had hidden away under their wraps, and the fight was on.

I wanted to run because. I felt like I was facing some sort of unbeatable creature but the wolves quickly convinced me that was not the case as they tore four or five of the oncoming creatures to pieces.

These devils were not scared of the wolves, and they ran right over them making the necessary sacrifices in their numbers to get to us. In my experiences whenever gun powder and lead faced off with steel, the powder and lead always won. This case was no different, and we mowed those poor devils down with our fire.

They would not stop coming, not till the last of them was gone.

Captain Pike kicked the dead devils away from his path and yelled, "We are running out of time here, mates! Let's get to it."

As soon as we touched the treasure the thirteen skulls began to glow brightly in the torch-lit darkness. We all stopped dead in our tracks and looked at them. Out of their large, ruby-red eyes came a great red beam of light almost like that the crystals gave off back on Devil's Den, except this light was not cool or refreshing; it was red hot.

The light came from each of the skulls and hit the floor of the ice cave just in front of them. The ice cracked and spewed and lit the cave with an awesome red glow as each of the thirteen light beams burnt their way toward a center spot in the cave.

When all of the beams joined up together in the center, the light was so bright I could barely look upon it. A great hole began to burn out from the floor of the cave. We all stood there with our mouths open watching the spectacle take place, burning deeper and deeper down until it hit the rushing water below and set off a great explosion that knocked us all off our feet. Then up came the Witch of the Sea.

As she rose up out of the hole, she came with all her beauty, and not a sound she made. She looked around at us all and just smiled. The thirteen skulls went quiet as if they had done their job as sentries and had called for their master to appear. Not a sound could be heard except the rushing water in the background. The sound of the water seemed far away, but we all knew how close it really was. We all just stood and stared. The witch came forward toward us with her smile and began to walk in and out of us all. The President and Captain McCartney stood their ground but I knew they wanted to run. But run to where the question is?

"She has legs, Captain," I whispered.

The captain just sneered.

She walked over to the captain and got really close to his face and said sarcastically, "Well, if it's not Captain Ethan Pike himself come to visit." Running her finger down the front of the captain's shirt, she said,

"And I see you have brought all your friends too. Isn't that nice?" The captain did not say a word.

She walked over to Tamantha and said, "Captain, I see you have even brought me a gift."

The wolves began to growl and Tamantha asked, "How does it feel to be alone in the sea, witch?"

That's when the fight between the two women began.

And like she was some sort of snake Miranda pulled out a dagger and hissed at Tamantha.

Tamantha began to walk slowly around the witch in a circle. When the witch went for her, Tamantha, in a second, changed into that white wolf. The first round between the two ended in just a few seconds. Tamantha, or should I say the white wolf, really tore that witch up. Miranda, at first, looked shocked at what had just happened to her. She looked down at her body only to see her torn to pieces clothing wrap that she was wearing that was now drinking up her own blood from injuries.

Miranda then looked up slowly, almost with a look of satisfaction, and a smile grew across her face.

Miranda then invoked the captain's curse he had sent to her on Triton's spear. She too changed into a great wolf and she came up snarling and snapping.

In the blink of an eye, Princess had her. Princess grabbed that witch by the back of her neck and shook her like she was a rag. Then she slammed the witch up against the side of the cave. To our surprise Miranda just stood up snarling, seemingly unscathed.

Miranda then made a leap for Tamantha, and Princess went for Miranda. The result was two thousand pounds of teeth and fur colliding in mid air. When they hit the floor of the cave they all rolled about in a ball of blood and fur.

Again that round only lasted a few minutes. Tamantha had a big cut above her nose and was bleeding badly. Princess had another big cut across her leg and one on her back. Miranda was the one that was really in bad shape. What she had given she had gotten back two-fold.

That's when Kodiak, Klondike, and Avalanche moved in. They looked like they had enough of setting on the side as their pack was being attacked.

Miranda was now standing in the center with our five wolves, including Tamantha, surrounding her.

Then, in another attempt, Miranda went for Tamantha. All five wolves unleashed their fury on her. When it was over Tamantha had Miranda by her throat, pinned to the floor of the cave. Miranda changed back to her somewhat human form and gasped for breath.

Tamantha also changed back to human form. Tamantha grabbed her dagger, and, holding the witch of the sea by her throat, she went to finish her.

As the dagger came down, the witch grabbed Tamantha by the hand, stopping her final blow. With the two of them struggling at the dagger, Miranda whispered, "Will you kill your own sister this day and violate the law of the sea?"

Tamantha pushed her away, threw her blade to the cave's floor and rolled away to regain her head. That's when the witch again went for it. Miranda grabbed up the dagger and went right for Captain Pike screaming like a banshee.

She did not make it. A second later there was Miranda with Captain Pike's sword right through her heart.

Looking at Captain Pike's sword in her chest Miranda began to laugh. She grabbed the captain by his shoulders and pulled herself farther onto the blade. As she inched her way onto the sword, she smiled a hideous smile and said, "You will never be rid of me, Captain Pike."

"Bunk," replied the captain, and he drew his sword out of her quickly and stood back.

He took his boot and pushed her over to the floor. To our surprise he pulled a handful of crystals out of his pocket and assembled them in his hand. The lightning cracked as the tunnel of lights opened.

It was a tunnel to that horrible world of fire I had made fun of the captain over. As the tunnel pulled on us we could feel the heat on our faces. Hotter and hotter it became till I thought we would for sure burn.

The witch stood one last time and made a run on the captain.

"I have had enough of you, Miranda, Witch of the Sea," the captain screamed.

With that the captain kicked her right into the tunnel, and we all watched as Miranda was gone into its light. Captain Pike closed the tunnel and threw the crystals across the cave.

He looked over to us all and said, "I told you I would one day get that witch and send her to a very special place."

"I guess I will have to find another place for my honeymoon Mr. Newly" said the captain laughing at me. I was not amused.

"We are running out of time," yelled Captain Simpson.

"Grab all you can, mates, and get out of this place," screamed the captain.

With the witch gone, so went her power over the many she held in their frozen tombs. As we ran down the ice corridor and headed back to the cave's entrance loaded with treasure, we could see the ice that entombed them began to melt. They began to fall out of their iced niches in our path.

They were all so grateful for their freedom, but we had no time for them. We just told them to get up the ropes and then run for their lives.

I was standing at the exit of the cave looking down at the water raging below us. Time was up. There was only about fifty feet of ice left before the great falls would take us.

I felt a hand on my shoulder, and I turned to see who it was. There stood the Captain's Adams and Bongeorno with their gals. Apparently they too had been taken and held here to serve the witch and were now free. I had no time for the reunion.

"What can we do, Mr. Newly?" asked Captain Adams.

"Next rope down, get up it," I screamed. "And help with getting the wolves back up.

"Where is Captain Pike?" asked Bongeorno.

"He is back in the cave with Captain Rickle and Simpson. If they don't show in the next few minutes they will be lost," I replied.

Four or five ropes fell back down from above right in front of us. I threw the bags of treasure I had on my back at Captain Adams and ordered them all up the ropes.

"What about you, Mr. Newly?" asked Captain Adams.

"I'm going back to get them," I answered.

I ran back as fast as I could back down the ice corridor for the Captains. Of course they were after the 13 skulls. When I arrived they were loading them in a chest. Captain Rickle was going for the thirteenth one.

He snatched it off its perch and threw it to Captain Simpson, who in turn flung it over to Captain Pike. The captain paused for a moment and staring that last devil right in the eye he said, "I don't know your story there, mate, or who you thought that witch was, but I am the keeper of the map, and you will serve me now."

I could see the map of the sea as it began to glow inside the captain's coat. The thirteenth skull's big red ruby eyes also began to glow brightly.

"We have to go captain," I screamed. "We have no time for this."

"Show me the last key of the sea, devil, or your fate will be worse than the one you suffer now," yelled the captain.

The skull's eyes just faded away and again went dark with no answer. Captain Pike shook his head and tossed the thirteenth skull in the chest with the others.

"It is not here," the captain screamed. "Get this chest back to the ship."

Finally, the last of the treasure, the crew, and the newly freed slaves came up the ropes, and off we all ran for the exit.

As we all spilled out on the beach, Captain Pike ordered a signal fire built, and the smoke ran high into the air. The crocs had returned to the beach, but as we all ran up on them, they scattered into the sea. We were in such a hurry I think we would have all walked across their backs to get to the ships.

"I am glad you all made it!"

"How about that Mr. President?

"How about that Captain McCartney?"

Smiling at Captain Adams he said "You owe me a ship and I had to rescue you."

"Same with the rest of you" smiled the captain.

"And Lady Jane, you were supposed to take care of them all" she got a big huge. I never Captain Pike huge anyone before.

Everyone just smiled bach.

It seemed like an eternity, but the ships all came on shore. Our urgency was quickly spread about all the ships, and they too went to triple stride. We all loaded on the ships, and we had somehow managed with the help of the freed slaves to get nearly every single jewel and piece of treasure there was to be had.

As we sailed off the shore, Captain Pike looked back at the island in his glass and said, "Have a look, Mr. Newly."

We watched as the island sank into the sea.

"It's gone back, Mr. Newly," said the captain.

"What about the last key, Captain?" I asked.

The captain smiled back and said, "I have the thirteen skulls, Mr. Newly, and I'll bet someone's going

Twenty-One

Captain Pike yelled, "Set a course for Calcos so we can sort out this treasure! Mr. Newly, signal all ships to follow and tell them our intensions."

"Where is Calcos?" I asked Jonesy.

"It is fine little patch of sand that is isolated and deserted, Mr. Newly, and just a day away," said Jonesy.

I looked about the ships, and all the crew were going about their work with large grins on their faces. All the ships had been just stuffed with the great treasure as fast as we could have thrown aboard, and all knew a treasure day was coming with the next day's sun.

I walked down from the wheel and joined Tamantha, the captain, Captain Bongeorno, Joedea, Captain Adams, and Lady Jane. It was good to hear them laughing, as we all knew what they had been through. Captain Pike was telling them that he was going to take the costs of his two lost ships and the two American ships out of their measure, and we all laughed.

The next day we arrived at Calcos, and all the ships anchored up side by side. We all transported the great new treasure ashore and lay it out across the beach.

What a site is was too, as the thousands of emeralds, rubies, and diamonds sparkled in the sun. There were more golden escudos and silver doubloons then a man could count in a lifetime. Piles and piles of the finest jewelry hung everywhere. The only thing on that beach that was not made out of gold were the crabs.

It took a couple of days to get it all arranged and to split it all up between ships. The President was really thankful and again offered us a spot in his country if we ever need a country to call home. It would be the individual captain's job to give each of his crew their deserved measure.

When the ships were all loaded Captain Pike yelled out, "This be our last night together mates as we all leave in the morning. Enjoy yourselves! Prepare the feast!

That's when our good friend Triton showed up.

The sun was just going down, and we saw him and his cohorts coming up fast in its fading light.

"Oh great," yelled Captain Rickle. "I hate dragons almost as much as I hate crocs."

Triton and his sea witch hunting party came up fast and landed their Dugan's right on the beach and dismounted. Triton and his twelve Lemuria guards walked quickly up to us. The Lemurian's, as usual, had nothing to say as they stood with their serious look. Triton on the other hand had a big smile on his face, and he said, "Well, Captain Pike, I see you have a nice haul here. Where did you find such a fine treasure?"

"Can't say," I have been saving up" replied the captain.

"Now, Captain Pike," said Triton. "You can tell me, as we are old friends."

"I have been saving up" replied the captain again.

Triton looked surprised and asked, "Have I done something to offend you, Captain?"

"Oh, let's just skip the pleasantries there, Triton, and get to it," said the captain.

"I'm afraid I have no idea what it is that you are talking about, my friend said Triton":

"Now, Triton," said the captain. "I know you know that Witch is gone, and you have not even mentioned it. I also know you know I have the thirteen skulls and that, my good fellow, is why you are here. Tell me the tale about the thirteen skulls, and tell me their importance to you. And while you are at it, mate, you can tell me where that last key to the map is."

Now Triton got an attitude and said, "Very well, Captain, if you insist. Indeed I do know about Miranda being gone. What did you do with her? I want her returned."

"Not much of a chance I'll be answering that question there, Triton but a little key might just loosen my tongue"

Triton just ignored him and said, "I want the thirteen skulls returned also. You can keep the rest of the treasure."

"Well, now ain't that neighborly of you, mate," said the captain.

I could see the captain was getting mad and so could the Lemuria guards as they had focused all their attention on him.

"Captain Pike," said Triton. Miranda must be returned to the sea for us to deal with in our own way. I know she has wreaked havoc on your lives, but that gives you no rights to her. As far as the thirteen skulls are concerned, no mortal man can possess them."

Captain Pike just stood there staring at Triton with a smile on his face.

"Don't make me extract the information from you, Captain, nor put me in the position of having to take the skulls back by force," said Triton. "Don't push our friendship that far."

"You see, Mr. Newly," said the captain, "it's getting so you can't trust anyone."

I did not say a word, and the captain just stood there smiling.

Triton motioned the Lemuria guards to move on the captain and said, "Very well then, Captain, have it your way."

To our surprise and Triton's, the Lemurian's did not move a muscle. They showed no emotion at all as they completely disregarded the order.

Tamantha and the wolves came forward and walked right past Triton to talk to the Lemurian's. The wolves ran about them all wagging their great tails. Kodiak even jumped on one of the guards placing his outstretched paws on the guard's shoulders trying to lick him in the face. As we had seen back on Devil's Den these guards too lost their stern looks and began to pet the wolves.

Whatever Tamantha said to them worked out for us because those Lemurian's just walked away, boarded their Dugan's, and off across the sea they went leaving Triton standing there with his mouth open.

Captain Pike laughed and said, "Well now there, Triton, what was it you were saying about forcing me to do something?"

Triton was furious. He huffed back across the sand, boarded his Dugan, and flew over top us. Before he left he said, "I must consult my father about this. I will return."

Captain Pike yelled to him, "Don't forget me key there, Triton, or you'll not be laying your hands on those thirteen skulls anytime soon."

Triton just sneered back, and off he went.

"Who did he say his father was there, Mr. Newly?"

I just laughed.

"Let's consult the map about all of this," said the captain.

With that out came the map of the sea. When captain pike rolled it open, it glowed a strange red-like color we had never seen before. The captain blew on the map to change it from its world scene to our local scene. As before, the map shimmered, and what we saw surprised us all.

A strange portrait appeared across the face of the map, and it showed the thirteen skulls sitting in a circle on their perches, in a dimly lit hall or cave. In the center of them was the map of the sea glowing brightly and all the skull's eyes were glowing bright red.

"Mr. Newly," said the captain.

"Aye, sir."

"Fetch those skulls."

"Aye, Captain."

When I returned with them, the captain told us to assemble them in a circle in the sand. When we had them all in place the captain said, "Watch this, Mr. Newly."

Captain Pike walked over and lay down the map of the sea right in the middle of them. The captain had barely dropped the map in place when things began to happen. First the map glowed bright red and then all the skulls' eyes lit up. Then the skulls shot that red light beam out of them like we had seen back in the cave. When all thirteen light beams hit the map it began to rise up in the air. The whole scene was really quite beautiful. The map looked like it was gathering up the light and growing in power. Brighter and brighter it glowed until we could barely look at it. Then in a second, the map seemed to take all the light it had gathered and shot it back to the skulls in a great burst. All went quiet! The skulls just sat again dark eyed, and the map of the sea fell back into the sand.

Captain Pike walked over and picked up the map to have a look. We were all right behind him looking over his shoulder. There before our eyes the third key had been placed on the map. This key's head was fashioned to look like one of the thirteen skulls. Now the map had three of the forbidden keys in place, and the captain had the other one in his cabin.

"Mr. Newly, go fetch that other key."

"Aye, sir."

When I returned with the key I asked, "Captain Pike, you're not going to place this on the map too are you?"

"Of course not Mr. Newly, there's no tellin' what's locked up in there that we don't know about. I'm only interested in a few of them."

The captain reached out his open hand, and I nervously dropped key on to it.

What we did not want to happen did. The fourth key got sucked up out of the captain's hand and was placed onto the map.

"This is not good Mr. Newly" said the captain.

According to the Oracle of the Sea's tale, the captain now had control over the map and could release anyone he wanted. We studied the map closely looking for any sort of clues as to how to proceed.

"You would think the map would through some sort of grand party or something to celebrate Mr. Newly" said the captain.

"They are all hiding" said Tamantha.

"Hiding from the worst monster ever created" she said.

"Who or what may that be?" asked Captain Pike

"You" answered Tamantha "You"

"You have the Map if the Sea and its four keys along with the 13 skulls"

"You have the curse of curses that you can lay down on anyone or anything.

"Well I just may have to go INSIDE THE MAP OF
THE SEA to get this all straightened out"

Arrrrrrr!!

www.ingramcontent.com/pod-product-compliance
Lightning Source LLC
Chambersburg PA
CBHW030814210726
48290CB00002B/588